praise for

THE IRON DREAMERS

"If you've ever been captivated by one of Ashley's science and tech videos, this book will sweep you away entirely. From the very first chapter, I was hooked. It's everything we love about Ashley—her rich storytelling, scientific rigor, and deeply human perspective—woven into a world that feels as real as it is extraordinary."

—***Camille Bergin,*** Galactic Media

"A haunting journey... Challenges our assumptions about reality and asks what it takes to adapt, endure, and build a better world for those yet to come."

—***Sarah Al-Ahmed,*** astrophysicist and host of *Planetary Radio*

"Ashley's talent for storytelling is obvious and pervasive throughout this work. Her creativity in bringing scientific concepts mainstream makes her writing both accessible and exciting."

—***Alexandra Doten,*** Astro Alexandra

"Ashley Christine is a strong voice and will shortly be your favorite new writer. Watch this space. Great things to come!"

—***Tom Julian,*** author of *Timberwolf*

THE IRON DREAMERS

THE IRON DREAMERS

by

ASHLEY CHRISTINE

Miami

Published by Mango Publishing, a division of Mango Publishing Group, Inc.

Cover, Layout & Design: Megan Werner
Cover Illustration: Andrew Haines

For permission requests, please contact the publisher at:
Mango Publishing Group
5966 South Dixie Highway, Suite 300
Miami, FL 33143
info@mango.bz

For special orders, quantity sales, course adoptions and corporate sales, please email the publisher at sales@mango.bz. For trade and wholesale sales, please contact Ingram Publisher Services at customer.service@ingramcontent.com or +1.800.509.4887.

The Iron Dreamers

Library of Congress Cataloging-in-Publication number: 2025934198
ISBN: (p) 978-1-68481-738-2 (e) 978-1-68481-739-9
BISAC category code: YAF015000 YOUNG ADULT FICTION / Dystopian

Printed in the United States of America

"There are more things in heaven and earth, Horatio,
than are dreamt of in your philosophy."

—William Shakespeare, *Hamlet*

CONTENTS

CHAPTER ONE

The itch had begun two days ago.

Yesterday, Lexi slapped the back of her neck so loudly that Mr. Adams stopped his lecture to stare at her and ask if something was wrong. No, everything was fine.

As if she could explain it.

It had felt like a mosquito bite. A sensation that drew her attention to the tiny hairs on the back of her neck. She tried to ignore it, forget about it, and then the itch returned. An hour ago, she could have sworn that she'd heard it buzzing.

"Hey, Lex," a voice nearby said.

She wondered if maybe she should go to the nurse's office tomorrow? It would be her first visit of the year, so no one would be suspicious. She didn't miss nearly as much school as her sister. Although, she had to admit, it would be a convenient way to miss the chemistry quiz.

"She isn't listening," a gentle voice replied. "And besides, she doesn't know what you're talking about."

The school bus lurched forward, and the rows of heads in front of Lexi rocked.

It was the slowest portion of the ride to Cannon Mountain. The highway ran in a curved line to the base of the mountain, all uphill. While the cars racing by were light enough to maintain a decent speed, the bus crawled. Lexi didn't mind the steady pace. It gave her time to stare out the window and admire the fresh snow.

The North Country was beautiful. Hostile, but beautiful. The kind of terrifying beauty known only at the bottom of the sea. Captivating from a distance, but cold and ruthless up close. Not many people lived in the North Country—a term lovingly coined by the locals who lived in the White Mountain National Forest of New Hampshire—but those who remained were well-suited for its subzero temperatures and hurricane-force winds.

"*Lex.*"

Lexi blinked. "Sorry, what?"

Michelle, the only person who called her Lex, was facing her, propped up on her knees in the row in front of her. Michelle was glaring, but she always looked like that. Her blue eyes weren't particularly striking, but her voice could be heard from miles away. Even above the mechanical roaring of the bus, and the excited cacophony of fifty students wanting to train, Michelle could be heard.

Michelle brushed her blonde hair to the side, a warning sign that she was growing impatient. Lexi had learned that the best way to deal with her was just to agree with everything she said. Michelle was, after all, her best friend.

"Told you," Gui said, cracking his knuckles, a physical tic of discomfort over being in the spotlight. Lexi's neighbor Gui—a French name, short for Guillaume, which no one could pronounce correctly but rhymed with "key"—sat next to Lexi and said, "She was complaining about your weekly ritual."

Lexi smiled at that. "Ah."

"I wasn't complaining," Michelle snapped. "I was *trying* to explain to Jonathan over here that it's all reruns."

Michelle gestured to Jonathan, who was sitting beside her. Jonathan was at least a head taller than them, but his posture and unkempt hair made him look five years younger. Lexi could only see the back of

Jonathan's head, but judging by his silence, he was likely grinning with that unshakeable arrogance so commonly found among adolescent males.

Jonathan had joined their group last September, having migrated to their lunch table one day for reasons unknown. He was a grade below them, but he assimilated into their faction nicely. He was lanky and lean, with dark brown hair that appeared almost black in contrast to his fair skin. A common combination for British descendants whose families had been in the northeast for centuries.

Time moved slowly in places like rural New Hampshire. A constant ticking of the clock without change, or progression. So, although Jonathan had been sitting with them for months, and Lexi knew where he lived and what his father did for work, she didn't *know* him, know him.

"What reruns?" Lexi asked. She regretted it immediately.

Michelle rolled her eyes.

There was only one television show that they watched, and it had to be at Michelle's house. Lexi's family didn't own a television. Most families in the North Country didn't. She and Gui had to drive to Michelle's house every Thursday night to watch their favorite show.

The bus hit a pothole—or a frost heave. It was difficult to tell in the middle of winter.

"*CSI*, duh," Michelle said, nearly snapping her neck on the seat. "What the hell was that, a moose?"

"If it was a moose, the bus driver would be dead," Gui said. "And we probably would spin off the highway, sustaining multiple injuries and concussions."

Gui's wasn't condescending, he was pragmatic. It was one of the reasons why he was set to be the class valedictorian next year, along with his twin sister Eilish, who had safely secured second place. He would probably become a doctor or a rocket scientist, something that required an inhuman level of determination. He would be brilliant at it, of course, but Lexi worried about his patients.

His voice would be calm, his gestures smooth, and then he would deliver a cancer diagnosis with the same bored demeanor as if he were ordering a cannoli.

"Perfect," Michelle said. It was her usual response to Gui's deadpan statements. "So, what are we doing? It's reruns this week."

"No, it's not," Jonathan said, chiming in.

"Yes, it is."

"Nope." Jonathan turned to face them, bracing himself between the seats as the bus hit another obstacle. "The reruns start when Mass goes on winter break, and then we go on break, and then Canada. The show doesn't start again until we're all back in school. That's been the pattern, anyway."

Jonathan's voice was astonishingly low. There was a roughness to it, as if he was out of practice talking. He had once told Lexi that he was content with silence, even preferring it. She'd warned him there would be none. Not around Michelle.

"How would you know?" Michelle demanded. "You don't even watch television."

"I watch *CSI*," Jonathan said.

"Since when?"

"Since now."

Her eyes narrowed. "What, out of spite?"

"Whatever shuts you up."

Michelle let out a sharp laugh. The quickest way to her heart was with a spear. "Fine," she said, relenting. "But you better be right."

"Usually am."

Lexi chuckled.

Jonathan's gaze turned to Lexi, the way it usually did when she managed to squeeze in a word around Michelle. His expression was unreadable, a gentle fog of contradictory thoughts, like he was trying to figure out the next thing to say in the wrong language. He didn't always have that cloudy look, but it was becoming more common.

Under normal circumstances, she would wait for a private moment to ask what the problem was, but she knew that Jonathan wouldn't tell her. He didn't let anyone dig. It wasn't that he was shy or nervous, or self-conscious. He was an independent nation. If he didn't like a question, he simply didn't answer it. He would let silence hang in the air until the discomfort made Lexi nervous enough to withdraw her inquiry.

A student at the front of the bus opened a window. The ice-cold breeze moved through the aisle, rustling Jonathan's hair. The taste of metal filled Lexi's mouth. It was a strange flavor that she didn't recognize. It was too strong and made her nose wrinkle.

Blood?

Maybe they'd run over a dead animal.

The students rocked forward as the bus driver released the gas pedal. It was the steepest part of the highway, and a bad spot to lose momentum. Lexi sat up, trying to see what the driver was doing. The older woman shivered violently, and then pressed on the gas again as if nothing strange had transpired.

"What the hell was that?" Michelle said, pulling herself up after slamming into the seat in front of her. "Is she *trying* to hit every single frost heave?"

"Michelle," Lexi said warningly.

She needed to sit down.

"Yeah, yeah, yeah." Michelle settled into her seat and chatted with Jonathan. Their heads bobbed; one blonde, the other black. They had nothing in common, not in appearance or personality, yet they never grew bored of each other. Lexi supposed that opposites did, in fact, attract.

Gui leaned into Lexi, his measured voice barely audible. "Should we expect to see more of him?"

"You mean Jonathan?"

"Clearly."

Lexi scratched at the ice forming along the edge of the window. "I guess so."

"Hm." Gui's scrutinizing eyes landed on the back of Jonathan's bobbing head. "I don't see the appeal."

Lexi laughed.

Gui's passive disinterest could be unsettling, but it was one of her favorite aspects of him. She could always count on him to see the bigger picture, or at the very least, through the eyes of a critical mind. Jonathan and Michelle were too engaged to ask what was so funny.

"Maybe Michelle wants to film him?" Lexi said. "She has to submit a project to get into that art school in Philly. She needs to do a documentary or something."

"Why would she choose him?"

"I don't know."

Gui cracked his knuckles. He was growing agitated by the expanding population of their group. He wasn't meant to be in large gatherings. He dutifully sat at the lunch table and went to the movies with them, but Lexi suspected that Gui wished to go back to when it was just him and Lexi, and their sisters. His own little tribe at the end of a dead-end dirt road in the middle of nowhere. But then Michelle shared most of their classes during sophomore year, and they all became friends.

And now there was Jonathan.

"Speaking of college admissions," Gui said, "have you written your essay yet?"

"Oh, that." Lexi exhaled, picking at the ice. "Early admission isn't for another six months."

"Yes, but still."

"I have time, Gui."

He eyed her suspiciously. "You're still planning on going to college, right? You're not the best student, but it would be unfortunate if you stayed here without a plan."

Lexi huffed. "Yes, *Dad*. I'll get the essay done when it's due."

Students in small towns fantasized about leaving. It was an understandable aspiration for any teenager living in isolation. They had an itch that needed to be scratched. A desire to fly toward the bright city lights like a moth to a flame.

Lexi was dreading it.

It wasn't that she was afraid of change. It was just that knew what she liked, and she was already doing it. She didn't want to give up skiing and hiking, or the smell of mountain air, for a piece of paper that did nothing but prove she wasn't an idiot. She was content. Why did she have to want more?

The bus climbed over the top of the hill, where Cannon Mountain rose above the window like a tidal wave. Tiny figures were scattered across the white trails. From a distance, the people appeared to hardly move, but Lexi knew that the skiers on the rightmost trail were traveling at sixty miles per hour because that was the racecourse.

Every Wednesday, their school took the students to the mountain for lessons. They didn't need to take lessons anymore. The icy conditions made them some of the best skiers and snowboarders in the country. By the time sophomore year rolled around, most of them were expert-level. The teachers knew. The parents knew. But nobody stopped it. That was just the way of things in the north.

"*Finally*! We're here," Michelle announced. "Ready to freeze your nuts off?"

"Those need to be removed," Gui said, pointing out the window. A row of icicles hung from the main lodge's roof. They were massive.

"That would be a good way to kill someone," Michelle mused.

"Excuse me," Lexi said, chuckling—"what?"

"Think about it," Michelle said. "There'd be no murder weapon because it would melt away. If they don't have a murder weapon, they can't prove you did anything. Seriously, it's brilliant. It's like that guy who made bullets out of ice—"

"That was a *CSI* episode," Gui corrected.

"Those shows are based on real events," Michelle countered. "I mean, obviously they dramatize it, but if you look up the crazy episodes, they're almost always based on an actual case."

"Someone should tell one of the managers," Gui said, surveying the icicles. Many were so long they were about to touch the ground. "They're a hazard."

Michelle looked down at her nails. "Death is the one thing meant for everyone. Maybe it gets better after this."

Lexi, Gui, and Jonathan stared at her. It was a remarkably metaphysical comment to come out of Michelle's mouth. Perhaps it was her detached tone, or the words themselves, that left a haunting aftertaste in Lexi's mouth. Michelle, who couldn't be bothered with a conversation three inches deep, had managed to scrape together such an insightful remark that it left the three of them speechless.

Jonathan's head cocked to the side. He studied Michelle's face, as if trying to find a smudge of dirt on her cheek. There was a strange weight to his voice when he asked, "Where did that come from?"

She shrugged. "Just popped into my head."

"Really."

"What?" Michelle threw up her hands. "Jesus, you're all looking at me like I ate a live rabbit."

"That would have been less surprising," Gui said.

Michelle's laughter cut through the tension and Gui smiled, pleased with himself. Jonathan's face darkened.

The bus stopped at the main lodge near the base of the mountain. There was a flagpole on the front lawn with an American and a New Hampshire flag. They whipped violently in the wind, snapping against the pole. If those were the conditions at the base, it would be worse at the higher altitudes.

The students unloaded their gear. Gui scooped up a handful of snow. His fingers were slender and delicate. "This will be an excellent day."

"Hold on, hold on," their teacher, Mr. Adams, said. He jumped off the bus, attempting to wrangle the students before they broke off into their respective groups.

Mr. Adams didn't grow up in the North Country, but he was from northern New York and that was close enough. He was young, early thirties, and didn't like winter sports, but he appreciated the northern life. The parents liked that about him. Locals complained about the conditions in jest, but they didn't appreciate it when outsiders did it. No one wanted to be judged for their way of life.

It helped that Mr. Adams was attractive. Naturally, that made him Michelle's favorite teacher. Even in the woods, beauty had currency.

Lexi slapped the back of her neck.

Itch.

There was that itch again.

She pressed her hands to her temples. It wasn't a headache, or a migraine. She rarely had those. It was something else. She lost her balance and bumped into Gui.

"What's wrong with you?" he asked, gently pushing her away.

It felt like Lexi's brain was being kneaded. A kind of lightheadedness that made her legs buckle. She worked her way across her head with her fingers, following the sensation. There was a single point at the base of her skull that seemed to be the source. When she pressed against it, a sharp pain surged through her body.

"I don't know," Lexi said. "I have a headache that started two days ago, or neck pain. I don't know. It's getting worse."

"Did you drink enough water?"

"No, Gui. Why would I ever do that?"

His brow furrowed. "Is that sarcasm?"

She let out a weak laugh.

Gui expressed himself through medical concern. It was the only method he had to communicate affection. He pressed a hand to his mouth, curling his fingers as he studied Lexi's face. "That's interesting."

"What?"

"Your eyes have changed colors." He waved a dismissive hand. "It's not that noticeable, but they're a bit too silver."

"Maybe it's puberty," Lexi joked.

"That's unlikely."

Lexi sighed. Gui truly had no ear for sarcasm.

The pain in her head softened to a dull ache. She decided to wait until she was home to figure out what was wrong. If the itchy pain didn't go away by then, she would tell her parents. A conversation that would undoubtedly lead to a hospital visit, which Lexi wanted to avoid.

"Someone's missing a glove." Mr. Adams held up a black glove that looked like every other black glove. "Speak now or forever lose your fingers."

The students looked around, making half-assed attempts to check their pockets. Everyone was already wearing gloves.

"No? No one?" Mr. Adams shrugged. "I guess it's a spare. Alright, head on up."

Gui's long strides catapulted him halfway up the stairs before Lexi could put on her backpack, and Michelle ran to catch up with him. A shadow lingered by Lexi. Jonathan was waiting for her to collect her things, watching in his trademark silence.

Unable to bear the empty space between them, she said, "Nice goggles."

Jonathan snapped a pair of light gray lenses into his goggles and cast a sidelong glance at her. "Thanks."

"Did your parents get them for you?"

He shook his head.

It wasn't awkward to be around Jonathan. She had known him—or at least, known *of* him—her entire life. There were fewer than nine hundred families in their hometown, and most of them had been there for generations. She couldn't go to a gas station without seeing a familiar face. Like a distant cousin she hadn't seen in years, Lexi was familiar enough with Jonathan to initiate a conversation, but not enough to know where to go with it.

"Have any spares?" she asked, partly teasing. She pointed to a pair of old goggles strapped to her helmet. "I only have the one."

"Nope."

Lexi didn't know what to say. He seemed to be in their friend group for Michelle. She'd started to make her way up the stairs when Jonathan stepped in front of her.

"Wait," he said, shifting his weight awkwardly as if debating with himself. A gust of cold wind rose up, carrying waves of snow that pounded into them. Nothing could snap a person into making a decision quite like a North Country wind. His lips parted, but Lexi couldn't hear a word.

"WHAT?" She shouted over the howling wind.

He took a step forward, closing the gap between them. "*What. Is. Wrong?*"

"NOTHING."

Jonathan was wasting time. If they didn't reach the chair lift soon, they'd be the last in line, and Michelle and Gui wouldn't wait for them. Once the rhythm between chair lift and slope was disrupted, it was difficult to line up again. Not without someone waiting at the top of the trail for twenty minutes. And Michelle didn't do that.

Jonathan looked toward the mountain's notch as if he could see the air and follow its path. He shifted to the left, blocking the wind. "You've looked funny all day."

"Well, thank you," Lexi laughed.

He was one to talk.

"No, I—" Jonathan tried to formulate his words.

A set of doors flew open and slammed against the walls. Gui and Michelle stepped outside and looked around. The wind was pushing everything in the wrong direction. The doors swung back and forth and hit against the building. Gui tried to close them, ever the good Samaritan. Michelle's eyes landed on Lexi and Jonathan, and her irritation transformed into intrigue.

"It's just a headache," Lexi said.

Jonathan looked over his shoulder to see what she was watching and realized that he had ten seconds before Michelle entered his personal space. He turned to Lexi. "You can talk to me, is what I'm saying. "

"Okay?" Lexi chuckled. "You are so weird."

"Oh, I know."

Michelle jumped on the stair between them. "Did I miss something? You two look like you're finally bonding."

Lexi and Jonathan exchanged a glance. The lightness that had been between them seconds ago dissipated. The tension returned to Jonathan's shoulders like a backpack sinking into the old familiar indents.

"I *did* miss something," Michelle said, clapping her hands.

Jonathan shrugged. "Not really."

"You're a terrible liar."

"I'm actually pretty good at it," he said, an admission that surprised Lexi. "It's just none of your business. Ergo, you didn't miss anything."

"Fine, fine," Michelle said, crossing her arms. "No need to get pissy over it."

A wave of pain surged through Lexi's entire body. It was the strongest, most disorientating blow she'd ever felt.

She fell to her knees.

Someone was talking. Everyone was talking. She couldn't hear anything until a high-pitched ringing entered her brain. Lexi looked up to find everyone staring at her. It was a ringing that no one else could hear, a loud steady alarm that didn't change, no matter what position she moved into.

Lexi had experienced pain before. Concussions, broken bones, torn ligaments. Lexi knew pain. She could even determine an injury based on what kind of pain it was. Bones throbbed, muscles ached, and punctures were cold. But this was something new.

Lexi reached to the back of her head and scratched at the area just above her neck. *Itch, itch, itch, itch.* Another part of her seemed to be scratching at the same spot, like a phantom limb.

A pair of cold hands grabbed Lexi's face. Startled, she sucked in her breath. Jonathan's fingers felt like ice. The numbing sensation should have been a relief, but it made her feel worse. She was going to vomit.

"I'm sorry," Jonathan said, pulling her toward him.

Lexi was too stunned to speak, too wrapped up in agony to ask what he was talking about. He angled her head against his chest. If an icicle had fallen from the roof and into her neck, then he needed to leave it there. Pulling an apparatus out of a wound would only make it bleed worse. Michelle and Gui would know that—though for completely different reasons.

Lexi was not a stranger to death. Accidents happened all the time in the woods. Her decisions weren't centered around prolonging her life or avoiding danger. It was an unreasonable expectation in a landscape where having fun meant jumping off a cliff.

Jonathan removed one of Lexi's gloves and held her hand to the back of her neck like she was plugging a wound.

"Breathe," he whispered.

The darkness behind her eyelids morphed into bright lines. An unnatural blue cracked through the darkness. A phantom limb—*her* limb—grabbed a wire behind her neck. She let go, shocked. Jonathan must have placed something there, a device or a charger. She didn't care. She needed the pain to stop, and that was the thing in the way.

She reached for the cord and tugged. The resistance sent another wave of pain through her skull. It was not going to dislodge easily.

In a last-ditch effort, she leaned her weight into Jonathan and with both hands, pulled on a thing that shouldn't be there.

The tension released, and a wall of water came crashing down.

She opened her mouth to breathe, but the air was gone.

CHAPTER TWO

Moisture is the killer.

In subzero temperatures nothing can be wet. People think that it's the wind or the heat that gets you, but nothing kills quite like moisture. It can breed lethal conditions within a few minutes. Every child in the north knows that. Lexi needs to escape. *Immediately*. She thrashes in the water, too confused to question her predicament or the source of it.

She raises her arms and gropes in the dark.

There's a cover just above her head. She clenches her jaw to fight the urge to inhale. Something is wrong with the water. It's thick. Her arms move slowly through the liquid. It's like she's either exhausted from running a marathon, or did nothing at all for three years.

A corner of the cover gives way and Lexi pulls it to the side. She sits up and gasps for air, but only a shred of it makes it to her lungs.

Something is caught in her throat.

Lexi touches her face. A strange apparatus is covering her nose and mouth, and it's hard as metal. A soft tube in the center extends down her throat. She convulses, wanting to gag, but the tube is unforgiving. How did it get there? How long has it been there?

And why is it *pulsating*?

She tries to breathe past it, but the device is controlling the airflow with an unrelenting rhythm—far too slow for her racing heart. She fumbles for the tube and grips it with both hands. She pulls slowly, one hand at a time, suppressing the urge to vomit as every rib of it rubs against her tongue. The tail end of it slaps against the top of her throat, and she retches out a swell of yellow bile.

Lexi coughs so harshly that blood comes up. She's finally able to breathe. The cold air fills the bottom of her lungs. It's a sharp pain with little relief, and too thin to be the North Country. She's at an altitude of 12,000 feet, if she had to guess. Which doesn't make sense. The closest mountains at that altitude are thousands of miles away.

How long has she been intubated?

Why? Where?

Just before panic rises, her training snaps into place. A kind of tunnel vision sharpened by years of nature's abuse. Every crisis has an order of operations, and the first inventory to take note of is her physical status.

Lexi rubs her eyes, but the pain is wrong.

It's not that the skin on her face is too smooth; it's that she shouldn't be able to feel it. Multiple bouts of frostbite over the years have damaged the nerve endings, and all that was left was the sensation of pressure. She rubs a finger over her cheek, amazed by the tickle.

Her eyelids hurt. Her fingers cramp.

Lexi can't seem to catch her breath. She doesn't know what a heart attack feels like, but she imagines it's not that different from whatever she's experiencing. She grips the edges by her knees, and cracks open an eye.

She's in a tub.

Water sloshes in a shallow basin. It's one foot deep and twice her length. It's too dark to see clearly, but the water doesn't sound as thick as she first thought. It isn't the slow drip of honey, but the viscosity of swamp water made worse by the contents of her stomach.

Lexi flexes her hands. There's just no strength in her fingers. Was there an accident? Her last memory is of leaning against Jonathan, his hands searching the back of her neck. She reaches behind her head and grazes her bare scalp. Her long wavy brown hair has been shaved off, leaving nothing but silky-smooth skin.

She's bald.

Totally and wholly bald.

She wants to scream. In the exact spot where Jonathan had touched her is a flat metal square embedded in her skin. She jerks her hand away. Terror overrides her senses. Another spasm of bile rises up in her throat.

In, out, in, out.

Breathe.

In.

Out.

Her fingers trace along the surface, exploring the minuscule ridges and valleys. There's no USB slot, or any adapter that she can identify. The device is small, and connects to her spinal cord, possibly her brain. The thought of that makes her tremble. There's a series of wires attached to the bottom half of the square. She follows the trail with her hand. The wires stretch down into the water behind her, and through the back of the tub.

She's plugged into the tub like a coffee machine.

Lexi has never seen this kind of technology. Perhaps she had been paralyzed, and the accident occurred years ago, and the device was invented during her time in a coma? She decides against sabotaging the equipment. If it is a medical device, then it's in her best interest to wait for the doctor, or her parents.

Oh, God.

Her family.

"Hello."

Lexi jumps. She scrambles in the water like a rat in a sewer, slipping to the opposite side of the tub.

"Relax," a woman says flatly, as if bored. "I'm not going to hurt you."

Lexi squints, trying to make out the shadow. She opens her mouth to speak, but the initiation of speech causes mucus to lodge in her throat. She hunches over and coughs. The woman reaches into the tub and cradles Lexi's side. Her hands are firm and warm. It's in this moment that Lexi realizes that she isn't wearing any clothes.

"Don't bite me," the woman warns. "I'm serious, Alexandria."

No one calls her that.

The woman grabs Lexi's jaw and pries open her mouth. Her skin is rough, as if she routinely force-feeds prisoners. If Lexi bites down, she will bite her own cheek.

The woman reaches into Lexi's mouth and pulls out the mucus lodged in the top of her throat. Thankfully, her fingernails are short. Lexi gags as her probing fingers scrape out the mucus. She coughs, more out of reflex than need, but her breathing comes easier.

"Don't swallow," the woman says. "Spit."

"W-wh-where?" Lexi manages to squeeze out.

If shrugging has a sound, then it is the loudest that Lexi has ever heard.

"Anywhere," the woman replies.

Lexi leans over the edge and spits onto the floor. She isn't sure what difference it makes. The water is already mixed with her vomit. She wraps her arms around herself. Shame is added to the list of emotions rattling her brain. Who is this woman? Where are the doctors? Gui should be around somewhere. Every time Lexi has a concussion or breaks a bone, Gui is there to observe. He loves the hospital.

Does a coma patient have rights? Lexi has no idea, but it's strange to be stripped naked. Even with hydrotherapy, there are bathing suits. She hopes this isn't one of those educational operations where a classroom is brought in to witness a medical miracle.

"Clothes would deteriorate in the solution," the woman says.

Lexi's throat is sore and her muscles can barely move. It's a bone-deep exhaustion that's left her frail and partially blind. If she was in a coma, then she's been unconscious for decades, and the world has moved well past her.

But she hadn't spoken.

"You're still connected to Beta," the woman says. "Until I detach this last data cord, your thoughts are recorded."

"R-re-corded?" Lexi stutters.

"Yes. You're something of a celebrity around here."

Lexi looks to her body, trying to gauge if all the parts are still there. Half-expecting to find a gaping hole in her chest, she asks, "Did I d-die?"

The woman doesn't look up when she says, "That depends on what you consider living." She reaches into the tub and grabs a loose cable, pulling it out of the water like a snake charmer. A gentle vibration sends ripples through the water as she traces the cord to the back of Lexi's neck, and places a hand on her head. "It would be best if you didn't scream."

Lexi grips both sides of the tub, and the woman rips out the cord. Pain tears through her skull like fire. She grinds her teeth, determined not to scream. It doesn't hurt as much as the cord she removed herself, but it still feels like her insides are being pulled out of her body through her head.

The woman steps back and wraps the cord around a floating spiked ball. It isn't held up by wire, or atop a pole. It must be magnetic.

The blue light below Lexi sharpens the image around her. The room isn't a room at all, but a long corridor that stretches into the darkness.

She leans over the tub—which is at least three feet in the air—and stares at the floor in wonder. Water trickles off her fingertips and splatters onto the floor. The woman rushes forward and pushes Lexi into the tub, plunging her underwater. Lexi scrambles and grips the sides as if she's hanging from atop a cliff.

"You'll fall out," the woman says, as if that explains it.

Lexi scoffs.

Her parents have been working at the hospital since she was a child. They take one of the doctors out on the boat every summer. She repaired a nurse's generator with her father during a thunderstorm. Her mother trades eggs with an occupational therapist in return for zucchini. Lexi knows everyone.

She does not know this woman.

"Wh-what's—" Lexi coughs. She doesn't recognize her own voice. "Who a-are you?"

The woman tilts her head; her rosy cheeks would give the impression of tenderness if not for the calculating silver-blue eyes. She looks young, about the same age as Mr. Adams, but there is something aged and weathered about her. Dark blonde hair is woven into an intricate braided pattern above her head—an unusually laborious practice for a medical professional.

Lexi peers past the woman, widening her eyes as if she can manually override her vision. There are metal squares cut into the walls. Hundreds of them. They're gray and flat, without markings or texture, and curve toward a ceiling that doesn't end. She's watched enough *CSI* to know where she is.

The woman follows her gaze. "Ah," she says, pursing her lips. "I would advise you to not think about that."

Lexi looks behind her. Her own tub is sticking out of the wall, a quarter of it still within. "Is-s this—" Lexi gulps, the mucus dislodging again in her throat—"a...m-morgue?"

The woman offers Lexi a blanket and says, "They're not dead."

The material is too thin, but Lexi is desperately cold. She wraps the blanket around her shoulders and relaxes under the heat. An electric blanket in water? It could probably electrocute her, but she doesn't care. For the first time in a long time, she is truly freezing.

"What's y-your name?" Lexi asks.

The woman pauses. Her expression is curious, but distant. Like Gui, she appears to be content with silence. Perhaps they'll just glare at each other for an hour.

"Artemis," the woman finally says.

Is Artemis a code name? Is this a military operation? *That* she might be able to come to terms with; little else can explain the ambiguous environment. They might not be in a morgue, but Lexi is a body in a drawer among other drawers with, presumably, other bodies.

Lexi waits for an explanation, but the woman doesn't elaborate. For a doctor, she is certainly tight-lipped.

Lexi stifles a laugh. "Right, okay."

"I have no reason to lie," Artemis says. "Spread your legs."

"*Excuse me?*"

"You have a catheter."

Lexi jumps. A cramp shoots its way through her abdomen so fiercely that it drags her under the water. The entirety of the catheter's size becomes known to her, and its depth. Horrified, she squeezes her eyes shut.

Artemis reaches into the tub and secures a hand on Lexi's knee, the other on her shoulder. There are callouses on her fingertips and palm. She could be from the North Country. Rough hands are not an exceptional feature there.

"I would tell you to relax," Artemis says, "but I can see that's a lost cause." A smile tugs at the corner of her lips. It's a practiced motion, a natural shape to the woman's face. It folds into her mouth and above her eyebrows like a faded line in worn jeans. Either Artemis is a seasoned liar, or humor is an intrinsic part of her personality.

Lexi peeks an eye open. "Are you...trying to m-make me feel b-better?"

Artemis looks to her hand in the water. "I'm afraid you won't be feeling that for some time. I'm going to cut here first." She points to a spot a few inches along the cord. "And then pull the catheter out. Do not move."

Lexi can only nod her head in response, tightening her white-knuckle grip. She hates to admit it, but she is frozen with fear. Artemis leans over the tub, and her sleeve appears to move. It shimmers like water, extending past her fingertips and transforming into a needle. Lexi has never seen clothing move before, let alone shape itself into a tool. It cuts the cord so gently that Lexi doesn't even feel it.

"Wh-what is that?" Lexi asks.

Artemis studies the area between Lexi's legs. It would be a good time to crack a joke, but she's too nervous to think of one. She closes her eyes as Artemis's hand inches closer. The interaction is far too intimate, too invasive, and Artemis is oblivious to the awkwardness.

Maybe she really is a doctor.

There are medical procedures that Lexi hasn't prepared herself for yet: childbirth, mammograms, colonoscopies. There are procedures that will happen to her, but not for many years. It's all wrong. A burning sensation rises between her legs as Artemis pulls. The woman is moving too slowly. It takes all of Lexi's mental fortitude to remain still as a fire burns inside her. Another second and—

"Done," Artemis says, stepping back. She wraps the catheter around another spiked ball, which expands the blue light beneath them, presumably so that she can see what she's doing.

The woman is wearing a fitted bodysuit that covers her from wrists to ankles. Elaborate blue lines cut into a muted black like rivers in a canyon. It could be an optical illusion, or the suit has multiple layers stacked on top of each other. She pushes the ball, and it floats beneath the tub, out of sight.

Lexi has never seen technology like that in a hospital.

"Is-s that it?" she asks. She checks the rest of her body for wires. The piece in Artemis's hand appears to be the last of it. Whatever it is.

"You're fully disconnected." Artemis enters a command on the side of the tub. The screen darkens, and then the water around Lexi drains with a gentle *swoosh*.

Lexi is left exposed. There are no more cables, no swamp water. The cold in the air is unfamiliar. Lexi has been freezing before. The North Country could reach temperatures of –20 degrees Fahrenheit for weeks, when it's too cold for clouds to develop and the sky is a piercing blue. Mornings like that, she knew it would be dangerous to go outside.

This cold is different.

Lexi can't quite put her finger on it, but there is a hollowness to this cold. Her fingers move through the air as if nothing was ever there. Not moisture, nor heat. For a moment, she fears she will suffocate in the nothingness, the cold determined to slither beneath her skin.

Artemis walks down the corridor, and the blue light beneath her follows. Lexi doesn't have time to ask about it before she's left in complete darkness.

This is her chance.

She could run.

"Unless you want hypothermia," Artemis says, "I suggest you take these." The woman holds up a set of clothes from twenty feet away. A cloud of blue light surrounds her feet as if she's standing on the only solid pillar in an endless black sea. There are no windows around them, no cracks of light beneath a door. No signs of the outside world. It could be nighttime, or they're underground.

What *is* this place?

Lexi glances around the room for anything familiar. A desk, a whiteboard, *something* to tell her where she is.

"I thought y-you couldn't read m-my mind," Lexi says—words she never thought that she would utter.

"I can't."

"Then how—?"

A sound escapes the woman's throat. Something between a laugh and exasperation. " 'There are more things in heaven and earth, Horatio, than are dreamt of in your philosophy.' "

Lexi snorts. "Okay."

Artemis's lips tighten. On a different face it might be a condescending smile, but on Artemis it looks more like admission. She knows that she is dodging direct questions. The firm line of her lips acknowledges that the ambiguity is probably maddening.

"We have programs that learn your pattern of thought. We can trace your logic, visualize mental images and inner monologues to an extent, but it isn't perfect because it isn't necessary. I just know you. Now, take it," Artemis says, holding her arm higher.

Lexi isn't sure how a woman that she's never met could possibly know anything about her, or why her thoughts would be recorded. What was so special about Lexi's dreams if she was in a coma? Why would anyone go through all this trouble at all?

She leans over the edge of the tub to catch her breath. Her heart is racing from the mild physical exertion, and her eyes burn. Everything feels wrong.

Moisture is the killer.

Lexi swings a leg over the edge, and takes a good look at her legs for the first time in what she's beginning to suspect has been months. Even in the dim lighting, she can tell that her legs are half the thickness they once were. Of all the nightmares—the implant in her brain, the catheter, the cord in her neck—it is her bony legs that horrify her the most.

Tears well in her eyes. Those burn too.

Lexi rolls onto the side of the tub. The edge crushes into her chest as if to cut her in half. Apparently, her rib cage is just as weak as everything else about her now. She throws her weight over the tub and slams onto the ground.

She wheezes in pain, groping her sides. She might have cracked a rib. The floor lights up beneath her, but does not turn blue immediately. A split second before, it flickers gray.

"Mm." Artemis surveys the light. "Interesting."

Lexi coughs. "W-what is-s happening?"

"You have less than a minute."

Lexi doesn't know whether to be confused, or afraid. What is the alarm for? What happens in a minute? She holds out her hand in the universal signal for help, but Artemis drops her arms, tilting her head in a way that Lexi is beginning to suspect is irritation.

Lexi isn't sure that she likes her, but it is not in her best interest to appear vulnerable to the woman who holds all the cards. She rolls onto her stomach, hoping she can leverage herself with her arms. She pulls one of her legs toward her chest and shifts her weight. Her hand slips, and she smacks her shoulder into the floor again.

Lexi moans, trying to massage what little muscle is there.

"By all means," Artemis sighs, "take your time."

Lexi restrains her aggravation, and reaches up with both hands to grab the rim of the tub. She has never been particularly good at pull-ups, but she can do a few. One look at her arms, though, and she is reminded that those are not her arms anymore. Her feet slip and slide on the floor like a drunken skater's. She's doing worse than a newborn foal.

How did this happen?

She doesn't remember a crash, or an ice shard plunging into her neck. As easy as it would be to blame Jonathan, he isn't to blame, she's sure of it. One moment they were on the mountain, and the next thing she knew she was in a tub. It would have taken months of lying in a coma for time to chisel away at her muscles like that.

Lexi clings to the side of the tub, the rim digging into her armpits, and manages to pull herself up. She's standing, technically.

"Halfway there," Artemis says.

Lexi croaks, semi-hysterical.

"What?" Artemis asks.

"That's what my dad always says." Lexi releases one hand and straightens. " 'One more hill,' even though it's like ten more hills." She finds the sweet spot above her feet where a skeleton can support itself if it stands just right. A light breeze would blow her over, but she's on her own. "Then we get to the top of the mountain and he says, 'We're halfway there.' "

"I always enjoyed that."

The silence is a beat too long. Artemis lifts her head with a moment of unguarded surprise, and they stare at each other.

A chill runs down Lexi's spine.

"Quickly now," Artemis says.

Lexi's legs are too heavy to lift. She slides a foot forward, and then the other. The gray light beneath her follows. A touch-activated floor is an unusual installation for a hospital. She lifts an arm in the expectation of falling, and as if on cue, her foot slips and her chest slams onto the floor. Her elbow feels sticky. It's bleeding.

"Listen to me very carefully, Alexandria."

Lexi releases a groan and rests her head on the floor. Her voice shakes between her chattering teeth. "That's not m-my name."

"Fine, Lexi." Artemis kneels beside her, folding the clothes and flattening them over her knee. "The safest you've ever been is inside this room. If you don't adapt, you will have no place in our world. That's not a good position to be in."

Lexi chokes back a laugh.

Artemis drops her head. "Maybe you won't survive this place."

"I know h-how to survive," Lexi says, offended.

"This will be different."

A high-pitched ding comes from Artemis's hip. She pulls out a device—a thin bar that extends into a transparent screen—and her fingers flutter over a holographic image. Before Lexi can ask, the screen dissolves and returns to the form of a pen.

"What's going on?" Lexi asks.

"You'll know soon enough." Artemis stands. Her voice is without compassion, but it's not hostile. "A firm hand," as they say in the North Country. Artemis may actually be trying to help in a way that Lexi understands.

Lexi lifts herself to her knees and rises to her feet. She's never been so cold in her life. Artemis stands ten feet away. With Lexi's gait, that's four steps.

She can make four steps.

Lexi slides one foot forward and then the other, wobbling. She slips once, and then twice, but remains standing. On the verge of tears, she makes it three steps and lunges. To her surprise, Artemis doesn't shift to the side and let her fall, but instead lets Lexi crash into her chest. She pulls the clothes over Lexi's bare back, and lets her cry angry ugly tears.

She should have listened to the heavy footsteps of people approaching, and their muffled voices. Anyone could sneak up on her in her current state. But she was too desperate for the clothes, too confused to think straight. Artemis's arm stiffens around her, and a different set of hands grabs her shoulders.

Someone presses a finger to Lexi's neck.

And the world goes dark.

CHAPTER THREE

Lexi opens her eyes to black.

The forest is without city lights or pollution, and the sky has too many stars to count. If the moon isn't out, then the gaseous arms of the Milky Way galaxy are visible from her porch. She's learned how to decipher shadows in a backdrop of black and purple, trying to determine if it's a coyote in the distance, or her own imagination. She knows the dark.

This is something else.

Her head is spinning, but otherwise Lexi is lucid. Whatever they gave her, it wasn't a typical sleeping medication. She can't remember a single dream—which is unusual for her. And she awoke without drowsiness. If she didn't know any better, she could almost believe that she had teleported.

She sits up slowly, unsure if her head is going to hit an obstruction and knock her out again. She waves a hand in front of her face, trying to detect even the slightest movement. She closes her eyes and squints.

It's *all* black.

Lexi sits on the floor, naked. Her skin isn't sticky from the solution in the tub, and the implant at the base of her skull doesn't itch. They must have washed her while she was unconscious—a position that makes her shiver—but a nurse should have dressed her. Leaving her naked in the dark is either a careless oversight, or the callous pretext of discipline.

Her parents must be freaking out.

Lexi can't imagine a scenario where her parents would have agreed to this. Not only are her parents untrusting of the government, and organized authority in general, as many people in the "Live Free or Die" state are, they are actively engaged in Lexi's life. They attend every ski race and take her to practice. They are *always* there. They would never have handed her over to a military facility without setting up their own bed next to her.

Lexi runs her hands over the floor and finds the blanket from earlier. She wraps it around her shoulders and curls into it, surprised that it's still providing warmth. It's an odd thing to fixate on, but she doesn't understand how the blanket works. Her fingertips trace the edge, and she finds no batteries or wires.

Odd.

She pulls her legs toward her chest, covering every inch of skin as best as she can under the blanket. She wraps her right hand around her left bicep, and her fingers nearly touch. She's all bone.

She should explore the room, feel out the parameters and determine if there are any objects that she could use to escape. She can't muster the energy. Her body is too tired. Her eyes fill with tears. She wants to go home. She hugs herself tighter, letting the tears spill down the side of her face.

"So, this is her," a child-like voice says.

Lexi jumps.

She scrambles to the back of the room until she hits a wall. Reflexively, her eyes dart back and forth, but of course, she can't see anything. The room is small. She can tell by the way the girl's scratchy voice reverberates off the walls.

"A second Iron Dreamer to roam our halls." The girl releases a heavy breath. "What an unmitigated disaster."

"I will need your approval to investigate," a familiar voice replies. "If we don't move quickly, he could release another."

Artemis.

Lexi is strangely relieved that the woman is there, though she has no reason to be. Artemis has been cold and distant with her since the moment they met, and she could be the one to blame for drugging Lexi and throwing her in a cell in the first place. But at least Lexi knows her, sort of, and that's something.

"My approval," the girl echoes mockingly.

Lexi is beginning to suspect that is not a little girl at all.

"This is only the beginning," Artemis warns.

"Had she been anyone else, this would have been an easier vote to secure. But look at her." The stranger sighs. It is neither dismissive nor angry, but uneasy. "The council must decide this one, my dear."

Lexi should say something. She could speak up, but she cannot think of a single word to say. What accusation is she defending herself against—waking up too soon? Nothing makes sense. Confusion snuffs out every thought before it reaches her lips, leaving her a bystander to her own fate.

A pair of feet shuffle across the floor, moving closer to Lexi. Warm breath blows against her face. She presses her back closer to the wall, wishing she could disappear into it. Artemis and the stranger must be able to see her. They move with confidence.

Is the room truly dark, or did they blind Lexi with some experimental poison?

"She looks so much like him," the stranger says.

Perhaps it's the intimacy of proximity, but Lexi detects a hint of sadness in the high-pitched voice. The touch of emotion calms her pulse. She isn't dealing with shadows or demons; these are people. Lexi has battled against the impartial whims of greater powers all her life. Nature is a formidable foe of mountains and hurricanes. People are small.

"Who do I l-look like?" Lexi croaks.

"She speaks," the stranger says.

Between the disorientation, her broken body, and the darkness, a wave of frustration rises within Lexi. If they're going to talk about her like she isn't there, then she'll have to force their attention. She tries to sit up, but her chest cramps.

"Who—" Lexi grits through a clenched jaw, "—who are you talking about?"

"You, my dear." The feeling of human presence drifts to the back of the room. Something is off about the woman's foot placement. It sounds like she's carrying a heavy load or walking with a limp. "Chen, the door." The stranger exhales uneasily. "I hate this fucking room."

Lexi can't see or hear a door, but she can certainly feel the effects of one. A gentle *whoosh* of air rushes into the room. Lexi is struck by how much colder the outside air is. Intuitively, she knows it isn't less than 50 degrees Fahrenheit, yet she's shaking. Her sudden intolerance for winter conditions is just another adjustment that she'll need to understand.

"Why is she naked?" the stranger asks. "Where is her balat?"

"I can't issue identification without your approval," Artemis replies. "Excuse me, the council's approval."

"Fine, granted. We don't need them ogling her."

"Thank you, Hatshepsut."

Lexi has never heard the name before. It sounds like hot chicken soup.

There is a long silence as fresh air flows into the room. Though "fresh" isn't exactly the term that Lexi would use. It's sterile. A kind of unnatural nothingness that has little in common with the wind between trees. There must be a considerable temperature difference from the outside air for the atmosphere to take this long to balance.

Lexi holds her breath, waiting for an indication as to whether or not the women have left. Unease clings to her like a fog and unsettles her stomach. If she moves too quickly, she might hurl. She considers rummaging through the dark to search for a door, but remains frozen in place. She decides to count down from sixty and then she's running, naked or not.

Fifty-nine.

Fifty-eight.

Fifty-seven.

"Hold out your hand." Artemis materializes inches from her. The walls must be insulated.

Lexi tenses. It takes all her willpower not to jump. She doesn't want them to think that she's a caged rat *and* a frightened one. She reaches up, and a wrapped bundle is dropped into her arms. She falls forward.

The black material is thick and unyielding, with textured layers that feel a few centimeters deep. It could be clothing, or a suit of armor. It's difficult to say when even her hands feel alien.

"I haven't been given permission to fully instate you yet," Artemis says. "The High Councilor has the authority, but as you heard, she's deferring it to the rest of the council to vote. Take this."

"What is it?"

"A balat. It will regulate your body temperature." Artemis's voice changes when she says, "Don't ever take it off."

"Okay." Lexi frowns at that. "What's a 'b-balat'?"

"It's the Filipino word for 'skin.' "

Lexi looks around, a useless reflex given the circumstances, but she assumes that Artemis's usual demanding tone has returned because Hatshepsut has left.

Lexi stares into the void where her hand is, hoping that her face isn't twisted into blatant disgust. "I'm not—" She searches for the words. "This isn't human skin or something, is it?"

"It's synthetic."

"You have a way of answering questions by not answering them, you know."

"Mm." Artemis takes the bundle from Lexi and unravels it, pulling at the ends as if it would be too rigid for gravity alone to straighten. She returns it to Lexi. "Put it on, you'll feel better."

"Is this w-what you w-wear?"

"Yes." Artemis sucks in air between her teeth as if answering questions directly pains her. "Every citizen needs one."

Citizen.

Of what, Spain?

Lexi runs her fingers over the material. She doesn't know what will happen when she puts it on, but anything is better than freezing to death. She leans back and lets her foot feel its way into the leg openings. The suit suctions to her skin like wet spandex, resisting as she pulls. The material is thicker than she expected. More metal than cloth. Weirdly, it has elasticity once she starts moving, as if it's coming to life.

"I'm going to seal the back," Artemis says, kneeling beside Lexi. "Once the final section is connected, it will constrict." Her hands tinker with tiny ridges rubbing against Lexi's skin.

"What's wrong with my eyes?" Lexi asks.

Artemis doesn't answer. She reaches the bottom of Lexi's neck and connects the final piece. The suit vibrates, and constricts around her throat.

Lexi collapses.

She pulls at the collar, but the suit tightens around her like a boa constrictor. It snaps and bends, squeezing tighter and tighter around her legs and throat. Lexi gasps for air for the second time in a day. She reaches over her shoulder and claws at the material for a release, but there is nothing to grab, nothing to pull.

"Moving will only make it worse," Artemis says. "It's fitting to you."

When Lexi doesn't stop struggling, Artemis presses Lexi to the ground with a firm hand. She might as well be held down by a wooden bat. Artemis is shorter than her, but the woman's strength is considerably greater.

"Breathe," Artemis says, in what Lexi assumes is her attempt at a soothing tone.

Lexi yelps in pain as a section pinches her inner thigh. She closes her eyes, meeting the same darkness as when her eyes are open.

In, out, in, out.

Breathe.

In. Out.

Ten more times.

Within seconds, the suit slackens. When Lexi takes a deep breath, the balat moves with her. There is not an inch of excess space—no gaps at the elbows or creases behind the knees. The material rises to the needs of the user, and then fades back when no longer needed. It really is a second skin.

The cold Lexi felt is gone, yet a ripple of goosebumps travels down her arms. The balat responds, evenly sweeping warmer temperature throughout her body. Is it experimental tech, a medical device, or a toy for rich people?

A small screen is embedded into her forearm. She can feel the change in texture by her wrist.

"We need to be aware of every resource and expenditure," Artemis says. "We can't suffocate because someone wanted to run a mile." She chuckles to herself. When Lexi doesn't match her humor and only stares in confusion, Artemis's voice drops. "You'll need this as well." She slides a soft fabric over Lexi's head.

Lexi has never felt her head before, not really. There has always been a thick net of hair in the way. Now it feels numb.

"What is this?" Lexi asks.

"A hat. It wasn't easy to locate. I spent twenty minutes describing it to the cataloguer before he understood what I was talking about. Your hair should grow long enough within the month."

Lexi is on the verge of tears. "Why did you shave m-my head?"

Artemis doesn't answer, and hands her a pair of socks. They reach to just below Lexi's knees and compress in a similar fashion, though Lexi is less dramatic about it this time. She doesn't need to breathe through her calves. The soles make a metallic sound when she sets them down onto the floor. They're too firm to be socks, too soft to be shoes.

What an odd gadget.

Lexi tries to collect herself despite a whirlwind of questions that she suspects will not be answered. She starts with the most critical. "What's wrong with my eyes?"

"Nothing."

Lexi would laugh if she wasn't so frustrated. "You know what I'm asking."

"I do," Artemis concedes. "But I am limited in what I can tell you until the council approves otherwise. They should be arriving soon." The last sentence trails off as Artemis turns away. "Stand up, and keep your head down."

A *whoosh* of air enters the room, but doesn't sting as before. The balat does an excellent job protecting Lexi from the cold. She stands shakily, trying her best not to lean on Artemis.

Footsteps shuffle into the room. She can't track how many people there are, but it's at least ten. She waits for the feet to settle. Most of them are random, but a couple are thumping in rhythm. Soldiers, maybe.

An uneasy murmur descends upon the room. The people's voices wander as their heads turn to inspect the space. They sound restless. Whatever room they've all gathered in, it's not somewhere anyone wants to be.

The murmuring ascends into a crescendo when they see Lexi. Shocked, they openly voice their protest and displeasure. Unsure where to fix her eyes, she closes them. She's never been more uncomfortable in her entire life.

"Council members," Artemis says.

The room hushes to silence.

A final pair of footsteps slides along the farthest wall. If silence can judge, then the jury is not leaning in the late arrival's favor. A pair of women in the corner giggle.

"Artemis," a shrill voice says. Hatshepsut. "The council has responded to your urgent notice. This is most alarming news."

"High Councilor Hatshepsut," Artemis says, engaging in what Lexi assumes is a bow. They are behaving as if Hatshepsut wasn't just there minutes ago. This is for show. "At approximately 0900 hours, I received an alert from column 1,227 pod 32,905 that an anomaly had occurred, and the pod needed repair. Following protocol 24 subsection A, number 220, I mobilized the pod for inspection, and found the inhabitant awake and disconnected."

Someone gasps, two women grumble, and a man whispers something conspiratorial. Their accents are predominantly American, but there's a hint of something else—British or Swedish or something—as if they had moved to another other country and their accent assimilated after years of exposure.

Lexi hadn't considered the possibility that she is no longer in the United States. She didn't detect an accent in Artemis's voice, but now that she's listening to them as a group, it's clear that Lexi is not on a U.S. military base.

"Councilors!" Hatshepsut shouts, followed by a clicking sound. "Councilors. I suggest that we hear the information in its entirety before jumping to conclusions, yes?" When no one challenges her, she says, "Continue, Artemis."

"Following protocol 24 subsection L, number 5," Artemis continues, "I inspected the nodes and found them to be fully operational. The primary data cord had been removed, along with the oxygen, carbon dioxide, and nourriture systems. Following protocol 24 sub—"

"Yes, yes," a man interrupts. "We're well aware that you followed all of the protocols. We don't hand out sentinel positions to just anyone. Consider your ass covered. Get to the point."

Artemis has been growing into an indomitable figure in Lexi's mind. An all-knowing force with a mastery of the tools around her. Artemis exerts a certain kind of command on the elements around her, yet the man has silenced her. Either he is Artemis's superior, and this is the first crack in her armor, or she doesn't like him.

"I appreciate the exoneration, Councilor Farhad," Artemis replies.

A different voice audibly chokes a laugh, standing in the same area as the late arrival. Lexi suspects that they are the same person. She isn't sure why, but she's keeping track of allies and adversaries based on their responses to Artemis, suspecting that whoever is on her side is likely also on Lexi's.

Farhad scoffs. "That is hardly an ex—"

"Following the final protocol," Artemis continues unabated, "I removed the secondary data cord, and waste systems."

The detached manner in which Artemis summarizes one of the most traumatizing experiences in Lexi's life is off-putting.

"Good thing you were close by," a woman says. "Which Iron Dreamer is it?"

Artemis stands beside Lexi and says, "Alexandria Carvalho, number 422y."

A flurry of voices coalesces into a single stream of piercing white noise.

"How—"

"Uncanny."

"Carvalho?"

Lexi's head cocks to the side. Her last name isn't Carvalho. That's her mother's maiden name. Maybe this really is an innocent mix-up of identities.

"Now there are two of them. High Councilor," Farhad says, approaching Hatshepsut with a tone of respect. "I vote for an immediate investigation into the anomaly. A committee will be assembled to validate Artemis's claims, and to ascertain the actions that must be taken."

"Are you suggesting that this was done intentionally?" a different man asks. "The actions of the Dark Angel, perhaps?"

The room hushes at the name.

Farhad uses the silence to take in his moment. "We are closing in on the Dark Angel. Luna denies knowing his whereabouts. He could be on a satellite station. Until he is captured, I suggest that no security clearance is permitted to number 442y until its fate is decided."

"She's not an *it*, Farhad. And you can't keep her in here," a melodic voice says. The woman speaks with such distaste that Lexi wonders if there's mold growing on the walls. "This isn't why we built the Forest."

"This is precisely why we built it," Farhad counters.

"You don't have the authority. That's for the High Councilor to decide."

The chaotic rise of voices is painfully loud. Lexi covers her ears. The strangers are so agitated by the room that it sounds like they're merging together to avoid touching the walls. Just as Lexi's about to crush her own skull and drown out the cacophony, a pair of fingers pinch the back of her hand.

"They can see you," Artemis whispers. "Show them nothing."

Artemis steps away and Lexi lowers her hands. Complying with her orders seems like the best bet in a bad hand. Farhad, on the other hand, is revealing his, and it is not in Lexi's favor. If he had been the one to find her in the tub, he might have pushed her back under.

A *click-click-click* cuts through the air.

"Councilors," Hatshepsut says. "We will take Councilor Farhad's suggestion and assemble a seven-person committee to investigate. We will vote at 0800 hours tomorrow. Until that time, Councilor Sophie is correct. Alexandria is no longer within Beta. As such, we cannot treat her like a prisoner and keep her in here. I will restrict her security clearance to base level 1A. Where is Mostafa?"

"Here, High Councilor," a young man says. It's the late arrival.

"See to Miss Carvalho's security detail, and a room assignment."

"Room assignment?" Farhad sneers, shifting uncomfortably close to Lexi. "Is it not enough to allow it free rein? We have to provide guards so that everyone can know how spectacularly we have failed to maintain security?"

Lexi has no idea how she could be a threat to anyone's way of life, but she takes note of his relentless determination to call her "it."

"The main levels are hardly free rein," Hatshepsut replies. "But if you are concerned that she'll wander into your wing, we can assign additional security for your protection."

There is an undercurrent of tension that cuts between them. The rest of the council members babble amongst themselves, preferring gossip over the delegation of duties and oblivious to the exchange. Lexi can't see Farhad's face, or read his body language, but he doesn't speak.

Hatshepsut claps her hands. "Dismissed!"

Most of the footsteps move out of the room quickly, the sound of people happy to be released, but a few of them inch closer to Lexi. She winces, prepared to be poked and prodded by curious fingers that never reach out. After a pause, the footsteps fade.

Lexi counts to ten, takes a breath, and snaps her fingers. The echo returns higher.

The door is open.

"No communication privileges," Artemis huffs, waiting until the rest of the council has left. "What would you like me to do, leash her?"

"It was that or keep her in here," Hatshepsut replies.

"Gal will file a claim against Lexi to ensure that her estate isn't challenged. Farhad will back her. The more you bend to him, the more he takes."

"Do not lecture me on Farhad," Hatshepsut snaps. "And where were you?"

"Apologies, High Councilor," Mostafa says, entering the mix. "I was occupied by a prior engagement."

"I'm sure you were." Hatshepsut's patronizing tone sounds strange coming from such a shrill voice. It's like a child learning a new word and thinking that no one else knows it.

"Why do I need guards?" Lexi asks.

Lexi imagines the three of them turning to stare at her. Her legs have been shaking from the effort of standing for what feels like hours, her ears are ringing, and her neck hurts from holding up her head. She needs answers before she passes out.

"It is quite jarring," Hatshepsut says gently.

"How do you think it's been for me?" Artemis replies.

Lexi needs to see their faces and know who she's talking to, and who's making decisions on her fate, but she doesn't need eyes to hear the conflict in Artemis's voice.

"Zuchiris!" Hatshepsut shouts. "Where is that brute?"

"Here," a voice behind Lexi says.

Lexi jumps into a stranger's hands. They grip her shoulders so tightly that they could be made of marble. The man waits until she regains her balance and lets her go. There had been a wall behind her, she was sure of it. How could a man have been standing there the whole time?

Was he there when she was sleeping?

"Nice, Zuchiris," Artemis says dryly.

"What?" He shrugs so hugely that Lexi can hear his arms move. "You asked for me."

Lexi has never heard the name Zuchiris before, or Hatshepsut.

Who are these people?

"Take her to her room," Hatshepsut orders him. "Do not let her leave until I tell you otherwise. Artemis, a word."

Zuchiris takes Lexi by the arm—not roughly, but not kindly either. She doesn't protest, instead following the lead of the rest of the council members and withdrawing from the room as quickly as possible. If they don't want to be here, then she doesn't want to be there either.

Zuchiris drags her through what sounds like a hallway. Without being able to see, it's a challenge to find her balance. Thinking about a sloped floor builds a ramp in her mind. Her knees buckle at the imagined incline, forcing Zuchiris to dig deeper into her arm.

"You have the wrong person," Lexi says. "Please, just let me go."

"What do you mean?" he asks.

Lexi is thrown off by the question. Zuchiris speaks as if *she's* the one with the authority to decide that she's the wrong person, and he is simply the last to be told.

"I, uh..." Lexi hesitates. "I don't know. I just know that I sh-shouldn't be here." Artemis told her to keep her head down, not that she couldn't ask questions, and Zuchiris doesn't seem to have the same rigidness. "How far from New Hampshire are we?"

Zuchiris laughs. It's devoured by the walls without a hint of feedback. The silence is oppressive. Wherever they are, the walls are low, narrow, and well-insulated. "Pretty far," he says.

"As in, I would need a plane to get there, or-r could I drive?"

Zuchiris pauses. "I can't say it."

Lexi's eyes well with frustration. Finding her way home is sounding more and more arduous. Are her parents close, or is she on her own?

He pulls her up by the waist when she trips over her feet. His fingertips flare out as if he's afraid to squeeze her to death. He holds her in place until she stops wobbling. She doesn't like being dependent on people. She hasn't spent her whole life training on the mountain just to become helpless.

It will take months to recover the physicality that she's lost, and she doesn't even know why it's happened.

Lexi takes a breath and clutches Zuchiris's forearms. He's wearing the same material she is—the same that Artemis is wearing. Lexi's fingers barely reach halfway around his forearms. Perhaps Hatshepsut calling him a brute wasn't an exaggeration. Judging by his arms and the distance from his voice, he towers over her.

Zuchiris guides her down the hallway. He's more careful this time, slowing their pace and loosening his grip.

"Were you there the whole time?" Lexi asks.

"Yeah."

"Why?"

His arms shift into another huge shrug. "Artemis told me to."

"To spy on me?"

"Hah. You don't know anything. That's why you still have options."

Zuchiris has a similar cryptic methodology of answering questions that Artemis has, but at least he's responding to them. His voice is relatable, and less formal. He talks like they're friends, like he wants to help. He loosened his grip, didn't he?

"Why couldn't anyone see you?" Lexi asks. "Is it like why I can't see? When will I get my eyes back?"

"You still have your eyes."

"But they don't *work*!"

They turn a corner, and then another. The halls are a maze. Lexi fumbles at every step until Zuchiris is half-carrying her. If they're passing people along the way, she can't hear them. The walls absorb everything, like the forest after a snowstorm. Even her footsteps are muted.

"Why couldn't anyone see you?" Lexi asks, determined to squeeze an answer out of him. It's not the most pressing issue, but for some reason it's the one that bothers her the most. She can't see—for no real reason that she can ascertain—but for no one else to have seen him when he was standing *right behind her* the whole time?

That unnerves her.

"It's a new piece of tech," Zuchiris says. "The High Councilor wasn't supposed to say anything. I mean, she can do whatever she wants. Sort of. But it was weird."

A thread in the web unravels.

It seems that the threads of this place aren't woven into an impenetrable administration. There are fault lines between the players. Lexi might be able to pull on one of them to escape. She knows that not everyone who gathered in the strange room was on the same page. Farhad made that clear. But the intricacies between the council members are far from orderly and succinct.

Zuchiris slows to a crawl. The palm around her arm rises and then lowers, as if Zuchiris is turning one way and then the other. He's reading door numbers, lost in his own train of thought.

"How long I was in that tub?" Lexi asks.

"The whole time."

Zuchiris is either oblivious to her confusion, or purposefully contributing to it. He doesn't strike Lexi as the nefarious type.

She isn't sure what concerns her more—the possibility that no one knows what's going on, or that someone does, and they're intentionally remaining hidden.

Zuchiris tugs on her arm and they stop. A breeze rushes past them. It's the same shift in air that used to happen in her high school before they fixed the heating system. The hallways had weak spots in the infrastructure, and did a poor job of shielding them in the winter. The classrooms were set to one temperature, and the hallways struggled to keep up. Every time a student opened a door, air would rush past them.

Wherever they are, the outside temperature is freezing.

Zuchiris grabs Lexi's shoulders and guides her into a room. She lifts her hands, worried that she'll bump into something. Thankfully, Zuchiris doesn't shove her. He allows Lexi to cautiously explore the space.

"Careful," Zuchiris says, just as Lexi's right foot bangs into something.

Her balance should be better than this. Her body is unrecognizable. How long was she in a coma?

"What year is it?" she asks.

Zuchiris whistles. It's not a pretty whistle, or melodic. The final note drops to the base of his throat like a stone. She's heard of patients being in a coma for months, or even years. Has it only been a few days, and he's simply constrained by the limitations of the orders he's following? Or is it worse than that?

Lexi turns to face him. "Can you not tell me?"

"I can," he admits tentatively. "You have base level 1A security clearance. Which isn't much, but technically, all security levels allow the year. I think, anyway. I'm trying to remember what happened last time."

"Last time? Is that the other Iron Dreamer—or whatever—that someone was talking about?"

"Yeah, Cillian 3124."

Lexi's face contorts into confusion. "Is that the door code?"

"No," Zuchiris says, releasing his grip. "That's the year."

CHAPTER FOUR

Lexi doesn't sleep for days. At least, that's the way it feels.

It's difficult to determine if and for how long she sleeps when everything in her world is darkness. If she dreams, she doesn't remember it.

Artemis comes by to drop off food in the form of small packets. They remind Lexi of the MREs that her parents like to bring on long backpacking trips. They're good in a pinch, but they taste awful. She asks Artemis for solid food, but she only replies with some cryptic rationale about how solid food is a bad idea for her body at the moment.

Artemis doesn't linger, or answer any of Lexi's questions. One time she dropped off food and left without saying a word. It might have not even been her. Zuchiris stays longer. His company provides a brief relief from the loneliness that grips Lexi when the quiet beats against her skull.

A deep vibration fills the room like humidity. She can't hear it, but she can feel the it in the space between her lungs.

The room is never truly quiet.

Two guards stand outside her door. One has a deep voice, the other's is raspy, and the third is a woman. It's the same three people on rotation. Lexi hears them when they acknowledge Artemis. They call her Sentinel Artemis, a designation that rouses Lexi's curiosity.

She waits for the woman guard's rotation to ask to use the bathroom. The bathroom is nearby, and the toilet flushes like they're on an airplane, but without the water. Lexi considers the possibility that they're on a jumbo jet or an airship, but she hasn't felt turbulence.

Zuchiris brings toys that he claims are good for Lexi's cognitive health. It gives her something to do. Her favorite toy is twelve tiny cubes carved from rock, bound together by a single rubber band that snaps the apparatus into different shapes. Her dexterity hasn't returned—her fingers continue to struggle to rotate the cubes—but the toy helps.

Aside from a cot that she sleeps on, and a chair, the room is empty. Sometimes she thinks she hears the sound of footsteps walking toward her while she sleeps.

"Why can't I see?" Lexi asks one day, sitting cross-legged on the chair, fiddling with the cubes.

Lexi has learned the differences between Artemis's quietly graceful steps and Zuchiris's heavy ones. There's a part of Lexi that doesn't want to know where she is—that if she wakes up to find herself in a white padded room, or a dirty cell, she'll have a mental breakdown.

"A couple reasons," Zuchiris says.

"Like?"

"I can't say it." He says, debating. "They don't want you learning the language."

"The language," Lexi replies flatly.

Zuchiris sits on the floor opposite her, watching a screen and occasionally chuckling to himself. She's asked him what the device is for. He says that it's above her security clearance, which has been increased to base level 1B in the last few days, but it still doesn't provide her with much information.

"I can hear you talking, and I understand," Lexi says. "What language are you talking about?"

"Not any you know," Zuchiris says. He pauses for a long while. He does that a lot. "Well, not that you ever knew this kind."

Lexi wonders, and not for the first time, if they're in a cult.

It would explain their commitment to the narrative that the year is 3124. How ridiculous. Zuchiris provides no explanation, and hasn't answered any questions about it since, which gives her the feeling that he wasn't supposed to tell her that they believe the year is 3124. If they're trying to induct her into an apocalyptic covenant, they've chosen a dreadful tactic.

Lexi releases an uneasy laugh. "I'm not going to be able to learn a whole language in a few days. Why not just let me have my eyes back? Am I being poisoned?"

"It's not worth the risk," Zuchiris says.

Lexi huffs.

One question at a time.

"Are you poisoning me?" she asks.

Zuchiris jerks so quickly that she flinches, unsure if his huge size comes with any grace, or if he might accidentally kick the chair out from underneath her.

"I'm not poisoning you," he says, offended.

"What, not your style?"

"No, I didn't say that." He chuckles, as if telling himself a joke. "Poison is a woman's weapon."

"That's a bit sexist."

Zuchiris sets the entertainment device on the floor. She imagines him folding his hands or crossing his arms over his knees. There's a calculating energy to everyone she encounters. From Artemis to the guards, and now Zuchiris. As if they all have nothing better to do than to play mind games.

"How tall do you think I am?" he asks.

"What?"

"How big?"

She imagines his dimensions. "I don't know, pretty big."

"Would you rather hit me right now, or strike when I'm asleep?"

The apathy with which Zuchiris presents the question unnerves her. He doesn't sound weathered by violence, or naïve to it; he sounds indifferent.

It's almost worse.

Lexi balks. "I-I wouldn't hit you."

"But if you had to, if your life depended on it. Would you rather attack when I *definitely* can fight back, or when I can't?"

Lexi imagines Zuchiris's huge form hurtling toward her. She would be helpless, truth be told. She might be able to bite or claw, or punch his groin, but otherwise she wouldn't walk away from the altercation unscathed.

"Yes, you're bigger," Lexi huffs, "and I would lose, but that doesn't mean poison is a *woman's* weapon. Anyone can use poison."

"You're five-foot-seven," he says. "That's not short, but you're not tall either. Most men will be bigger than you, and it's not just a matter of size, testosterone is also a factor. Even if you trained every day for years, you'd never beat me in a straight fight. Sure, you could get a hit or two in, or throw me off my guard, but you'd lose to my size nine times out of ten, and that's being generous. Do you want to take those odds?"

Lexi isn't sure if she should be scared or irritated by the turn in conversation. It's an arrogant declaration; that she will always be unable to defend herself and Zuchiris holds the upper hand. But there is nothing hostile or proud in his voice, no pleasure extracted from the exchange. If anything, he sounds tired.

"It's not fair," he says quietly. "But it's the truth. If you're going to survive here, you have to be realistic. And then know your weapons."

His tone reminds Lexi of her first encounter with Artemis. When Artemis wanted her to crawl toward her from the tub, soaking wet and naked.

"You sound like Artemis," Lexi grumbles.

"Trust me, it's a good thing."

"You're making it sound like being a woman isn't a good thing at all."

Zuchiris snorts. "I would rather fight a hundred men than go head-to-head against her." His voice trails off, returning his attention to the entertainment device in hopes of putting an end to the conversation. "You should probably get some sleep."

Another five days pass, and still no updates.

Lexi worries about her family. They must be stressed out of their minds. Are they at home, calling up the local politicians and protesting on social media, or are they on the road, making their way to her?

The boredom is unbearable, even with Zuchiris's efforts to distract her. Each hour blends into the next, and the next. The days are a fog of timeless suspension. She's learned every inch of her cell—which is what she's decided to call it, since her situation amounts to imprisonment. It's eight feet by ten. The door is very strange. It melts away, becoming a featureless section indistinguishable from the wall. No gap, no lines of any kind.

The walls have a few peculiarities of their own. They're hard, but have pliability. Like the difference between glacial ice and an ice cube, where the former is significantly denser from hundreds of thousands of years of time and pressure, and the latter comes from a refrigerator. She knocks on the walls and can't find the support beams. It's a single unbroken unit.

"You should do your exercises," Zuchiris says one morning.

"I really don't want to," Lexi complains. "I can barely do twenty squats."

"That's two more than yesterday."

Zuchiris gives her exercise routines that she can do in her room. Simple, boring activities like jogging in place, pushups, and squats. He says that her form is bad, and corrects her squats whenever her knees twist outward. She's never liked working out in the traditional sense. Her extracurricular activities have always been enough to keep her out of the gym, but the pain provides a convenient distraction from an existential crisis.

"It's more than that," Lexi says, fiddling with the cube toy. "I feel heavy. Which I know doesn't make sense because I'm sure I lost forty pounds."

An awkward tension settles between them. Lexi's noticed this happens when she asks a question too close to territory that Zuchiris doesn't want to explore. If she comments on a strange smell in the air, or a humming behind the walls, he shuts down.

"Am I crazy?" she asks cautiously.

Zuchiris takes a breath, deliberating. "You're heavier. Well, your mass is the same, but it'll feel different every now and then."

"What does that mean?"

"Weight and mass are different."

Lexi is tired of everyone speaking to her like she's an idiot. "I know that," she snaps, having only just remembered that weight and mass are different.

The door slides open. It's Artemis. Lexi can tell by her inaudible strides. Zuchiris jumps to his feet and the room is quiet.

Zuchiris mumbles a protest. A week ago, Lexi would have been curious about the reaction, but the humdrum of a small room and little company for nine days has rendered her detached from the happenings between these people. What would be the point in asking? They wouldn't tell her what's going on anyway.

A different set of footsteps enter the room. A new set. Graceful, but delayed, as if pulling an empty sled. What fresh humiliation will this new prospect offer?

"Lie down on the bed, Lexi," Artemis says.

Lexi's hands ball into fists. "No."

"Do you prefer being blind?"

"You're going to give me my vision back?" she asks, careful not to sound too excited.

"We didn't take it. Your eyes are covered. Doctor Singh here is going to remove the covers, and then you'll have your full vision."

"That will take some time," a man interjects. "It may take a few hours for the blurriness along the edge of your vision to withdraw, but you will be able to see, yes. The procedure is quick and painless."

There's a doctor on site, which means that they expect complications of some kind to arise from whatever shady business they conduct. They are well-sourced and well-funded. That, or a cult leader has brainwashed a doctor.

Lexi bolts to the bed. She lies on her back, hands by her side, vibrating with excitement. She will have her vision back. *Finally*. She can't remember the last time she was this excited, or relieved, about anything.

"Tell her the pill thing," Zuchiris says, shifting in the way that Lexi has identified as anxiety.

"She knows too much," Artemis says. "It's already too late."

"Oh my god," Lexi fumes, turning her head toward them. "Please stop talking about me like I'm not here."

Zuchiris's heavy footsteps stomp toward Lexi. He kneels beside the head of the bed, wound tight like a rubber band. "Right, so," he says, "there's this movie I used to like. The main character was given two options: a red pill or a blue pill. This is like that. If you get your vision back, that's like taking the red pill, and your life will change forever. If you turn it down, that's the blue pill, and it'll be like this never happened. You don't know anything, so you still have choices."

"Zuchiris," Artemis says, with a warning tone.

"She's not Cillian," he says.

Lexi turns over the words in her head, but doesn't understand. Of course she wants her vision returned. She can live with an implant at the base of her skull—maybe look into having it removed someday—but she couldn't sacrifice skiing and biking for the rest of her life because of a misunderstanding. She wants to go home. They have the wrong person.

"I want my eyes back," Lexi says.

Zuchiris moves wordlessly to the back of the room. She's never appreciated her vision before, or having freedom, or her own bed. There are a lot of things that she's going to change after this ordeal.

"I'm going to place a device over your eyes. It'll feel like..." Doctor Singh's voice drifts upwards, as if looking to the others for instruction.

"Ski goggles," Artemis says.

"Yes, yes," Doctor Singh replies. "Ski goggles. It will take a moment to begin, but once you hear the buzzing, keep your eyes open, and do not blink."

Lexi becomes immediately concerned by the lapse. He could be distracted by other parts of the machine he's managing, or he's a forgetful doctor. Who doesn't know what goggles are? She holds her breath, unsure of how loud the buzzing will be. She doesn't want to accidentally burn her eyes out. For the briefest moment, she wonders if the whole demonstration is a ploy. If the technology doesn't exist and they have, in fact, permanently blinded her.

A gentle buzzing moves up and around her face. It feels like tiny, sharp gusts of wind blowing into her eyes. It takes all of her willpower to keep from blinking, but the reaction is involuntary. She blinks twice, three times, and then can't stop. The wind sensation has been pulled *underneath* her eyelids, vibrating. The machine's humming rises from the resistance.

Lexi's heart races.

"Please don't blink," Doctor Singh says. "The nites are moving too much."

"Nites?" Lexi is blinking rapidly now.

"Yes, yes. Nearly done."

She manages to keep her eyes open, and the sensation migrates to the edge of her eyes, then disappears. The machine stops humming. Doctor Singh is giving Lexi instructions, but she's not listening. Panic grips her as she opens her eyes and closes them, and there's no difference. Everything is pitch black.

She's blind.

"Give me your hand," Artemis says.

Lexi is on the verge of hyperventilating. "It didn't work. It didn't—"

"It worked," Artemis says. "It's the goggles. We're going to remove them, but I need to show you something first."

Lexi takes her hand and sits up. The woman still manages to have a body temperature five degrees warmer than everyone else—even with Lexi wearing a balat that pulsates heat through her body, Artemis's skin is a furnace. She pulls Lexi to a standing position, and together they make their way down the hall.

Zuchiris's disgruntled footsteps follow closely behind, along with two bodyguards. All of Lexi's attention is focused on not tripping in front of an audience. The exercises have helped a bit, but she feels heavy one moment and then light the next. It's as if she's on a boat, and the waves underneath are rolling slower than molasses.

A set of doors opens, and a cacophony of noise erupts through them. Men and women at various volumes conversing in a massive space. A light breeze brushes Lexi's face. The room is significantly warmer than the hallway.

No, not a room.

"It sounds...big," Lexi says.

Voices, both close and far, echo and combine into the white noise of people in a market, or at an event. Lexi almost believes she's outside, but the sound is too tight. She's in an area with hundreds of people, maybe a thousand. Either the space has zero insulation, or it's the size of a football field.

"This is my second favorite place," Artemis says.

"Can I take these off now?" Lexi asks.

Artemis takes a deep breath. There is no lightness to it, no relief. The jagged cuts in her exhale are subtle, but Artemis is troubled.

Lexi doesn't know what her problem is, and frankly, doesn't care. She wants to see, and go home, and forget that any of this ever happened.

"This is a bad plan," Zuchiris says, voicing the words in a singsong.

Artemis's hand flexes against Lexi's shoulder. She radiates when she thinks. There's a pressure applied to the air around her, like she's exerting her will against it. "I am sorry," she says, and peels the goggles off Lexi's face.

A piercing white light stabs Lexi's retinas. She cries out and covers her face, falling to the floor. After weeks of darkness, the light is painful even from behind her closed eyelids. Her head is ringing and tears well in her eyes. No one reaches for her. No one asks if she's alright. They stand in silence.

Lexi slowly opens one eye, but the searing light causes another round of high-pitched ringing in the front of her head. They're trying to blind her with a different tactic.

"The sun is brighter here," Artemis says. "It was tricky developing a filter that could mimic Rayleigh scattering without completely diminishing the stars during the night rotation. We didn't think it would be a problem, but everyone complained about it."

It's such a specific answer that Lexi nearly loses her balance. "What?"

"We can dive into the quantum mechanics of the dome later, if you're interested. I'm also working on securing an estate for you," Artemis says. "With property comes certain rights. Not that different from life as you knew it, actually."

"I own property?" Lexi is taken aback. She has never once considered owning land, at least not for another ten years. The idea of securing property thrills her. A little piece of dirt to call her own.

Maybe she could camp on it.

Wherever it is.

"It's in litigation," Artemis tells her. "Fortunately, the courts generally rule in our favor on these matters. You may remember me mentioning a woman named Gal when you were first presented to the council. She is one of Farhad's. She originally held full claim to your estate, but now that you're here, you've been granted a small portion of it. Hopefully more in the future."

If Lexi could figure out where she is, she might be able to narrow it down to either a military facility, or a cult hidden in the woods. It wouldn't be her first interaction with a cult. Rumor has it there's a cult hidden in an encampment three miles off Sugar Hill Road. Lexi and Michelle drove around for hours trying to find the trailhead.

A hand grabs Lexi's wrist and pulls her out of the memory. She yanks it away, startled.

"Mostafa," Artemis chastises.

"High Councilor has requested vitals," Mostafa replies.

Where did he come from?

Lexi doesn't like being grabbed, especially when she can't open her eyes. "It's alright," she says, holding out her hand to him. "I need a few minutes to...I don't know, adjust."

Mostafa turns her hand over. She's been careful to avoid touching the screen so that she doesn't press the wrong button and accidentally suffocate herself, but that hasn't stopped everyone else from touching it. He releases her arm and takes a step back.

Lexi presses a hand to her forehead like the visor of a baseball cap and focuses on her balat. What appeared to be a muted black matte is far more intricate.

Layer upon layer is interwoven into the material with an assortment of patterns. She twists her foot, bending the knee to test the suit. It adjusts to her movements like water. The suit folds into itself and then stretches, shimmering like a mirage, leaving not a single gap of air. What she thought was a breeze squeezing through the gaps in her suit was actually the tiny movements of nanotechnology.

"Carbon nanotechnology," Artemis says. "One of our more impressive inventions. You can change the colors if you want."

"Why do you call it a balat?"

"The inventor is Filipino. It'll adapt to temperature and pressure, and create a basic shield to protect the wearer in hostile environments."

Lexi lifts her head. In the distance are hues of blues and greens and black, all curving up and over into a foggy funnel. The raucous noise of the space lowers, and the voices hush to a gentle chorus. She suspects that she's become the main event.

Lexi rubs her eyes, and gasps.

A massive funnel unfolds into a garden of Eden, lush with greens and speckled with warm colors beneath a dark black sky. The stars don't twinkle or shimmer, they're static, scattered like paint across a glass ceiling. The night sky in the North Country is clearer than in most parts of the world, but this is a whole other level. The gaseous arms of the Milky Way galaxy stretch across the ceiling. If it's a painting, it is the most realistic that Lexi has ever seen.

The ground twists into space farther than Lexi's eyes can see. Hundreds of rows of trees and flowers weave through the garden and up toward the edge of the funnel, where it curls up and to the left. The trees are perfectly trimmed and massive, stretching at least a hundred feet high.

Maple, pine, oak. Men and women stand beneath their massive branches, chatting in groups, but never taking their eyes off Lexi, who stands atop a wide platform above them.

Lexi's balance wavers, and she turns left, only to be blinded by the sun. It should be impossible. The sun, the Milky Way, and a garden of Eden in one place beneath the stars. It's breathtaking. It's astonishing. It isn't real.

She staggers toward the sun. The platform hovers a few feet above the tallest tree, and she peers over the edge of the railing. She can't see all the way down and through the dome, past whatever is beyond the curved glass, but it must be full of stars.

Which is impossible.

"Where are we?" Lexi asks, voice hollow. "What is this place?"

Lexi turns to Zuchiris, taking in his size and appearance for the first time. He wasn't wrong before when he told her to know her weapons. She would never win in a fight against him.

She steps back.

Zuchiris raises his eyebrows, his most prominent feature. They're large and dark, and a bizarre contrast to his dirty blonde hair, giving him the appearance of a disgruntled Neanderthal. There is not a single effeminate feature to his face, nor any delicateness to his frame. He is tall and broad-shouldered, a body designed for the sole purpose of barging through doors.

Where Artemis's features allow her to blend into any crowd, Zuchiris is the most distinct and imposing figure on the platform. He holds up his hands, approaching Lexi as if she's a wild animal. The two guards step forward, but he sends them back with two curled fingers and a swift motion of his arm, followed by a series of hand motions.

Sign language.

Lexi bends over, resting her hands on her knees and suppressing the urge to vomit. Every muscle in her body tenses. Her heart races. She shakes her head, thoughts jumbling and catching fire before rising up again for another round. Incomplete sentences that she can't bear to finish suck the air out of her lungs.

She catches a glimpse of fingers reaching for her. "*Don't touch me.*" The motion throws her off-balance and she collides with the floor, hip first.

The impact should hurt, and maybe it does, but Lexi doesn't feel anything. She closes her eyes and focuses on her jagged breathing. Artemis is there, lifting her off the floor.

There are a million explanations for what is happening. She could be in one of those Hollywood domes that look like real places, where actors merge themselves into distant landscapes. She saw a special about it after a night of watching *CSI*. Maybe this is just an exceptionally pervasive dream. It could be a prank, but what is there to gain?

Lexi curls onto her side and pulls her legs toward her chest. "Where am I?" she croaks.

Artemis and Zuchiris stand over her like hunters come to collect their prize. Artemis kneels. When Zuchiris doesn't follow, she tugs on his arm and he kneels beside her, one arm resting over his leg. He slouches his shoulders as if he could make himself smaller.

"Space," Artemis says flatly.

Lexi's mind reels so violently that she would fall over if she wasn't already lying on the ground.

"You should open your eyes," Zuchiris says.

Keeping her head on the floor, Lexi leans to the side and looks toward the ceiling.

The stars are brilliant and piercing. She recognizes the Big Dipper, able to identify the constellation by the three stars of the handle. She looks for Orion's Belt next, and then Vega. They should be twinkling. Stars shimmer because of the atmosphere and vast distances. Uniform stars suggest remarkable attention to detail. If this is a virtual reality game, then it certainly is a convincing one.

"Where are we?" Lexi asks, for the umpteenth time.

"In an orbiter," Artemis says. "A city-station in orbit around the sun. We've built two of them. This one is called Sol. It's positioned at Lagrange Point 4, and the second, Luna, is at Lagrange Point 5. There are a handful of smaller stations, but Sol and Luna are the main orbiters."

"I don't know what any of that means."

Zuchiris shifts his weight, uncomfortable with the tension of consequential moments. He's much easier to read now that Lexi can see his face. Artemis, on the other hand—even when she's frank, she's indecipherable.

"You're in space," Artemis says, picking at her fingernails.

"Well, send me back," Lexi pleads. "Just send me back."

"If we could do that, then none of this would have happened." Artemis sighs, her patience fading as a restless tone bites out her next words. "The Earth has been dead for a thousand years. This is all that's left."

CHAPTER FIVE

Lexi is confined to her room for three days.

She spends most of the time crying.

One of the guards had to carry her from the Solarium after she refused to walk. He had cradled her like a child, and she probably weighed as much. She cracked open an eye to watch the guards' footsteps illuminate the floor. It was like watching a surfer wade through bioluminescent water. The grace with which he walked, combined with the captivating way the floor responded to him, eased her mind into a trance that she eagerly accepted.

Her room isn't what she expected. It's small and bare, without windows or features of any kind. She had assumed that there would be wear and tear since it was a storage space, but the walls have the same shiny gray shimmer as the floor.

Sometimes she thinks she hears footsteps pacing near her cot, but now that she can see the entirety of her room, she realizes that no one is there. It's just an echo of the bending and cracking of a space station.

Someone tells her that she can walk the halls and explore the Solarium—which is what they call the big open funnel with trees and stars—but she has no desire to. Her hands clench at random times, and her heart races erratically. She can't sleep. She can't eat. Every few hours, she needs to remind herself to breathe. If she doesn't, she's afraid that she might stop breathing altogether.

She lies on the cot, unwilling to eat or speak. Her back is turned to the room, so that what she sees is only the wall.

It's not solely out of stubbornness.

Lexi's legs give out from beneath her whenever she tries to stand. She sways as if trying to balance on a tightwire hundreds of stories above the ground. She can see the solid floor, feel its hardness, but a tingling sensation in the back of her mind tells her that she's going to fall through.

The guards continue to stand by her door. Chen—the raspy-voiced one who carried her from the Solarium—stands motionless. Every time Lexi catches a glimpse of him, he is in the exact same position. His jet-black hair is cut short, with chart-like markings that look like a topographical map. It could be artistic, or cultural.

The second guard, Olaf, looks similar to Zuchiris, but shorter and broader. They could be cousins, if not for the drastically different facial features. Olaf has a softer face and light red hair, and stands a few inches shorter than Chen. He's even shorter than Lexi. She doesn't doubt his skill, though; he maintains the same motionless pose as Chen, and his shoulders reach from one side of the doorway to the other.

What is all the security for?

"Hey," Zuchiris says. He hunches in the doorway, careful to avoid hitting his head. The balat he wears is black, with hints of red lines across his chest. They glisten like blood when he steps into the room. If his voice weren't so welcoming, she might be afraid.

"I brought you food," he says, holding up a tray. "Real stuff, mostly. Doc says you need to eat."

The tray has two metal ovals and one clear cylinder that appears to contain a milkshake, or yogurt. There are no plastic materials, only metal and glass. She can't determine which meals are inside the opaque containers, but she spots a red apple.

Lexi's mouth waters at the sight, but the surprise of seeing an apple reminds her why she's surprised. The Solarium. The stars. The year 3124. The garden beneath a black sky. Even her sleep is restless. She wakes up every few hours in a panic, momentarily forgetting where she is until the white walls and eerie silence remind her that she's floating in space.

"Look, I get it," Zuchiris says, placing the tray on her chair. "This is probably a lot to take in, but you'll accept it faster if you look at it. You should go outside."

"Outside?" Lexi mumbles miserably.

"Well, our version of it. Not space," he laughs. "I thought the lack of sound would be the problem, but it's the spinning. I get nauseous every time I look down. You're supposed to keep your eyes on the same reference point so you don't vomit, but there really aren't any in space. Anyway, I'm ranting. What I'm trying to say is that space sucks, and you shouldn't go."

Lexi tightens her arms around her chest. She feels safer in her room than anywhere else. The walls are plain, and there's nothing to look at aside from her cot and a chair.

"So, what's left of humanity is trapped on this rock," she says.

"This isn't a rock."

It's hard to feel offended by a man whose every gesture is genuine. His brashness isn't for lack of empathy. He isn't trying to get a rise out of her. He's simply trying to communicate in the only way he knows how.

Bluntly.

Lexi reaches for the milkshake container and twists open the top. She takes a test taste. It's surprisingly not terrible. She holds it out in front of her and asks, "What is this?"

"Bacteria."

Lexi coughs. "Excuse me?"

"Everything is made of the same stuff. Just got to figure out how to arrange the atoms to get what you want. That," he says, pointing to the container, "is kind of like yogurt, except the bacteria are eating asteroids instead of milk. It shouldn't work, but it does. Everything is made of carbon, even the asteroids we mine. That's what organic means; a thing that has carbon. So, that's milk, asteroids, bacon. Did you know water isn't technically organic because it's just hydrogen and oxygen?"

"Oh, cool." Lexi takes a sniff of the light brown froth and detects a hint of caramel. It doesn't taste bad. Her head is spinning.

What else can they make?

"We mine a lot," Zuchiris continues. He rubs a hand over his chest—a strange physical tic that appears when he explains things. "We always need something, and asteroids have most of what we need. Psyche 16 turned out to have a pocket of platinum. That was neat."

"I want to go home," Lexi says, overwhelmed. "Send me on a ship. Obviously you have the technology. I'm sure you have ships to refuel or what not, right? I won't say anything, I swear."

"Yeah, we can't."

Lexi buries her face in her hands. Zuchiris lowers the food tray to the floor and takes a seat. The chair bends beneath his weight, crackling like firewood as he shifts back and forth.

"I'm not good at this," he says, mostly to himself. "You should probably talk to someone. We have a bunch of therapists here, obviously. Not everyone has adjusted well. And people have a mental breakdown every other solstice."

Zuchiris chuckles.

They did this to her—whatever this is—and that made them the last people she wanted to speak with. Zuchiris's gesture could be authentic, or perhaps he is the mastermind behind it all. Lexi doesn't trust anyone. Not their words, nor their offerings.

"Well." Zuchiris purses his lips and leaves.

How difficult would it be to build a jumbo screen the size of a city? Lexi could have a friend who won the lottery and decided to trick her into believing that the apocalypse had come, and the world had been destroyed. It certainly would be in line with North Country humor.

Many of the people in her hometown, including her parents, are what Michelle likes to call "doomsday prophets." They prepare for the end of the world as if it's right around the corner. They teach their children how to build a shelter and start a fire, but also how to make soap from goat's milk and filter water with charcoal, sand, and bark. They put up solar panels before the rest of the country thought about it.

The North Country is a breeding ground for resourcefulness. Maybe that's just the nature of a small town, or maybe that's the nature of isolation. It could be an elaborate rite of passage—survive in space and find your way home—but they don't have those kinds of resources. They can build a house out of pine cones, but a jumbo screen and nanotechnology?

That's too much.

"—wants to know where she stands," a voice says.

Lexi turns her head, having missed the first part of the sentence. An attractive young man stands in front of Chen, tapping his finger against a clear screen the size of a notebook. His brown skin is perfectly smooth, and caramel eyes so bright that Lexi can see them from her cot. Every detail of his face looks photoshopped, from his perfectly curved nose to his smirking lips.

He might be the most beautiful person she's ever seen.

Chen looks down at his screen and frowns. "You were supposed to arrive twenty minutes ago. Does the High Councilor have you working all hours of the night, or just a few minutes' worth?"

Olaf snickers. He maintains a forward gaze, with his hands clasped behind his back, but his body leans slightly toward the conversation.

"Why don't you join me next time, and you can inspect my work," the young man replies. The pad he was holding evaporates into a slender piece of metal the size of a pen. He slides it into a pocket that appears near his hip.

Chen gives the man a humorless smile. "Maybe I will, Mostafa."

This is Mostafa?

Lexi had no idea that he was only a few years older than herself, or that he looked like a movie star. He's so quintessentially dark and handsome that it might be a joke. His voice resonates differently now that she can see him. If she had known that he was the one grabbing her in the middle of an existential breakdown in the Solarium, she might have not rebuffed him.

Chen's mouth tightens. He nods to Olaf and they both step aside.

Mostafa enters the room, looking from one corner to the other in the casual way of a tourist perusing an unexpected detour, but then his focus locks on the wall.

She follows his gaze, perturbed. There could be a crack in the reinforcements, or an opening leading to the vacuum of space. For all she knows, her room is on the outermost layer of the station and susceptible to punctures.

Mostafa shakes his head. He smiles, but it doesn't reach his eyes. He gives Lexi a once-over, and shuts the door behind him. Lexi catches a glimpse of Chen's disapproving glower before the door seals, melting into the cracks like quicksand, leaving no impression of a door. If Lexi had to draw a room of horrors, it would contain that feature.

The walls absorb every frequency of sound. No one could hear their conversation. No one could hear her scream.

Mostafa grabs the top of the chair and pulls it toward the cot. He sits down, crossing one hand over the other, and studies her. His balat is black with hints of gray, quite ordinary by Sol's standards. Of all the suits she's seen, his is the least colorful.

"Finally, some alone time," Mostafa says. His eyes roam her face. "So, you're the shiny new toy. I can see why he wants you. He never met a mirror he didn't love."

"What are you talking about?" she asks.

"The Dark Angel." He smiles to himself and pulls the chair between his legs. "You could say he's the reason you're here."

Mostafa sits so closely that his knees brush against her cot. Lexi isn't uncomfortable with the proximity. Gui has no sense of physical boundaries and is always checking her pulse. Her mother loves hugs, and Michelle slaps her shoulder whenever she's caught in a laughing fit.

But Lexi doesn't know Mostafa. She shimmies away, pressing her back against the wall.

Mostafa nods. "You shouldn't trust anyone."

"That would include you," Lexi points out. Her voice is as rough as sandpaper. "Why should I listen to anything you have to say anyway?"

"Maybe you shouldn't," Mostafa agrees, leaning back. The chair crackles under his weight. "It's hard to say, when you've never really listened to anyone."

Does he think that the condescending comments are going to help? As if she doesn't know that this place sucks, and the undercurrent of danger isn't as omnipresent as humidity in July. The youthful beauty that she was stunned by warps into aggravation.

Lexi scoffs. "What's that supposed to mean?"

"Everything in your life was fabricated," he says. "All of your problems were a series of lines in a code. They were thought experiments by the engineers and sentinels. You've never spoken to a living person until now. How would you know who to trust, when you're dealing with the human condition for the first time in your life?"

It takes every ounce of strength not to sink into the cot. She doesn't know what he's talking about, or why he's talking to her at all. She doesn't want to look confused, so she doesn't ask.

Mostafa leans back in his chair, crossing one arm over his chest as if reading her thoughts. "They want to deliver the bad news to you in pieces, in case you lose your mind, which I voted against. But I have no vote."

Lexi's family isn't religious, but she remembers being shown bible stories by her grandmother before she died. The stories were drawn onto large cut-outs that her grandmother would hold up and narrate. The drawings were colorful and lively, and one of them had an angel. It was a beautiful man—muscular, luscious hair, with massive dove-like white wings. Her grandmother had told her that the card was a lie. Angels weren't beautiful. They were horrifying to behold, a nightmare to imagine.

"You'll need to be quicker than that," Mostafa says, disappointed. "The faster you learn the rules of the game, the better your odds."

Lexi frowns. "Well, I don't want to play."

"The moment you pulled that cable out of your head, you entered the game, and the clock is ticking. Every moment you waste puts another Iron Dreamer's life at stake. We haven't had a good game in years."

Mostafa was obedient and subservient just a few days ago. He had shown no signs of individuality. He had been a quiet bystander, or maybe it had just seemed that way because Lexi couldn't see his face. It shouldn't make a difference being able to see eyes and mouths, but it does.

Lexi feels like a rat in a cage, cowering in the face of greater forces. From the moment she woke in this place, she's been pushed and pulled by the will of other players. The Solarium. The stars.

"What's an Iron Dreamer?" she asks.

Mostafa grins, and his head cocks to the side just like the Cheshire cat. It would be endearing if it weren't so unsettling. The metal pen by his hip dings. He lets out a frustrated groan and snaps it in the air. The pen extends into a full screen. It's not glass or plastic like an iPad—it's a hologram.

It may not be the year 3124, but some years have passed since her coma began. The technology is decades ahead of her time. From the balats, to the doors, to the hologram in Mostafa's hand.

He scrolls through a series of texts that Lexi can't read from the back, though she's not sure she could read it from the front either. She doesn't recognize the command symbols or the program.

"What is that?" she asks.

He holds the hologram up. "Arabic?"

Lexi has seen pieces of the language in movies and images in textbooks. She's never known anyone who could speak Arabic. The only languages in her hometown are English, French, and German. It still doesn't explain his mystified daze.

"Was I supposed to know that?" she asks awkwardly.

His attention drifts through her, past her, as if his eyes are turning into a memory buried deep within his mind. "I forget how young you are."

"You're not that much older than me." She bites the inside of her lip, embarrassed. "How do you know Arabic?"

"I was born in Egypt." Mostafa looks up, registering her confusion. He presses a button to collapse the screen and leans forward. "We're a diverse group." He points to the door, moving from Chen to Olaf. "Chinese. Norwegian. We have every country in Sol. Should be impossible, no?"

Lexi tries to play along. "I guess you have a really great human resources department."

"Or maybe we're here against our will."

She takes a moment to consider the possibility that everyone in the facility is being imprisoned. If so, they certainly have free rein over the premises. It's just another layer of confusion growing on top of her ignorance. She hasn't witnessed anyone trying to escape. If Zuchiris and

Artemis are being held against their will, then they're doing a piss-poor job of planning an escape.

This should be when Lexi says something clever and crafty to establish her intelligence, so they'll stop tossing her around like a rag doll, but she doesn't know where to begin.

"You haven't figured it out," Mostafa says, realizing.

The door opens. A gentle rush of air brushes Lexi's skin and sweeps out of the room. High pressure to low. Chen stands in the doorway, arms by his side, an imposing figure in a black balat. He doesn't walk into the room. He doesn't have to. Mostafa's body stiffens in response.

"Time's up," Chen says.

Mostafa smiles, a smile so seemingly genuine that it almost reaches his eyes. "One minute." He grabs Lexi's arm.

Instinctually, she jerks her hand away. She doesn't know why. Mostafa hasn't done anything to her. He reaches for her again, and she crawls back.

"That's enough," Chen says, stepping forward.

The presence of two men in a room that she doesn't want to be in overwhelms her. She's a prisoner. A caged rat. The Solarium. The stars. The year 3124. The garden beneath a black sky. She jumps off the bed and runs for the door.

Chen doesn't stop her. Olaf, too, makes no moves to restrain her. His eyes remain locked forward, as if she's invisible.

She turns down the dark hall and sprints, her footsteps illuminating the floor with blue light. Her balance is unreliable and she smacks into one wall and then the other, like a car in a high-speed chase trapped between two semi-trucks. She stops, leaning over her knees. She used to be able to run five miles. Now she can barely run five feet.

Her fingers reach almost all the way around her leg. Her body is gone, her mind is frayed. She's certain she's lost everything. She can feel it like a pit of despair taking root in the depths of her spirit.

Where is her family?

Where is everyone?

She pivots left and races down another empty hall. Since the doors seal into the walls, she can't tell how many rooms she's passed, if any.

Lexi comes to a halt. Unlike the plain characteristics of the rest of the halls, this section has an archway carved into it. The designs curve up and over her head, different languages woven together in vines and leaves. It is colorless, but beautiful. The light from the floor overflows the edges in streaks of blue.

She reaches forward and the door opens to the platform of the Solarium.

The open space is as crowded as it was before. Men and women in colorful balats cast her judgmental glances before going about their business. Lexi grabs hold of the railing and makes her way down the stairs.

The stars are different. Lexi has never left North America, but she remembers learning about a couple of constellations in the Southern Hemisphere. It makes sense, considering that the sun pierces her eyes from the right side this time.

Sidewalks curve around massive trees, whose bright green leaves are a striking contrast against the black sky. Patches of short grass, long grass, flowers, and ponds with fish are scattered throughout the Solarium. Lexi's mother grows flowers. They have a basil plant the size of her sister in the living room. Her mother's green thumb could grow anything, even in the frigid climate of the North Country.

Lexi isn't sure if her mother could grow a garden like this.

She walks to the edge and presses her hand against what she imagines is glass. There is absolutely no give to the material, or feedback. It's as if nothing exists on the other side of the Solarium's borders. It truly is a void out there.

Lexi sits in the grass by the base of a maple tree. She's always loved maple trees. They're the most colorful in the fall, and take up significant space, which she greatly appreciates at the moment. The upper branches block the stars and most of the black sky. If she holds still, she can watch the trees' shadows move across the grass. The station is in rotation to simulate gravity, but it makes her feel like time is rushing past her.

She lies down and curls her body around the trunk, rubbing her fingers along the stubble growing on her head.

Minutes pass, maybe hours. The murmuring voices are a strange relief, melting together like wind. If she closes her eyes, she can almost believe that she's home.

"Hello," a familiar voice says.

Lexi grumbles, tightening her arms over her chest.

Artemis takes a seat beside Lexi and leans against the tree as the last lip of sunlight plunges them into the darkness. The stars twinkle brightly during these periods. The plants must hate the quick intervals of night and day.

Lexi certainly does.

Artemis's hair is woven into another intricate design. She crosses one leg over another, her calves stacked in a yoga position that would hurt most people. She must sit a lot.

"I take it you've accepted that you're in space," Artemis says.

"It's pretty convincing," Lexi admits grudgingly.

"I'd say."

Lexi picks at a blade of grass. It looks real. It feels real. She plucks it and licks it, expecting it to taste like plastic, but it's the way she remembers it. Artemis watches, but says nothing, allowing Lexi's rudimentary experiments to be conducted.

Lexi twists the blade between her fingers. "You lied."

"I did not."

"You said I owned property. We're in space. What property is there?"

"Every citizen owns something. Many of us built our own spaces in the beginning of Sol's construction. Some have contributed more to the domains than others. Lucky for you, you were entitled to one of the largest estates on the station."

"I didn't build anything."

"And you were entitled to it nevertheless."

Lexi huffs. "Vague. So, where is it?"

"Nearby."

In Lexi's short time on Sol, she's learned that prying will not advance her. Artemis is as stubborn as a goat.

Lexi sits up, facing the glass and a universe of stars behind it. She's taller than Artemis, which gives her a fleeting sense of satisfaction. She can't be a caged rat if she's bigger. She's not stronger, but someday she could be. It's not much, but that hopeful surge of vengeance gives Lexi something to hold onto.

"Why am I bald?" she asks. "I don't have hair anywhere—and I mean *anywhere*."

"Teenagers." Artemis makes a disapproving sound. "I shouldn't be surprised that your curiosity orbits around vanity."

"Vanity? It's not vanity, it's traumatizing. What right do you have to shave my head? To take anything from me!" Rage and confusion pound through her chest, but the fatigue hits her immediately and she struggles to catch her breath. She doesn't even have the strength to feel rage. Ridiculous. She closes her eyes before she vomits and embarrasses herself even further. As soon as the urge passes, Artemis speaks. She has an unnerving intuition of Lexi's body.

"There is a solution added to the pods to inhibit hair growth," Artemis tells her. "Without it, the maintenance would be unmanageable. Hair finds a way into everything."

Lexi holds up a blade of grass. "Is this real?"

"We shouldn't start there."

The ambiguity is maddening. Lexi tosses the grass and groans.

"There isn't a guidebook," Artemis says. "We have protocols and procedure, rules and security clearance, but how to change someone's reality without completely destroying their psyche isn't well documented. We thought it best to approach slowly."

"So, I was in a coma for a thousand years, is that what you mean?"

"No." Artemis tilts her head up toward the tree. "We spent the first two centuries without this, you know. The station was just a tiny aluminum pod. There was no greenery. Everything smelled like metal. Even the food started to taste like rocks after a while. It was awful. At first, this was built to be an office garden. It wasn't meant to be anything more than that, maybe a tomato plant or two, but people flocked to it. We fought over their allotted time. There were protests. It wasn't tenable. So, the council approved expansion. It took eighty years to build, but it's been a significant morale booster."

Lexi's eyes survey the garden with a newfound appreciation. She has to admit that there is a significant amount of care and detail that has gone into the flora. She shivers at the idea of being locked in a tiny space station without it. She couldn't imagine a more contrary life to her own. She's grateful for the people who fought to build the Solarium.

"Mostafa said you were here against your will," Lexi says. "Not you like, you-you. But all of you."

Artemis leans back, scratching the side of her neck. "He is right, I suppose."

"Who put you all here?"

"Mm. They're long gone."

Artemis looks over her shoulder and makes a gesture to Zuchiris with three fingers, and then angles her wrist. He hovers by a pine tree in his black and red balat, and nods. At some point, Lexi will have to learn their sign language. It doesn't come across as traditional. There's a dramatic element to their version.

"I have so many questions and I don't even know where to start," Lexi says.

"I suggest at the beginning." Artemis picks at her fingernails, searching for the appropriate starting point. "In the year 2076, a deadly virus appeared, and no one could find the source. It wasn't unlike the coronavirus of 2020 in your world, except that if you contracted this, you would die. The mortality rate was 76 percent among adults, and children and the elderly almost never survived. A quarter of the world's population died within the first eight months.

"Then there was a vaccine. There were minor adverse effects, but for the most part, people survived. Unfortunately, the population never fully recovered. The supply lines fell apart and there weren't enough people to maintain them. The work force was abandoned, schools shut down. By the early 2090s, people were having fewer children in the face of famine, war, and climate change. And something odd had been growing in the shadows for decades.

"Twenty years after the virus, rumors began to spread of people who had abnormal reactions to the vaccine. It was hard to detect at first. It was a gentle change, so quiet that it took years to be documented. A very specific reaction had manifested in less than .001 percent of the population. It became apparent that people like myself weren't aging at a normal rate. We could be injured, but our bodies didn't change. Somehow, the vaccine had become a key to immortality for one in 100,000 people. They called us the Senex, which is Latin for 'old man.'

It's not grammatically correct. '*Senes*' would have been the plural form, but the term spread regardless. What was left of the world's governments realized that the Senex had become immortal in a sense, because they had contracted the virus before the vaccine and just didn't know it. We had a natural immunity.

"Construction on the orbiters began shortly after the Second Nuclear War. Perhaps it was a last-ditch effort to spread across the galaxy, since humans couldn't spread across Earth anymore. India and Australia began construction on Luna, and the United States and China built Sol. Earth was poisoned and the orbiters were our last hope for survival. Now we're here."

Lexi's blood runs cold. The balat continues to pump heat into her skin, but she is numb to it.

Artemis's story might make sense. People behaved something like what she described during the coronavirus, though Lexi doesn't recall trigger-happy nuclear nations. Even from a biological standpoint, immortality doesn't sound completely out of left field when turtles can live for hundreds of years. Humans are obsessed with living forever. It was only a matter of time until humanity stumbled upon the key to life—whether intentionally or by accident.

It could explain why they're in space, how a technological wonder like the Solarium can exist, and why she can't see Earth.

But it doesn't explain Lexi.

"Why leave me in a coma for a thousand years?" Lexi asks. "You could have taken me out at any time."

Zuchiris's footsteps quietly approach.

Lexi surveys the Solarium to find it empty. The hundreds, maybe thousands of people who had been meandering along the sidewalks have been discreetly nudged out. Chen and Olaf stand by the doors on the platform, bracing for impact.

"What's going on?" Lexi asks nervously.

"You were born seventeen years ago." Artemis flexes her hand, preparing to divulge information that weighs heavy on her. "There's no way to know for certain, but it appears that at some stage, the Senex became infertile. The cloning program is the only reproductive capability that we have. We can't stay in the orbiters forever, and there aren't enough of us to figure out how to save Earth. We need the computing power. We need to present enough people with enough problems to see which of them can solve it."

Lexi crawls backward, physically separating herself from Artemis's words. Her lungs tighten under the grip of time, every shallow breath wrenching her from the past and accelerating toward a future she doesn't understand.

Lexi's back slams into Zuchiris's legs. "So, I'm...?"

"A clone," Artemis says, as gently as she can manage. "There are just over 700,000 of you kept in amniotic pods, like the one you woke up in. You were connected to a simulation called Beta. It's overseen by people like myself, called sentinels. The engineers manage Beta, and the sentinels design it. At the moment, Beta is in the mid-2020s. Sometimes we program it for the 1950s; other times, it's the 2130s. It depends on our needs. The Beta program has been the most successful project in the last five hundred years. The discoveries your people have made, Lexi, the inventions. They're saving our species."

The world crashes and Lexi drowns in the current.

War. Simulation. Clones.

Her parents disintegrated. Her friends turned to dust.

Lexi closes her eyes and sees her father gifting her a pair of skis for her fifth birthday. Her mother is reading her bedtime stories. She smells the pine trees after an early spring rain and remembers the feel of snow on her palm. They are the moments that build a person, and the pieces that hold one together. From the defining points in her life, to all the inconsequential ones she can't remember, not a single component that has glued her together is real.

Lexi's memories melt into dreams, as all of it blurs into a fog that she can no longer grasp.

If she isn't her memories, if she isn't the collection of events that have happened to her and the people she's loved, what is she?

Lexi's voice is hollow when she says, "My people."

"Clones, yes," Artemis says. "We call you Iron Dreamers."

CHAPTER SIX

Artemis doesn't escort Lexi to her room, or give her time to digest the information.

Instead, she leads Lexi down a series of windowless hallways with Zuchiris, Chen, and Olaf in tow.

Lexi keeps her eyes fixed on the blue steps beneath Artemis's feet, listening to the strange hollow pounding as the sound is absorbed by the station. She doesn't know their position, and has no sense of orientation in Sol. They could be on the bottom level, and there could be nothing but a few millimeters of aluminum floor separating her from the nothingness outside. There are no windows or signs. Everyone just seems to know where to go.

It could be her muscle atrophy, but walking in this direction takes more effort than walking from her room to the Solarium. If the floors are sloped, it would explain the lack of elevators.

They pass no one along the way. The Solarium could hold 10,000 people, and that was only one section of the structure that she's seen. She can feel her mind anticipating being rewired, but unwilling to move toward it. It's like the ruin of a battlefield, where the horror of man stretches across the countryside. Once Lexi climbs over the hill and sets her eyes on the aftermath, there will be no unseeing it.

Is everyone she knows in one of those tubs, or were they all fabrications of an artificial reality since the beginning?

The blue lights come to a halt. Lexi throws up her hands and accidentally pushes Artemis's back. The woman barely flinches. A slender man with skin dark as night and short curly hair stands in front of a wall. He holds one of the hologram pads in his hand. A hollow, as Artemis calls it. His onyx eyes jump from Artemis to Lexi to the men behind her.

"This is Azi," Artemis says to Lexi. "He's one of our engineers—one of our best, in fact. And he's going to give us an update on an issue we've been having."

Lexi notes that Artemis doesn't introduce her. It makes sense that everyone would already know who Lexi is, but she still prefers a modicum of manners.

"Yes, but—" Azi points to the group—"this as well?"

"I wouldn't have brought them just to stand out here," Artemis says. "You'll find number 442y's clearance in your hollow."

Lexi's eyes scan the wall behind Azi, searching for markings or indents, anything to indicate that a door is nearby. It seems that they all dissolve, leaving every door to look like a hallway, and every hallway to look the same as the next.

"Yes, I received that, but—" Azi takes a step toward Artemis and lowers his voice, but it's a courtesy more than an effort to speak privately. "There are a handful of people cleared already, and that number is growing too large."

"How many people would you prefer to handle a crisis?" Artemis asks, eyes narrowing. "One?"

Azi appears to agree with her, but is visibly stressed by the prospect of consequences. Lexi can't help but feel the push and pull of personalities, and wish she could just shrink into the background and avoid every single one of them for the rest of her life. Whatever *that's* going to look like.

Azi swipes one finger on his hollow. He sighs, as if hoping to find a different result from the one that he had expected.

"I would like my objections to be documented," he says.

"Noted." Artemis gestures toward the wall. "Show us, please."

Azi presses a palm to the wall, which illuminates in a similar blue as the floor. Edges of a door materialize around him like sand slipping through the cracks. Dr. Singh mentioned nanites when he returned her vision. The technology must have found a way into other applications. Is Sol controlled by nanotechnology?

A door slides open to reveal a wall of darkness.

Normally, Lexi loves the dark. The winter nights are long in the mountains, and life learns to navigate through shadow. It's comforting in its own way, like being wrapped in a warm blanket before falling asleep. But this is a different kind of darkness, an empty one. As if the void is omnipresent, watching with its cold dead eyes from every room, waiting to devour them.

Azi walks over the threshold, his body visible only by his footsteps. Artemis follows.

Lexi turns to Zuchiris. "Do I have to go in there?"

"Yeah," he says. "This is just the Iron Sector, where we keep the Iron Dreamers. It's not actually made of iron. It was just the easiest material to mine when we first built it. But that's been replaced by nanotech and other junk now. We should probably rename it. It's not like you're made of iron, or dreaming." He reads her confused distress, and his eyebrows furrow. "You're doing well."

"What?"

"I don't know. Arty told me to say it." He shrugs. "Does it help?"

"Not really."

"I'll let her know." He walks toward the doorway.

"No, wait." Lexi grabs his arm. His balat has no give. The suit is like a sheet of armor. At least one person is warming up to her, and showing a semblance of humanity, regardless of the inhuman feel of their clothes. "It does help," she admits. "A little. I think."

"Okay," Zuchiris says, and then he's swallowed by shadow.

Chen and Olaf wait behind Lexi. There is no sense in trying to negotiate with them. They're just following orders. Lexi sighs and walks through the doorway.

The room is large, though how large Lexi can't determine. Azi, Artemis, and Zuchiris walk in tandem at a faster pace, growing smaller and smaller. Their light doesn't reach a single inch of wall. Zuchiris looks to the left, and tilts his head back. Lexi focuses on his steps. Orienting her body is difficult enough as it is; if she mirrors his drifting gaze, she'll fall over.

Chen closes the door behind them and gives Olaf a hand signal. They spread out on either side, peering into the shadows. They look tense.

So, she's not the only one who doesn't want to be here.

Azi, Artemis, and Zuchiris congregate around a tube protruding from the left wall. Lexi quickens her pace, recognizing the contraption.

"Is that..." Lexi runs up to them. "Is that one of the pods, with the simulation thing?"

"It was," Artemis says grimly.

Lexi looks down into the tub. A naked man lies submerged in the same amniotic fluid, except that all of the wires are still connected to him. The breathing mask, the neck cord, even the catheter. A few weeks ago, that was Lexi.

She shivers at the memory.

She tilts her head back, taking in the rows upon rows of people above them. Clones. What does it mean to be a clone? Does that make her less of a person? She doesn't feel less. She's as alive as anyone else.

Thousands of people like her are locked away in drawers, each of them oblivious to the horror of their true reality. They don't know that their planet has been gone for a thousand years, and that everyone they know either is dead or never existed. Lexi is jealous of their ignorance. There must be a way to bury her memories. If these people can build a space station the size of a city, surely they can remove the last two weeks from her mind.

Lexi stands on her tiptoes to get a better look at the man in the pod, and jumps back. "Oh my god!"

The man's eyes are closed. He looks to be in his forties, Western European, maybe Brazilian. He could be sleeping, but the gray skin is unmistakable. Lexi has seen that particular shade enough times to recognize when no one is home.

So, the pods aren't invincible. The Iron Dreamers are vulnerable.

It's a helplessness that Lexi can't stomach. At least in the forest the animals can fight back, they can run. There are hundreds of thousands of people sleeping in these pods, and they can't defend themselves. They just lie there, naked, waiting to be crushed like newborn chicks.

"Was anyone here when it happened?" Artemis asks, her gaze locked on the lifeless man.

"No one was present. The engineers ran a systems check and everything was stable," Azi says. "Approximately three minutes later, pod 31,766 opened. They found it like this during the shift change thirty minutes ago."

"I'd like to speak with them."

"Of course." Azi pulls up his hollow. "I'll send for both of them."

"All of them," she emphasizes. "The engineers who ran the systems check, the ones coming in, and anyone else within spitting distance. If there was a pulse in this room that is not in a pod, I want to speak with them." Artemis turns to Zuchiris and changes her tone. "That's four now. He's getting sloppy."

Zuchiris reaches into the tub and pulls out the man's hand. Viscous water drips from his arm as he inspects the Iron Dreamer's fingers. Rigor mortis hasn't set in yet. He died less than two hours ago.

He was just there.

And now he's gone.

An unwelcome thought slithers into Lexi's mind as she watches Zuchiris probe his body: anyone could have touched her while she was asleep. It could have happened all the time and she would have never known. How difficult would it be to commit an unspeakable violation on an Iron Dreamer? What are the protection protocols for clones, anyway?

"It doesn't seem sloppy to me." Zuchiris points to the section of the breathing mask that meets the man's cheek. "I don't see scratch marks. He's figured out how to keep his hands clean."

"I don't think this was his intention." Artemis crosses her arms.

"What do you call this?" Zuchiris shakes the dead man's hand in a limp wave. It would be comical if it was a prop, but no one is laughing.

The man's fingers are dull and lifeless compared to Zuchiris's fair skin. It's not the color that makes her stomach uneasy. It's the emptiness. A shade of gray that can't be painted onto a canvas, or described in passing. It's felt. She's seen it before.

She hates that color.

However, Lexi is comforted by the perturbed expressions on everyone's faces. Zuchiris's jaw hasn't unclenched since they walked into the room, and Azi is jittery as a rabbit. For all the flaws of Sol, murder is not a casually accepted occasion. A murdered body means there is a murderer nearby, and in a place where there's nowhere to run, how far could a culprit possibly get?

Zuchiris pinches the man's fingertip, his eyes distant and unfocused. It's not a scientific motion, but an absentminded one. A dead body is nothing more to him than a broken hammer with which he can no longer interact. He turns to Azi. "What pod number did you say this was?"

"It's 31,766," Azi says.

Zuchiris and Artemis share a look.

Curious about their exchange, Lexi looks around the room for a landmark. Every drawer and column look the same. The room is painfully bland. If there was ever a moment to risk asking a question to try to unravel the chaos before her, now is the time.

"Where was I?" Lexi asks.

The three of them turn, having forgotten that she was there. Their startled expressions are disheartening.

Is she that forgettable?

"You were there," Artemis says, pointing behind Azi. "The tubs can rotate behind the drawers. Otherwise, we couldn't access them. At the current configuration you were about a thousand pods away, and two columns."

"We were right next to each other," Lexi realizes.

"You were close," Artemis corrects.

Lexi is standing in the worst moment of her life, and she didn't even notice. It's impossible to tell in which pod she spent the last seventeen years. The pod could currently be empty, or there could be another clone inside it. A clone of her. It's an assembly line of slaves sedated into submission, solving problems that they didn't cause.

Is the clone in her pod right now truly identical to Lexi? How would that even work? Inside the simulation, Lexi's mother couldn't be pregnant again. It would be suspicious for seventeen-year-old Lexi to disappear, and a statewide search, only for her mother to become pregnant with a carbon copy weeks later. People would ask questions.

Lexi's heart races at the possibility that her friends and family are being blamed for her disappearance. They could be in jail, or on trial for murder. They didn't do anything wrong, and there would be no evidence because there was no crime. Lexi hasn't heard a word of what's happening inside Beta since she left.

Chen appears on the opposite side of the tub, snapping Lexi out of her inward spiral. His hands are locked behind his back, but there is a hint of strain in the guard's voice when he says, "It's clear."

"Yes, well. I didn't expect him to hang around." Artemis says it mostly to herself. She enters a command onto her screen, and her balat begins to shimmer. The edges of her suit stretch past her wrist and crawl up her fingers. The balat changes shape and extends into a glove. She runs a finger down the edge of the tub, and rubs the residue against her thumb. "Is it too much to ask for a trace of physical evidence?"

"Visible and infrared are negative," Olaf's voice announces. The second guard is prowling somewhere in the shadows. The way his voice echoes off the walls suggests that the room is incredibly large. "Checking the other EMs now."

"You won't find anything," Artemis says. The balat retracts from her hand, returning to the form of a normal sleeve. "He can do it remotely now."

There is no growing accustomed to death, no matter how many times Lexi crosses its path. Death is an omnipresent force in the wild. The look, the smell, the excrement. It always renders the same feeling of emptiness.

Artemis dips her finger into the water and watches the ripples spread. They move in tiny succession through the solution, one after another, until they slap gently against the corpse. A set of muffled footsteps approach from the distance. Walking toward them are one man and two women. Their illuminated footprints stroll through the abyss like mythological messengers from one of Lexi's nightmares.

Artemis's head snaps to Azi. "Where is the fourth?"

"The engineer called out," he says. Her accusatory tone makes him jumpy. He consults his hollow and adds, "He doesn't appear to have been present when the incident occurred."

"None of them were present when the incident occurred," she reminds him. "Let me see the report."

Azi gives her the hollow. She zooms in on a time stamp and compares it to another. Her head tilts to the side, calculating. When she returns the hollow to Azi, her eyes are closed, meditating through her next course of action.

Three engineers stand in line, shoulder to shoulder, and bow their heads. It's militaristic in nature, but informal, as if they do it out of respect and not duty. Artemis stands in front of each of them. She's an inch shorter than one of the women, and a few inches shorter than the other two. She observes their faces, eyes darting back and forth as if reading a row of scrolling marquees.

Lexi spots a glowing blur in the corner of her eye. It could be a consequence of having been blind for weeks, but she can hear the confidence in the stranger's gait. There is a swagger to their rhythm. They don't have a care in the world.

The young man stands in line with the others. He bows to Artemis with an exaggerated flourish, his shaggy brown hair hangs past eyes so dark they might as well be black, and his balat is rolled up past his forearms for some reason. It's the first unkempt appearance Lexi has seen. He's attractive by conventional standards: wavy hair, tan skin, chiseled jaw. But there's an arrogance to his disposition that she finds off-putting.

"You're all free to go," Artemis says, pointing to the young man. "Except you."

The three engineers don't need further encouragement. They scurry out the door as quickly as possible.

"Sentinel," Azi interrupts, watching them retreat. "We should question them. The council was very clear in their orders that the report must be thoroughly comprehensive."

"They don't know anything. This one, however." Artemis takes two strides and stands inches from the young man. "How did I know it would be you, Cillian?"

The name rings a bell.

Cillian places a hand to his heart and gasps dramatically. "What would I ever do to displease you, my liege?"

Lexi stifles a laugh. The snarky response is so quintessentially human in such a rigid place.

Cillian's head swivels to Lexi, and he grins. It's a boyish grin, a quirky contrast to his otherwise haughty attitude. It doesn't make her uncomfortable, but she prefers not to be the center of attention.

"The famous escapee," he says. "I thought the council would space you. I had a hundred hours betting on it."

Lexi blinks. "Space me?"

Artemis steps in front of Lexi, blocking his line of sight to her. "What did he promise you?" Artemis asks. "Luna? Swipe your memory and send you back in? You know it doesn't work."

"Ah, you wound me," he replies. "I would never be so ungrateful as to betray your trust."

"If only you had it."

Cillian's laugh is drier than a desert. He looks toward the rows of Iron Dreamers. It's doubtful that he's able to make out the different drawers, but it allows him to avoid eye contact with Artemis.

"I did once," he says. "But I guess eight years is nothing to you. How long does a person take to matter around here? A few centuries, or just a few pounds of flesh?"

Artemis points to the dead man. "You were the only one even remotely close enough to this pod all week."

"Why would I risk that?" he demands. "Or no, even better, be sent to Earth to die? Even being here and treated like a second-class citizen is better than that."

He makes a good point, and he sounds genuine. Lexi thinks that he's telling the truth. But nobody cares what Lexi thinks.

Artemis studies him in the way she studied the other engineers, utilizing centuries of proximity to analyze a face that she has seen thousands of times. But Cillian isn't like the other engineers. He said "go back." He was inside Beta, inside the fabricated reality that the entire human species is built around. Now she remembers.

Cillian is an Iron Dreamer.

He's like Lexi.

"I swear, Cillian, if you weren't so full of shit all the time I might actually believe you," Artemis says. "Azi, have Cillian put into the Forest. If this happens again, we'll know it wasn't him and he'll be cleared of all suspicion."

Cillian's face falls. The façade of arrogance is replaced by sheer and unadulterated horror. His eyes widen. He doesn't try to hide his emotions, and neither does anyone else. Even Zuchiris's massive eyebrows furrow.

Azi's fingers hover above the hollow, as if checking to be sure that he heard Artemis right. When she doesn't alter the order, Azi enters the command.

"You can't be serious," Cillian says, his eyes darting back and forth between them. "The Forest is for criminals. I haven't done anything wrong! You're crazy."

The hatred on his face is so wildly explicit that Lexi gasps. Whatever affability Cillian was feigning caves to reveal his true feelings toward Artemis. His disgust cuts through every syllable.

Artemis doesn't flinch. "Olaf."

The redhead materializes from the shadows and grabs Cillian. Lexi isn't sure she'll ever get used to that. Cillian tries to shove him off, but the stout man is unmovable. Olaf's meaty hands grab him and drag him out of the room. She spots the implant on the back of Cillian's neck as he thrashes against Olaf. His shouts of protest blend into a single stream of panic that falls on deaf ears.

If this is how they treat Cillian, what could Lexi possibly expect her treatment to look like? Guilty until proven innocent? It doesn't look space is a democracy.

Even after they're gone, Cillian's pleas ring in Lexi's ears.

Zuchiris whistles. "Well, that was something."

Artemis stares into the darkness. If she's bothered by the exchange, she doesn't show it. A game of chess is being played by beings older than the Holy Roman Empire. Under different circumstances, Lexi might be fascinated by it.

"The council thinks Cillian is the Dark Angel," Artemis says.

Zuchiris snorts. "But he's an idiot."

"And the easiest target." Artemis walks around the tub, her eyes locked on the dead man's face. "An Iron Dreamer trying to destroy Beta makes more sense to them than a sentinel, even a disgraced one. The sooner we eliminate Cillian as a suspect, the sooner we can get to the real problem."

Zuchiris rubs his chest. It's not sensual, but Lexi still feels like she's watching a private moment. He doesn't seem to realize that he's doing it.

"So, he's the patsy," Zuchiris says.

"He's whatever we need him to be to get this over with. The Dark Angel hasn't approached him yet, but he will soon. Once that contact is established, the council will deem Cillian guilty of treason whether or not he decides to join him. This protects him from that."

The Dark Angel is an overly dramatic designation for a society rooted in science. How did that slip into their lexicon? If he's the one who murdered the man in the pod, then someone has had enough time to inspire otherworldly status among a population seemingly immune to mystical hysteria.

A dark angel, indeed.

"He wouldn't approach him," Zuchiris says, looking more confident than he sounds. "What would he want with Cillian?"

"They believe in a lot of the same things," Artemis says. "Can you honestly say that you don't think Cillian might at least entertain the idea? He'd love to release the Iron Dreamers and think of himself as a hero. He hasn't exactly had a smooth transition. For now, he's safer in the Forest."

The engagement between Artemis and Cillian had sounded like an interrogation, not a play for Artemis to keep him out of danger. Lexi could just as easily be a tool to her. The precision of Artemis's evasiveness is surgical. She hadn't lied to Cillian, yet he had walked right into her trap.

And yet there is something about Artemis that seems trustworthy. She has been methodical, maybe domineering, but never evil.

Artemis rests her hand on the edge of the pod. Her gaze drifts through the dead man, and the lifeless motion of his floating arms. The room holds its breath, waiting for her orders. Lexi's watched enough *CSI* to recognize inner conflict when she sees it. This is no simple murder investigation. Whoever committed the heinous act, Artemis knows them.

"Sentinel, if I might ask," Azi says. "At this rate, it would take him over two thousand years to disconnect all of the Iron Dreamers, and not before we replenish the ranks. Why is he killing them?"

"That's not his mission," Artemis says. She touches Lexi's balat, as if picking dust from her shoulder. The gesture is almost motherly. In another life, they might have been friends, although Artemis was born closer to Shakespeare's time than to Lexi's.

"Tell the High Councilor what happened here," Artemis orders Chen. "I'll bring Lexi to her room. Zuchiris will stand guard until you return."

Chen nods and departs, leaving Artemis and Zuchiris to share a wordless conversation. Their arms cut through the air, their gestures appearing to be more theatrical than anything, but even the subtle flick of a pinky finger has significance.

Artemis grabs Lexi's arm and pulls her out of the room. "He's getting close."

"Who?" Lexi asks, tripping over her feet. "Is someone trying to kill us?"

They round a corner and hasten up a narrow hallway. Every direction feels like an upward slope. Between their pace and Lexi's weak cardiovascular system, she struggles to breathe.

"The Dark Angel was one of the original architects of Beta," Artemis says. "A brilliant programmer. Without him, it's unlikely that a simulation would have worked. He knew how to incorporate Sol's problems into Beta for the Iron Dreamers to solve without them growing suspicious of it. Every challenge he assigned, they devised a solution for. It was so natural. The way he saw the world—" Her voice breaks as they approach a corner.

Zuchiris consults his hollow. He looks up to Artemis and gives a stern nod. They move to the middle of the hallway and lean against the wall.

"That's what I told her," Artemis laughs. "Can you believe it?"

"Makes sense, coming from her," Zuchiris replies, matching her casualness.

Lexi is glancing back and forth, utterly perplexed, when two young women holding a hollow between them appear around the corner. The women jump upon seeing them, and stand straight when they catch sight of Artemis.

They bow slightly, and then their eyes fall on Lexi.

Their faces contort as if smelling something rotten. Lexi imagines that her sudden emergence into their world has caused mixed reactions. It hadn't occurred to her that the citizens' opinions were as passionately held as they were diverse. Maybe they hated the simulation.

Maybe they hated her.

Artemis gives the women a hand signal and they scurry off, whispering to each other as they fade into the darkness. She grabs Lexi's arm, and they hurry.

"What are you going to do with the man in the pod?" Lexi asks. She doesn't even know his name. Is anyone mourning him? Does anyone in Sol care? There could be another Iron Dreamer nearby within Beta—a living person who actually cares—but the odds of them having come into contact with each other are slim. Any grief or sadness felt by those around the dead Iron Dreamer is fabricated.

The only entities to mourn him are lines of code.

"He'll be recycled," Artemis says, loosening her grip.

"What does that mean?"

"We don't have the luxury of waste. Everything is recycled. Even if one of us were to die, the procedure would be the same."

"Yeah, but you don't die." Lexi imagines her body floating in a pod for a thousand years. "So, that's how you clone people? You just use the same parts over and over again?"

"It's not that different from Earth, really," Artemis says. "The process on Sol is simply faster."

Lexi reaches for the implant on the back of her neck, and strokes the rounded metal corners. She misses the feeling of her hair. Playing with the locks was a nervous tic of hers when she needed something to do with her hands—now it's just another comfort that she's been robbed of. The painfully slow growth of fuzz is more depressing than the implant.

"Who's the Dark Angel?" Lexi asks.

"A terrorist," Zuchiris replies from behind them.

"He was a sentinel once," Artemis says, her voice unusually low. "But not everyone is in agreement that it's him. The council doesn't believe that anyone would self-sabotage. It doesn't matter what the evidence is; the council refuses to believe that one of their own would stoop so low."

Lexi snorts. "Sounds about right."

Artemis looks over her shoulder. The light from beneath their feet casts an otherworldly shadow on her face, turning her eyes black.

"Be careful with that, Lexi," she warns. "It's easy to point a finger at another, but I've watched you your whole life. You're not exactly the poster child for an open mind."

Lexi recoils.

She's done fine, all things considered. She was raised in the wilderness, where adapting is the key to survival. Lexi can construct a shelter of wet branches and start a fire from pine needles. She can walk two miles through rough terrain with a twisted ankle and carry a fifty-pound pack. Her current predicament is an extreme circumstance beyond even her parents' imaginations.

"His name is Tiago." Artemis's voice catches on the last syllable, but she continues before Lexi can ask how they know each other. "A few years ago, he raised concerns about Beta and the general utilization of an entire population for our own means. He argued that resources could be put to better use, and that we should wake up everyone in the simulation." She scoffs. "Can you imagine setting 700,000 people loose? They outnumber us two to one. What do you think will happen when we tell them that Earth is dead, and they're fated to spend the rest of their lives trapped in space? They would rebel, and no one would blame them for it."

"Isn't that what you're doing to me now?" Lexi demands, trying not to let the resentment inside her rise to the surface.

"You're one person. Releasing hundreds of thousands of people into a city that can't support them is a different matter. We don't have the resources for that kind of influx. They're in a sedated state now, and consume less energy. Their release would overwhelm us, and cause a war. They would be children in a world that they don't understand. They could end the entire human race simply because they pressed the wrong button."

Even after weeks, Lexi still doesn't have a handle on Sol, or its people. She finds herself agreeing with Artemis. How could the sudden release of 700,000 people not cause a conflict? Food doesn't just grow in the desolation of space. Resources need to be harnessed or manufactured, and it can't be easy.

"If Tiago is trying to set the Iron Dreamers free, why is he killing them?" Lexi asks.

Artemis doesn't look to Zuchiris, but she can feel their silent interaction. Maybe after centuries of friendship, humans become mind readers.

"That was an accident," Artemis says carefully. "He can be...obsessive. Knowing him, he rationalized it as a necessary evil for the greater good. He's made mistakes before. That's why the 'Dark Angel' name stuck."

Lexi asks, almost afraid to know, "What mistakes has he made?"

Artemis is quiet.

Lexi assumes it will take her a moment to choose an example—given their age and the complexity of the simulation—but Artemis gravitates toward one point in time.

"What do you think happened to Hitler?" Artemis asks.

Lexi is struck by the question. The wars of history and the twentieth century feel so far removed from Sol that they might as well have happened in another universe.

"He died?" Lexi says, though it comes out more like a question. "He killed himself in a bunker at the end of the war, right?"

"That's not what happened." Artemis takes a breath. "In your simulation—the most recent version of Beta—Hitler committed suicide before the Allies could capture him. But in our reality, what really happened is that he was alive. Sure, he let his wife take a cyanide capsule, and everyone else in the bunker, but he was too proud. He waited for the Americans to capture him. It was the trial of the century. It took a few years, but eventually he was put to death in New York. They broadcasted it on live television."

"Whoa." Lexi can't imagine that series of events. She's not particularly fond of history, but Hitler being alive is certainly not what happened at the end of World War II. That would have been crazy.

What else didn't happen the way she thinks?

"In reality, mutual disdain for the Nazis kept the United States' and the Soviets' interests aligned for some time," Artemis continues. "There was no Cold War. A race to space, yes, but not nearly so hostile as the one designed for your simulation, and not until a century later. The reason The Cold War was programmed into Beta is because four hundred years ago we had a problem with a fusion reactor. It's been the standard storyline ever since."

Lexi's blood runs cold. "You created a war in my world so you could fix some stupid part in one of your machines?"

"That is the purpose of a simulation, Lexi. To run scenarios."

"We're just a calculator for you. Some tool you mess around with so you don't have to fix any of the problems yourself."

They come to a stop. Zuchiris catches himself before slamming into them, and backs up toward the wall as if physical touch disturbs him.

Artemis tilts her head to the side in the same way she did when she examined the engineers. "You sound just like him." Her face drops, and she marches down the hallway.

Lexi turns to Zuchiris and he shrugs. It's not a shrug of confusion. He knows precisely what Artemis is talking about, he just can't say it.

"So, in real life Hitler was alive and the Cold War didn't start for another hundred years," Lexi says, catching up with Artemis. "Where's the mistake the Dark Angel made?"

"In one version of Beta," Artemis says, "Tiago created a history where the Soviets found Hitler, not the Americans. The Soviets were not as keen on global cooperation as the Allies had been. The Americans weren't invited to the trial in Moscow; neither were the British, nor the French. The conflict accelerated The Cold War and eventually led to nuclear destruction. It was a complete disaster. Beta had to be rebooted three decades early, and all of the Iron Dreamers were scratched. It was a tremendous waste."

The implication of being "scratched" is a detail that Lexi doesn't question. It could be like switching a game off, or it could be outright genocide. The technology to wipe an Iron Dreamer's memory and implant a new life, down to the smallest detail all the way to birth, sounds complicated. It probably would be easier to just start the simulation from scratch.

Lexi shivers, imagining 700,000 people being murdered in their sleep.

"Isn't the simulation a program that you control? Why not just stop that from happening?" she asks. "You could literally end all wars, and you just let us suffer."

"We're not gods," Artemis says. The weight of the statement drops her voice, as if she has had to say it many times. "We only enter the initial conditions. Decisions are made by the Iron Dreamers. One move affects another, and so on and so forth. It truly is a world on its own."

"Sounds like a god to me."

"Mm."

"So, where is he?"

Artemis massages the back of her neck. "He took a ship four years ago and never returned. He could be on a smaller satellite station near Earth, but it's Luna that would have the tools he needs. I don't think they would risk a diplomatic incident and provide him aid. Our relationship with Luna is...tenuous."

Lexi takes a breath. "Is my family here?"

It's a question that she's been dreading, but she needs to know. She needs to know how much of her life has been real, and how much has been lies. All of the little moments she shared with her parents, the games she played with her sister—was it all just lines of code? A bunch of holograms meant to trick her into solving other people's problems?

"Your parents and sister died in the First Nuclear War," Artemis says. "You were the only one from your family that we were able to retrieve a viable genetic sample from."

Lexi loses feeling in her fingertips. The world around her spins. She has no firm ground to stand on. No one to hold onto. She is utterly alone in a place where she doesn't belong. Her parents' faces slip through her fingers like fog. What right did they have to clone her? Why hadn't they left her alone? She imagines lying dead in the dirt by some battlefield, bloody and mangled, and a man in a hazmat suit rising out of the trenches to rub a cotton swab against her mutilated arm.

What right did they have?

"Tiago's objective is not to kill you. Never you," Artemis says.

Lexi suppresses a laugh. "Me? I'm nobody."

"Normally, that would be the correct assessment, but you were chosen to be in Beta because Alexandria was his favorite. We have the genetic material for millions of people, and we prefer to circulate them since diversity yields the best results. But he insisted that she be included in every iteration."

Lexi's heart sinks.

She is a copy of someone else—someone who had existed a thousand years before she was even born. A girl who had the same body and the same brain, whose wavy hair knotted at the bottom, but who preferred to be called Alexandria instead of Lexi. She lived an entire life, and wandered through a world that Lexi thought was hers, but it never was. It hasn't been real for a thousand years.

A small part of Lexi had hoped that she was chosen to be cloned because she had accomplished something great. After all, wouldn't the Senex only clone the most critical players in human history? The presidents, the thinkers, the creators—the people who mattered most? But Lexi isn't important. She hadn't contributed anything at all.

She's just related to someone who did.

"He's discovered that you're awake." Artemis's head tilts back, as if the Dark Angel is hovering above her, watching. "I can only image that his newest intention is to reunite with you."

"I'm not even real," Lexi says, her voice barely a whisper.

Artemis turns to her, provoked by a hidden undertone. It could be empathy, and the innate inclination to comfort a human in distress, but it's quickly overridden by exasperation. "So, you're the genetic makeup of one person instead of two. What difference does it make?"

"I feel like it makes a bit of a difference. It's not like I'm Alexandria's daughter. I'm *her*."

"You are not her," Artemis says firmly. "What do you think asexual reproduction is? It's reproducing from one source instead of two. Tapeworms. Sponges. Earth has been cloning long before humans stumbled upon it."

"Great, so now I'm a tapeworm."

"Don't be dramatic."

"How am I a real person if I'm just a copy of someone else? I don't even have Alexandria's memories—at least those would have been real. My life and the people I know aren't real. What am I now?"

"That's something you need to figure out, same as anyone else," Artemis says, softening her voice. "The circumstances may be different, but the task is the same. You are alive, and to be alive is to be in an existential crisis. Who you are is a question only you can answer."

Lexi audibly groans. She wants empathy. If she's being honest with herself, she wants someone to feel bad for her. She's tired of the Senex's stoic expressions. Space and cloning might be perfectly normal to them, but for Lexi, each new piece of information about the future is an earth-shattering revelation.

So, she isn't Alexandria. Fine.

Then who is she?

From the moment Lexi was born, she was raised by a computer. A series of ones and zeros changed her diaper and tucked her into bed. An algorithm held her hand as she learned to ride a bike, and hugged her at her grandmother's funeral. A roomful of engineers designed her life and every single person around her. It was a computer that she loved, and a computer that taught her how to live.

If a human being is a collection of memories and events from a lifetime of interactions, but then it turns out that none of it was real, what's left behind? What is a person if not their life?

"I won't know anything about Tiago," Lexi says as a deafening void grows in her chest. "I can't be whatever it is he wants me to be. You could be wrong."

Artemis bites back her words and says, "I could be."

"So, who am I to him?"

"His name is Tiago Carvalho," Artemis says. "He was your uncle."

CHAPTER SEVEN

Lexi is given her own hollow.

Her activity is strictly monitored, and most of the features are disabled, but the device allows her to send messages and watch what's happening inside Beta.

Apparently, Beta provides a kind of entertainment on Sol—which is a much larger station than Lexi realized. She spends most of her time studying the map and zooming in on the live feed from public spaces like the Solarium. Some of the sections are blacked out. Zuchiris says it's because her security clearance isn't high enough.

The city has a population of 346,001 people, and 250 square miles of floor space, which is a little more than half the size of Los Angeles. The station is sleek and aerodynamic, though there is no atmosphere to move through to necessitate that efficiency.

Sol's two arms curve around each other in a rotating corkscrew, as if to embrace an invisible friend. They are separated by a mile of space, with three connectors to transport materials. Since the station relies on centrifugal force to simulate gravity, with the outer edges feeling nearly the equivalent of Earth's gravity, the connectors can only be accessed by trained personnel, since the push and pull fluctuate the closer they move toward the center.

The station looks alien, and not like anything Lexi would have imagined humans building. It could have been designed by a species similar to humanity, but godlike. A Mount Olympus of ambition. It is quite beautiful.

In a creepy, apocalyptic opera sort of way.

If humanity had just taken as great care of Earth as they do of Sol, then the world wouldn't have ended. Lexi could be living in the future every child of the twenty-first century imagined. She could be vacationing in a hotel at the bottom of the ocean or driving a car through a cloud city. Instead, she's in a pressurized tube in the vacuum of space, forbidden to take a single step outside.

Lexi places the hollow on the grass beside her and tilts her head toward the night sky. The sun should appear in a few minutes. The glass dome dampens the star's intensity, but the transition from night to day is jarring, especially since it happens every few hours. She rubs her eyes. Her eyelashes have grown in, and her eyebrows. Finally.

It will be a few more months until there's enough hair on her head to blend in with the Senex, but at least there's a semblance of personality coming in, and not a blank canvas. During one of the early hours, when the sun is shining just right, she's able to use the reflection to gauge her face. From what she can tell, she looks the same as she did in Beta. At least they haven't changed that.

Lexi spends most of her time in the Solarium. It's the closest thing to a real place that exists on Sol. She reads maps and archives to catch up on the last thousand years of history. It's like uncovering a new world. When she notices differences in events—an assassination that didn't happen, or a drought that did—she finds herself captivated by the story of what is, essentially, a parallel universe, yet enraged by the depth of the deception. Couldn't the Senex have given them the same history? Why did they change things?

Iron Dreamers.

A chill runs through her.

Over 700,000 people are living in a fantasy world on the edge of a graveyard. They're working at jobs that don't matter, eating food that isn't real, and loving people who don't exist. The Senex call the programmed characters "phantoms," which is most of the population. Roughly 99 percent of them aren't real. Meaning that almost every person the Iron Dreamers meet is just lines of code.

Lexi grabs the hollow and takes a deep breath. She decides to study the landscape of the city before the stress sends her into cardiac arrest.

The largest arm of Sol hosts the Solarium, businesses, and other communal spaces, while the other arm is primarily residential. The arm with the Solarium is newer and has a shinier aesthetic, with big windows that can be seen from the residents' homes across the narrow passage of space. The residential arm is more utilitarian, with rows of small windows and bulky compartments. Lexi hasn't been permitted there yet.

An alert on the hollow hovers above the screen.

"President Horris experiences déjà vu."

The Senex love the simulation. BetaVu is a national pastime on Sol and the main source of entertainment. They have their favorite Iron Dreamers, they bet on outcomes and gossip over the most tantalizing stories. They watch football games and celebrities, and pretty much everything else that people did in Lexi's world.

Lexi's hometown is a particular point of interest, but Artemis won't say why, and the hollow prevents her from accessing the archives relating to the North Country. She can only access the current footage. Her fingers have hovered above the command a dozen times, but she can't bring herself to watch her friends and family carry on as if nothing has happened.

As if the end of the world wasn't two feet outside of their pods.

Inside Beta, Lexi has been replaced by a phantom: an avatar that talks like her and acts like her. No one's noticing the differences because the overwhelming majority of the population is simulated anyway. What's one more character to the mechanical hum? Even her family hasn't noticed. It feels like Lexi has died and no one cares.

She wipes a tear from her cheek, embarrassed by Chen and Olaf seeing her cry for the hundredth time.

She's so tired of crying.

"The president experiences déjà vu."

Lexi waves her hand under the notification, expecting the image to glitch from the obstruction of the projection, but it doesn't even flicker. Zuchiris told her that the holograms are redirected from multiple angles so that the images are undisturbed. She could switch the device to a flat screen if she wanted, but she doesn't remember how to do that. The mechanics of the hollow are strange to her.

Human, yet faintly alien.

Sol has incorporated aspects of their sign language into the devices to allow for more complex commands. Lexi tries to remember the one for "select." She makes a few attempts, bending and twisting her fingers until the screen finally expands the notification.

The president of the United States is sitting at his desk in the Oval Office, signing a pile of documents. A woman with a tablet in her arms stands beside him and places another document on his desk. He looks up at her, and his eyes drift to the wall behind her. He shakes his head and returns to his paperwork. Another alert appears.

"Engineer Cortez to address the glitch."

As with most events on Sol, Lexi is perplexed by what she's witnessed. She digs for an explanation, scrolling through pages of text, until she finds the backstory.

Déjà vu is a hiccup within Beta affecting most, if not all, of the Iron Dreamers. When Beta runs a system check, or a section of code needs to be altered, there is a fraction of a fraction of a second when there is no visual information relayed to the Iron Dreamers in that sector. The human brain, acknowledging the breach of reality, scrambles to fill the gap by repeating the previous millisecond, causing the moment to repeat itself, and the Iron Dreamers to experience déjà vu. To maintain consistency, the phantoms are also programmed to experience a version of it, but at random moments.

Not even déjà vu is a real thing.

Lexi tosses the hollow. It slams against the trunk of a birch tree. The device is light and paper-thin, yet impossible to break. If the ceiling of the Solarium collapses, she could use the hollow as a shield.

Lexi pulls her legs to her chest and drops her head onto her knees. She rocks back and forth, letting the pressure massage her temples, until she catches a set of eyes watching from across the field.

The woman's long black hair hangs past her shoulders. She is slim and graceful, weaving around the vines like a mountain lion on the prowl. Her intense focus is not the flash of disdain to which Lexi has become accustomed from the other Senex in the Solarium; it's personal. The woman glares into Lexi's very soul, as if she's known her since birth. Given the circumstances, it's not that outlandish a presumption.

The grass beeps. Lexi hasn't heard that particular tone come from her hollow before. Assuming that it's a message from Artemis, Lexi crawls through the grass, appreciating every inch of dirt that pushes through her fingertips.

"I figured you'd be here," Mostafa says.

Lexi stiffens.

He walks carefully toward her, his steps cautious over the grass. People are meant to stick to the trails, but Lexi has been granted permission to wander through the fields. Between her shaky legs, nausea, and incessant fatigue, her adjustment to life in space has been rough. The only way to reach her is to violate the rules. It's a convenient way to be spared the whispers of passers-by who try to catch a glimpse of her.

Mostafa's black balat may be the least personal of them all. Its smooth matte hampers the light's reflection like a shadow. It's as if he's has chosen the plainest appearance for the sole purpose of challenging his ability to glamor people. The sunlight over his shoulder is white, with a slight hint of yellow to imitate the way it would appear on Earth, accentuating the warmest features of his skin.

Even space suits him.

"It is a lot to take in," Mostafa says.

Lexi's head swivels for the woman, but she is gone. The ceiling is glass, and the space is wide open. The Solarium is not a hiding spot.

Lexi stands, wiping the dirt off her balat. "You could say that."

"You've arrived during one of our more glorious eras," Mostafa says. "Though I enjoyed the mining boom."

Mining boom?

He tugs at a branch above Lexi's head, rattling the leaves in a wistful song from her childhood. He's being too rough, but the branch doesn't snap. She realizes that this might be the first time he's been allowed to touch a tree.

"I'm afraid to ask because I don't know much about..." Lexi holds out her hand toward the sun. "But I'm pretty sure we're getting blasted with radiation, right?"

"Not anymore." Mostafa picks at a piece of bark. "Radiation doesn't affect the Senex, but it can kill everything else. It took years to develop a force field for the plants."

"A force field," Lexi repeats.

"Not the science fiction sort you're thinking of. It's not a wall of energy that solidifies when an object hits it. It's suspended around the station like an orb, designed to repel high energy and allow everything else to slip through, like visible light, a ship, or even you. Brilliant, no?" He regards her skeptical expression, and a small smile breaks across his face. "Think of it as a filter for ionizing radiation."

"Yes, I'll be sure to do that." Lexi has no idea what ionizing radiation is. "Is that something an Iron Dreamer thought of for you?"

"The beginning workings of it. We don't give the Iron Dreamers the same technological access. It's normally their calculations that we use. Math comes before the science."

"So you keep the best of us locked up in your fantasy world."

Mostafa's eyebrows furrow as if in thought, but without the sincerity. He wants to give the *appearance* of empathy without the emotion to back it. The facial reactions are slightly off. They don't quite reach his eyes. There is a power displacement in Sol; she just doesn't know how it's shaped, or who benefits.

"What do you want?" she asks.

Mostafa grins, as if he's been waiting for that question. "What do *you* want?"

"I would say it's fairly obvious."

Real or not, Lexi has no place on Sol. She doesn't understand the technology, or the language. She's an outsider. A visitor from the past. She has no place among immortal beings, or the stars. She wants to go back to her life. She doesn't want to be trapped in a claw-shaped snow globe in the middle of space.

Mostafa measures her with a cold gaze, his eyes roaming down her body. It's more clinical than predatorial. Lexi still shrinks from the scrutiny. "You want to return to Beta," he says, amazed by her desperation. "I'm afraid that's not possible."

"Why not?"

"We've tried," he says simply. "We could send you back, but there will always be a part of you that knows something is wrong. You'll question every person you meet. Distrust every interaction. It will drive you mad until you trust nothing at all, not even your own thoughts."

It might have been Cillian who tried to return to Beta. He's the only other Iron Dreamer that's awake. He has the biological mechanisms to be connected to the simulation. Maybe that's why no one trusts him, and why Artemis threw him into the Forest. Maybe Cillian is losing his mind.

"You don't know me," Lexi says. "You don't know that will happen."

Mostafa leans against the tree. "I'm something of an expert. A PhD in molecular biology, and others in psychology and nuclear medicine." He looks down at his fingernails. "I was bored that year."

Lexi tries not to sound impressed. "Is everyone a genius here or something?"

"Life would have been much easier if that had been the case. No, we just have a lot of time."

"Well, then there must be a way to drug me."

He seems amused by her pleading. "Memories are complex things," he says. "It's not as simple as deleting a file. They're interwoven into other aspects of your mind. Removing a memory of eating ice cream when you were nine years old could hinder your ability to walk. We can't unravel the web. You're not the first to wish this, but it cannot be done."

"I don't *care*," Lexi says, trying to gather the fragmented pieces of what she fears is hopelessness. "So, what, you're all gods and I just have to do what you say?"

"We are not gods."

"Fine, immortal. Same thing."

He scratches his jawline. "We die eventually."

"From what, a broken heart?"

He snorts, offended by the notion. "We deteriorate at a slower rate. Estimates put us at...I forget now...18,000 years? We can still die, or starve. We're not immune to death, just to aging."

Lexi doesn't know what to do with that ridiculous information. Being alive for 18,000 years? It sounds terrible and thrilling at the same time. The Senex will live long enough to explore the galaxy—if they haven't tried already. They could master every art, sport, and language before the insanity of infinity shatters their minds.

If humans were meant to live as long as rocks, then they would. Nature is about balance, and they've tipped the scales. There has to be a price.

Lexi runs her hands over the grass, reaching as far as she can. She has no flexibility in her lower back or hamstrings. Her body is alien to her. She sighs. "What is it you want again?"

"That is complicated."

"Leave me alone then."

Mostafa watches her, and his shoulders drop. He softens into a younger version of himself. It is a transformation so noticeable that she can feel it in the air between them. If she were to pass him on the street, she would think he was an easy-going teenager on his way to school, not a demigod from another world. Maybe it's the psychology degree. Mostafa can be anything he wants, and he's had centuries to perfect his art.

Sol is a nest of vipers.

"The High Councilor has requested your presence," he says, holding out his arm as if it were the most normal thing in the world. "I'm here to escort you to the command deck."

"Where's Artemis?"

"She'll meet you after."

Lexi looks at his arm, and she finds herself taking it. She regrets the moment of weakness immediately. There is no comfort in the contact. No warmth to Mostafa's touch. What should feel human is like a statue made of rock. The balat is a suit of armor, as cold and unyielding as Sol itself.

An older couple walks by and glares at them. She hasn't been told why the Senex are having such a negative reaction to her. Lexi is no stranger to a reclusive town, but the culture in space takes isolation to a whole other level.

"Why isn't Artemis here, or Zuchiris?" Lexi asks.

"I don't know where Zuchiris is," Mostafa says, an admission that seems to bother him. "Artemis is preoccupied at the moment."

"Like you were with the High Councilor?"

Mostafa's jaw clenches.

Lexi isn't sure what she's insinuating. She's only repeating the snide comment Chen made, hoping it would strike a nerve and set Mostafa on edge, like she's on edge.

She untangles herself from Mostafa's arm and strides quickly up the platform to Olaf. The long years of life in the void creep into Mostafa's face as he stands motionless at the bottom of the stairs. For a moment, she questions the cruelty of the jab.

The red-headed guard chuckles. "Good instincts."

If anyone is privy to the inner workings of Sol, then it's someone as ideally positioned as Olaf. He might even be willing to divulge information.

"Is he trustworthy?" Lexi whispers.

"Mostafa?" Olaf follows her gaze. He inhales through his nose, conflicted about sharing information. "He's committed to keeping Sol operational, which is more than I can say for some of the Senex. It's how he goes about it that I question."

"How does he go about it?"

The guard rocks his head. "Gently."

"You mean he sleeps around."

"There are many ways to extract information."

Lexi watches Mostafa walk up the stairs. Is this what Zuchiris was talking about—finding your weapons? Zuchiris is a brute. Artemis is cunning. Is Mostafa's tool just the scandalous kind?

"He looks too young," Lexi says. "I mean, I know you're all old, but he looks so innocent."

"Mostafa was an interesting case. He received the vaccine when he was fourteen years old. He aged for a time, but then stopped at around twenty. It happened to a few people; they got the vaccine when they were kids, but didn't stop aging after puberty. I am grateful. I wouldn't have liked to see children behave like old men. We're all between twenty and fifty."

It must have taken decades for Mostafa to realize that something was wrong. After his siblings' wrinkles set in, and his parents died. At what moment did his family realize that he was frozen in time? If the ancient world had cast their gaze upon him, they would have worshipped him as a sun god and made him king.

A man trapped in the prime of his life.

Lexi's hollow beeps. Olaf looks down with a quizzical expression. She's only meant to receive messages from a few people.

"I put everything to the same sound," Lexi lies. She smiles awkwardly and turns her back.

The command symbols are gibberish—a bunch of lines and slashes that mean nothing to her. A tiny alert in red font appears in the corner of the screen.

Time to talk?

The message is from a sender with no private access. She closes the hollow and stands at attention, letting herself be distracted by the way the sunlight brings out the different shades of brown in Mostafa's hair.

"Shall we?" Mostafa asks. Notably, he does not offer his arm this time.

Lexi nods, and follows him into the belly of Sol.

The hallway from the Solarium on the way to Lexi's room is more difficult to walk than the others. She's deduced that it's because her room is located near the edge of Sol where the pull is strongest. It's hard to know for certain where they are without windows, but a station built around a centrifugal system and rotating arms means that the edges will feel more of a pull than the center.

Around the third corner, Lexi's heels don't reach the floor. She glances at Olaf and Chen, trying to gauge their reaction in the low light, but they walk normally. There is a muffled clicking sound coming from their heels. She keeps her focus on the illuminated steps in front of her, hoping she doesn't float away.

"Would you like my assistance?" Mostafa asks. "This must be your first time in the center. You can adjust the settings to automatically magnetize to the floor, or have it done manually. Judging by your flailing limbs, I'd say it's set to manual."

"I'm not flailing." Lexi rotates her wrist to reveal the small screen on her forearm. "How do I change it?"

Mostafa enters a command on her balat. The sole of each of her feet thickens into a flat layer, and her body sinks to the floor. The boots snap to the ground.

She holds out her arms to test her balance. There's a bit of resistance in her step as she pulls her heels up, but otherwise the magnetization isn't noticeable. It's almost like normal walking. The temporal distance between her and Sol is the same as between her and medieval England. She needs to learn the symbols of their technology.

"Thanks," she mumbles.

"This is like your hike down Mount Lafayette, no?" he asks. "When you were a little girl, and your father chose the more challenging trail. Your knees buckled every few feet."

Her heads snaps to him so fast she nearly decapitates herself. "How do you know about that?"

"BetaVu."

"How much does everyone watch?"

Mostafa shrugs. "Quite a lot."

Lexi feels the oncoming mutiny of another panic attack. Her breaths grow rapid and shallow. She lowers herself to the floor and brings her head between her knees. Every aspect of her life has been an invasion.

"Lexi?" Chen asks tentatively.

Lexi waves her arm to shoo them away. "It's fine. I'm fine." If she can control her breathing, the dizziness will fade into the background.

"It's impressive that her mind is still intact," Mostafa says. "I had expected it to be unsalvageable."

Chen lowers himself to the ground. His balat swirls as it adjusts to his position. The nanotechnology shimmers like rainwater, leaving no gap around the joints. A cocoon to safeguard one of the universe's strangest creations.

"Would you like a distraction?" Chen asks.

She nods.

"I was thirty-nine when the virus struck," Chen begins, leaning back onto his heels. "I was living in southern China working as a guide. The Yellow Mountain was a popular destination for tourists, and I enjoyed meeting the people. It wasn't too unlike where you're from. It was beautiful." Chen's voice fades as he drifts through memories long forgotten. "My wife was pregnant with our first child when the lockdown started. They said it would only be a few weeks, but a few weeks turned into a month, then two months, and then three. By the sixth month of lockdown, my wife tried to deliver the baby at home, but there were complications. We went to the hospital, and that's probably where I contracted the virus. I must have walked by the room of someone infected, or I brushed against them in the cafeteria. I don't know. The vaccine was administered a few months later. My wife made a full recovery, our baby was healthy. All seemed well.

Fifteen years later, at a wedding, my cousin spoke of joint pain. We were the same age, and grew up together. At some point, even my wife began to notice the differences between us. I didn't understand it at the time, she was perfect to me, but there was a rift that had been growing between us, and I was helpless to stop it. When my daughter married is when I knew. She married at twenty-eight, and her friends thought I was her brother. We heard rumors about a side effect of the virus, of people who were never sick. Men and women in their seventies who looked twenty. I was one of them. I was cursed."

Chen runs a finger along the designs in his hair, tracing one of the patterns. The silence drags on for what feels like an hour. Lexi is too stunned to rush him. It's the first vulnerability she's witnessed in Sol—the first signs of *humanity*—and she doesn't want to ruin it.

"My daughter was an artist. I never understood it. There was no realism to it, nothing I could look at and say, 'Ah yes, I recognize that.' But after she...I found a painting in her belongings. It was wedged between the pages of her favorite book. I kept the painting with me for years. After I made my way to Sol, I found someone who was able to tattoo it, and cut the designs into my hair so she is always with me."

Lexi's been so wrapped up in her own situation that she's failed to acknowledge the horror that everyone in Sol must have experienced when the world ended. There are thousands of stories in the city, and all of them are as tragic. They are the last survivors of the greatest war in history.

"I'm sorry," Lexi says, her voice catching. "I-I didn't..."

"I didn't mean to upset you," Chen says. "Sol is a beacon of hope, but it has come with a price. We can never escape what we've done, or restore the ones we love. But we can honor their memory."

The four of them walk in silence, the echoes of Chen's story playing in her mind. Judging by the awkwardness between Chen and the others, the citizens of Sol don't discuss their past often. There wouldn't be any point. The past offers them nothing. And besides, they could just look up each other's stories on the hollows.

They stop in front of an ornate section of wall that is almost upside down. Lexi is still feeling nauseous, but follows the others, watching her feet take one impossible step after another up the wall. Like the entrance to the Solarium, there are designs carved into an arch, but instead of vines and leaves, they are dots. It could be a kind of Morse code. Mostafa presses his palm to the wall, and the sides of a door illuminate with that familiar shade of blue.

The edges slip away like sand, and the door opens to a bright space of worker bees buzzing at their stations.

Rows upon rows of panels, videos, and interactive maps are organized in rings. Dozens of people are reclined in chairs, their bodies unmoving, as lines of code appear and disappear faster than Lexi can fathom.

The ends of Olaf's hair float, their motions delayed as he turns his head. Gravity is hardly present. If Lexi jumps, her head will smack into the ceiling.

The outer walls are the best part. Where the Solarium is a night sky with flowers and trees, the command deck is fully transparent. They could be in a floating bubble. The entrance behind Lexi seals, and it too transforms into a window. The double arms of Sol wrap around them, twisting into space, and the floor ripples like water around her feet, allowing her to see them both through the station. If she hadn't been counting her steps, she might think that the command deck was a separate space station, but they are standing in the innermost compartment.

There are no real windows.

"This is the command deck," Mostafa says. "It oversees everything in Sol. Navigation. Maintenance. Power. It is the heartbeat of the station."

Lexi's mouth hangs open. "You built this?"

“Yes,” Mostafa says, pleased by her wonder. It appears to give him a dose of appreciation himself. His attention drifts to the far side of the room, as if imagining taking it in for the first time.

Lexi can’t resist the smile on her lips. In her wildest dreams, she would never have believed that humanity could build such a magnificent structure. Sol isn’t one town made of one people. It is a slice of every place in the world. It is what every child imagines the future will be: a shiny city with flying cars in a technological utopia. Humanity built a garden in the face of darkness.

The first thought that comes to mind is telling her father. He would love this. He loves to tinker with gadgets and imagine the shape of the future. A sharp pain in her heart reminds her that he isn’t real. He was a piece of programming designed to nurture and raise her, but he doesn’t really exist.

“I’m glad you like it,” Mostafa says. “Now there’s someone who would like to speak with you. A word of advice: don’t stare.”

Half a dozen people stand on the right side of the room. An older man and a girl are in a heated debate. The girl’s back is to Lexi, but she can see their frustration when his arms swing in their quiet language. The group disperses and drifts toward the back, flowing past the young girl like water around a rock. She stands hunched, her bony hands resting on a cane in front of her.

She is no child.

The woman hobbles toward them, applying her weight to a cane that doesn’t make a sound when it strikes the floor. To avoid being rude, Lexi’s eyes drift back and forth from the floor to the woman, but the woman’s scrutiny is striking.

“May I introduce the High Councilor Hatshepsut,” Mostafa says.

This is the High Councilor?

The woman who decides her fate is not anything that Lexi expected. Hatshepsut is the height of a child, with the body of a woman battered by her own genetics. Her face is sunken, the skin clinging to the irregular bone structure. In her own time, she might have worn baggy clothes to conceal her disfigurement, but on Sol, the nanotechnology is only a few centimeters thicker than spandex. Lexi can make out every irregular crook of her body.

If Lexi were offered immortality and power for the price of residing in the High Councilor's body, she would respectfully decline.

"Close your mouth, girl," the woman says. Her bony fingers curl around her hand.

Lexi's cheeks redden with embarrassment. "Uh, sorry."

"It's been some time since a fresh set of eyes looked at me. I've missed the dumbfounded shock. Come."

Lexi follows Hatshepsut, maintaining a steady pace behind the leader of humanity. It's the first time Lexi has felt physically imposing since arriving in Sol. Despite Zuchiris's best attempts, her body has been slow to regain muscle. It could be the low gravity, or the simple fact that her body has never been strong before. Standing next to Hatshepsut, she feels like a giant.

They stop in front of the transparent wall that faces the sun. The arm of the Solarium is about to rise above them, uncovering what should be a piercing white light, but is instead subdued by filters. The sun is tinted dark red with black spots, sharpening the stormy nature of the most tempestuous life force of the universe.

Hatshepsut adjusts her weight between two uncoordinated legs. "Navigation. Show us the Libra and Scorpio constellations."

"Yes, High Councilor." A young bald man seated behind them rotates his chair, twisting one of the screens near the ceiling. The man's gaze drifts past them, as if he's daydreaming.

The stars in the distance glow brighter, gradually becoming connected by a series of lines. There are no manual controls; everything is being managed by his mind.

Hatshepsut lifts her cane and points toward a constellation over Lexi's shoulder. "Do you see that one on the left? Sagittarius. And to the right, Scorpius. If you look at the bright light in the middle, that is Earth."

A heavy lump forms in Lexi's throat.

Earth is a smidge larger than the stars, but otherwise appears no different. Its color is light gray, instead of the lush green and blue she remembers. It could be an illusion of the screen's filters, but it's a shade of death. How many times has Lexi stared in that direction from the Solarium and been completely unaware that she was looking at a graveyard?

"Does anyone go back?" Lexi asks.

"Not if they want to live." Hatshepsut taps the cane between her feet. The screen highlights a spot to the right of Earth and enlarges it. Lexi has navigated by the stars enough times to recognize a spot that shouldn't be there. It's not a star, or a planet.

It's a ring.

"Luna," Hatshepsut says, dropping her chin. "India began construction shortly after Sol. When they ran out of money, Australia chipped in to secure their own spots aboard. There was a mass exodus in the twenty-second century, and the station went radio silent for sixty years. We still don't know what happened. We opened the channels of communication and sent supplies, engineers, food." Hatshepsut faces Lexi, standing just far enough away to not have to tilt her head back. "What have they told you about the Dark Angel?"

Lexi hasn't given much thought to her uncle. She's familiar with the shadow of him that she knew in Beta, but that was years ago. She enjoyed his brief visits from Portugal and the sweet *pastel de natas* that he brought when she was little. But she doesn't know him.

She only knows the ghosts of people.

"Not much," Lexi says. "Just that that he's trying to destroy your simulation."

"My simulation," Hatshepsut repeats.

"Well, it's not *mine,*" Lexi says. "I wouldn't lock a bunch of people in a prison without telling them. I wouldn't enslave an entire group just to let a thousand people watch them pee."

Hatshepsut erupts with laughter. It's a pained, wheezing laugh that causes the feeble woman to cough. "Have you heard of a *kouros*?"

"No."

"It's the Greek word for a standing sculpture of a naked young man." Hatshepsut drums her fingers like a professor gathering her thoughts. "In 1983, a man approached the Getty Museum claiming to have a *kouros* dating back to the sixth century BC. There were only a couple hundred of them at that time, so it was quite a remarkable find. Naturally, the museum was thrilled, and they paid millions for it. Shortly after its public debut, sculptors and curators took one look at it and said, 'Fake.'" Hatshepsut chuckles to herself, a strange short sound, like a bird choking on a worm.

"The experts were asked what the problem was," she continues. "But not a single one of them could answer. They simply knew something was wrong. Months later, the museum discovered that it was a fake. The surface of the marble had been aged using potato mold. Potato mold. *Hah*!"

Hatshepsut hobbles a few steps to the side. She balances herself between her feet and the cane, rocking with the incoordination of a gangly body.

Lexi follows, careful to keep a safe distance. "How'd they know it was a fake?"

"That's the million-dollar question, isn't it? How could a few people know within seconds what took the museum months of analysis to realize?

An expert mind trained in their field will forget more than most of us have learned in a lifetime. The subconscious picks up on the tiniest of details, and helps us make snap decisions in the background, remembering the things that fade with time. And when you reach my age, girl, there is an entire world you'll forget." She closes her eyes and tilts her head back. "It's still in there somewhere."

The woman appears to be in a meditative state. As a semi-immortal, time probably means nothing to her. Lexi isn't sure what to do in the silence.

"I know it's Tiago," Hatshepsut says, opening her eyes. "I cannot be sure how, but I know it's him. I've lived too long to doubt my judgment. Your uncle is one of the most brilliant, cunning men I've ever had the displeasure of working with. He learns from his mistakes, which is what makes him a formidable adversary. He has been missing for four years, presumed dead, but a man like that wouldn't space himself, no. He's alive, huddling behind a processor somewhere."

"What does any of this have to do with me?" Lexi asks.

Hatshepsut taps her cane onto the transparent floor. For a moment, it appears to slip through space. "We need someone who can follow him into both worlds. Someone he wants," she says. "We need you to return to Beta."

CHAPTER EIGHT

Return to Beta?

Lexi could go home. She could see her friends and family again. They could hook her back up to the simulation and she could forget that any of this ever happened. This could be her chance at a normal life.

She nearly jumps out of her skin. "When can I leave?"

Hatshepsut closes her eyes, unsettled by Lexi's eagerness. "It would not be permanent," she warns. "And you will not be in a pod. There is a deck below the Iron Sector called the Nest, where our engineers monitor Beta. Your only responsibility is to go unnoticed. You will go to school, do your chores, and spend time with your friends. Artemis and Mostafa will handle the rest."

Lexi shoots Mostafa a fleeting glance. "Why is he coming?"

"Mostafa will present himself as a tourist, or something or other. You need not be worried about him."

"So, I'm the bait."

"Would you prefer to take on a more active role? Tag your uncle, trace the code, utilize advanced interrogation techniques?"

Lexi clears her throat. "Um. No, thank you."

"I thought so."

"Has it agreed to the terms?" a man asks, emerging from the lower platform.

It's the older man Hatshepsut was arguing with earlier. He is tall and skinny, towering over her with a critical eye like a father without affection. His short curly hair is black as night and closely trimmed. He appears to be only a few years older than Artemis, but his eyes are aged. He was attractive once, with sharp cheeks and a straight nose, but time and resentment have chiseled away at whatever innocence he formerly possessed. Referring to Lexi as an "it" can only mean one thing.

Councilor Farhad.

"It appears that a terrorist has taken an interest in you," he says. "Assuming that you are not a co-conspirator, or withholding information about an impending attack."

Tiago must have left quite the impression for everyone to so adamantly deny his role, or Farhad is unable to accept the possibility that one of their own is sabotaging their way of life.

"I'm here to tell you that either you apprehend the terrorist," Farhad says, "or three clones will be scratched to compensate for your presence here."

Lexi's jaw drops. "I'm sorry, *what*?"

"We did not prepare for your escape," Farhad says easily, as if bored. "Were you aware that the consumption rate is greater outside of the pods? Two clones utilize the resources of one citizen of Sol. For you, this means we do not have enough to spare."

If the Iron Dreamers are so critical to the advancement of their society, then why is Farhad looking down at Lexi like she's a spilled septic system? What are the Iron Dreamers and their brainpower, if not the most valuable asset on Sol?

Lexi looks to Hatshepsut for reassurance, but the High Councilor's face is unreadable.

"The resources weren't rationed with your arrival in mind," Mostafa interjects. "According to the analytics from your room, you have been consuming an unusual amount of oxygen. More than the average citizen. We need to compensate for what you've used."

Thinking about an artificial atmosphere is enough to make Lexi feel like she's suffocating. As if the protective bubble could explode at any time. She forces herself to take shallow breaths.

"Have you thought that maybe it's because I've never breathed before?" she argues.

Mostafa's posture is hunched, as if bashful. He nods, contemplating the situation with an indifferent academic curiosity. "There is a mission from Earth set to return in six weeks with additional resources. They're scheduled to replenish the oxygen stores, but without a recalibration, a part of the system could suffer."

"Then just put me back into a pod. You don't want me here. I don't want to be here. If you put me back, I'll just use the same supplies as before and everything will be fine."

"It's not that easy," Mostafa says. "We've never reinstalled an Iron Dreamer like that. It would be a major medical event. And if your mind rejects it, your reaction could set off a chain reaction that brings down the entire simulation."

"The point is, you know the truth," Hatshepsut says impatiently. "You would be a valuable voice for the Dark Angel's cause. It's safer to keep you here."

Sol is the size of a city. One additional person shouldn't make a difference. They monitor every breath, every bite of food and bowel movement. There is a computer storing all the data and scheduling the output. Lexi doesn't know much about programming, but surely there is a way to adjust the numbers. To conserve oxygen, they could tell everyone to walk instead of run for a few weeks.

Is human life so cheap that they would kill three people just to keep a bed of roses?

"You're saying that I have to stay here. But if I do, I'm consuming too much oxygen. And if we don't find the Dark Angel, you'll kill three of my people," Lexi says. "Is that about right?"

"Clones," Farhad corrects.

She shoots him an irritated look.

Centuries of procedure have lulled the Senex into complacency. The moral dilemma behind the development of a simulation and the cost-and-reward calculus to preserve the human species could be argued until they're all blue in the face, but the inflexibility of resources is absolute. The conditions have changed, and the people must change with them.

An unyielding branch breaks.

Lexi doubles over, shoulders rising and falling with each labored breath, barely able to bear the weight of her stress. They'll kill an Iron Dreamer every few weeks if she fails to, what, stand around? She doesn't know which Iron Dreamer it'll be. The decision could be random, or precise. She couldn't live with herself if three people died because of her. She couldn't live with a dog dying because of her. How is she supposed to work under those conditions?

This is how things are handled in the future.

Through a clenched jaw, Lexi asks, "How much time do I have?"

"Three months," Mostafa says.

"Oh."

"It will come sooner than you think," he warns. "We've been searching for him for four years."

Hatshepsut hobbles toward the wall and gazes upon the pit of stars. One knee is permanently stuck in the wrong position. "The Dark Angel will seek you out," she says confidently. "An Iron Dreamer reentering the simulation will send a flag he's unlikely to miss. We think he might try to recruit you to his cause. He'll know it's a trap. He'll come anyway."

"How do you know?" Lexi asks.

The woman shrugs, her bony shoulders pushing through the balat like a row of marbles. "He has a savior complex. Now, do I have your assurances? You will not run around announcing from the mountaintops that it's a simulation. You will not disturb the protocols. You will not risk another Iron Dreamer, should you happen to stumble upon one."

Lexi hadn't considered the possibility of actually knowing another Iron Dreamer. For every 25,000 people in Beta, only two are real. There are three thousand people in her hometown. The odds aren't in her favor.

"If I help you," Lexi says. "Which I will—under one condition."

"The girl is learning." Hatshepsut sounds impressed, before she notices Lexi's excitement. Her mouth twists in disapproval. "But you are young, and your concerns lie directly with yourself. What is it you want?"

Lexi doesn't appreciate the High Councilor's tone, but she's not wrong. Lexi *does* want to go home. She was never meant to live in Sol. Her plan is to protect the Iron Dreamers and then return to where she belongs. She'll go to college in Boston and find a high-paying job. The rest of her days will be spent skiing and biking and hanging out with her friends.

Two birds. One stone.

"Let me stay in Beta," Lexi says. "I'll help you find the Dark Angel, and then you'll hook me back up *permanently*. I don't ever want to come back to this place. I don't care if I remember. I'll figure out how to live with it. Just send me back."

The High Councilor regards the crew. She is their commanding officer, responsible for every life on Sol. If she's coming to Lexi for help, then she must be desperate. Hatshepsut is in no position to negotiate. She will have to find a way to make it work.

"We'll send you back," Hatshepsut agrees. "Mostafa."

A wide grin breaks across Lexi's face. She would shake the woman's hand if she weren't worried that she would snap it in two.

"Yes, High Councilor," Mostafa says, stepping forward. It's a sentence, yet also a question. Every time he speaks, he walks a fine line between asking what the High Councilor wants and already knowing the answer.

"She has agreed to the terms."

"Yes, High Councilor." Mostafa leads Lexi toward the door. She isn't sure what to say to Hatshepsut without feeling inclined to address Farhad, so she scurries away from them both. Lexi gives Chen a nervous grin from across the command deck. He reads her expression and frowns, seeming to register the bargain that has been struck.

"This is not a good idea," Chen whispers.

"It's my best chance of going home and back to my life," Lexi replies. "You didn't tell me they'd kill someone because I'm here." Her voice sounded more accusatorial than she intended, but it feels like a betrayal. He could have warned her.

"Lexi." Chen gently places a hand on her shoulder. His expression is tender, despite the warlike designs on the sides of his head. "They're not your responsibility."

She rips her arm away. "How is it *not*?"

"You're a child, and Tiago has had centuries of experience."

"You don't think I can hold my own? You don't even know me."

He raises an eyebrow. "If you get in his way, he will not hesitate to kill you."

"They think he wants to recruit me."

"And what do you think will happen when you refuse?"

Lexi hasn't had a moment to catch her breath, let alone consider the plan if Tiago reaches her before Artemis and Mostafa can capture him. She doesn't know what she'll do.

Mostafa waves a signal to the crew, giving no indication as to whether or not he's listening. One of the controllers enters a cerebral command, and the section of wall behind Lexi shimmers, shifting from a starry sky into a flat gray door. The modifications of reality are another element of space that she struggles to accept. How can she trust the people when the windows aren't even real?

Mostafa ushers them into the hallway and the door seals behind them. Grains of nanotechnology trickle between the cracks of light and snuff out the buzzing noise of the command deck, pushing the three of them into darkness. Silence used to be the forest after a winter storm when Lexi couldn't hear a sound; now it is nothingness.

Absolute nothingness.

Mostafa waits for the door to finish sealing before dropping the façade and transforming back into his earlier self. He appears to grow three inches by sheer willpower. What's the point of becoming a different person in different company after all these years? What does he have to gain from putting on a show for the High Councilor? He must be tired of it by now. Maybe he lives for the game. Lexi tells herself that she doesn't care because she's going home.

Lexi's eyes struggle to adjust to the blackness, and she trips over her feet. Concentrating on the light beneath Mostafa isn't helping when nausea rises up every other step.

"Lexi," someone says. She's not sure who.

"I'm fine," Lexi says. "What's the plan? Once I'm in and disrupt the code or whatever, you swoop in and grab him?"

"The less you know the better," Mostafa says. "All you have to do is pretend everything's normal."

Lexi snorts. "Yeah, because that's easy."

Mostafa stops so abruptly that Lexi slams into his chest. He takes a step forward and she scuttles back. He won't harm her with Chen and Olaf nearby, but the light beneath his feet carves a pair of half-circles under his eyes so dark that he looks to be a man barely containing demons.

"If you fail to play along, it could cause a chain reaction," he says. "The last time that happened, we couldn't contain it. The sentinels will restart Beta to avoid a system-wide failure."

"Wh-what does that mean?" Lexi stammers.

"They scratch everyone. The program starts over."

"Okay?" Lexi glances between Mostafa and Chen. Their silence is telling.

If the standard procedures of the Beta program were morally secure, then they would have no problem clarifying what it means to scratch all of the Iron Dreamers. It would just be one of many maintenance protocols required for such a complex system. But they don't want to say anything. Somewhere deep inside their dusty souls, they have doubts. Lexi's fresh eyes gives them a new swell of shame.

"They kill the Iron Dreamers," Chen says.

They continue down the hall.

Lexi should have done the math. Keeping Beta within a certain time period for a hundred years means that at some point, it needs to be restarted to keep the timeline within a specific century. Lexi has been too overwhelmed by her body and playing catch-up to the last thousand years of history to assess the technicalities of Beta.

The simulation is in the early twenty-first century, which means they'll need to restart the program in a few decades. Tiago may have delayed the inevitable, but how long did Lexi have before they would have pulled the plug and killed her anyway?

Lexi's breath is shaky when she decides. "I hate this place. Everyone pays a price but you people. Everyone dies but *you*. You just play with us like toys. You push all these players around the chessboard and never have to pay any consequences for it."

"That's not true," Chen says.

Lexi doesn't move to face him. No one should live above consequence. The Senex may have been human once, but now life is cheap. If an Iron Dreamer dies, they can just clone another. There is no value in a life if a carbon copy can be reset at any point.

"What's the Forest?" Lexi asks.

Mostafa turns his head. "Where'd you hear that?"

"She was there for Cillian's sentencing," Chen says.

"Interesting," Mostafa says. "It's a prison. The walls are layered with a material that reflects no light. It replicates a void so that you have no orientation."

"What's the point of that?"

He shrugs. "It drives you crazy."

It's not enough to have a prison, or rehabilitation program for whichever sociopaths and criminals passed through the genetic barrier and became Senex. They can't allow one grain of rice to fall and encourage disorder. They'll break you if they must.

The future has a ruthlessness Lexi thought was meant for the past. The cold calculation of kill or be killed, she'd thought, belonged to the animals. How could such incredible technology be wielded by beings who thought it easier to break someone than rehabilitate them? Wasn't the whole point of evolution to improve their way of life? Not to rely on archaic, reptilian methods when something goes wrong.

"Punishments are difficult to enforce on Sol," Chen says, attempting to dull the sting. "We created different methods to deter criminal behavior. We have not had an incident in a very long time. Sometimes we—"

"Sometimes you throw an innocent man into prison." Lexi finishes his statement before he can try to flower it with some benevolent spin.

She's taking everything out on Chen, and she doesn't know why. "Does Cillian have an estate?"

"No," Mostafa says. "Why?"

"Is this like medieval England, where owning property gives you more rights?"

"Something like that."

Lexi is beginning to suspect that the second arm of Sol and its living quarters are directly linked to the oldest roots of their civilization, and are clinging to the present like a disease. The people who contributed to the construction of the station have built up their plots, and therefore will wield more power. They should be entitled to enjoy the fruits of their own labor, sure, but what about those who arrived later, or don't know how to build like that?

Not *everyone* can be an engineer.

"You have a higher claim to Tiago's estate than Gal," Chen says. "She is a very distant cousin, but you are his half-sister's daughter. After Alexandria's mother died in the war, Tiago adopted her and raised her as his own."

"I was like a daughter to him," Lexi says, realizing. "That's why he's looking for me, or her."

"Alexandria was never a Senex. Whatever gene he carried that turned him into one was not passed down to her. He took her death hard." Chen turns his head, looking past the featureless halls as they rush by what could be several different rooms. "Sometimes I am grateful that my family was not cloned. I'm not sure I could look into their eyes and see nothing looking back at me. It would be their bodies, but it would not be them."

Lexi does her best not to take it personally. She can understand why Chen would be reluctant to embrace a shadow of what was once his family. Watching his daughter learn to walk, or drive a car, all through the veil of the simulation would be haunting. Chen couldn't interact with her, or comfort her. It wouldn't be her anyway. Not really. It would be her body and her DNA, but not her memories and experiences.

Isn't that what makes a person a person? What they've done and who they've loved?

Lexi can't imagine how Tiago's response will be any different. He'll look at her with the same disappointment. She is not Alexandria. She is a clone. A physical copy with all of the same blueprints, but none of the color. Lexi doesn't have Alexandria's memories or life experiences. To Tiago, she'll be nothing more than a shell.

She's not sure how to feel about that. It shouldn't matter what a terrorist thinks, yet she finds a strange lump forming in her throat. It's human nature to want to be liked.

"What happened after she died?" Lexi asks.

"Tiago was recruited as a materials scientist by what was left of the United States government after the First Nuclear War to work on Sol," Chen says. "He threw all of his focus into it. He refined the mining process and accelerated the stores. It gave him influence. As soon as the Beta program was created, and Luna agreed to supply the Iron Dreamers, he included Alexandria's DNA. He wouldn't agree to help unless she was there."

"There's another version of me right now, isn't there?" Lexi asks. She doesn't know what makes her think of it, but if Tiago's one demand is that his niece stay on rotation, then a replacement would need to be waiting in the wings.

The council wouldn't risk upsetting one of the builders of Beta without a backup plan. Look at the damage he's already caused. He would have been too consequential to upset. There's a clone of Alexandria in a test tube somewhere. What stage of life she's in is anyone's guess, but someone is waiting to replace Lexi as soon as she dies.

Mostafa might be impressed. "What makes you ask that?"

"Everyone walks on eggshells as soon as Tiago's name is mentioned," Lexi says. "It seems like you all want to make him happy. I could have died in a car accident in Beta, or hit a tree while skiing. It makes sense that there would be backups in case that happened. I don't think you would have wanted to piss him off."

Mostafa nods once, very slowly. He is not a man who is easily surprised. The caramel in his eyes shimmers with amusement. Lexi could stare at his eyes all day and not catch every detail. Who knew that shade of brown could transform so much.

"There are backups of you and many others," Mostafa tells her. "They are kept in the second trimester until needed."

"I have twin sisters."

The glow of the hallway darkens his cheekbones, as if they've walked halfway through a portal. "You're taking it well."

She laughs, but the sound is hollow. "I'm not sure about that."

"I am."

Chen clears his throat, uncomfortable with whatever turn the conversation is about to make. "Tiago's sector is impressive," he says quickly. "He had the resources, and the means. If you were not here, Gal would still have to fight for it after he was declared dead. He left no instruction on inheritance. Death is not something we think about."

All the riches of the kings end up in wills.

"Why is Artemis helping me?" Lexi asks.

"The Iron Dreamers are her responsibility," Chen says simply.

"Cillian's an Iron Dreamer. She should be taking care of him too."

"He was not in her sector."

Lexi snorts.

That is the most middle-management thing she's ever heard.

She doesn't know Cillian, but he's an Iron Dreamer—the only other one living outside the simulation. There may be no one else who cares about what happens to him. It should be her responsibility to keep tabs.

"What's going to happen to him?" she asks.

"There will be a trial."

"By combat?" she asks dryly.

"Not if you catch your uncle in time," Mostafa interjects. His hollow dings, and he flicks his wrist to expand the screen. The gray light casts a deep shadow in his jawline.

Chen steps beside Mostafa, the lighting engraving into his hair like war paint. "What is it?"

Mostafa holds up the screen for him. "She thinks this is his next target."

"What's going on?" Lexi asks. Now that her security clearance has been increased, they don't have to resort to sign language and stoicism.

"Artemis thinks she's found Tiago's next target," Mostafa says. "If he finds an Iron Dreamer from within Beta, then it's not to wake them, but to convince them to wake themselves up. He's recruiting."

Lexi doesn't see the problem. Waking from inside Beta is how she survived. It's better than Tiago's last approach, which left a man dead. At least he's trying a new tactic.

"That's not a big deal, is it?" Lexi asks.

"Yes, it is," Mostafa says, frowning. "There is no safe way to disconnect an Iron Dreamer. They have spent their entire lives connected to hardware. Waking up, even from the inside, could kill them."

"I lived."

Mostafa shakes his head. "Before you and Cillian, there were only two other Iron Dreamers who woke from inside the simulation. One drowned, and the other had brain damage that left him in a coma. It is a complex transference of information moving in and out of the brain.

Cillian survived because a sentinel was nearby. An ordinary engineer wouldn't have been able to handle it. You survived because—"

"Artemis," Lexi says.

"You were lucky."

Lexi doesn't feel lucky.

It wasn't a computer glitch that caused her to wake up, or the council would have blamed it on that, and it certainly wasn't by her own doing. She's not a genius, and she didn't will herself out of the simulation on sheer brainpower. Everything seemed fine in her world. She had absolutely no idea that anything was amiss.

She shouldn't be here.

"Who's his target?" Lexi asks.

A smile tugs at the corner of Mostafa's lips, like a fisherman whose bait finally caught. "A friend of yours."

"I thought everyone I knew wasn't real."

"Sometimes we group Iron Dreamers together." Mostafa hands her the hollow. "Your town has three of them."

Three.

Lexi can hardly believe it. This makes her life so much easier. Knowing who the other Iron Dreamers are means that she can find them and protect them. She grabs the hollow, half-expecting to see two familiar faces, but is instead met with a video from the afternoon at Cannon Mountain when it all went to shit.

She sees herself lying on the snow, her hair blowing in the wind as her empty eyes look to the sky. Teachers and students are scrambling to call an ambulance. They don't know that she's already gone. That she's looking down on them from a dimension of reality that she couldn't explain to them if she tried.

Everyone is panicking. Everyone is concerned.

Except for one person.

One set of arms that is cradling her body and placing a hand on the back of her neck. One person who had maneuvered his way into Lexi's friend group a year earlier without explanation. He's leaning on one knee, staring at her lifeless body with a mixture of curiosity and unease.

Jonathan.

CHAPTER NINE

Artemis and Zuchiris are waiting for them in the Iron Sector.

They stand beneath an ornate archway of symbols that look like hieroglyphs. The Senex went to great effort to incorporate language and art into their framework. She just wishes she could understand the tools around her, rather than roam the halls of an alien civilization that isn't her present, or her past.

Artemis and Zuchiris are a comical sight. Artemis, the short and resigned figure in a blue balat with her hands loosely clasped in front of her. And Zuchiris, the black and red lines in his balat cutting into his body like the scars of an animal. His brutish figure shifts back and forth. He doesn't like this plan either.

Artemis gives Lexi a curt nod, and then waves her hand with two straightened fingers. Chen and Olaf respond with a palm to their wrists. They engage in a quick wordless conversation, either out of habit or to hide their concerns from Lexi.

"I see Farhad was calm and collected when he explained the terms," Artemis says. She gives Lexi an encouraging smile, an attempt to bring her into the conversation. "Would you believe he has mice?"

Lexi blinks. "Like as pets?"

She can't picture the bitter man nurturing anything.

"We used to train them to carry wires in tight spaces," Artemis says. "The first few years were scrappy. Once our technique improved, we had no need for them, but Farhad kept a pair. He's been breeding them ever since."

"Hapsburg jaw," Zuchiris says.

Artemis chuckles. She is always able to follow Zuchiris's logic, no matter how far it veers from the original source material. Their minds seem to be connected by wires while the rest of them watch from the outside. A millennium of proximity has made the two telepathic.

Zuchiris gives them a quizzical look, as if it's their fault for not following. "The genetic disorder?" he says. "It was that jaw deformity passed down through the royal families in Europe because they were boning their cousins. The mice are inbred."

"You should see Farhad with them. You might think he has a soul." Artemis takes a heavy breath. "Let's begin, shall we?"

Lexi cranes forward, watching Artemis press a hand against the wall. The nanotechnology of Artemis's balat rushes to front of her palm and shimmers against the skin. She remains very still as the nanotechnology aligns perfectly against indents that appear on the metallic surface of the wall. A kind of call-and-response between Artemis and a hidden door.

It's not fingerprints that regulate the doors, it's the balats.

The suits are not only for life support; they're intrinsically connected to the station. A balat is a Social Security number. All commands move through the suits, each with its own unique code. No wonder Artemis was so quick to give one to Lexi. Without it, the station wouldn't know she exists.

The door slides open to a long corridor with low ceilings. Each wall is an unbroken panel of moving images stretching to the end of the room, which curves out of sight. It's similar to the command deck; the screens are so crisp and lifelike that Lexi could fall through if she didn't watch her step. A hundred men and women recline on chairs, wearing clear helmets connected to cables that hang from the ceiling. Their hands slide over unseen consoles above their laps.

"We call it the Nest," Artemis says. "It's where the engineers manage Beta, and the sentinels monitor the Iron Dreamers."

"This is where you control the world."

"Mm."

Lexi takes a step forward, trying to maneuver for a better view of one section. A family of four is vacationing in London. They're smiling in front of the gates of Buckingham Palace on a partly cloudy day. The youngest child, a girl in a red sweatshirt, is illuminated in a way that the other three are not. As she moves, the outline of her pops off the screen.

She's an Iron Dreamer.

"The decisions she makes are what influences her world," Artemis says. "The artificial intelligence follows her actions and intentions. We control very little."

The little girl laughs at something her father says. They seem like a perfectly normal family. The simulation is an overly complicated place to extract a few golden eggs.

"Why even have us?" Lexi asks. "It looks like you could just have AI solve your problems instead of real living people."

"We couldn't," Artemis assures her. "We tried for centuries to crack artificial general intelligence, or the self-aware kind you saw in movies, but it never worked. Think of it like connecting dots. AI might be able to connect dots, but only if we create basic instructions to follow. Like signs on a road, it can be guided along designated paths, but it can't navigate off-trail. Humans are just better at it. Nothing compares. If it did, then that's what we'd use. For now, all AI does is maintain reality to keep the storyline flowing."

Lexi chuckles. Maybe she's losing her mind, but it's ironic that, even with all the powers of a demigod and the technology of the thirty-second century, people still need each other to help with their math homework.

"We keep certain events consistent between our world and Beta to maintain an adequate level of technological progress," Artemis continues. "AI that's self-aware is purely theoretical, and no one's sure what it would look like anyway. What does it mean to be sentient? How do I know that you're self-aware, or anyone else in this station, for that matter?"

"Solipsism," Zuchiris says, standing beside Artemis.

"What's that?" Lexi asks.

"You can't prove that anyone else is as real as you are. You can't get inside their head, not really," Artemis says. "You can watch or listen, but you're not truly inside of a mind. It's a particular form of evidence that's difficult to generate. So you have no proof that anyone else is as real as you know you are."

The little girl on the screen smiles with her family, kicking a piece of wrapping paper on the sidewalk. Her mother holds out her cell phone and shows the picture to her husband. They smile. The little girl stares off toward the river, watching the boats pass as she follows her parents over the bridge. Blissfully unaware.

"After this, I'm not sure *I'm* real," Lexi says, mostly to herself.

Artemis cocks her head. "Does it matter?"

Lexi's lips part, but no words come out. It's a thought she's never had: What does it mean to be real—to be alive? Is there a set of classifications they learn in biology? Lexi doesn't have the answer, but she's pretty sure it matters. Artemis's cavalier approach to reality is a convenient stance for a semi-immortal. She doesn't have to question if she's alive or not, she has 17,000 years to figure it out.

Artemis pivots to Chen and Olaf. "Wait out there."

The guards move to the hall and stand on opposite sides of the entrance. They don't have the clearance to be in the Nest.

"You too," Artemis says to Zuchiris. "Sorry, buddy."

Zuchiris shrugs his huge shoulders. "Scream if you need me."

It's not hard for Lexi to imagine herself screaming. Everything about Sol sets her teeth on edge.

Lexi walks in step with Artemis's brisk pace, thankful that she stands a few inches taller than the woman, or she wouldn't be able to keep up. Most of the screens pass too quickly to follow. The engineers freeze and slow the moments to track the action. There are Iron Dreamers all over the world, in different cultures, speaking different languages. The engineers must be polyglots. Lexi's always wanted to learn French.

"Wow," she whispers to herself.

"What was that?" Artemis asks.

"I was, uh, just noticing how hard they work," Lexi says. "The engineers seem really focused."

"Flow state," Artemis says, looking to the row of them. The white lights accentuate her profile, highlighting the upward curve of the tip of her nose. "It's when the challenge slightly exceeds your skill. Or just enough to require a steady stream of attentiveness. It's like solving elementary math problems. Not too easy, not too hard. Keep an engineer at that level, and they can stay engaged for hours. The system learns an engineer's specific flow state, and keeps them locked into it. It's how tasks are distributed."

Lexi's not sure if she should be concerned, or impressed. What other human phenomena have the Senex uncovered and harnessed to fit their needs?

They pass a dozen more engineers before stopping in front of an empty set of chairs.

Chair is a generous term.

The seats are only partially built. Holes are scattered from the armrests to the feet, as if torn apart and eaten by mice. If they expect Lexi to sit on a cheese grater for ten hours, they'll need to bring a cushion.

Artemis grips the headrest. At her touch, the edges along the chair illuminate in the same blue as her balat. It's a sentinel station, *her* station. This is where Artemis was when she saw Lexi yank herself into existence and spin a thousand years in the wrong direction.

"I suppose there's not much I can say to prepare you." Artemis casts a warning glance at Mostafa. Her expression hardens. She takes a step toward him. "In a hundred years, we haven't had anyone outside of the engineers and sentinels in the Nest. I could have tagged the Dark Angel myself."

Mostafa inclines his head, making himself appear smaller. "The High Councilor thought it best you had reinforcements."

"And that's you, Moose?"

Lexi perks up at the nickname. She doesn't know much about Egyptian culture, but she knows there are no moose in Africa. Have they ever even *seen* a moose? They're large, cumbersome creatures that can flatten a truck.

Mostafa looks toward the sentinel chair, his mouth tightening to conceal a grin. He's never been inside Beta. The excitement is plain on his face. "I do want to help."

Artemis studies him with those piercing silver-blue eyes. Whatever advantages Mostafa's beauty granted him on Earth have long since lost their influence over Artemis. How could anything hold sway after a thousand years? Every rock has been upturned, every shadow brought to light. They probably know everything about each other.

Lexi is a bit jealous.

"It's not just Tiago we're looking out for," Artemis says. "The Watch has assured me that he hasn't broken through the security wall, but until he's captured, any set of eyes could be his." She lowers her voice and says, "I'm operating under the assumption that accomplices come from within, and without."

Meaning: Mostafa is not above suspicion.

He straightens, collecting himself. It must be difficult keeping track of his many personalities. "I understand," he says.

"Mm." Artemis turns to Lexi. "For you, it's business as usual. We'll provide you water and nutrients through your balat. You can carry on with the day as you normally would. If you're worried about what Hatshepsut said, don't be. You couldn't convince another Iron Dreamer if you tried."

Lexi isn't sure that's a compliment.

Every time she wakes up in her sterile room, it takes a full minute to remember where she is and why—and that's with physical evidence. Convincing an Iron Dreamer, who's never been outside of Beta or even heard of Sol, would be the equivalent of explaining Socrates's work to a golden retriever.

"If I don't help you, you kill three Iron Dreamers," Lexi says. "And it all rests on me being the bait? There has to be a better plan than this."

"There are a few other tactics in motion," Artemis says. "Don't look so surprised. We don't take chances on Sol." She rests her hands on her hips and shifts her weight to one leg.

During the summer Lexi spent in Portugal with her family, one of her aunts told her they could always spot an American by how they stood. Europeans stand evenly, perfectly centered between their feet. Americans lean.

Artemis is an American.

"Maybe now you can understand what it feels like to have the responsibility on your shoulders," Artemis says. "For all we know, our failure here could bring about the final breath of intelligent life in the universe."

It hits Lexi like a gut punch.

She hadn't considered the possibility that they were not only the last of humanity, but all life as well. She just wants to go home and protect the

Iron Dreamers, not only from the Dark Angel, but from herself as well. In a place where breathing has a penalty, Lexi has no place in keeping an entire species alive.

"Hang out with your friends," Artemis says, reading her pensive expression. "See your parents. We'll be dropping in during the last week of June."

"*June*?" Lexi counts the months on her hand. "I've been gone for three months?"

"Time flies when you don't look at it."

Azi drags a cord behind him, wrapping it around one of the floating balls as he approaches. It's the same spiked ball that Artemis used when Lexi pulled herself out of Beta. She still hasn't learned how they work.

The nervous engineer who showed them the murdered body has not relaxed his shoulders since. His onyx eyes settle on Mostafa, and the crease in his forehead deepens. Mostafa's presence in the Nest is more disturbing to him than Lexi's presence. It's nice to not be the target of mistrust for once.

Artemis points to Mostafa. "Him first."

Azi attaches the end of the cord to the adjacent chair, leaving the ball to float beside him. Mostafa places his hand on the headrest and twists his wrist like he's dancing with the chair. He's excited. Azi explains the controls, and Mostafa's smile grows wider and wider.

"He's applied to be an engineer for years," Artemis whispers. "He actually qualifies for it. His cognitive scores are some of the highest we've tested."

"Why not let him do it?" Lexi asks.

Artemis hesitates before replying. "Politics."

Having to choose a university and decide on a career that Lexi would have for the rest of her life at seventeen was bizarre enough, but the prospect of holding a position for centuries was even more daunting. How did one wake up every day for that?

Mostafa finds a comfortable position on the cheese grater. At his touch, the balat snaps into place and the chair comes to life. The metal underneath expands, crawling up his chest and legs, and spreading across his body like a cloud. It doesn't cover Mostafa so much as it diffuses into him. He tries to contain his shock as his head is snapped back against the headrest. He may have been told what was going to happen, but he can't logic his way out of surprise.

"The engineers are outside observers," Artemis says. "They can capture moments, repair the code, but they don't interact directly. Mostafa and I need to interact. That's why it's different. The sentinel chairs sedate us and allow us to move within the world."

"So you become an Iron Dreamer," Lexi says.

"In a way."

It's a relief to finally hear Artemis explain things. She's been dodgy on a few questions, but she's disclosing the key points with more detail. The feeling of falling behind is improving. Maybe Lexi will catch up soon.

"I didn't know you guys were in there with us," Lexi says.

"We try to avoid it."

At least 35 percent of the station is watching Beta at any given time. When they're not tuning in, they're talking about it. Lexi found thousands of chat rooms on her hollow dedicated to storylines and characters. An ordinary person living an ordinary life in Beta could be a full-blown celebrity and never even know it.

"Most of them watch Beta, but there are some who try to connect like this," Artemis says. Unlike the engineers, whose limbs are moving through the controls, Mostafa is entirely still. He could be asleep. "This is as close to full submersion as you can get without installing an interface into your head. The data drain is considerable. Outside of the Nest, only a few others can manage the supply for those willing to pay in whatever manner they deem appropriate. They call those places the grottos. We've been trying to root them out, but they're mobile and difficult to track."

"I don't see what the problem is," Lexi says. "People should be allowed to have a retreat. How is it different from playing video games?"

"Remarkably different. Life on Sol can be difficult, Lexi, and Beta is highly addictive. There, you're free to be anyone you want and go anywhere you want. The past can be intoxicating, especially for those with regret. If the council allowed it, people would stay longer and longer until the station fell apart."

A thousand years trapped in space with no hope of returning to a forest, the sea, or the first cool breeze of autumn. No rain clouds, or open skies, for the rest of their long, long lives. The Senex may be godlike, but they're still human. Their bodies have evolved through millions of years of living beneath a wide sky. The thirst for open spaces and freedom will never wane for a species meant to run.

A thousand years to find a solution, and this is the best they can come up with.

No wonder there's a black market for sentinel chairs.

Lexi casts her gaze down the rows of engineers. Their balats shimmer as if they're swimming under a dark sea. The engineers' fingers ripple over invisible controls while the sentinels are motionless, their minds relocated to a different plane of existence. Mostafa doesn't want Lexi to call them gods, but they're nearly there. They built a world and control the fate of all those who live in it.

That's the working definition of a god.

Mostafa's body relaxes as the nanotechnology rhythmically swirls around him. He could be standing in a field somewhere in the North Country, waiting for Artemis and Lexi to arrive, or he has his own agenda.

Azi approaches with a helmet tucked under his arm, looking over his shoulder to Mostafa. He seems worried by Mostafa's presence in the Nest. Does Azi know from personal experience how addictive it is, or is the man perpetually nervous?

He hands Artemis the helmet, and she holds it up in front of her. She enters a command into her forearm. The balat moves down her arms and toward the edges of her fingertips, flickering asynchronously across the helmet as if preparing to swallow it whole. Artemis is deeply distrustful. The balat is performing an inspection of some kind. Wherever her trust lies, it is not with the engineers. Not anymore.

If Azi is offended, he doesn't show it.

Satisfied, Artemis's balat returns to its standard position. She swings the bulky helmet over her shoulder like a backpack. "Who will be his sentinel?" she asks.

Azi pauses before answering. "Councilor Gal."

"What?"

"Sentinel Salvador was assigned for this mission," he replies quickly. "But it was changed moments ago. The order came directly from Councilor Farhad."

Artemis rolls her head back. "Of course it did. Where is she?"

The chairs come in two types: recliners with wires and cables sticking out, and the cheese graters of the sentinels. The balats neutralize most of the body's shape, and with everyone wearing helmets, it's impossible to tell who is who. Azi points to a woman lying on her back. Nanotechnology ripples across her body. She looks to be asleep. There is no way to discern her face, and the balat covers her fingers and skin. Lexi can't tell anything about her.

"My deepest apologies, Sentinel," Azi says, and he truly means it. Which is ridiculous. It isn't his fault.

"We need to hurry," Artemis says.

Lexi runs to catch up with her. A sharp pain shoots up her thigh. Her body is so underused and inflexible. She refrains from wincing, and points over her shoulder. "Will we be safe with her there?"

"Gal? She's not going to do anything," Artemis says. "As soon as she disconnects from Beta, she'll crawl back to Farhad and report our activities. She's a whisperer. She doesn't have a spine."

They stop in front of a gray cot.

Most of Sol is a technological masterpiece. Between force fields, nanotechnology, and transparent walls, every inch of the city is meticulously considered. And yet here's a plain old cot slapped in the middle, indiscernible from a cot from the Middle Ages—aside from the small hole cut into the headrest.

Some amenities just don't change.

Lexi crawls onto the cot. It creaks under her weight. She's not disappointed to miss out on the experience of a sentinel chair, but there is something surreal about a dinky cot being able to access one of the greatest and most complex technological achievements in the history of mankind.

Artemis wraps her fingers around Lexi's lower head and guides her neck above the hole. It suddenly occurs to Lexi that connecting to Beta could hurt. Ripping the cable out the first time didn't hurt because adrenaline was pumping through her veins. Now she has the peace of mind to frighten herself.

Lexi keeps her eyes fixed on the ceiling while Artemis works. The ceiling is made of small hexagonal pieces. They don't glow like the floor, or dissipate like the doors, and only a few are openings for the cables. The pieces are plain and simple, aside from the scratches where they were assembled by hand. If the Senex were willing to commit so much time to millions of hexagons throughout the city, then it's because they needed it to last, and in a certain way. A ceiling on Sol isn't just a ceiling, it's an additional layer of protection against the hostile choke of nothingness. Lexi appreciates every effort at protection. Too bad she's never going to learn about it.

Artemis stands over her, the view upside down. "We're going to drop you at Upper Falls. We've moved your avatar out of sight to the other side of the bridge, where the cross-country trail starts. Do you remember where that is?"

"Yes." Lexi's caught between excitement and nausea. "Where will you be?"

Artemis tugs at a stubborn cord by her waist. "The less you know, the better."

"Ominous."

"You don't need to do anything other than act like a normal teenage girl in the woods—if there ever was such a thing." Artemis smiles to herself. "If you knew what Mostafa and I looked like, you'd give us away."

"You're not going to look like yourself?"

"Neither will you, technically speaking. Your hair is two inches long."

Lexi touches her scalp. She hadn't considered the possibility of choosing her appearance. Maybe one day they'd let her look like a supermodel, or a man.

That could be interesting.

"No one will notice, but you should make your way back to the waterfall as soon as you arrive." Artemis checks the time. "You've been gone for...fifteen minutes. Are you ready?"

Lexi looks to the cord in Artemis's hands. It's thinner than the one she pulled out in the pod. "Can you read my mind with that thing?"

"No, not that we would need it. You're an open book, Lexi."

The way she says it doesn't sound like a compliment.

Artemis places a palm on Lexi's forehead and pushes her head against the cot.

"Wait, wait." Lexi's mind is racing. "What if I die? Do I die here too?"

Artemis sighs. "If you were an Iron Dreamer in a pod, then yes. They're programmed to match the events in Beta. Out here, it's no different than a dream. If you die, then you'll be booted out. You'll be fine."

"What if Jonathan talks to me? What if he asks me if it's real?"

"He won't."

Lexi thinks of that day on Cannon Mountain. "He might."

"Hold still, or I might jam this in your eye."

Lexi stiffens.

Artemis's fingers blindly probe Lexi's neck, aligning the cord with her implant. Lexi tenses, waiting for the pain, but all she feels is something rubbing against her neck. She hears the connection more than she feels it. Artemis stands and scrolls through her hollow.

Lexi taps her fingers on the edge of the cot, waiting for the program to start. She tests the resistance, lifting her head to gauge the weight of the cord.

"Sentinel," Azi says, rushing over. "Did you sedate it first?"

It isn't until that moment that it registers: Azi thinks of Lexi as a thing. Just like Farhad. From the moment they met, Azi has not directly addressed her once. Rage clouds Lexi's vision.

When Azi takes a step toward her, she recoils. "Don't touch me," she snaps.

Artemis steps in front of him, twisting her wrist in their sign language. "Let me."

Azi's face is awash with confusion. He is alarmed by the hostility, oblivious that he brought it upon himself. He leaves. Artemis gives Lexi a knowing glance. She's aware of the prejudice on Sol, and is saving that battle for another time.

"Take a breath," Artemis says, and presses a patch to Lexi's forearm.

Lexi's balat flutters around the patch. It doesn't hurt, but there is a pinch. Before Lexi can ask what drug is being administered, darkness swallows her.

At first, nothing happens. There are soundless blurry images. They're distant, as if happening to someone else. Lexi waits for the images to approach, or for her to walk toward them. She can't tell what she's supposed to do. It's like falling into a dream.

Cool air entered her lungs.

A gentle breeze blew against her skin.

Lexi blinked, attempting to see through the haze that settled around her like a fog. She dug her toes into the ground, astonished by the way it gave in so easily.

Dirt.

Lexi fell to her knees at the sight of a lush green forest. Rows upon rows of bright leaves shone in the sun, rustling against the touch of summer. The blanket of trees stretched into the distance, stopping at the foothills of a familiar rocky range. It was a scenery so enduring, so utterly perfect, that it could have existed since the dawn of time.

She pushed her hands into the dirt, letting the soil swallow her fingers. The realism was astonishing. Every layer was a different texture with all the shape of randomness. The degree of creativity was beyond her ability. Even knowing that it wasn't real didn't change the illusion. The simulation was *flawless*. She would never be able to convince an Iron Dreamer it wasn't real. She could hardly believe it herself.

A scream ruptured the air.

Lexi jumped, orienting herself to the new setting. To the untrained eye, every tree would look the same, but she knew the juncture. It was an intersection for cross-country skiing in the winter, and in the summer it was a bathroom for thrill-seekers.

Lexi ran toward the sound.

Her muscles were as developed as she remembered, with the callouses in all the places she left them. She was strong again. Her feet pounded on loose dirt and pine needles until she reached the bridge. She rested her hands on the wood railing, taking in the scenery of kids swimming in the river below. Boys and girls laughed as they dove into the crystal-clear water. The granite cliffs were narrow and dangerous, but those who had been swimming in the river for years knew precisely where to jump.

Lexi was transfixed by the joy. A mindless joy whose only purpose was to motivate a few people, she remembered. The only point to the complexity was to push three people within a one-hundred-mile radius to fulfill their purpose.

An older boy approached the edge of the cliff. He crouched, took a breath, and sprinted. He pulled his feet and spun backward over his head. For a moment, it seemed that his legs would hit the rocks behind him. He crashed into the water, landing only slightly crooked. He had been working on that jump since last summer.

"Jesus Christ, I was wondering where you were."

Her best friend walked toward her.

Michelle was squeezing the water out of her hair, probably heading toward the woods to go to the bathroom. She was heavy on her feet, her strides landing heel-first. The rhythm of her footsteps audibly beat into the wooden bridge. She watched the boy climb out of the river, scrambling up wet rock to attempt his jump again.

"Ugh. He's going to smash his head before he pulls that gainer," she said.

Michelle was talking to Lexi—*standing* by her, chitchatting as if everything was right in the world. Lexi wanted to touch her face. If she peered closely enough, would she see a glitch? A scrolling marquee in the retinas? Maybe Michelle was an Iron Dreamer. That would be great. She could handle the future better than Lexi could.

The water cascaded underneath them, tumbling over the edge into a waterfall that even locals avoided. If she jumped, she could be trapped by the waterfall and sucked into the underwater alcove behind it, never to resurface. She would die. But not really.

"Yo, Lex," Michelle said, sounding more annoyed than worried. "What's wrong with you?"

Normal. She had to act normal.

They were watching.

Lexi said the first thing that came to mind. "I think I ate something."

"That's what you get for packing cheese. It's probably growing mold in the car. Anyway, I'm freezing my tits off standing here." Michelle marched to the cliffs, committed to pulling a gainer before her younger brother. She was all business.

At least *that* part was normal.

The parents were chatting by the end of the bridge, drinking beers. The North Country didn't have hot days. Maybe one or two in August, but temperatures were moderate even in the middle of July. Most of the adults avoided swimming in the rivers near the mountains because the water was runoff from the higher altitudes. Was Mostafa one of them?

Artemis should be there by now, assuming that she was dropping into Upper Falls as well. Lexi couldn't very well go up to the parents and ask if they were real. They were programmed to believe it. They would defend their own existence wholeheartedly. How could a phantom prove their existence to Lexi, or to themselves? Could the Senex have created sentient beings and not know it?

Lexi groaned and counted down from sixty.

Fifty-nine.

Fifty-eight.

Fifty-seven.

She couldn't think about Sol, or the Dark Angel. For all she knew, Artemis and Mostafa were masquerading as billionaires in the Bahamas. Maybe they weren't doing anything at all.

Lexi passed the set of parents and smiled politely. She was going to jump into the river like she would on any other summer day. She had been working on a back flip, and hoped that the avatar of her hadn't managed it already. At some point, she would need to review the photos on her phone to catch up on the last few months.

Michelle was peering over the edge of the rock ledge, shouting to her brother in the narrow pool. Gui was standing by a birch tree, staring at his fingernails. He was at Upper Falls simply because that was what they did every summer. He was a creature of the forest, and just wanted to be with his friends. When he looked up at Lexi, her breath caught.

Seeing Michelle wasn't shocking. The girl was a force of nature. If she wasn't an Iron Dreamer, then she would will herself into existence out of spite. Gui was different. Seeing him smile so innocently made her heart ache. He had to be real. He just *had* to be.

Michelle and Gui began to bicker. Michelle wanted Gui to jump in first, so he could perform CPR on her if she smashed her head. Gui was telling her to stop trying to do the trick. He couldn't reconcile the risk and reward. Lexi grinned, warmed by the familiar banter. Everything would be fine.

"Hi."

Lexi looked behind her to a towering figure. He had grown a few inches since she the last time saw him. His hair was longer, and his face looked older. But it was him.

"Jonathan," she breathed.

He was real.

She wasn't alone.

The world emptied, and the cacophony of laughter retreated into the distance. She and Jonathan were alone in a room together. The walls were soundproof, and the floor was hard as porcelain. Somewhere in space, Jonathan's body was submerged in an amniotic pod a thousand years away. He was hairless. There were cables in his head and mouth and genitalia.

Lexi might have heard her name being called, but she didn't notice.

Jonathan smiled. "I see you finally showed up."

CHAPTER TEN

The car ride from the river was awkward.

Lexi sat in the back seat next to Jonathan, who wouldn't stop looking at her. Michelle and Gui were in the front, trying to decide on a song that everyone knew the words to so they could practice their harmonies. Michelle wasn't a great driver, but even less so when she was distracted.

"Give that to me," Gui said, taking her phone. "You're going to kill us."

Michelle's head swiveled. Her neck was strained from hours of backflips. She needed to lift her butt to see in the back. "Do you guys have your seat belts on?"

Lexi and Jonathan tugged at their seat belts, and said in sync, "Yeah."

"See? They'll be fine." Michelle pointed to Gui. "It's you and me that would die."

"Not today, if you don't mind," Gui replied. He scrolled through her phone, settling on a song that everyone knew. The intro had a short instrumental section. It gave them a few seconds to prepare for their harmonies. If they didn't hit each note, Michelle would demand that they start over.

"I don't know," Lexi said, pulling out the humor cobwebs. "I think the purple wagon could handle a deer or two."

Michelle snorted. "It couldn't handle hitting a *rock*. I know how fast I'm going by how many pieces are falling off. You guys ready?" She turned up the volume until the windows shook. The first verse was between Michelle and Gui, the soprano and the tenor. Their voices were almost drowned out by the volume.

Lexi nervously tapped her fingers against her leg. The car was louder than a jet engine, yet the space between her and Jonathan felt quiet. One moment he would gaze out the window with his hand blowing in the wind, the next he would stare at her. His face was guarded. His expression was so muted that it could have been a statue's. The more nervous she became, the more he allowed himself to be distracted by the music.

What was Jonathan to the Senex?

What had a small-town boy from the North Country been in a previous life that drove a space station to recreate him over and over? He was an A-B student, nothing exceptional. He didn't like art. He played the piano with moderate skill. There wasn't anything outright about him that struck. But clearly he had done *something*. He had carried out an act significant enough to convince demigods that he was worthy of being reborn.

Perhaps what made Jonathan exceptional needed to be triggered by an event that hadn't happened yet. Perhaps he was a fire waiting to be lit.

The windows were rolled all the way down, and the wind was thrashing inside the car like a wild animal. The trees rushed by them, curling overhead as if to devour the street. It was starting to feel like the old times.

Lexi pinched her eyes, unable to stop the rush of intrusive thoughts.

What was happening in her hometown right now? The real version. In the future. Was greenery eating away at roads and homes that were once part of the North Country, or was everything scorched beyond recognition? Nothing but a wasteland sweltering in the nuclear fallout of a few powerful nations that wanted to take the world down with them.

Fifty-nine.

Fifty-eight.

Fifty-seven.

"Lex, we're here," Michelle said.

They were parked in Lexi's driveway. Had she even been singing? Her parents were home. On a day like today, her father was working in the yard, and her mother was baking, or everyone was painting the walls. Her family painted the living room so often that they were going to need to start pulling in the furniture.

Gui exited the car, preferring to walk up the dirt road to his house rather than spend another minute in Michelle's purple wagon. Lexi followed and gave an awkward goodbye. Whatever conversation was brewing between her and Jonathan could wait. The rear tires kicked loose rocks and sand into the air, and Lexi couldn't resist chuckling at the sight. Michelle hated driving on her and Gui's road in the summer because the rocks damaged the undercarriage. Although it wasn't any better in the spring, when the road was mud. Or in the winter, when it was a sheet of ice.

They watched her car fade into the distance until nothing but the chirping of blue jays and the wind blowing through the trees was left. Children of the forest didn't mind silence. They could stand in it for hours. The world was loud. There was so much noise in a city and rumbling on the streets. Like the light pollution of a metropolis, the sound contaminated everything. This was the last gasp of fresh air left, and it wasn't even real.

"What are you doing for the rest of the day?" Gui asked.

"I, uh, don't know," Lexi admitted.

Everything had happened so fast. One minute she was in a cold room with wires sticking out of the floor, and the next she was jumping into a river. She hadn't really considered what to do once she was home.

Her uncle was out there somewhere, wandering through the North Country, scheming and plotting. Nobody had seen him for years, but he could appear as anyone. The clock was ticking. Three months sounded like a long time, but Mostafa hadn't radiated confidence when he heard the deadline. Lexi wouldn't be responsible for the systematic slaughter of three people simply because she was breathing. The sooner they captured the Dark Angel, the safer the Iron Dreamers would be. And then she could go home.

The only question: where was he? Aside from Jonathan, her uncle could be any character. Her mother. Her father. She cast a sidelong glance at Gui.

Lexi couldn't trust anyone.

"I think my dad and me will do some chores," Lexi said.

"Dad and I," Gui corrected, holding up a bony finger. "Since when do you volunteer to do chores, anyway?"

She shrugged. Lying wasn't her strong suit.

"Well, as long as he's not designing a wind turbine, I think I can join you," Gui said.

"Uh, that's okay." She scrambled for an excuse. "He's probably shoveling the coop. I can meet up with you later. What are you up to?"

Normal Lexi wouldn't be in a hurry to do chores. Normal Lexi would hang out in the driveway for as long as possible until someone shouted for her to put on a pair of gloves and lift something heavy. She had to act normal.

"There's a new series Eilish wants to watch," Gui said. "Desperate something or other."

"Is that like reality television?"

"I don't care. I'll read."

Gui's twin sister had very different tastes from him. Eilish enjoyed drama and romance novels like Lexi's younger sister, Rose. Gui preferred documentaries and science fiction. Whenever the two families were in the same house, Eilish and Rose went into a separate room to watch their show, while Gui and Lexi settled in for something more interesting—like *CSI*.

"Would it be legal to watch people who didn't know they were being filmed?" Lexi asked.

Gui frowned. "What do you mean?"

"Do you think it would be wrong? You know, if a bunch of people were being watched by another group."

"Why would they do that?"

"I don't know." Lexi shrugged. "To learn from them? Maybe they're a really smart group of people. And they wanted to learn without intervening."

"Do you mean like aliens watching us?" he asked, coming to life.

Gui enjoyed thought experiments related to intelligent life. He always said that, mathematically speaking, the odds were in our favor. Humans existed, and so that meant it wasn't *impossible* for life to exist. It was simply a matter of population size, and in a universe with an incomprehensible population, that meant it was a matter of when, not if.

Lexi didn't want to veer too close to the truth. The Senex weren't aliens, but they might as well have been. They acted like it sometimes.

"No," Lexi said, rocking uncomfortably on her heels. "Just regular people."

"Oh. Then I think it would be more efficient to just ask."

Lexi nodded silently.

There had never been an awkward silence between them. Friendships as old as Lexi and Gui's were worn in at the edges. Silence should have been a normal setting, yet it felt like an exposed nerve. Gui sensed it too.

"Well, let me know if you get bored," he said.

"Okay, bye." She didn't wait for Gui to leave the driveway. She rushed toward the field to look for her father, but he wasn't there.

The grass was an inch too long, which would drive him crazy soon enough. She couldn't understand why he didn't just let the field grow out. They weren't using it for anything. But her father was adamant about having open land.

Lexi made for the house.

Their home was an open cathedral style: two stories with massive windows and a wood ceiling. The front wall was floor-to-ceiling windows facing south. The positioning provided additional heat in the winter by providing sunlight from sunrise to sunset, and spared dozens of trees from being chopped to fuel the wood stove—which was their only source of heat for eight months of the year.

"Rose, you can't beat the butter so aggressively, it changes the texture," her mother said.

A knot caught in Lexi's throat.

It was the first time she had heard her mother's voice in months. It was the softness that surprised her most, like her favorite song. Even when her mother was giving instructions, there was a tenderness.

"It's taking too long," Rose complained. If she were a few years older, she would have been Michelle's best friend, and not Lexi. Rose and Michelle were similar in almost every way, aside from their appearance. Where Michelle was fair-skinned, Rose's skin was olive-toned and her hair dark brown, like their mother.

The bathing suit in Lexi's hand slipped from her fingers. She walked slowly toward her family, her mouth slack. She never thought she would see them again.

"*Alexandria*!" her mother chided. "Your clothes! Don't leave them on the floor."

Lexi blinked, startled by the name.

She looked to the floor, where water was leaking into the cracks. Her parents were particular about the floors. They were hardwood, and difficult to maintain if not cared for. No shoes. No dirt. Lexi mumbled an apology and rushed to the bathroom to hang up her bathing suit. She could hear her father's footsteps through the ceiling. The top floor of the house was her parents' bedroom, with a balcony overlooking the living room.

If her father was directly above her, then he was in the closet looking for music to play.

The house smelled normal. Her family looked normal. All Lexi needed to do was act normal. If she managed that, then no one would be hurt, and this would be her life again. She would be reinstalled into the simulation where she belonged. She walked into the kitchen and leaned onto the counter, watching her mother and sister.

Rose was a terrible cook.

One night she had tried to make instant muffins from a box. They deflated in the oven. Lexi wasn't sure how that was possible. There were only two ingredients to add, eggs and milk. Leave it to Rose to unwittingly desecrate the laws of chemistry.

"About to deflate some muffins?" Lexi teased.

"No, we're making cookies," Rose replied, pushing Lexi out of the way. "And don't eat any!"

"I'll wait until you fall asleep."

Rose's eyes narrowed. "Then I'll hide them in my room."

"Your door doesn't lock." Lexi poked the dough. It had the proper consistency. Rose hadn't ruined them yet. "What are these for, anyway?"

"Katie's throwing a birthday party tomorrow and I told her I'd make, like, a hundred of these things, so I have to finish them tonight. Who has a birthday in the summer? Gross. Get out of my *way*." Rose shoved past her.

Lexi looked to her mother, who was pretending not to pay attention. "Did you know that poisoning children carries a minimum twenty-year prison sentence?" she asked.

Her parents were an easy laugh. Her mom tried to resist smiling, though, for Rose's sake, as she was easily flustered by stress and deadlines.

"Maybe if you would *help*," Rose complained. "Instead of just standing there watching. You're better at this than me."

Lexi held out her hand. Rose sighed and placed the bowl in Lexi's arms. Cooking was therapeutic. Lexi loved the rhythm of cooking. And of course, there was nothing more rewarding than eating the final result.

Music blasted from the upstairs speakers. Her mother preferred silence, but her father loved noise. Lexi could hear his arms swing as he descended the stairs, favoring his right leg. He walked into the kitchen and grinned at the sight of cookies. His hair was fairer than her mother's, though his skin was permanently stained by dirt and oil. There was filth under his fingernails that, no matter how hard he scrubbed, would never go away.

"Ooo," he said. With dirty, calloused fingers, he grabbed one of the hot cookies and bounced it between his hands.

Rose reached for it. "These are for my class!"

"This is the father tax," he said, taking a bite.

"That's not a thing."

He smiled with his mouth full. "When you build a house and pay the bills, then you can take all the cookies you want."

Rose rolled her eyes.

On a different day, Lexi might be triggered by the power play, but today she couldn't help but laugh. It was such a normal exchange. The monotony of cooking, the familial teasing, the smells of fresh food. Why had she ever argued with them? Words that Mostafa had said crept into the corners of her mind. Like jumping off a cliff mid-scream, she could hear it growing closer and closer.

Memories are tricky things.

It would take time for Lexi to adjust to Beta and fully integrate into her old life. It could be years before she forgot about Sol. Years before her shoulders relaxed, and her chest didn't ache. Years before she no longer jumped to the conclusion that anything bad happening was the fault of an engineer. But she would get there.

She had to.

People were fine with divine intervention; how was this any different?

Since the beginning of time, humanity had believed they were under the watchful eye of gods. They followed the agenda of higher powers, and those faiths endured for centuries. What difference did it make if the higher powers had a name, and a birthplace? At the end of the day, the Senex were no different. They oversaw an entire world with the same detached interest, focusing only on the characters that served them, and the sacrifices placed at their feet. As far as Lexi was concerned, it was the same old, same old.

"What did you do today, honey?" her mother asked.

Lexi almost laughed. For starters, she had sat in a field of perpetual twilight. Explored the command deck of a space station. And had a cable attached to her skull that pushed her into an alternate reality where hundreds of thousands of clones performed tasks to the pleasure of an immortal species that observed them from above.

You know, normal stuff.

"I hung out with Gui and Michelle," Lexi said, handing the bowl back to Rose. Her sister could handle it from there. Hopefully. "We went to Upper Falls."

"It was just the three of you?"

Her mother always seemed to know when Lexi was holding back. She would say that her mother could smell omitted information, but she could hear it over the phone too. It could be the dumbest, most minute detail, and somehow her mother knew that Lexi was dodging something.

Lexi washed her hands in the sink, being careful to avoid eye contact. "Another guy from school," she said.

"Another guy?"

"Some sophomore. Well, he's a junior now, I guess." Lexi cleared her throat. "He started hanging out with us last year."

"Uh-huh," her mother said, reaching into the fridge for eggs. "What's his name?"

"Mom, come on." Lexi was becoming increasingly annoyed, but by what, she couldn't say.

Her mother chuckled, as if finding a sweet spot. "I'm just curious."

Lexi's nerves were on edge. She didn't feel like being interrogated, or revealing too much information about Jonathan, or anything else that had to do with a world that seemed more and more ridiculous the longer she thought about it.

An unwanted idea crossed Lexi's mind: could the Dark Angel be her mother? Tiago could appear as anyone. *Look* like anyone. Jonathan was the only person Lexi could be sure was real. It also made him valuable. If she was being watched, then she needed to watch her words.

Lexi chose the path of least resistance, hoping that would deter her mother's curiosity for a few hours. "Guinness."

"Guinness?" Her mother looked up from the counter with a mixed expression. "You mean Jonathan Guinness, right?"

Lexi tensed.

There was no reason why her mother would know the name of a boy in a different grade. Lexi had never once mentioned him, or brought him to the house. At least, not the real her. The avatar could have brought him home in the past few months, come to think of it. She needed to review the photos on her phone as soon as possible.

Lexi opened the oven and pulled out a tray of cookies. Busy hands were steady hands. "How do you know him?" she asked, vibrating with nerves.

"You don't remember what happened to his parents?"

"Is it one egg or two now?" Rose interrupted. She stepped between them, holding out the bowl of batter for her mother to see.

Her mother wiped the flour off her hands, adding another trail above years of cooking stained into the apron. She didn't look down when she answered, "Two."

Would a notification be sent to the engineers that Lexi was stressed? Would she be pulled out of the kitchen because she was consuming even more oxygen? She was torn between locking herself in her room and screaming for someone to pull her out before she screwed up the plan.

"They were in a drunk-driving accident, almost ten years ago now," her mother said, returning to the conversation. She glided toward the drawers and grabbed a rolling pin. "Accidents happen there all the time. You know the area. It's a wide road, but there's this one stretch of hill heading to...where is it?"

"Lancaster," her father said from his rocking chair.

Apparently, the inquisition had piqued his interest.

"Lancaster, that's it," her mother said. "They were coming up the road and a truck driver was heading down, and they collided head-on. His sister and her husband have been taking care of him ever since. I hear the husband is very nice, though. It's all so tragic. Can you imagine losing both of your parents at such a young age? And to a drunk driver. I never found out if he went to prison or not."

"Oh yeah, he did," her father said.

That's how Jonathan's parents died? In the year Lexi had spent with him, he had never once mentioned his parents.

In true small-town fashion, no one talked about the accident once the rumors dulled.

Perhaps that was the motivation behind Jonathan's interest in Lexi and her friends. Did he need a new environment? A fresh group of friends who wouldn't ask questions? Death wasn't a rare occurrence in the North Country, but losing both parents at the same time was unheard of. If there was an Iron Dreamer who could handle a different reality, it was Jonathan. He was already halfway to the truth without even knowing it.

"I've been meaning to ask you two," her mother said, smiling widely. "How would you feel about spending Christmas in Porto this year? The flights are cheap, and your father and I were thinking about jumping on it."

Rose jumped, clapping her hands. She loved Portugal. "Oh my god, yes! That would be so cool. We haven't spent a Christmas there in ages."

Since when did they leave the North Country for the holidays? People traveled from as far as Boston to buy Christmas trees at the local 1,400-acre tree farm. And every town within an hour radius went above and beyond with street decorations. It was one of the most popular times of the year for their area, second only to leaf peeper season in the autumn. Why would they go somewhere else?

Lexi was skeptical that flight prices were the reason behind the sudden interest in Portugal. There was one other pull to the small city in northern Portugal.

Her uncle.

Her father put the paper down and took a seat at the counter. "Well, hold on, girls—we haven't booked the trip yet. Remember, it's a long flight. We have to drive to Boston, and then there's that layover in Lisbon."

"Zurich, actually," her mother said. "For some reason the flight doesn't connect in the usual spot. Must be because of the holidays."

"Who cares? Get the tickets!" Rose demanded. "I haven't had one of those custards in so long."

"Well, alright. If that's what everyone wants to do." Her father looked to Lexi. "What about you?"

Her mother released a quick laugh, tossing the rolling pin into the sink. "Since when does Lexi say no to Porto?"

"She'll be old enough by then for caipirinhas too," he said.

The trip was suspicious, but there was no viable reason to say no. Normal Lexi would have said yes before Rose.

"Sure," Lexi said.

"Yay!" Rose squealed. "Oh my god, this is going to be so great. I can't *wait* to tell everyone. They're going to be so jealous."

Lexi spent the rest of the night in the kitchen, lost in thought. Rose escalated the cookie count from three dozen to no less than two hundred cookies. Lexi was secretly pleased. It was an excuse to keep the family in the same room, even if everyone was preoccupied. Her father continued to read from his rocking chair while her mother scrolled through flights on her laptop.

Rose's phone dinged, and Lexi was pulled out of the daydream.

"Michelle is trying to call you," Rose said, reading the texts. "She wants you to call her like, right now. Why is she calling me?"

The only people who called Lexi were her family—who she was currently with—and her friends, who she just saw. If Gui needed her, then he walked down the road, or used the walkie-talkie from their childhood that should still be on her dresser. Her phone never rang.

Lexi ran through the possible scenarios as she dug through her backpack. The picture of her and Michelle at Cannon Mountain flashed across the screen. Michelle was calling.

Lexi answered immediately. "Hey, what's going on?"

"Well, well, well," a woman said. "You are a difficult person to reach."

She didn't recognize the voice. It could be a joke, but Michelle wasn't a prankster—she lacked the creativity to torment.

"Is now a bad time?" the woman asked, as if knowing that it was in fact a bad time.

Lexi gave her family a reassuring smile and ran to her bedroom. She closed the door behind her without turning on the lights, and whispered, "Who is this?"

"I'm Mai, and I've been trying to get a hold of you for weeks." The woman laughed cheerily, as if they were old friends catching up. "Imagine the commotion in Sol when we were found out an Iron Dreamer was roaming our halls. Wonderful! How *did* you manage that? They say it's impossible."

The pause was heavy and intentional. Lexi waited for the woman to fill it with her babble, but the line was silent as a graveyard.

Mai was breaking the rules.

Lexi studied her bedroom, searching for lights or a camera. She knew that Beta was a pastime on Sol, and there was a possibility that anyone could be watching her at any moment. Weren't there more interesting people to watch?

Seeming to sense the suspicion, Mai said, "Don't worry, it's just us. All anyone sees is you texting your friend. Although it would make Boole's job easier if you could turn on your lights."

Lexi moved away from the door and stumbled toward the bed, certain that Mai was watching her. "Who are you?"

"Mai."

"Yeah, I heard. What are you?"

"Oh, *that's* what you mean. I'm a Senex, silly." Mai giggled. "Your sentinel has made it quite difficult to get an interview. I've never seen anyone go so far out of their way to hold back a tsunami, but that's what makes her a sentinel. We send only our best to the Nest. Oh, that has a recruitment ring to it, doesn't it? Best to the Nest. *But*," Mai said, singing the word, "now that we have a moment, I was hoping you and I could have a little chat. We have so many questions for you. I hope you don't mind."

"I'm pretty sure I'm not supposed to talk to you." Lexi looked out the window with an unfocused gaze. It was pitch black. No one was coming. Artemis was busy on her own mission, and Lexi wasn't given a panic button. She was on her own, thrown into a sea of consequences that she wouldn't feel until she hit the bottom.

"How are you even doing this?" Lexi asked. "Are you in a grotto?"

"Oh, no," Mai replied with the first hint of discontent. "Those are filthy places. Promise me you won't ever go to one. I have Boole. He was one of the best engineers in Sol before he was so rudely fired for writing a very interesting line of code that we don't have time to discuss now, but he is the best Beta hacker in, well, all of space! Don't worry, it's just the three of us."

Lexi snorted. "I doubt that."

"Hah!" Mai whooped. "You learn quick. Yes, the truth will out. I'm a reporter, you know, and we've all been starved of the truth. The council is quite good at keeping secrets—you didn't hear that from me. A city needs answers in a time of crisis. You would ease so many minds by giving us whatever you're comfortable with, and nothing more, I promise."

Judging by the hostile reception Lexi received in the Solarium, and the open prejudice from Farhad and Azi, it wasn't hard to assume that fear and confusion were germinating in the isolated city. The council kept information from Artemis, and Artemis kept information from Lexi. Secrecy was currency.

Lexi needed to hang up the phone. "I don't know."

"I totally understand," Mai said. "I wouldn't let you tell me anything about the conversations between council members, that would be in poor taste. I just want to know about you. You're free to talk about yourself, aren't you? How did you wake up? The rumor is a disgruntled janitor pulled you, or something along those lines. Which is absurd. They would never have been given access to your pod. How did you do it?"

"I don't know," Lexi admitted.

Mai seemed to understand the response was born out of genuine ignorance, and not a rebuff to her line of questioning. "It must have been a very scary experience for you," she said. "You're so young, even by your own world's standards."

It was the first time that anyone had acknowledged her trauma. Most of them behaved like it was normal to straddle realities, and she simply needed to get over it. She woke up in what she thought was a morgue. A giant cable had been attached to her brain. She was weak, fragile, and hairless, and then a stranger pulled out a catheter. It was a moment that made her panic whenever she thought about it.

"It wasn't great," Lexi mumbled.

"Tell me about it," Mai insisted. "Please."

Lexi imagined her nodding and scribbling onto a notepad. "Well, I mean, it's what you'd imagine, I guess. I'm just trying to figure it out now."

"I can't imagine, *woo!*" Mai shivered. "They were never designed for that, you know, to cause trauma. The Iron Dreamers were meant to live long, peaceful lives. Most of them are born and die in quite mundane circumstances. Only a few ever really contribute anything."

"Wait, really?" That surprised Lexi. No one had mentioned the success ratio. The simulation had been in operation for so long, Lexi assumed the program had always performed well.

"Oh, it's very difficult to extract anything functional. The storylines have to be laid out perfectly, and it can take years to squeeze out even one useful tool. The program has been very successful, but over the course of centuries."

"I didn't know that."

"I'm sure there are plenty of things they're not telling you, lovey. And even more they're not telling us poor plebeians."

Lexi held back a laugh.

"What was that?" Mai asked.

"Sorry, I just didn't imagine a hierarchy like that. You know, rich and poor. I thought they would tell you what's going on. You all seem to be in about the same shoes."

Mai made a clicking noise with her teeth. "Oh, dear. It sounds like there's a lot you don't know."

The conversation was putting Lexi in serious trouble. The engineers may not have been aware that a hacker was altering their screens, but someone would eventually discover the breach. There were a hundred ways it could go wrong. Lexi didn't want to face the same fate as Cillian and be thrown into a prison cell that drove her mad.

"One second." Mai moved away from the phone and whispered to someone else. "Right, okay. Listen, Lexi. We don't have much time, so I'll get right to it. It's unusual to send an Iron Dreamer into Beta after they've left. I'm sure you've heard of Cillian. He petitioned for years to return, but alas, to no avail. They made him an engineer instead. It must have been torture for all those years. It's no wonder he lost his mind!" Mai giggled. "Anyway, we're quite confused why they would send you back. Is something wrong in Beta? The citizens are worried about what's happening in the simulation, and with you. We only want what's best."

The tone in Mai's voice implied that she knew exactly what was wrong in Beta. Whispers of the Dark Angel had spread through every layer of Sol. Lexi had seen the chat rooms. The entire city was talking about him, arguing over their theories on who the shadowy figure could be, and speculating on the diplomatic implications of Luna aiding his efforts.

Whether or not Mai knew that the Dark Angel was Lexi's uncle, was a sentinel, or had already killed an Iron Dreamer and was actively tracking down another remained to be seen, but there was no question that the Senex acknowledged the threat he posed.

"I'm not supposed to do anything," Lexi said.

"I see. They want you to act normal," Mai deduced. Her voice fluctuated, as if she was walking back and forth. "If you're acting normal, then it's a performance. But why would your performance matter? Unless the *performance* is a trap, and you're the bait. This is about the Dark Angel, isn't it? Of course! What do they expect you to do? What are your qualifications for such a mission?"

Lexi wanted to slap herself.

Mai sounded like a teenager, but she had survived the end of days. The woman with the sweet voice had managed to secure a ship to the last stronghold of humanity in the midst of war. Either she had been remarkably resourceful, or remarkably lucky. It didn't matter how discreet Lexi thought she was being; Mai had had more experience facing opposition.

"Don't worry, no more questions!" Mai said happily. "I have everything I need. Thank you so much. You're making a real difference, you know. Can we schedule another time to speak? Perhaps we can get to the bottom of this together."

No, Lexi was not making a difference.

She had made a huge mistake.

"If you ever need to get a hold of me, just say your coes are told. I hope this is the beginning of a great—"

Lexi hung up the phone. She was not going to have a relationship with Mai. She was never going to speak to Mai again. The reporter had risked the entire operation, and compromised Lexi's chance of returning to Beta for good. If they failed to capture Tiago, if they failed to put a stop to the sabotage, then Farhad would order the deaths of three Iron Dreamers, and Tiago would find Jonathan.

A sharp pain shot through her skull.

The walls of her bedroom pulled away like mist. Lexi fumbled forward, reaching for the foot of her bed, but her arms fell through the blanket. She was being lifted through the fog, out of her house, and into a coldness that was unlike the chill in the mountains, or an icy lake. It wasn't the lack of warmth that froze her bones, it was the nothingness of it.

The absolute nothingness.

CHAPTER ELEVEN

"That went well," Artemis says sardonically.

"I know. I'm sorry." Lexi sits up, feeling lightheaded.

Coming out of Beta is not the way she remembers it. The adrenaline pumping through her veins the first time must have clouded her senses. It's not a smooth transition, but a violent roller coaster. She feels sick, as if she had been drinking all night and is just now sobering up.

She presses a hand to her forehead, and squeezes her eyes shut. "Why does my head hurt?"

"You need to sleep," a man replies. "I told you she is malnourished. She needs to exercise and strengthen her cardiovascular."

They have three months to capture the Dark Angel before three Iron Dreamers are killed in her stead. She doesn't know how they'll be selected or in what way they'll be "scratched," but Jonathan is still in there. What if he's the one they choose? Lexi wouldn't put it past Farhad to elect Jonathan just to punish her. She couldn't live with herself if the only real person she knew was murdered because she was breathing too hard.

"I'm fine, really," Lexi says. She doesn't have the time to build endurance.

"This is Doctor Singh," Artemis says, gesturing to the man on the other side of Lexi's cot. "He was the one who returned your vision, if you remember."

"And the one who removed it," Mostafa adds. He moves behind the group, disappearing from view.

"Mm." Artemis locks her hands in front of her.

Lexi cracks open an eye to find a tall dark man with narrow shoulders looking down at her. His brow is furrowed with concentration. He appears to be around her parent's age, but of course, he's not. He takes a step back, and the white in his balat shifts to gray. They're lucky they had a doctor who happened to have the right genetic makeup to become a Senex.

"Azi called Doctor Singh when your heart rate jumped," Artemis says. "Apparently, the disconnecting process is stressful on your body. We're going to have Zuchiris design an exercise plan for you."

"Sentinel," the doctor protests, "I must advise—"

"Noted," Artemis says, holding up a hand. "We'll warn her next time before pulling her out."

"It's not the withdrawal that concerns me." Doctor Singh moves his arms in sharp angles. Lexi can't understand their conversation, but he appears to be voicing a strong opinion.

She didn't enjoy their first meeting, but she appreciates the doctor's advocacy for her well-being now. He walks out of view and is replaced by Mostafa, who looks down on Lexi with a disapproving glower.

"Why did you talk to the reporter?" he asks.

"I don't know," she says.

"You don't know."

"I didn't think I was saying anything important."

Mostafa leans forward. The artificial lighting dulls the caramel in his eyes. If he weren't so angry, Lexi might lose her breath from the closeness.

"Her job is to extract information," Mostafa says. "Even your silence tells her something."

"I'm sorry. I-I'll lie next time."

He keeps his voice low when he says, "Lies tell her something too."

Being in the presence of an expert extractor just means that Lexi is vulnerable no matter how it goes. Whether she told the truth, told a lie, or told Mai nothing at all, Lexi was an open book.

But why is Mostafa so upset?

Lexi was under the impression that he didn't care about anything, and that every interaction was a game with prizes only he could win. A Casablanca of space. Chen mentioned that he cared about Sol—which is logical, since there's nowhere else for them to go—but she didn't expect Mostafa's unease. Does he care about the fate of the Iron Dreamers, or is there some other prize to be had? She just can't get a read on him.

"Tell me about Mai," Artemis says. She pulls one of the floating spiked balls toward her. She starts to wrap the cable that was attached to Lexi's head, until Azi holds out his hands, insisting that he do it. A dutiful servant. "Did she have help?" Artemis asks. "And what's this thing about Portugal? The flights aren't cheaper."

"Oh, uh," Lexi rattles her brain, scrambling to be useful. "Yeah, she said something about an engineer hacking into Beta, or however that works. He had a weird name. Who was the guy that killed Abraham Lincoln?"

Artemis and Mostafa stare at her.

"John Wilkes Booth," Azi says. He pushes a screen back until it hovers near the wall, scrolling through the images for them all to see. "He shot the sixteenth president of the United States in 1865. Then Booth was tracked down and shot by a Union soldier. He died a few hours later, at the age of twenty-six. That is both the Senex history and the current iteration of Beta. The storyline has been included since the eleventh iteration."

"An engineer wouldn't have chosen that name. It's not Booth," Artemis says.

"Why are we looking for a historical figure?" Lexi asks. Artemis. Zuchiris. Hatshepsut. They couldn't be the names these people were born with. They're either ancient, or made up.

"Half the station kept their birth names," Artemis says. Her voice is stiff. "The other half chose new ones when they boarded. A new name for their new lives."

“So your name isn’t really Artemis.”

Artemis gives her an incredulous look. “Did you think the High Councilor was a pharaoh too?”

Lexi shrinks. She probably deserves the attitude after the blunder with Mai, but how could they expect her to know anything? There is so much history in the future. The least they can do is be patient as she tries to catch up with a thousand years of nuance.

A young woman with hair tied into a high ponytail whispers into Artemis’s ear. Artemis nods and gives Mostafa an unreadable look. The woman runs off, walking alongside an older man near a web of floating wires.

“Did you guys find him?” Lexi asks, trying to decipher the exchange.

Artemis says stiffly, “No.”

“I found a nexus!” Azi exclaims. “Lucy Hale. She was engaged to Booth around the time he assassinated the president. The engagement was called off, and she died much later, in 1915. She was buried in New Hampshire. A connection, perhaps?”

Artemis grabs the hollow, and a smile tugs at her lips. “Look at that. Dover, New Hampshire.”

Dover is a small town near the coastline between Massachusetts and Maine. It’s not even directly on the coast, it’s inland. The only people who know about it are the locals who live there. Why would it make Artemis smile?

“Not Booth,” Mostafa says in an academic daze. “Boole. It has to be him.”

Lexi vaguely remembers the name Boole from math class. He was a mathematician. He developed a kind of algebra that Lexi hated. Where 0+1=1 and 1+1=1 and other nonsense, but it’s an important principle for computers, apparently.

"That's it—Boole," Lexi says. "No wonder I couldn't remember it. I'm terrible at math."

"You weren't always." Artemis holds a hand to her chin in thought. Each word is carefully separated, as if hearing the words for the first time. "His sentence isn't over for another 120 years. How could it be him? That prison is a fortress."

"Mai must have found a way to free him," Mostafa says.

"She couldn't have broken him out of prison on her own. She doesn't possess those kinds of skills."

"No." Mostafa's voice drops, pulling Artemis down to a conclusion that she doesn't want to draw.

She reads something in his face, and her eyes narrow. "You can't possibly think Tiago's working with them? Boole's a sociopath."

"It's not a bad idea," he says, sounding impressed. "Who else would have the capability? Tiago wouldn't risk contacting Lexi directly, so he sends someone else. Boole wouldn't help—it was Tiago who caught him—but if Tiago extracted him from Luna and sent Mai as the emissary, he could hide in the shadows. Boole probably doesn't know Tiago's the one who hired him."

"Tiago doesn't work with anything he can't control. And what would be in it for Boole? We're just going to throw him back in his cell."

"Freedom, even if only for a few weeks, is better than none," Mostafa says. "It gives Mai access to Beta without going through a grotto and tarnishing her reputation for a story. Everyone wins."

Artemis's hesitation to bring Mostafa along on the mission must have a backstory, or perhaps she finds him as unpredictable as Lexi does, but his insight is valuable. He's earning his position. Artemis gives Mostafa a tentative nod.

Azi coughs noisily, drawing their attention. He shifts his eyes, signaling to a woman sitting up on a sentinel chair a few rows away.

Gal pulls off the helmet and hands it to an engineer. It's the woman from the Solarium. The one who had been watching Lexi from the vines.

Unlike Artemis, and most of the people with long hair, Gal does not wear hers in a tight bun, or elaborate braids. Her dark hair flows around her shoulders in waves, shimmering from the blue light beneath her feet as if challenging gravity itself to dull her fire. While free-flowing hair must be cumbersome in space, it certainly makes her stand out. It accentuates the sun-kissed olive skin so prevalent in Lexi's family.

Gal is a Carvalho.

"She doesn't know about the Mai thing, right?" Lexi whispers.

As if able to hear her from across the hall, Gal's head tilts with intrigue. Her calculating eyes move past her, as if Lexi is too uninteresting to warrant a second thought. Distant cousins separated by centuries of war and turmoil. For a moment, it appears that Gal is considering approaching them—maybe to rub the fiasco in Lexi's face. Instead, she bows her head to Artemis and turns on her heel.

"She knows," Artemis says. "And now Farhad does too."

"All things considered, it could have gone worse," Azi says.

Artemis and Mostafa look at him with raised eyebrows. Azi doesn't expand on his comment, but Lexi suspects that it has something to do with the low regard he holds for her. As if Lexi was expected to fail spectacularly because she's an *it*.

Artemis stills, an idea coming to her. "Take Lexi through the gates at the back end," she tells Mostafa.

"Through the gates, or *to* the gates?" Mostafa asks.

"Through."

The word triggers an unsettling calm. Mostafa assesses her with that quiet intensity she's becoming accustomed to. She's not sure why he inspects her in such a manner, but he has yet to find what he's looking for.

"Take Zuchiris with you," Artemis adds, leaving to follow Gal. "But keep him by the gate."

Mostafa bows his head.

A sour taste fills Lexi's mouth. She shouldn't care what Artemis thinks of her. The sentinel is a direct line to the North Country, and Lexi becoming an Iron Dreamer again. Her approval shouldn't matter. Yet Lexi feels the sting of disappointment.

"She seems mad," Lexi says.

"She's always like that," Mostafa says.

"What were you guys doing in there?"

"Looking for Tiago, as you know."

"Yeah, but how? If he's some tech wizard, how do you find him in a world that he created?"

Mostafa pauses before answering. "Artemis has a way of knowing what he's going to do."

They could be tracking him like an animal in the forest, reading signs in the tea leaves, or it's more technical than that. Beta is a simulation, meaning that every rock and cloud in the sky is a line of code. Surely Tiago's presence leaves a mark. But why is it Artemis who leads the search? What does she know about him that the rest of them don't?

"I bet there's a story there," Lexi says.

Mostafa snorts. "There's a story with everyone."

Lexi follows him past the rows of engineers and sentinels. Some of the screens are dark, it's the middle of the night on the Eastern Seaboard. The engineers in that designation take a quick break, chatting to each other with their feet hanging over the edges of the chairs. They drink out of glass tubes, and suck food out of the smaller ones. She can feel their gaze as she passes.

Mostafa tells Zuchiris that they're going to the gates. Zuchiris laughs. Not in the warm, friendly way, but with an amused disbelief.

Lexi follows them down the halls, taking a turn at an intersection she doesn't recognize. The details are subtle, but she's beginning to notice the differences between the patterns in some sections of the wall that indicate where the doors are. Sol was not built for tourists, so there is no point in carving signs or directions. Everyone knows where to go because they've been looking at the same muted patterns for years.

Mostafa and Zuchiris's hands occasionally communicate in their sign language. It appears to be an argument, but fades into submission. Lexi is tired of the tension.

"Why do you guys even have sign language?" she asks.

"When we were first constructing Sol, we had communications issues," Mostafa says, keeping his eyes forward. "Like Earth, the sun has seasons that run on an eleven-year cycle. During the solar maximum, the sun has more solar flares. That first period was especially active, and the flares were damaging our communications. Even an inch of space between compartments meant there was no sound. At first, we used military signals, and that evolved into a language when we discovered the value. We call it Sessiz."

"Sessiz?"

"*Sessizlik* is the Turkish word for silence. A pair of brothers from Istanbul were the first to record the commands. Some had trouble pronouncing it, so it devolved into Sessiz. They still correct us."

Lexi perks up at that. "They're here?"

"Of course."

It's strange to remember that anyone who did anything is on Sol. All the figures from history are still roaming the halls, unaffected by the ticking of time and continuing on with their work. It's the Iron Dreamers who live in the memory of the old world. The only creatures dying for a cause they know nothing about.

"If you wish to learn Sessiz, it would be wise to ask the sister." Mostafa says, leading them down a hall that grows wider with each step.

"Do the brothers have bad people skills?" Lexi jokes.

"The cloning program is controversial."

"Oh." Understanding dawns on her. "They don't think I'm a real person."

"You're real," Zuchiris interjects. "They're just idiots."

A group of people gather in front of a doorway, waiting for one of them to open it. A *whoosh* of air and what sounds like a thousand people speaking at full volume bounces off the walls. Light pierces her eyes. Unlike the familiar blue glow of the floor, the light coming through is pink with flashes of yellow, as if people are walking in front them.

"This is neat," Zuchiris says. "This is the Trough."

A hall longer than the Solarium stretches farther than the eye can see. Swarms of people stroll beneath fluorescent signs surrounded by hanging plants that extend halfway to the floor. Some of them have bright flowers, others are entwined around statues depicting figures from the ancient world. The sector is a mix between Times Square and the hanging gardens of Babylon.

At first glance, it appears that the ceiling is one massive screen, but it's the same assembly as the Nest. The honeycomb ceiling is illuminated to match the sunset of Earth. It must be late afternoon. Light fluffy clouds float across the panels. A set of birds fly by. Lexi has seen the Trough on her hallow, but walking through it is a far more enchanting experience. She counts six floors, each narrower than the floor below like a pyramid.

"Restaurants, gyms, and bars. This is where we keep all the fun stuff," Zuchiris says.

It's Lexi's first time exploring the second arm of Sol. The Trough was one of the first places Lexi wanted to visit because it's the most realistic sector, designed specifically to mimic the cities of Earth. Even the air smells better, as if they're misting flowers through the vents. Most of the station smells like metal, or blood from the high levels of iron. Even the Senex and Lexi's skin smell like raw materials. Outside of the Solarium, the Trough is the best-smelling part of space.

She expected demigods to be boring. She imagined humans of the future to be above reproach, evolved to a monk-like state in their worldviews. Having thought every thought there was to think, and nothing new left to enjoy, they would be disinterested in the tastes of lesser beings.

"So, people in the future still like this stuff," Lexi says, surprised.

Mostafa's brow furrows. "Why wouldn't we? For thousands of years, people have enjoyed entertainment. That's not going to change because of the location."

The first pair that walked through the door take a seat at a bar. The screen by the patrons' legs glows dark blue with colorful fish and coral reefs. The shapes don't distort as they swim past the corners. They could be real fish, Lexi realizes. Fish don't need much to survive.

Three men sitting at the bar stare at her warily. She's tired of the strong reactions everywhere she goes. Her existence shouldn't be controversial. She hasn't done anything wrong.

Well, maybe with Mai.

But they don't know that.

"This joint has the best whiskey," Zuchiris says. He takes long strides toward the bar. He tilts his head back and rubs the top of his chest, reading the menu. Zuchiris is a bit strange. Not enough to be overtly noticeable, but there are little oddities. Balats are tough as armor. There is no feeling temperature, pressure, or even movement through them. If Zuchiris is rubbing his chest, it's not because he feels an itch underneath.

"Joint?" Lexi asks Mostafa. "Is Zuchiris from New England?"

"Boston. That's where he met Artemis."

"They knew each other before all this?"

"Yes. They were lucky. Most of us didn't know anyone."

Lexi takes in the Senex around her, wondering who else is from the northeast of the United States. She's warmed by the touch of familiarity. "I thought language would have changed by now," she says.

"It should have changed. If we lived and died as humans used to, then even English would have evolved to be unrecognizable to you. But everyone here was born in the twenty-first century, and most iterations of Beta are within a hundred years of that point. There's been no reason for language to change."

Zuchiris stares at a floating screen with a soccer game on display. He likes to stare at things. The stadium is massive, and full of people drenched in the rain. It can't be real.

"BetaVu," Mostafa says. "The goalkeeper is an Iron Dreamer."

"That's sad."

"Why?"

"I don't know. Because he's not playing against anyone who's real?"

Mostafa stops in the middle of the walkway and lets the current of people brush past him. It reminds her of the beginner skiers on expert trails, and how they just sit in the middle, unconcerned with how they've made themselves a danger to everyone around them. Self-centered and annoying.

"What does that mean?" Mostafa asks.

"Should we be standing here?" Lexi looks around. Most of the Senex glance quickly, but some of them glare as they pass. It wasn't officially announced on BetaVu, but somehow everyone knows that an Iron Dreamer is in their midst.

"Tell me, what is real?"

"I don't know," Lexi snaps. "Something tangible. Like, you can touch it, or it thinks. You know, *real*."

“No, I don’t know. You didn’t describe anything that couldn’t be in Beta. The Iron Dreamers are real. Their thoughts and feelings are real. You don’t think they’re valid because the pixelation is different?”

By pixelation, she assumes that Mostafa means what their eyes are seeing in space, versus what the Iron Dreamers see daily in the simulation. Theoretically, the quality could be better in Beta. An Iron Dreamer born with poor vision could be altered to experience Beta in 20/20. But the quality doesn’t matter. It’s an artificial reality built by people. A fabricated world built by *people*. Higher pixelation or not, it’s not real.

“Come on,” Lexi scoffs. “You know this is different.”

“You’ve yet to define the difference.”

“Okay. How about I can go into Beta *and* be here, but the phantom characters you made can only be in Beta.”

“You’re suggesting that physical access defines the authenticity of reality?”

“Yeah, I mean, that’s one example.” Lexi has never considered what makes reality real. She’s not a philosopher. She’s not trained in the art of elaborating on what’s obvious.

“Have you read *Flatland*? It’s a satirical novel from the nineteenth century about a world that exists in the second dimension.”

“Sounds above my pay grade,” Lexi laughs dryly.

Mostafa grins. His beauty could soften the blow of a death sentence. As annoyed as she is, she finds it hard to stay mad at him.

“It’s one of the High Councilor’s favorite books. She talks about it often.” Mostafa holds out his hand and presses a finger to his palm to illustrate it to her. “A single point is one dimension. A line is two dimensions. And you and I are three dimensions, yes? A world that exists on a piece of paper would be full of two-dimensional creatures. The people there could move left and right, forward and back, but not up and down. If you were to lower your finger onto that piece of paper, it would look to them like you appeared out of thin air. But you didn't. You're just from a higher dimension. To them, you're not really there unless they can see you. But you can always see them."

"Okay, but you're still describing living, breathing things. The phantoms in Beta aren't in some other dimension, they're not real."

"You defined reality by what it can physically access, and I proposed that a higher dimensional being, above our world, might consider us not real because we can't see them."

"I don't have the words for it," she admits. "I'm not as smart as you people. But you know what I mean. This is real."

"Is it?"

Mostafa lowers his head. It could be to avoid prying eyes, but he has a tendency to move in close when he wants to toy with her. She pretends to be irritated by it, but she's not. It gives her a new detail to notice. There's a small mole near his nose.

Finally.

An imperfection.

"How do you know this isn't another simulation?" he asks. "You didn't realize it the first time."

"This is real," she says with a confidence that she doesn't feel.

"Possibly." Mostafa presses a finger to his chin. "I wonder about it. Someone could be doing to us what we've done to you. It would be poetic justice for the Iron Dreamers, I suppose."

"You think this is a simulation?"

"When the first version of the simulation was created—Alpha—we realized how easy it was to submerge the human mind. We considered the possibility that we were already in a simulation, and that someone else was doing it to us to solve *their* problems. So we set up systems that monitor for irregularities."

Lexi frowns. She doesn't like the possibility that there's another layer to the nightmare. "What kind of irregularities?"

"Mathematical ones," he answers. "Pi is a constant, yes? The number extends forever. If, three million digits out, one of the numbers changes for a fraction of a second, then we would know something is wrong. Like software resetting, we would identify the glitch and realize that the constant, and possibly everything else, isn't real."

"Who would even notice that?" Lexi asks. "I thought it would be more obvious. Like the same cat walking through a hallway twice."

"No, this is too perfect," Mostafa says, his suspicions considering the probability in real time. "Reality is impossible to define."

Lexi runs an unsteady hand through her short hair, wishing the halls had music, or rhythmic melodies outside of the low hum of machinery. The deep rumble adds an unsettling undertone, as if they're being watched.

Mostafa shrugs, and the window closes. "I'm simply saying that, for someone trying so hard to return to a simulation, you have unusually negative feelings against it. It must be real enough for you to want it so badly."

A wave of nerves moves through her. She hadn't considered the possibility that Sol was another layer to a simulation. That would be ridiculous. There's a quality to Beta that, once she was made aware, she couldn't ignore. Sol has no such qualities. Mostafa is overthinking it.

"Guys," Zuchiris says, finally tearing himself away from the screen. He runs up to them. "They're showing the North Country."

Most of the patrons disregard the change, choosing instead to scroll through their hallows, but a few of them look to the screen, and then to Lexi. As if to confirm that they are in fact seeing double.

The scene is from earlier today, of Lexi and her friends at the river. It's an entirely normal episode until Jonathan steps into view. From what Lexi has read, two Iron Dreamers rarely interact. Sometimes they're separated by hundreds of miles.

The screen zooms to Jonathan before he approached Lexi. She's talking to Michelle and Gui, all of them oblivious to Jonathan. From this angle, she can see his hesitation. His eyebrows are furrowed. It's an out-of-place expression in such a carefree summer setting.

Mostafa's mouth twitches. "Post shouldn't have released that."

"Why is he acting like that?" Lexi asks.

An older woman pauses on the walkway. She gives Lexi a curious look before her eyes widen. The features on Lexi's face are too similar, too quintessentially her mother's side of the family, to go undetected. Lexi has the ghost of a face with which the Senex are intimately familiar. Even if she weren't an Iron Dreamer, she would have a difficult time hiding from the long shadow cast by her uncle.

"Are you...?" the stranger asks, her voice leading.

A shorter man bumps into the woman. And then another. Within moments, a small crowd has gathered around Lexi, keeping a safe distance, but blocking the exits.

Mostafa grabs Lexi's arm and says, "Yalla."

Zuchiris waves his hands, seemingly amused by the word. "*Yalla, yalla.*"

The three of them weave through the crowd. If anyone follows, they have the decency to keep a wide berth. Zuchiris may not have Artemis's rank or prestige, but the Senex know an active assignment when they see one. Lexi has never been popular, or felt a semblance of fame. She's not sure she likes it.

She keeps her eyes fixed to the ground. The floor doesn't illuminate from her footsteps; rather, it maintains a steady dark green. She likes the color. Maybe that's what she'll change her balat to instead of the default black.

They rush into the hallway and Zuchiris seals the door behind them, snuffing the noise. "Think anyone noticed her?" he asks sarcastically.

Mostafa snorts. "Let's get this over with."

They make their way down the hall. The floor folds in every twenty or so feet, as if these sections were once puzzle pieces. This area of Sol must have been mobile during early construction. The path grows three times in width, and then a doorway leads to a cargo bay so large it makes Lexi's head spin.

The ceiling curves all the way up into a tube, with a diameter of precisely a mile to maintain the centrifugal force, according to Zuchiris. People walk along the ceiling, inspecting square containers the size of semi-trucks. The back end of Sol is one giant opening to allow different sizes of cargo and ships to exit. Some of them are open, revealing the black void of space. The cargo bay is easily the largest single section of the station.

Equipment glides through the center of the tube, floating along an invisible river where gravity's effect is negligible. A small figure hangs from the back of a box, its feet hovering behind it.

"If I jumped high enough, could I reach that?" Lexi asks.

Zuchiris tilts his head back. "With a pack, sure, but I wouldn't recommend it. The oxygen isn't super consistent near the center. You'd probably suffocate."

"What's wrong with the oxygen?"

"Nothing. It just moves and stuff. Gas is affected by gravity too. We have fans to keep the atmosphere moving, but it's not perfect."

Lexi never thought she would be spending so much time thinking about oxygen. She keeps her eyes fixed to the floor, nausea striking from watching the workers on the ceiling a mile away.

They walk through a row of shipping containers. A handful of workers are nearby. Their balats cover their heads, adding an extra casing of protection in case they fall out the back and drift into space. The worker closest to them inspects a container with exposed wires and boards. The worker waves a hand, and a wall of nanotechnology cascades down from over the lip like a curtain. The container snaps into a smooth, perfectly sealed, metallic box.

Lexi rubs her eyes, reminding herself that it's not magic, she just doesn't understand how the future works. "Where's it going?" she asks.

"Luna," Mostafa says, passing a row of smaller containers. "We have a trade agreement with them. We manage the asteroid mining, and send them supplies."

"What do you get in return?"

Mostafa glances over his shoulder, grinning with an unsettling amusement. "You."

Lexi looks to the containers. There is no indication that there are people inside. There are no windows or doors. No way to tell how human beings would be unknowingly transported across the vastness of space to where they would spend the rest of their lives.

There is something disconcerting about being moved like cattle.

"I'm from Luna?" Lexi asks.

"Divide and conquer," Zuchiris says. "It keeps everyone from blowing each other up."

Lexi needs to review the history of Sol and Luna and figure out why there are tensions between the two stations. She knows there were two nuclear wars on Earth, one right after another, but the records make it sound like all the major nations were equally guilty for their part. The orbiters were meant to be an escape pod for whoever was left—not politicians and world leaders, but the survivors of the great leveler of randomness: disease.

Statistically speaking, the Senex would almost entirely be made up of regular people. Not diplomats or generals. Wouldn't citizens have less quarrel with each other?

Mostafa stands to Lexi's right, and that is the only reason why she's able to catch a glimpse of his slight hand movement. A worker nearby—seeming to have been waiting for it—catches the motion and shakes her hollow.

"Hello," she says, addressing Zuchiris. Her black hair is cropped short with the tips flaring out. Once Lexi's hair grows out long enough, she's going to ask how to do that.

Zuchiris spins. "What?"

"I have a message from Sentinel Artemis for Zuchiris. That's you, correct?" she asks.

It suddenly occurs to Lexi that not all the Senex know each other. Lexi's town has fewer than three thousand people, and although she's seen most of them in passing, she doesn't actually know all of their names. Sometimes there's just no need to remember someone.

"I've been informed the message is classified," the woman says. She gives Mostafa and Lexi a distrustful glance.

Zuchiris takes the hollow and turns to Mostafa. "Cargo Bay 21A," he says. "But wait until I get back."

The woman follows Zuchiris across the bay.

Mostafa waits until he's out of sight before walking in the opposite direction. "Lexi," he says, beckoning her. She likes the way he says her name, even if it sounds like a warning.

She follows Mostafa to a section of wall that transports something large. He stands against one of the exposed panels. Unlike the hallways and main decks, no effort has been put into the shipping sector to conceal the guts. Everything about the cargo bay is an exposed nerve. There is no beauty. Mostafa presses his palm against the panel, and a door opens.

Lexi screams.

She loses her balance and falls to the floor. A few chuckles echo around her, but she's too embarrassed to make eye contact.

There's no glass dome, or sheen of plastic. It's a simple opening. Mostafa stands perfectly at ease with his toes an inch from the vacuum of space. The glare from the sun washes out most of the stars, but the light from Earth is enough to stand out. The station looms in the shadow of a graveyard.

"You could have warned me," Lexi says, standing.

"When we first constructed the loading bay, the pressurization was wasting air," Mostafa says, as if nothing has happened. "The field surrounding Sol to protect it from solar radiation is similar to this. The fields are designed to keep in molecules, like oxygen, nitrogen, and moisture, while allowing larger materials to pass through. These fields consume energy, so we don't keep them open, but it allows us to avoid recreating atmosphere every time we need to transport equipment."

The ground is solid enough, but the rotation of what few stars she can see makes her feel nauseous. She holds up a thumb, feigning appreciation.

"Very cool," she says.

"Come closer."

"No, thank you."

"Lexi."

It's as if Mostafa knows that she likes the sound of her name. Are the Senex capable of reading her mind outside of Beta? There could be an implant in her brain. She wouldn't put it past them. They have no sense of boundaries.

Lexi sighs, and takes one step forward.

She peers over the edge. She's not quite sure where the force field ends and where space begins. Looking down and seeing stars is a sight that she'll never get used to. Stars are meant to be above, not below.

Standing in silence next to Mostafa isn't like standing next to Gui. There had been an awkwardness in the North Country that she couldn't explain. She was fairly certain that Gui was a phantom anyway—another projection from the Beta engineers. Explaining to him how she felt would be the equivalent of talking at a book. With Mostafa, there's comradery. Their homes are gone. Their families. Their countries. The human race could be snuffed out in seconds, and with that, the last of life in the universe. It's chilling, but there is solace in facing the future together.

"Sometimes I come here and stare at the stars," Mostafa says wistfully. "We know about many of the exoplanets that orbit them. We've spent years mapping the routes, hoping to find a world that can support life. There are a few candidates, but it will take thousands of years to reach them. Don't act so surprised," he says, regarding her slack jaw. "You didn't think our plan was to stay in space forever, did you?"

Lexi blinks. "I, uh. Yeah, I did."

The Senex are human. If that hasn't changed, what is the likelihood of an unsuspecting planet meeting the same fate as Earth?

"So, at some point you take over another planet," Lexi says. "Another world where you consume, poison, and bomb it. Then what? Move on to the next place and do it again? I'm not sure how I feel about that."

"You sound like Artemis."

"Is that a good thing?"

"That depends. She always has a plan. What is your plan?" Mostafa asks. "Tell me, what is the alternative? We can't stay here forever. What would you like us to do, die?"

"Maybe that's what you deserve," Lexi says bitterly. "Nuclear war is insane. I'm still trying to wrap my head around how you all let that happen. I mean, not *you* you. But that's always been the problem, hasn't it? A few people decide to go to war because they want power or money or whatever, and they drag the rest of the world down with them. Maybe fate has already decided what to do with us, and this is it."

"And this is it," Mostafa echoes grimly.

He presses a hand to Lexi's back. She can't feel his skin through the balat, but she can sense the closeness. Startled, she freezes, unsure whether or not it's a friendly gesture. He takes a heavy breath, and shoves.

Lexi gasps, but there is no air to breathe.

CHAPTER TWELVE

Lexi floats in the nothingness, spinning head over feet.

She considers being at peace with death. Suspension has an unexpected calming effect that she's never felt before. It's not like swimming. There is no resistance when she swings her arms, no friction to work against so that she can orient herself. For someone who has spent months in space, it's absurd that she hasn't experienced weightlessness until now. The cold stabs her skin with a million knives.

Lexi snaps herself out of her shock.

She claws at her throat, gasping for the air rushing out of her. The nothingness is thick, as if the universe is plugging her windpipe. Her eyes burn from the sun. The balat reaches up her neck and wraps around her head, shielding her from the cold. It clings to her like a blanket. There is no way to breathe when it presses against her mouth.

So, that's it. That's how she dies.

Ridiculous.

Something grabs her ankle. She kicks at it. Another hand grabs her leg and pulls, bringing her eye-level with a dark mask. She would yell if her face weren't frozen in a scream.

The masked figure angles her so that her back is facing it. Something small is snapped to her suit between her shoulder blades. Her balat swirls, and nanotechnology molds to the device in a set of vibrating waves. Her mask pulls away from her face, transforming into a proper helmet. Finally, a blast of warm moist air floods the suit. It's as if every molecule has been squeezed out of her. She's breathing, but it takes multiple painful breaths to refill her lungs.

The figure throws out a hand, and a house-sized blanket extends behind them, blocking the searing light from the sun. They are plunged into darkness and a sky full of stars.

A voice enters her skull. She can't be sure where it's coming from, but then a screen appears at the bottom corner of her helmet. It's Mostafa's face clouded by shadow. His mouth is moving, and she hears the words, but her brain can't process them.

Until Sol, Lexi has never run from anything. She didn't freeze to death in a blizzard because she knew how to find her way home. Sports came easily to her because she practiced every day. She was prepared for life because she was given the tools. Since waking up to whatever twisted version of reality the Senex call home, Lexi has been blinded, imprisoned, and suffocated. And she's been helpless to stop it. Rage floods her system.

"Don't touch me!" she screams. "*Don't touch me*!"

"Calm down." It could be the darkness of space, but Mostafa's warm features have twisted into something dangerous. He's acting as if *she's* the one that tried to kill *him*.

She flails her arms, smacking his head, but the balat performs its duty and protects him from her attacks. "You tried to kill me! *Let. Me. Go.*"

"If I let go, you'll drift into space. That's an emergency pack on your back," he says, pointing over her shoulder. "But it's only enough oxygen for twenty minutes. Do you still want me to let go?"

The fear of drifting through space until she suffocates terrifies her. She stops struggling. Flexing to keep her arms down by her sides is a strange sensation. She strains to keep the tears from falling down her face, because they wouldn't fall. They would float and then cling to her eyeballs. And probably blind her.

"Now you know where you are." Mostafa's voice is full of annoyingly smug satisfaction. "There is no air, and no warmth. Look."

Lexi looks to the city.

Sol is drifting away from them. The rotating arms spin too slowly to notice, but the subtle motion gives the station a sinister appearance. It's as if the city is a claw reaching into the abyss to seize what's left of the universe's resources, and leaving Lexi behind.

"What about it?" she asks.

"That's it," Mostafa replies. "That's it. We have nowhere else to go."

"You have Luna."

Mostafa suppresses a laugh. "Do you think we're overwhelmed with options? Space doesn't have alternatives. There is no diversity of choice. We have what we have, and nothing more. Tiago won't stop at the simulation. He's delusional. Like you."

Lexi jerks away, but Mostafa's grip digs into her balat.

"Tiago thinks this is what we want," he continues. "He thinks that we're happy to keep people in a simulation because we don't have the resources to feed them. That we're satisfied living on a station when we were born on a planet. That we would choose a dome over open skies. Nobody wants this. We make decisions based on what we have, and what we have sucks."

Lexi snorts. "No kidding."

"That," Mostafa says, shaking her. "That right there is the problem. You whine and complain, and you don't do anything about it. You wish things were better. We *all* wish things were better."

Mostafa looks away, tilting his head to peer up at the stars as if they were standing on solid ground. His mask is shrouded in darkness. His steady breathing is so light that he could be asleep. Covered by the blanket behind them, the stars shine brighter, but they do not twinkle. It's hard to feel alone in a sky so densely packed.

"The air where I was born was polluted," Mostafa says. "We would wake up to dust storms, and the streets would be covered in centimeters of sand. We threw tarps and blankets over cars, but it still found a way in. What was created for you to breathe in Beta is just what we think the air smelled like, but most of us can't remember. We've learned how to program a stimulus that triggers the same part of your brain that would react if it was smelling the real thing. Each Iron Dreamer is smelling something different because it's in their heads. You have never breathed fresh air."

A few months ago, that would have disturbed Lexi, but given everything that could have gone wrong in the simulation, she feels a strange sense of appreciation that the Senex labored over the smell of air in the first place. They didn't have to do that. They incorporated the wind and the taste of strawberries to such fine detail that Lexi still aches for it. It's a consideration so laborious that it almost seems compassionate.

The Senex could have made their lives easier and removed the ability to smell altogether, focusing instead on producing workhorses to crank out products by the end of each quarter like machines. The Iron Dreamers wouldn't have known any better. But the Senex didn't do that. They created havens like the North Country.

And Fiji.

"*We* didn't decide to launch a nuclear war," Mostafa says, pressing a hand to his chest. "*We* didn't drop bombs on cities and poison the oceans. You're not the only one paying a price for other people's mistakes. It's been a thousand years, and we're still figuring out how to clean up the mess they left us."

The Senex population is just over half a million people. Statistically speaking, none of them were world leaders, or oligarchs. They had no say in world events of the nuclear wars. The vast majority of them started off as regular people going about their lives on Earth. They were thrust into space by the genetic lottery, victims of the whims of presidents and generals who would never experience the consequences of their own actions.

The Senex were the casualties of war, sentenced to remember their helplessness.

"I hadn't thought of it like that," Lexi admits.

"No, you haven't," Mostafa snaps. "Because you've been so concerned with yourself that you haven't thought about why Beta must exist. It's not about whose life is unfair, and who's been dealt the worse hand—we were trapped here and did what we could to survive. At least you were in paradise. I would have given anything to trade places."

She frowns. "You wanted to trade places with me?"

"*Yes*!" he exclaims. "Of course I do. I want to be with my family. I miss them every day, and I will never see them again. I could see the entirety of the universe, but never their faces. You don't know how lucky you are. Your life has been peaceful and full of love. Mine has been—"

Mostafa's voice drops. His face on the screen turns toward the darkness, hiding his expression from her.

Lexi looks at her feet. The stars dance around her legs. She can appreciate Sol's ability to thrive in the most hostile place, but Lexi is not a Senex. She's not a demigod capable of enduring the trials of their life. She just wants to find Tiago, and turn Farhad's attention from the three Iron Dreamers that he's foaming at the mouth to kill.

"This is where you are," Mostafa says. "Whether you return to Beta or not, this is where you are."

Lexi's eyes drift toward Mars, near the top of her helmet. Its red hues are unmistakable, even in the chaotic backdrop of a starry sky. The constellations she was raised to navigate by are obscured by the jam-packed view, crowding the patterns and identifiable markers into one giant mass. Yet Mars is easy to spot. Why couldn't they live there?

"What did you mean about me being like my uncle?" she asks.

"He hates Beta. It's ironic, since he is one of its founders."

"The simulation was *his* idea?"

"No, but he laid down the foundation it was built around. Him and Artemis. That's why they have so much influence. They're like the mother and father of Beta. I hate to admit it, but life would have been harder without their...creativity."

Lexi didn't realize that her uncle and Artemis had known each other. She can't shake the feeling that there are more secrets she needs to unearth.

"Tiago thinks the simulation is a prison," Mostafa says. "He's made good points, but he fights without presenting an alternative. You want to keep Beta, yet you do not fight to make it happen. You just want to complain about it. This is how you are alike."

Lexi winces. She hasn't been complaining *that* much. A healthy amount, she would say, given the circumstances.

"I'm just trying to figure this all out," she says.

"I know." His voice is softening, but he's still angry. It's not just that she's a threat to his way of life, it's that her carelessness could put other lives at risk.

"You really care about Sol," Lexi says.

He shrugs. "Of course. It's my home."

"But you care about the Iron Dreamers too."

"I'm not a monster. I hope not, anyway." His voice has lost its edge. It's as if he's beginning to feel guilty. Once the adrenaline rush from forcing Lexi to learn a lesson wears off, he's left with the secret plea that she won't think he's a monster. Deep down, we all just want to be understood. Lexi is the first new person Mostafa has interacted with in centuries; he wouldn't want her to hate him. He would want to be understood. It's human nature. Even a thousand years later.

"I don't know..." Lexi says, teasing him. "You did just try to kill me."

"I wouldn't have let anything happen to you."

She warms at that.

"You know this is the first real conversation we've had?" The words sound stupid coming out of her mouth, but she doesn't have friends on Sol. Technically speaking, she hasn't had a friend before, ever, not one that wasn't programmed. She would like to be friends with Mostafa.

"You're not so bad," he says, suppressing a smile. "You haven't pulled out the wires, or told your family they're NPCs."

"NPCs?"

"Non-player characters. Don't repeat that. That's what they're called in the grottos."

"Should *you* know that?"

"There are many things I shouldn't know."

Lexi bumps her shoulder lightly into his, which probably pushes them 17,000 miles per hour in the wrong direction. Mostafa is reluctant to warm up to her, but she sees a smile tugging at the corner of his lips. She doesn't ask him to elaborate, instead taking the small win and remaining silent as they float together.

Sol is in orbit at Lagrange Point 4, which means the station orbits the sun ahead of Earth. Moving in tandem with Earth would require too much fuel to stay in orbit. The Lagrange Points are different. They're locations in space near two celestial bodies whose gravity essentially balances out. An object can stay in orbit at Lagrange Point 4 without kicking on the boosters every few hours. It simply floats. Lagrange Point 5, which trails *behind* Earth, is the other stable point, and where Luna is located.

The Senex are a people adrift at sea. They have nowhere to anchor.

Earth is not Lexi's home planet. Technically speaking, Luna is. Earth is the birthplace of Mostafa and the other Senex. The rest of the lifeforms on Sol are creations of a station birthed from spare parts. Aliens, as far as Earth is concerned. Lexi has never been there. It's a memory. A digital blueprint of whatever the Senex can recall of it.

A warning flashes above Lexi's screen. There are two minutes of oxygen left in her tank. Like a storm on the mountain, she becomes aware of the cold wrapping around her, waiting to slip through the cracks in her armor.

Mostafa mutes the alarm. "Are you in the fight, or not?" he asks. "Because if not, I will leave you here. We can't send you back if you make another mistake like you did with Mai. You could get yourself killed, and the other Iron Dreamers."

"And the Senex," Lexi says. "Your life is on the line too."

Mostafa stifles a laugh, cutting through the tension. "Ah, yes. Me. The most important."

Lexi bursts out laughing.

It's not that Mostafa conceals his personality, it's that he presents too many versions of it to determine which one is real.

He clears his throat. "Let's bring you back before Zuchiris stabs me."

"Would he do that?"

"He has before." Mostafa taps his arm and the side of his leg snaps against hers.

The thrusters behind him ignite, and they hurtle toward Sol in tandem as if running a three-legged race. Lexi can't hear the device, but she can feel the reverberations move through their bodies. Sol grows in size until the mile-long back wall fills her entire view from within the helmet. A few autonomous machines move across the panels, transporting equipment and supplies along the bay doors. A ship near the center looks to be disembarking.

No one notices that two stray bodies are approaching the cargo bay at what is probably 70,000 miles per hour.

"Did you know the person before me?" Lexi asks. "The original Alexandria."

"No."

"That's too bad. I was hoping you could tell me about her."

Mostafa gives her a sideways glance. "You're curious about that?"

"Well, yeah. She's kind of like my mother, right? I have her DNA. It'd be cool to know stuff about her. See how alike we are."

He shakes his head, trying to distract himself with the screen on his arm. "You're not what I expected."

"What do you mean?"

"You're observant. You think." His neck flexes in what appears to be a shrug. "Cillian wasn't so flexible, and he was specifically chosen to be an Iron Dreamer. Perhaps, with the right stimulus, you would have been worthy of being an Iron Dreamer on your own."

It could be a compliment, or an acknowledgement that Lexi is the product of nepotism and didn't earn her place in the future. She doesn't belong on Sol. She knows that. She's no great thinker or artist. Her entire existence rests on her uncle whose capture, if it occurred, could mean her presence in the simulation is no longer useful anyway. They may stop making her after this is all over.

Is she sentencing her future twins to death? She knows it's not technically her being reborn, just versions of Alexandria with the same genetic code and different lives, but it feels like a death sentence all the same.

"You could ask Artemis what Alexandria was like." Mostafa enters a command into his suit, and their bodies orientate to a cargo door along the top edge, flipping them. "They lived together."

"Excuse me?" Lexi reaches forward, a reflex to stop them from moving when in fact she has little control.

"Don't move," he warns. "It's the computer that keep us from smashing into the wall, not my piloting abilities."

Lexi stiffens. When she compares the edges of Sol to the stars in the background, she realizes that they are moving at an alarming rate. She suppresses the urge to grab Mostafa's arm. With a press of a button, he could disconnect their legs, but he wouldn't be able to shake off her death grip.

"I thought Artemis was from, I don't know, Los Angeles?" Lexi says, trying to distract herself from their blinding speed. "She seems like a city chick."

"What would make her a city chick?"

"She's kind of ruthless."

"You have no idea," Mostafa says bitterly. He hesitates before blurting, "Artemis is from the North Country."

Lexi's eyes widen.

The North Country?

It would make sense. Artemis's personality, her knowledge of obscure coastal towns in New Hampshire, her closeness to Tiago. In another time, maybe they had grown up in the same town. Not only did Artemis know Lexi's personality, she knew the nature of her life. Before the end of the world, Artemis had lived it.

"Wait, how did she and Alexandria live together if Tiago is the one who adopted me?"

Mostafa drags a finger down his forearm, and they slow. "They were married."

Lexi needs a moment to catch her breath. The pieces snap into place, though in uncomfortable ways. She presses her palms together. "We're hunting Artemis's husband."

"Yes."

"We're hunting my uncle, and Artemis's husband. Because they're the same person. I'm not a forensics expert, but that's a conflict of interest, don't you think?"

"It doesn't matter what I think."

It's impossible to tell where they're going, or which doorway is the one they're going to charge through, but then Lexi spots the red slashes of Zuchiris's balat. They seem to be rippling with fury. He paces back and forth by the edge of the cargo bay door, never taking his eyes off Mostafa as they gently float through the invisible doors.

"She's fine," Mostafa says, holding Lexi.

Her knees buckle when she touches the floor, but she doesn't vomit. "I'm good," she assures Zuchiris once her helmet recedes.

"You tricked me." Zuchiris points an accusatory finger at Mostafa. "That's annoying."

Mostafa pulls the tank off Lexi's back. It's the size of a wallet. "I was following orders."

"That wasn't the order."

"If Artemis wanted her to be coddled, she would have asked you to take her." Mostafa hands the tank to a worker walking by and grabs Lexi's arm. He enters a command into the controls on her forearm, and the suit loosens. She hadn't realized that it was squeezing her.

Zuchiris's mouth tightens, unable to refute the point. He's the type of person that puts his faith in others, and that doesn't bode well for trickery. It's no wonder that he doesn't trust Mostafa.

"In other news," Zuchiris says, stepping to the side. "There's someone who wants to say hi for some reason."

A woman leaning against the wall watches their exchange. Unlike the black settings she wore in the Nest, her balat is in varying shades of dark blue to match her eyes. Lexi's cousin glides toward them, her hair flowing behind her.

Lexi isn't clear on the situation with her estate. She hasn't seen the property she supposedly owns in the residential arm. All she knows is that Gal wants it, and she herself is standing in the way. Gal could have been watching from the bay door since the moment Mostafa pushed Lexi through it. Maybe she thought he was doing her a favor. She must have been disappointed to discover that Mostafa's intention was to teach Lexi a lesson, not to kill her.

Hopefully, anyway.

"Well, that was fascinating," Gal says. Her eyes study the three of them, as if trying to determine which one she wants to devour first. "I haven't witnessed a spacing since the Second Expansion."

"Yeah, we're just a barrel of laughs around here," Zuchiris says.

Lexi wipes her nose and feels a sticky wet substance. She pulls her hand away. Her nose is bleeding.

"That's normal," Mostafa says.

Gal snaps her head to Lexi like a bloodhound. "There she is. You don't look much like him. I imagine they've filled your little head with all the things he's done. The tyrant. The terrorist. Sounds like a colorful character, doesn't he? With that resume, he could be a world leader."

"Gal," Mostafa says, with a warning tone.

"That's Councilor Gal to you," she says. "The High Councilor isn't here to defend you. I'm merely offering a different viewpoint. Don't you want your doe to have all the information? There is no evidence that Tiago is the Dark Angel. If such a figure exists."

"But he's in hiding," Zuchiris says.

"Maybe because coming forward would give the High Councilor the excuse she's been looking for to space him? It wouldn't be the first time she's tried." Gal's attention whips to Lexi. "The Beta version of him is a shadow of the real man, but you've met the real version a handful of times. Can you imagine that person carrying out a crusade?"

Truthfully, Lexi's memories of her uncle are fragmented. He never stayed in the North Country for long. Her mother was his half-sister with a considerable age difference. They had little in common, but he always made a point to visit when he was in the United States. He and her mother would spend the night drinking wine on the deck beneath the stars catching up. Nothing in those visits sticks out to Lexi. He was a bit of a recluse, but normal.

"What do you mean we've met?" Lexi asks.

"The sentinels are notorious for entering Beta," Gal says, running a hand through her hair. "I'm sure they've made it sound like they try to avoid it, but they're no different from the suckers in the grottos. And who can blame them? Beta is an escape."

"Weren't you a sentinel?" Lexi asks.

Gal speaks with the confidence of someone who knows from personal experience how addictive a simulation can be.

Her jaw clenches. "The Iron Dreamers might be comfortable in the twenty-first century, but did they tell you about the twenty-second century? When the air was so toxic that they suffocated before they could contribute anything? The last time we ran that era we lost a thousand an hour. All in the name of this." Gal presses her hand against the invisible barrier separating them from the vacuum of space.

An Iron Dreamer invented the force field that protects Sol. An Iron Dreamer invented the shield that protects them from asteroids and radiation. It wasn't just a tragedy that those people died having no clue how instrumental they were to the survival of the human race; it was *criminal*.

Zuchiris's hands ball into fists. His body is a useless hammer in a verbal scrimmage. Mostafa, on the other hand, is unmoving.

"The twenty-second century is next," Gal continues. "We need a new method to mine tritium for the fusion reactors. That was the beginning of the fusion engine age, and we have the genetic material of two of the researchers who worked on it. Once this round of Beta is scratched, we're going to put an entire population through famine and disease just to get two people to advance an engine. *That's* what the simulation does."

Lexi knows the regular toll of time doesn't drum the same in Beta. The simulation exists in segments based on the needs of the Senex. They're not going to start the simulation at the year 1911 and let it roll out for four centuries, day after day. That would be a waste of time. They rewind and skip ahead, extracting what they need.

How much longer is the twenty-first century scheduled to last?

Lexi could have fifty years left.

Or a week.

"What's the alternative?" Lexi asks, using Mostafa's words.

"I don't think you appreciate what's happened here, *cousin*," Gal sneers. It reminds Lexi of Farhad. "Tiago is complicated, but he's not a monster. I left the Beta program because I saw what was happening, and I couldn't be a part of that."

"Right," Zuchiris grunts. "Because you're the poster child for morality. What would you call your escapade through South Korea during the First Expansion, a thought exercise?"

Gal ignores the bait. "Have they told you what they'll do if they catch him?" she asks Lexi. "They'll space him and incinerate his samples so he can't even be an Iron Dreamer. He'll truly be gone."

There is an image of the dead man floating in a pod. Lexi fixates on his hands in the solution, trying to recall the shade of gray of the Iron Dreamer's skin. One morning he woke up to whatever life he lived in Beta without any idea that it would be his last. Like so many others throughout history. Except that he wasn't the victim of a car accident or bad weather. He died because of agents on the other side of a false world.

Sol is so far out of an Iron Dreamer's reach that the man couldn't have intervened or pleaded his case if he'd tried, yet he fell victim to it all the same.

"Everyone dies," Lexi says.

"Yes, they do. You're not some casual bystander. Your actions will lead directly to his capture. And whatever happens from that will be because of your help." Gal points to Zuchiris. "You think this one has clean hands? We were at war for 110 years. What do you think a life is to someone like him?"

Lexi thought her cousin would be selfish. An opportunist scavenging through the ashes because the humanity has been siphoned out of her. Lexi didn't expect her to be reasonable. Gal is trying to save the life of someone she cares about, and the truth is her weapon. But Lexi has seen the results of the Beta program. She's standing in one, behind one, above one. It has helped the Senex develop the technology that keeps the human species alive, and it allowed Lexi to live a somewhat normal life.

"It's not real to you, is it?" Gal asks, reading her expression. "You can't conceive of genocide. You can't imagine more than 10,000 people because the human mind can't imagine a population bigger than a village. But you don't need to imagine 700,000 individual faces to appreciate them. You're not *really* trying to understand their deaths."

"I don't want them to die," Lexi fires back. "The only reason I'm doing all this is to keep three of them from being killed."

"And then what, you go back in and never think about Sol again?" Gal stares at her as if truly seeing her for the first time. Lexi feels exposed. Her eyes seem to move through her skin. Gal shakes her head. "I don't know which is worse. The ignorance, or your apathy."

Lexi hasn't fully considered the Senex or their intentions because it's too much. It's too overwhelming to fathom the Iron Dreamer population and the future of the human race. She thought she was finally gaining some clarity after the spacing exercise with Mostafa, but what if Gal is right? Is it wrong to keep so many people in a fantasy world? Wouldn't it be better to release them and tell the truth?

Gal studies her. "Maybe you are getting it."

Mostafa steps beside Lexi. "You've made your point, Councilor Gal."

"What's the matter? Afraid I made a reasonable argument?"

"An argument without a solution is just complaining."

Gal clicks her tongue and regards each of them, angling her face from one set of eyes to the next. Mostafa is better practiced in discretion. He could have been a spy on Earth, or a politician.

Satisfied, Gal turns on her heels. The tension doesn't leave with her. It lingers in the air like a bad smell. Mostafa watches her fade into the shadows of the cargo bay. Whatever progress he and Lexi made in the abyss has taken a gut punch, and he knows it.

CHAPTER THIRTEEN

The next few weeks, Lexi spends little time in Beta.

Her awareness of the dual states has caused inner turmoil—the equivalent of practicing a song on the piano at home versus performing it live. The mind knows there's an outside perception. It feels the additional pressure. She knows she's being watched.

After the incident with Mai, the council has been on the fence on whether or not to use Lexi as bait. They say she's too young, in over her head. Lexi can't sit back and let others determine the fate of Jonathan, or three unknown Iron Dreamers, just because she's breathing.

She can't let people die on her behalf.

She needs to do *something*.

Artemis has been able to convince the council to allow her an hour a day until her health is adequate enough to be more involved, and they've removed the recordings of her from BetaVu. The less the station knows about Lexi, the better. The team in charge of broadcasting the footage from Beta has redirected the attention toward other regions in the simulation. So, as far as the other Senex know, nothing is amiss.

At first, she thought exercising next to Zuchiris's huge figure would be intimidating, but he's quick with a joke and doesn't criticize. They spend two hours every morning in the training center. It's located on the farthest edge of Sol's arms to take advantage of the stronger centrifugal forces. Gravity feels nearly the same here as on Earth. Not that Lexi knows that for sure.

She's never been to Earth.

"Good. Now let your forearms fall to your hips, and then bend over," Zuchiris says. He supports most of the weight of the kettlebell, letting it fall slowly as he shows her the motion of the swing. "I'm going to let go, and just let it swing back up so I can catch it."

Lexi nods and Zuchiris releases the kettlebell.

It drops fast, swinging through her legs and tapping her tailbone. When it swings back up in front of her, Zuchiris catches it. If he let it drop, she would have lost her footing and fallen on her face.

"They're kind of tricky, but they're the best when you get the form down," Zuchiris says. "You can let go now."

"Right, sorry." Lexi releases one finger at a time, her hand sore from gripping the handle for the last hour. She leans over her knees and takes a breath while Zuchiris continues with his own exercises.

She's been conscious of her breathing since the meeting with Farhad, weighing every breath against the lives of the three Iron Dreamers who have a death sentence hanging over their heads.

The council expects her to work out and regain her strength to return to the mission in Beta. Does that mean they took into account the additional oxygen it would take to *build* that muscle? Or do they expect her to take shallow breaths?

"I can go again," Lexi says, reaching for the kettlebell.

"If you overdo it, you'll just set yourself back two weeks. Are you hyperventilating?"

She looks up. "What? No, I'm just...uh, breathing shallow."

"Don't do that. If you pass out, you're no use to anyone."

She decides to breathe normally, though her chest is tight with unease.

The training center is as shiny and brand-new as nearly every other sector of Sol. Without dirt, all the equipment stays clean. Most of it she can't recognize, but some of the devices are familiar. There are curved treadmills and barbell stations, and an area with yoga mats. They're not moveable foam mats, but permanent features in the floor that can change their stiffness, color, and size via the commands on their balats. They're Lexi's favorite.

The view from the gym is spectacular. The entire back wall is made of floor-to-ceiling windows. When Sol's rotation shifts them away from the sun, Lexi can exercise beneath the intense spectacle of the night sky. Her room doesn't have windows, so she asks if the floor and wall lighting can be reduced so she can marvel at it, but Zuchiris says one of them would break an arm in the dark. Not to mention there are other people using the facility.

Lexi runs a finger over the kettlebell. "This is iron, right?"

"Cast iron," Zuchiris wheezes out between swings. "Iron is pure metal. Cast iron is an alloy made of iron and carbon. I think we put some silicon in there too. The magnetism is a pain in the ass, but it was easy to mine so we put it everywhere."

"Like the Iron Dreamers."

Zuchiris makes a face.

"You're not made of iron."

"No, I know. I just mean that iron is a theme around here."

"Oh, yeah. Definitely. Don't sit down."

Lexi groans, lifting herself from the bench. She was hoping he hadn't seen her. The room is spinning, and she's afraid to say anything. She would be mortified if she passed out. She places her hands on her hips and paces, distracting herself from her tender stomach.

"I know it sucks," Zuchiris says. "But doc says standing is, like, the bare minimum you can do."

She drifts toward the window. The planets are easy to identify. Mars's red tint is unmistakable. She tries to keep her gaze away from the sickly light of Earth.

"You know, I was pretty strong in my hometown," Lexi says.

"No, you weren't."

"I mean I worked hard growing up compared to the other kids."

"Yeah, but it wasn't real." There is no malice or taunt in his voice. He's genuinely confused as to what Lexi is trying to say. Zuchiris's innocent black-and-white view of the world makes it difficult to communicate with him sometimes.

Lexi sighs. "I guess you're right."

"Eight more minutes, and then you go again."

Lexi gives him a thumbs-up, which he doesn't see. He's already transitioned to the next routine, swinging the kettlebell over his head. She presses her head against the glass, realizing that it's probably not glass, but another invention by an Iron Dreamer.

She flattens her hands against the window, trying to determine the thickness of the medium. The incident with Mostafa was weeks ago, but her heart jumps whenever she remembers spinning through the void. She needs to force herself to face the outside. She takes these moments to look the stars in the eye, hoping that her blood pressure and heart rate will adjust to the reality of her situation.

Technically, she's still standing. Zuchiris can't scold her for leaning.

"A bit early for exercise," Mostafa says.

His voice reverberates through the gym. There are two other training centers in Sol, but since Lexi has appeared in their midst, the Senex have taken a special interest in this particular location. They give her a wide berth so they don't have to share equipment or wait for their turn, but they orbit around her like a school of fish.

Her guards watch from the entrance. It's a new rotation, with Chen and the woman from when Lexi first arrived. No one has given Lexi a straight answer on why they need to be there. Now that her security clearance has been raised high enough to give her free rein on Sol, it doesn't make sense to keep them. Who are they protecting her from, exactly?

Mostafa stands beside Zuchiris and observes his training. It's impossible to tell the exact body type of either of them. The only visible bits of skin are their heads and hands. Judging by the way their balats cling to them, they're both in excellent shape. It makes sense, given the vulnerabilities of space, like low bone density and the cardiovascular issues that Lexi is now facing.

"Are you just going to watch?" Zuchiris asks, dropping the kettlebell to the floor.

Mostafa shrugs. "Maybe."

Zuchiris points to Lexi and asks, "Is she supposed to be somewhere?"

"No, I'm here on my own."

Zuchiris's face is easier to read than most. Even after a thousand years, he's made little progress in concealing his emotions. His massive eyebrows rise up his forehead, signaling his surprise.

Mostafa seems to acknowledge the uncharacteristic behavior and changes the subject. "What's next?"

"Uh." Zuchiris pulls out the hollow from his outer thigh and flicks it open. He reviews a few lines and then slides his finger across the entire screen. Whatever he was looking at is now on Mostafa's hollow. "Two more sets of swings, and then we're going to move on to Turkish get-ups."

"No games?"

"Not until her heart rate stops spiking."

Mostafa flicks his hollow and shrinks it to pen size. He snaps it to his thigh and the nanotechnology absorbs it. His eyes roam her body in that nonclinical way they do. Lexi has grown accustomed to it.

"One game of wallball won't hurt," he says.

Zuchiris snorts. "That's the most hurt."

"What's wallball?" Lexi pushes off the window and approaches them, her interest piqued. A game sounds infinitely more fun than routine exercises.

"It's easy, rule-wise," Zuchiris says. "I don't know if your coordination is ready for that, though. Arty will kill me if you knock your teeth out. Our calcium supply is still two weeks out."

Lexi has no idea what a calcium supply is.

"I'll play," she says.

"There's a room downstairs." Mostafa turns to Zuchiris and smiles with triumph. The few sincere smiles he reveals have a way of making his face dazzling. "See? She wants to try."

Zuchiris blows out a heavy sigh. The guards are facing them, but too far away to hear the conversation. Without the use of Sessiz, their sign language, they're oblivious. Lexi can see the wheels turning in Zuchiris's head. He doesn't like to be left in charge.

"Fine," he sighs, a twitch of discomfort in his mouth. "Just don't push her into space this time."

Mostafa tilts his head to Lexi. Whether he feels guilty or proud of his actions in the cargo bay, he doesn't reveal it. She's not as skilled in the art of concealment. The distrust on her face is palpable.

They walk across a row of treadmills and down a sloped opening that turns where they had been standing. The walkway is darker than the main level, leading to a pitch-black space. The floor sensors illuminate beneath their steps. The room is no wider than a studio apartment, with the same plain gray walls as the main hallways. The only differences are the lines drawn on the floor, and a giant brick wall two stories high.

"Is that real brick?" Lexi asks. She rushes forward, running her hand along the rough ridges.

"The only brick in all of space," Zuchiris says proudly. "We thought we'd need the clay, but we ended up replacing that project with something else. It's actually not great for wallball because it's uneven, but, you know, nostalgia."

Lexi smiles to herself. Like so many things, it's the first time she's ever touched something that's a staple feature in New Hampshire here on Sol. "So, how do we play?"

Mostafa pulls out an off-white ball from behind his back. "It's simple. I throw the ball at the wall, it bounces off, and you catch it before it hits the ground. If you do, that's one point and then you serve. If you slap it back instead, that's two points. Whoever reaches twenty points first wins."

"That's it?"

"The game was different when I was a kid," Zuchiris says. "But when we first started playing up here, the gravity was wonky. So we just chuck it at each other now."

"What about kicking?" Lexi was never good at soccer, but backing up to allow the ball to slow down a bit would give her the opportunity to react, even if that meant with her feet.

"That's three points," Mostafa says.

"Expert level," Zuchiris adds. "Please don't try it."

Since Lexi is new to the game and there's an odd number of them, they spend the hour crisscrossing paths and ignoring the boundary lines. Most of the game is spent between Zuchiris and Mostafa, but they allow a few gentle returns to Lexi. When she protests, hating the baby treatment, they start throwing the ball. Hard. Fortunately, even a direct hit to the face doesn't hurt. The real challenge is not tripping over her feet.

She keeps her eye on the ball, never having considered the rarity of the brick, or rubber. Whenever she asks what something is made of, it's always the same raw materials. The only plastic in Sol is mixed into the outer shell of the station, a remnant from before the discovery of the force field that protects the plant life. Polyethylene—the same plastic that makes garbage bags—is weirdly resistant to solar radiation. It was useful at the time, but difficult to recreate without access to fossil fuels.

Today, there's no plastic anywhere inside the station. The ball must be made of rubber.

Lexi smacks the ball. It's too direct an angle and shoots straight at Mostafa. An easy shot, but it's still a score. Her first two points. Zuchiris gives her a thumbs-up.

Mostafa and Zuchiris do not hold back, and she simply cannot keep up. Out of breath from the exertion, she moves off the court. The balat around her chest loosens, allowing her lungs to expand.

"Is there someone else I could practice with?" Lexi asks. "A small child, perhaps?"

Mostafa laughs. He catches Zuchiris's return and tosses the ball up and down in his hand. "You requested fair treatment."

"Yeah, well." She swings her arm out. "This is all new to me."

"You're doing well," Zuchiris says. His voice is stiff repeating Artemis's words. It's not true, and the timing is off, but the effort is appreciated.

Mostafa throws the ball overhead, trying to trick Zuchiris on the return angle, but Zuchiris catches it. They counter back and forth, both of them unable to slap the ball for the extra points.

She should take this time to continue her studies. She's on the Second Nuclear War and barely through the geopolitical structure, the history of nations, and all the tiny cracks that come together to sink a ship. She's not sure she wants to know what happened. She decides to watch Zuchiris and Mostafa compete instead, because it's the first time she's seen them have fun.

They might actually be human.

In a completely nonsexual way, Lexi is curious what their bodies look like. The balats act as another layer of secrecy, preventing her from being able to identify even the basics of what lies beneath. The balats aren't spandex. They're thick, and move on their own accord, so there is no way to see the crease in muscle. Lexi imagines Zuchiris as mostly upper body, since he favors standing in place and reaching for the ball, while Mostafa is all lower body, zipping around the court and favoring speed.

"Isn't rubber a plastic?" Lexi asks, leaning against the wall.

"It's from trees, actually. We grow them in the Solarium," Zuchiris says. He smacks the ball instead of catching it. Mostafa lunges forward, kicking the ball with the outside of his foot. He does it so gently that the ball bounces off the wall only another foot or two high. Zuchiris is too far away to return. He throws his hands up in frustration. Mostafa takes the win.

The only reason Mostafa recommended playing wallball was to show off.

"Nice," Zuchiris says. "I still think you're a dick, though."

Mostafa nods, breathless. "Fair."

Even with the win, his emotions are concealed and tempered. Lexi used to think that it was a mask, but she's beginning to suspect that the mask became a part of his identity a long time ago.

They bump fists, not in the usual way, but with the backs of their hands, as if they're tugging in opposite directions on a rope.

It's nice to catch a glimpse of what life is typically like without a terrorist on the loose. When they asked students in elementary school a thousand years ago what they imagined the future would look like, it would be this snapshot: two people who looked nothing alike, playing an ancient game in a futuristic city in space. A place where no one got sick, and no one went hungry.

It gives Lexi a semblance of hope that life could be normal, even for her. The ball rolls to her and she picks it up.

"This came from a tree?" she asks, tossing it between her hands. "I don't know anything about rubber. How do you guys remember all this stuff?"

"It helps when you're bombarded with the same information every day for hundreds of years," Zuchiris says. "Anyway. I'm done. Can we eat?"

They make their way up the spiral walkway to the exit. Sweat drips down Lexi's neck and into her balat. There is no discomfort because the nanotechnology absorbs every drop. Theoretically, one could go forever without a shower. There is no dirt in space, and sweat is absorbed by the balat. Lexi misses showers. She misses the feeling of water running over her.

"You have spirit," Mostafa says, walking beside Lexi.

Her head snaps to him, astonished. Just a few weeks ago, she thought he was trying to kill her. He could have played wallball against Zuchiris any time, but he came when Lexi would be there. Had he come to check up on her? Did he feel anything about it?

About her?

She hates that she cares about his opinion. On the surface, she should hate Mostafa, or at the very least fear him. He's impulsive and difficult to read, and he pushed her out of the cargo bay. But she hangs onto his every word. Is that the power of beauty? Can they attract anyone? Lexi has heard that beauty is a weapon, but she's never seen it wielded before. There are handsome people in the North Country, in a small-town kind of way, but they are nothing like Mostafa.

To the left of the exit is a small pad with a handprint. Zuchiris places his hand on the pad. His balat reaches up over his face, covering his head with an airtight suction to remove the sweat, and then shrinks back down to his neck. It makes a gentle whirring noise, and he shivers. He pulls his hand away and rubs it against his chest.

"I hate that feeling," he says.

Upon leaving the training center, the pad sucks up the moisture from their balats, filters it, and circulates it back into the station's water supply. It's both gross and clever. Not a single drop can go to waste.

All of their hollows beep. It's an alarm that rings throughout the gym. Mostafa reaches for his hollow, frowning as he reads the text. "Mai's story is out," he says.

Zuchiris reaches for his hollow, and Lexi follows suit. She's growing accustomed to the navigation. It's more sensitive to the twist of her fingers than she first assumed. The Senex make it look easy, but the hollow demands precision. Lexi concentrates, moving her hand in just the right way to select the blinking red alert at the top of her screen.

She takes a breath, and begins to read.

Hello Reader,

I am pleased to report to you that I have spoken with the recently defected Iron Dreamer, number 442y, Alexandria Carvalho. Like her brilliant uncle, Tiago Carvalho—may he rest in peace—she has managed to do what only one other Iron Dreamer has done before: free herself from Beta.

As you might remember from Cillian Côté and his formal requests to return to Beta, a full submersion is impossible for an Iron Dreamer once removed. And yet, the council of Sol have decided to send Alexandria back to assess the Dark Angel threat. What makes her more qualified than Cillian to ascertain this terrorist, and why have the council decided to risk it? Our conversation was brief, but rest assured, readers, I got straight to the point:

Mai: How did you wake up? How did you do it?

Alexandria: I don't know.

Mai: It must have been a very scary experience for you.

Alexandria: It wasn't great. I'm just trying to figure it out now.

Mai: And now they have you hunting a terrorist. What are your qualifications for such a mission? You're so young, even by your own world's standards. What do they expect you to do?

Alexandria: I'm not supposed to do anything.

Mai: I see. They want you to act normal. It's a performance, and you're the bait. Is something wrong in Beta?

Alexandria: I thought they would tell you.

Mai: Can we schedule another time to speak? Perhaps we can get to the bottom of this together. The citizens are quite worried about what's happening in the simulation, and with you. We only want the best.

Alexandria: I'm not supposed to talk to you.

Mai: I hope this is the beginning of a great—

It was at that moment that someone cut the line. This recent development leads me to question the security of the simulation, and the ethical implications of the cloning program. Even members within the mission, such as Alexandria Carvalho herself—a young and inexperienced component of a plan that is far outside the realm of her capabilities—are not clear on the objective, which leaves me to ask: Who is in charge? And do they know what they are doing?

Though the Beta program has undeniably been an asset, providing us with technological breakthroughs from nuclear fusion to artificial intelligence, it might be time to sit down and assess the relevance of a 450-year-old program.

Lexi's eyes remain glued on the hollow. She can barely contain her rage. She lifts her head to Mostafa and Zuchiris, who look equally indignant.

"That's not how it happened," Lexi assures them. "Not exactly. The words are right, but she moved everything around. She made me sound like an idiot."

"I'm not surprised," Mostafa says. "Her reporting amounts to gossip. I wonder why she waited this long to publish it."

"Luna probably made her," Zuchiris says.

Mostafa gives him a hard look. "Watch that. Implicating Luna in a classified mission on Beta would create a diplomatic incident."

Zuchiris sobers, nodding quickly. "Right, yeah."

"The council will want a brief," Mostafa says. He shrinks his hollow and marches past the guards without saying another word. Either he's anticipating a reprimand, or he's about to deliver one.

Lexi is mortified by having made the situation worse. The council and sentinels already knew about the conversation with Mai. They have been holding their breath waiting for the hammer to drop. It comes as no surprise that it did. The rumors had grown, and it's Lexi's fault that they're gradually turning their attention away from the Dark Angel, and instead to the competence of the council.

"I'm hungry," Zuchiris says. There is no greater knife to cut through the tension than Zuchiris's insatiable stomach.

They eat lunch in the Trough. Lexi hasn't won over any admirers. Everyone stares. Zuchiris says it could be for any number of reasons, not necessarily because of the report. She makes herself small at the table, keeping her eyes on her food tray. The pink smoothie in the larger tube is her favorite. It's made of synthetic berries, and sometimes Lexi forgets that, technically, it's the first time she's tasted real berries.

Well, sort of real.

Most of the food on Sol is genetically modified. Even the best chefs on Earth couldn't taste the difference between a berry from the soil and a berry from the lab. The universe is made of atoms, and they can be arranged in any which way. It was one of the first major breakthroughs on Sol.

They can't make everything. They haven't been able to produce heavy elements like gold in large quantities, but they're able to make biological materials. Food is designed under the Botanical Wing near the Solarium, and built from the ground up with an identical molecular structure because it's just carbon, hydrogen, oxygen, and whatever else.

From a biology standpoint, they look the same.

From a chemistry standpoint, they *are* the same.

"Do you need anything else?" the server asks. The older woman is asking the table, but she's looking at Lexi.

"Uh, no," Lexi mumbles. "Thanks."

The server is overly nice to them to compensate for the passing glares. The Trough is a fishbowl. There aren't many corners to hide in. The server gives her a reassuring smile and moves to the next table.

"See? Not everyone hates you," Zuchiris says, sloppily chugging a dark green liquid.

"She's just being nice because she has to. I can't believe there are still servers. I worked as one for a summer. A bunch of rich Massholes." Lexi snaps her mouth shut and looks to Zuchiris, mortified.

It's what everyone from the North Country calls people from Massachusetts.

Zuchiris bursts into laughter. "*Massholes*," he says, choking on his food. He slams a fist into his chest to clear his throat. "I haven't heard that one in a while."

"I'm sorry."

"It's fine. I'm from outside of Boston, though, not the actual city. I just say Boston because people have no idea how to pronounce those stupid towns." Zuchiris releases a final, wet cough and says, "Anyway, servers are kind of a normal thing. We had them thousands of years ago. We'll have servers thousands of years from now too. It's just the way we are as miserable sacs of flesh."

Lexi chuckles. "Yeah, but wouldn't people prefer that robots do it?"

"Nah, Uncanny Valley."

Lexi frowns. "What?"

"It's that creepy feeling you get when you interact with something that's pretending to be human, and it's doing a pretty good job, but something's off. Like in old horror films when the bad guy has a really big mouth. There's a part of your brain that rejects it. We tried robots for a while. Didn't matter how good we designed them, everyone knew they weren't human, and it creeped us out so we just stopped using them. We send them outside for repairs. That's about it. Artemis is coming, by the way. I wasn't sure if it would scare you."

Lexi tries to mask her fear at the abrupt confession. "Why would I be scared?"

"Because you talked to Mai, and now everyone knows you screwed up."

"Right." Lexi swirls the bottle. "Why would she want to eat with us?"

"We eat every meal together."

"That's kind of cute."

One of Zuchiris's eyebrows rises. "Cute?"

"Yeah, you two are like besties for life."

"Something like that." He nods slowly, lost in a train of thought. A deep frown pulls his brows together, but then he purses his lips and the clouds dissipate. He's trained himself with physical triggers to pull himself out before the storm. "She's really good at keeping people alive."

Lexi knows very little of Artemis and Zuchiris's story.

She knows they were marooned in the northeast during the nuclear wars. They were also some of the last of the Senex to be brought to Sol. Where they were before they caught a ride to space, or how they managed to survive on a dying planet, isn't in the archives. Either they didn't tell anyone when they arrived, or even Sol doesn't want to know what they did.

Lexi casts her eyes to Zuchiris's hands. They're like Artemis's: thick-skinned, calloused, and permanently stained. It reminds Lexi of her father. He worked outside his entire life too. His skin was stained from working in the dirt, and butchering the chickens in the summer. Artemis and Zuchiris didn't live on a farm. They were surviving a nuclear fallout. They were able to survive because they are Senex, but they still felt hunger and the suffocation of poisoned air.

Lexi doesn't want to know what they've done either.

She shakes the berry bottle; the contents swirl without seeds to stick to the glass. "How did you guys meet?"

"In college," Zuchiris says. "Artemis's dorm room was across the hall from mine freshman year. Everyone in that corner just kind of became friends. I'm pretty lucky I knew anyone who made it this far. Not that I really knew Tiago. He was pretty quiet the first few years I saw him. He mostly kept to himself and just appeared wherever Artemis was. Then he would disappear again. Kind of a weird dude."

"Sounds like a North Country guy."

Zuchiris snorts in agreement. "It was nice to recognize someone. Most of the Senex came by themselves, and I managed to know two others. Statistically speaking, that's insane." He looks up and sees Artemis on the walkway. He waves an arm dramatically. It isn't Sessiz, just Zuchiris being Zuchiris.

Artemis sits next to Lexi and folds her hands. Little cuts around the knuckles highlight the fairness of her skin, though the softness has been gone for some time. The braids in her hair are neat and tidy. The patterns change weekly, shaping her face ever so slightly, depending on the thickness of the braid.

The server sees Artemis and inclines her head. She brings the same pink bottle that Lexi has, and Artemis gulps half of it down in a single swig.

"You drank that like it's Lagavulin," Zuchiris says.

Artemis scratches the side of her mouth. "If I waste half a bottle of Lagavulin, you can push me out the cargo bay."

They both chuckle.

Lexi tenses. She doesn't mean to react. It's an involuntary motion when she remembers being pushed out the cargo bay and spinning in the void, suffocating on a cold that wasn't cold, but an absence of. She never wants to experience that again, though the threat constantly lingers just beyond the aluminum walls.

Lexi smiles tentatively, unsure if Artemis is angry with her.

"Mai would have been a complication no matter what you did," Artemis says, reading her expression. "With or without you, she was going to publish a report with the same level of clarity, which is to say none. I'm not sure why Luna is protecting her, but I will find out."

"So, it went well," Zuchiris says.

"The council meeting went about as well as you'd expect. Although I do come with good news." Artemis turns to Lexi. "Doctor Singh is pleased with your progress. You've been approved for full shifts in Beta. It's tentative, but your vitals are promising."

A wide grin spreads across Lexi's face. She *has* noticed the pain in her chest subsiding, and the nausea fading. Her muscular strength isn't what she remembers back home, but it's enough to walk the halls and play wallball without passing out. Even her hair is long enough to give her face some character. She's starting to feel normal.

"I know this has been really hard," Artemis says. "Believe me, I know. But you've adapted well beyond our expectations. It may not feel like it at times, but you are a survivor. I know one when I see one. I'm proud of you."

Zuchiris dips his head in agreement.

They're the kindest words anyone has spoken to Lexi in months. They may be the only real kind words she's ever heard in her life. It's like a pat on the back from the goddess of the night herself. Lexi hadn't realized until this moment how much Artemis's validation means to her. She was the first person Lexi saw when she woke from Beta, and she's been the one protecting her ever since. Artemis has been by her side every step of the way.

"Thanks," Lexi manages to say.

Artemis rests a hand on Lexi's forearm. "Don't cry. You'll have it sucked out through the hand pads."

Lexi cracks a laugh. "Was Alexandria like that too?"

"She was," Artemis says without hesitation. "It's hard to say how much a person is born with, and how much of them is made, but you have the same genetic information and grew up in the same environment, so you are quite similar. There are slight differences, though, in case you're wondering how much free will you have."

"I try not to think about it," Lexi admits.

"I understand." Artemis spins the bottle, hovering her hands in case it falls. "I brought something for you." She enters a command into her balat and turns her hand upward on the table. The nanotechnology shimmers and collects on her palm, arranging itself into a small circular device that rises from her hand. Artemis pinches it between her fingers, holding it up to Lexi.

"What is that?" she asks.

"Mostafa told me that you wanted to know more about Alexandria."

Lexi suppresses a smile. "He told you that?"

"We didn't record much in those days," Artemis replies without answering. "But I was able to find a short recording from Tiago's belongings. At some point, you're going to ask questions that only you can answer. The nature of being alive, I'm afraid. I thought it best you had the resources to explore it without the existential breakdown."

Lexi inspects the coin-like device and says, "I'll probably still have one of those."

"Mm." Artemis takes Lexi's arm, and her balat stiffens, holding Lexi in an immovable seated position. She cannot lift a finger or turn her neck.

She has a love-hate relationship with the balat. It is both her life vest and straitjacket, the temperamental emblem of the Senex spirit. The patrons around them meander as if nothing unusual is occurring.

"Keep your eyes closed," Artemis says. She presses the device to the back of Lexi's neck.

The world doesn't activate with the same comprehensive submersion as Beta. This file is quicker. And meant for viewing, not for interacting. Lexi has no body or physical presence in this simulation. All she can do is watch.

A teenage girl a few years younger than Lexi had one leg tied to another girl's. They ran in tandem across the field of Lexi's high school in a three-legged race, their arms around each other's waists, laughing. It should be the North Country, but the sky was an ugly gray above the trees. As if a city nearby was bleeding smog onto the field.

The grass was a sickly green, not quite the autumn colors of hibernating foliage. It was all wrong. The colors. The smell. It looked like Winter Carnival, but it wasn't winter. The annual competition between grades was supposed to take place in the snow. Many of the games depended on it.

A small group of students and a couple of teachers stood nearby shouting their encouragement. Lexi made her way toward them. It wasn't like watching a movie. Lexi felt present in their world, like a ghost roaming through the trees to spy on the living.

The two girls crossed the finish line in second place. They bent over their knees to collect their breath. The second girl coughed a rough, wet cough. She'd had it for some time, and the dirty air wasn't helping. No one seemed alarmed.

Lexi felt a push toward the two girls. A pair of feet that didn't exist floated toward them. As she drew closer she realized why the girl looked so familiar.

It was Alexandria.

All of Lexi's senses dialed to the highest level. She was spellbound by Alexandria's face. She studied every mark, every scar and imperfection. How many details did Lexi share with her donor? Alexandria's hair was shorter. That was the first notable difference. She didn't keep it long like Lexi. And she had a small scar above her left eyebrow. Everything else was the same: her posture, her muscles, even the way she cracked her hip when the girl freed their legs.

Alexandria saw Lexi and ran toward her. Lexi sucked in her breath. She wasn't prepared to make conversation with herself.

"That could have gone better," Alexandria said.

It was Lexi's voice. Her inflection. An *almost* exact copy.

"It's still second place," a man's voice replied.

"Olivia's cough is getting worse," Alexandria said. She cast her eyes toward the girl. Her eyebrows furrowed in concern, the same way Lexi's did. "She tries to hide it, but she doesn't have much longer. First Stephen, now her."

The man exhaled sympathetically. Lexi couldn't determine where he was coming from. "All you can do is be there for her," he said.

"How many more do I have to watch until it's my turn?" Alexandria's voice was thick with emotion. Her gaze pierced Lexi's soul. The girl held a fury that Lexi had never contained. It was strange seeing her fourteen-year-old self so full of anger.

"It won't be," the man assured her. "That's not going to happen to you."

"I'm not you," Alexandria snapped.

Lexi tried to back away. She was intruding on a private moment. It made her uncomfortable to see a version of herself behave so aggressively. Was Lexi capable of that rage? Did the dying grass have something to do with it?

“I’ll find a way,” the man said softly. “I’ll figure out whatever this is and give it to you. I promise.”

“You can’t keep that promise.”

“They’re finding more of us now. It’s a matter of time until someone discovers the missing link. It can’t be that hard to find.”

Alexandria sighed with a quiet resolution far beyond her years. She lifted her head, eyes red with tears that would not fall, and said, “Not everything is a circuit breaker you can fix.”

Lexi couldn’t see the man, but she could feel his sorrow. His agitation. He wanted to work. He wanted to dig his hands into the problem and solve it *now*. The air buzzed with tension. He could comfort the girl, and assure her that everything would be alright. She didn’t want that, but he was going to try anyway.

“Do you want to go home?” he asked.

Alexandria shook her head, gathering her determination for the next challenge. An easier, immediate task that she could finish on a leveled playing field. “No, the next game starts in ten minutes.” And with that, she was gone.

Lexi’s head snaps back. Her chest drops onto the table as the balat softens to its normal flexibility. She lifts her head. The sentinel’s silver-blue eyes are studying her. Zuchiris clutches the bottle between his hands like it’s a rag getting wrung out.

“Was that real?” Lexi asks.

“Yes,” Artemis replies steadily. “That was the real world.”

Lexi reflects on the details of the video. The sky. The grass. The sound of coughing. That wasn’t a limbo state between the flu and a few days from recovery. That was a world in the final throes of death. “It’s worse now, isn’t it?” she asks.

Artemis nods. “Much worse.”

Alexandria was a girl who lived a thousand years ago. She lived in a world that Lexi recognizes, but has been lost for centuries. Their proximity was an illusion. Alexandria wasn't a girl across the horizon. She was a pile of bones buried deep within the Earth.

Lexi buries her face in her hands. "She was just a kid, and she knew she was going to die."

"She didn't for a long time."

"Who was the man?"

"Tiago." Artemis leans back, sliding her palms down the table. "That was a simulated assembly of the video so it could be experienced in Beta, if one wanted. He didn't mean to record all that. He was trying to record the Winter Carnival games. They were kind of a big deal back then."

"I remember," Lexi says. "We have them too."

Artemis smiles sadly. "Right."

It should have been more shocking to see Alexandria. Lexi's donor was both her mother and father. It didn't feel like watching a past life—like Lexi was a reincarnation with memories of Alexandria that hovered just beyond reach, and if she tugged on just the right string, she would be reborn into her former self. There was a tether between them. Lexi felt a pull to the young girl. But it was more akin to that of an ancestor. A distant and relatable call from someone who shared her genetics, but also something less tangible that she couldn't quite put a name to.

"It might not be that easy," Artemis says, her eyes narrow as if a marquee of code is scrolling across Lexi's forehead. It's unnerving how she seems to be able to follow Lexi's thoughts, even when she isn't plugged into Beta.

"I didn't see Jonathan," Lexi says.

"He was graduating college at that time." Artemis's voice is clipped. Her mouth closes at the end of the sentence rather than hanging slightly open like most people engaged in a conversation. She's hiding something.

"Since your absence, Tiago's signature has been all over the place," Artemis says, changing gears. "He's only nearby when you're in the North Country, which means we need you there as soon as possible. I'm certain he wants to convert you to his cause. An Iron Dreamer on his side would be a strong voice against the Beta program."

Tiago's agitation rumbles through Lexi. There was an intrinsic stress in the recording that lingered in Lexi's muscles, as if Tiago had been holding onto the pain for years. Was that the sort of ache that went away? The Senex had plenty of time to test it. Maybe that's why Tiago kept Alexandria in every iteration of the simulation. He felt guilty for not being able to save her. He was torturing himself.

"Is there anything I should know about him?" Lexi asks.

"He's..." Artemis holds the silence. She pulls the weight of the air in quiet command, funneling it toward her until Lexi is hanging on her every word. "He's convincing." Artemis smacks her palms on the table, wanting the sound to register, but not to echo. She's agitated. Like Tiago had been.

"So, what now?" Lexi asks.

"You go back in," Artemis says. "Before he tears down the world."

CHAPTER FOURTEEN

School felt like a dream.

It *was* a dream, but Lexi couldn't tell her friends that.

It had been almost two months of searching for Tiago, advertising herself as a perfectly normal teenager. She spent the autumn hiking with her friends and preparing the house for winter. She attended school and did her homework. Honestly, she had hoped the future would be more exciting than calculus. But so far, the Dark Angel hadn't taken the bait.

No one had mentioned the three Iron Dreamers since Lexi's agreement with Hatshepsut, though their lives still hung over her head. She secretly hoped that the council had lost track, and so long as she didn't ask about or mention them again, the Iron Dreamers would be safe.

There had been instances when the Dark Angel's digital signature was detected in the Iron Sector, and then a shadow in the North Country, indicating that he was keeping tabs on Lexi at the very least. Which was good for her, because it meant that she still held value to the Senex. Aside from that, the Dark Angel had been inactive. He seemed to have crawled back into the shadows from which he came. No one trusted that it would last. Even the chat rooms that believed his identity was some low-level engineer, or a stowaway from Luna, were certain that he would return.

The Dark Angel was planning his next move.

Artemis had been exceptionally stressed the last few weeks, but wouldn't say why. She and Mostafa didn't spend every day in Beta like Lexi did. They collaborated with the council and other agents who were attempting different methods of capturing Tiago, and that left Lexi free to do what she wanted.

The air felt different when they were there. Lexi couldn't quite put her finger on it, but the ground had weight when there was a Senex walking over it.

The pieces of Beta were beginning to settle. Lexi was reacclimating to her life and the old routines. There were no red flags or blaring signals to warn her that it was a simulation. The world ran on an impossibly smooth schedule. It was remarkable. She could get lost in the farthest reaches of Beta's corners and never find a flaw. She could live a long normal life. In time, she would forget all about Sol.

The school cafeteria wasn't much of a cafeteria. The students sat on a three-tiered platform that descended from the main level. Each platform could only fit one row of benches, so everyone sat on top of each other, as if watching a theatrical performance. A kitchen was slapped in the back, but the room was clearly meant to serve a different purpose. Even the fluorescents struggled to brighten the ugly brown carpet. There were steel bars hanging overhead that served no discernible purpose other than to swing in the wind. Either Sol's engineers had overlooked the features, or this was how Artemis remembered the cafeteria. This was her school, after all.

Her and Tiago's.

How did a shack in the woods mold them? How did its musty halls and classrooms contribute anything meaningful to the creators of humanity's greatest achievements?

"Yo, Lex," Michelle said, snapping her fingers in front of Lexi's face. "I swear you've been spacing for the past hour."

Lexi flinched.

The memory of Mostafa pushing her into space continued to give her nightmares. She didn't want to admit that she had been marked by the trauma. She didn't need to give the Senex another reason to think she was weak. It motivated her to exercise with Zuchiris more rigorously. One day she was going to be as fearless of the void as they were.

"Sorry," Lexi said. Her head dropped to the food tray. A slice of pepperoni pizza, yogurt, and berries. Eating didn't have the same pleasure it once had. Now that she knew what berries were supposed to taste like, she couldn't help but notice the difference. They were too sweet. The Senex were feeding the Iron Dreamers lotus leaves. "I was listening," she assures Michelle. "We're going to the movies—no, Lincoln. You want new snowboard boots first."

"Yeah, before all the Massholes come up and grab all of last year's stuff," Michelle said.

"It's already October," Gui said. "I'm not sure what you're expecting to find at this point."

A breeze moved through the cafeteria, rustling Michelle's hair. The air had a sudden weight to it, and the taste of metal filled Lexi's mouth.

One of the Senex had entered Beta.

It could be that a sentinel was plugged in directly next to Lexi, and they were sharing a power outlet, or it could be the side effect of a glitch. Now that Lexi was attuned to the sensation, it was impossible to miss. She wondered if the signs of the simulation had always been there, and she just hadn't noticed.

Lexi scanned the cafeteria, half-expecting Artemis or Mostafa to walk through the doors. They didn't, of course. They could be a thousand miles away.

"Is Eilish coming with us?" Jonathan asked.

Lexi had forgotten he was there.

"No, she has golf practice after school," Gui said, his eyes narrowing. "Why?"

Jonathan shrugged. "No reason."

“Do you have a crush on her?” Michelle asked.

“She’s nice,” Jonathan replied easily. “Just figured we don’t invite her to stuff that much.”

Gui didn’t press. He took a bite of food and said, “I’ll ask her.”

Jonathan wasn’t close with Gui’s twin sister, and Eilish hadn’t been part of their activities for years. As far as Lexi knew, they’d never had a conversation. There was no reason to mention her. The bell rang and the students dispersed to their last class of the day.

“Meet me out front after the bell,” Michelle ordered.

Jonathan nodded and swung his backpack over one shoulder. He had cut his hair short. It hardened the features of his otherwise kind face, making him look like a military recruit. He walked up the cafeteria tiers without saying a word. It was typical behavior for him, yet still off.

Considering how much time Lexi had been spending thinking about Jonathan, and the pressure she felt to keep him safe, it was becoming awkward that they didn’t talk. She wasn’t his fairy godmother protecting him from the clouds. They needed to be friends.

Artemis was pushing Lexi to spend more time with him. It should have been an easy task. His assimilation into Lexi’s group was a convenient coincidence, but talking to Jonathan wasn’t easy even under the best of circumstances.

He didn’t like to talk.

Unfortunately for him, he was slowly becoming the center of attention. The Dark Angel was tracking Jonathan, of that the engineers were sure. Tiago could take the form of Michelle or anyone else in Beta without detection, and push him across the chessboard. This made the sentinels nervous. Lexi didn’t know why. Who was Jonathan? What role had he played on Earth?

Jonathan walked in long strides across the locker area. A backpack was slung on his shoulder. His back was so long that it made the bag look like a toy.

Gui waited until Jonathan disappeared around a corner to ask Michelle, "You don't like him, do you?"

She recoiled. "*What*?"

"You've been showing a lot of interest in him."

"So what?" Michelle said, tossing her blonde hair. "I think he's cool."

Gui cracked his knuckles, unable to reconcile an unsettled ledger. "It's just curious."

It *was* curious. There had only been one person that Michelle had a crush on in high school, and he had had a girlfriend from a different school. Aside from that, Michelle hadn't shown an interest in anyone. There weren't enough students for an adequate sample size to deduce what caught her fancy. The students in their high school dated either different grades, or different schools. There were too few of them to risk the drama.

"I absolutely do *not* like him," Michelle said firmly. "He's a year younger, for crying out loud! I turn eighteen next month. That's statutory rape, Gui."

"I'm not asking if you want to—" Gui shook his head, quickly losing interest in the conversation. "I would rather not know the details of that, to be honest."

"Thank God." Michelle rolled her eyes so hard that she almost fell to the floor. "Can we fast-forward through this conversation?" She grabbed her backpack and stormed off, leaving Gui and Lexi by the lunch table.

"Well," Gui said, pursing his lips. "She's being defensive."

"It's probably nothing," Lexi said, hoping that was true. "Not everything is a love triangle, Gui."

"Maybe not an equilateral one."

"What?"

He shook his head, dispelling his own thoughts. "I don't want to be late for class."

"Uh, right. Okay."

The rest of the day went by without incident. After school, Michelle found a pair of snowboard boots in Lincoln, while Lexi and Jonathan roamed through the aisles, careful not to bump into each other. By the time the four of them returned to the North Country, the sky was dark.

The movie theater was a local landmark. It was always voted some travel magazine's "Favorite Small Town," or that newspaper's "Favorite Getaway Trip." Visitors came from all over to escape their congested city lives. They wanted to walk down a quiet road and marvel at the brick sidewalks. They sat on wooden benches overlooking the river and explored the covered bridge that stretched across it. The town was perfectly picturesque, situated on a hillside as if placed there for a postcard.

Lexi hoped that was what it looked like a thousand years ago.

Michelle parked her car behind the theater and explained why the movie they were about to see was set to win an Oscar for having some avant-garde narrative that Lexi didn't care about. She didn't like movies.

The four of them walked across the dimly lit main road to find Eilish waiting for them in front of the candy store.

So, Gui *did* tell her about movie night.

Eilish was similar to her twin in every way except socially. They were both intelligent, focused, and disciplined. But where Gui was contemplative, Eilish was bubbly and spontaneous. She had the same fair hair and eyes. She was bright, inside and out.

"Hey, guys!" Eilish said, skipping toward them. She was wearing jeans and a long-sleeve shirt. It wasn't warm enough to leave the house without a coat, but her optimism transcended weather.

"Hey, Eilish," Jonathan said, shoving his hands into his pockets.

The sound of his voice startled Lexi. He had barely spoken the entire afternoon.

"Hi! I feel like I haven't seen you guys in forever. I can't wait for a good storm." She opened the door to Chatters, and a bell chimed. "It's wicked hot in here though, geez."

Jonathan followed her into the store. Whatever reason he had for wanting Eilish to meet them was meaningful enough to relax his shoulders once she arrived.

Maybe he did like her.

Chatters wasn't a candy store. It was *the* candy store. The North Country didn't have much to be recognized for by the outside world, but they did have two records: one for the highest winds in the world, and another for the longest candy counter. The store was built shortly after the Civil War, and hadn't changed much since. The jars were old. The floorboards were old. American flags and the motto "Live Free or Die" were stamped on every trinket. Freedom was serious business in the north.

Everyone grabbed a pair of plastic gloves and made their usual rounds, unscrewing the tops of jars and digging for candy. Gui didn't eat it, but he grabbed a handful anyway. Michelle and Jonathan spoke between themselves, so Lexi decided to explore the back of the store. There were aprons, scented candles, and homemade soap in the shape of moose. It made her think of Mostafa.

Gui glided up to her. She would say that he wandered, but his actions were too intentional to be meandering. He picked at one of the wrappers with his fingernail.

"Is your experiment going as planned?" Lexi asked, tilting her head toward Jonathan, Michelle, and Eilish.

Gui followed her gaze. "I'm trying to figure out what's going on."

Lexi was as perplexed as Gui. She didn't understand Jonathan's intentions. The engineers were having trouble reading his thoughts as well. His mind was either quiet, or scrambled. They claimed that wasn't unusual during developmental periods, like infancy or puberty when the mind was establishing itself. But the timing was curious.

For Gui, it was like picking a scab. Once he started, he couldn't stop until the entire thing was torn off. Living with a mystery was unacceptable.

"Did you know about his parents?" Lexi asked.

Gui stared at her for a moment—or rather through her—as he tried to figure out what she was talking about. "Oh, that," he said eventually. "Yes, I knew."

"Why don't we ever talk about them?"

"Why would we?"

Lexi balked. "Jonathan's parents being dead seems like an important thing to talk about from time to time."

"It happened a while ago."

"That doesn't make it any less relevant."

"That's precisely what it does," Gui said. "Relevance is time-dependent. If it was a long time ago, then it's not relevant."

"Just because something died a long time ago doesn't mean it doesn't matter."

Gui cocked his head. "Something?" He picked up a bar of soap and sniffed it. His face wrinkled with distaste. He tested the next bar. "Are we still talking about Jonathan's parents?"

"Y-yeah," Lexi stammered. "I'm just saying that it matters, and we should, I don't know, ask him about it sometime."

"Feel free to do that."

For a moment, Lexi questioned the veracity of their deaths. What if Jonathan's parents hadn't died, and it was simply a new storyline being pushed since Tiago started disrupting the simulation? That couldn't be.

Jonathan was an Iron Dreamer. The story he believed was the one that had been there since the beginning. He couldn't be reprogrammed to believe something new, as the phantoms around him could. He was real. If memories could be so easily erased, then Cillian would have had his wiped so he could return to Beta.

The sentinels could have given Jonathan an easy life with parents, but they didn't.

Why?

"Is that why you've been acting strange?" Gui asked Lexi. "You two are quiet around each other. I thought maybe it had something to do with Michelle."

"No, I'm just trying to—"

Protect him.

Eilish materialized from around the cupboard, rescuing Lexi from the inquisition. Eilish smiled and stuffed a bag of candy into her shirt. She held her arms out and spun. If they lived anywhere else in the world, people would think she was trying to steal candy.

"How's that?" Eilish asked. A piece was poking through her sleeve. It was conspicuous, but not enough to raise suspicion.

Lexi gave her a thumbs-up. "Looks good."

"You have a Snickers bar hanging out of your shirt," Gui said.

Eilish looked down. "Oh, shoot."

"It's okay," Lexi said. "Movie theaters don't actually care."

"Yeah, but still." Eilish's lips rose in a mischievous smirk. "It's kind of fun to try and hide it."

Eilish's personality was impossibly endearing. She didn't hang out with them as often as she used to since she worked most nights at the local hotel. She liked to work. She couldn't resist making friends with the tourists, or chatting with strangers on hiking trails. She was a social butterfly, always on the move.

After the five of them bought their candy, they went outside and waited by the intersection. A few cars stopped at the light, and two kids jumped out of the back seat and raced toward the theater. They didn't look before crossing because they didn't need to. How many habits did the children of the North Country develop that wouldn't fit into the real world? Lexi wondered if she had been prepared to live in any other part of the simulation at all, or if she had been meant to stay in her small corner of the woods forever.

"Three dollars," the attendant in the ticket booth said. He looked to be Lexi's sister's age, maybe younger.

Gui and Eilish each gave him three dollars, and the attendant handed them two raffle tickets. Michelle and Lexi stepped forward.

"Three dollars."

Michelle and Lexi each gave him three dollars, and the attendant handed them two raffle tickets. Jonathan stepped up, and the attendant changed his tune.

"Six dollars," he said.

Michelle shoved Jonathan out of the way and leaned over the counter, having anticipated this exact exchange. She drummed her fingernails on the counter. "Look, we don't have an even number of people. Can you just give us the three-dollar ticket, please?"

"It's buddy night," the attendant replied, bored. "Three dollars a person if you bring a buddy. If there's just one of you, it's the regular price."

Eilish stepped forward. "Just give him the ticket, *Jason.* Unless you want to start paying for your own lift tickets."

The hotel Eilish worked at could print lift tickets to any ski resort in the area. The younger students tried to stay on her good side since they weren't old enough to work there yet. Unless their parents could afford a season pass, they had to beg Eilish or some other connection for lift tickets every weekend. Eilish was the more benevolent employee.

The attendant's eyes grew wide. "Hey, Eilish. Yeah, I didn't see you. Three dollars is fine. Here you go." He handed Jonathan a raffle ticket.

"Thanks." Eilish beamed and trotted toward the entrance.

The others passed Lexi as she fumbled through her pockets, having thought that she heard a ding from her phone. It could be Mai. She checked the screen to find no missed calls. It might have been the hollow stored in her balat on Sol. Could Lexi have heard that from inside Beta?

When she looked up, Jonathan was holding the door for her. It was a weird gesture, but it would have been weirder for Lexi to refuse. She bumped into his chest when he leaned down and said, "Did I even have to pay?"

"Uh, probably not," Lexi chuckled awkwardly. "Eilish can be pretty convincing."

"She is different."

His green eyes were fixed on Eilish, who was squeezing the candy in her coat to a less conspicuous location beneath her armpit. She laughed at something Michelle said—a full-throated laugh. Jonathan's gaze was unreadable. Maybe it was innocent. Just another tale of lust and love. Lexi followed them into the theater, determined to enjoy herself.

The theater was built during the golden age of Hollywood, and it certainly felt like strolling through the 1920s. It even smelled like it. The chairs were hard and squeaky. The concession stand was a hundred years old. And the slope toward the screen was almost flat, so everyone was sitting at roughly the same level. There were two screens, both of which ran the same movie for weeks.

The seating arrangement was an art. Michelle needed to sit next to Lexi because she wouldn't shut up. Jonathan needed to be in the aisle seat because his legs were too long. Gui needed to sit at the end because he didn't like talking through movies, and Eilish was flexible. They were like one of those math problems where person A was twice as old as person

B, and person C was lactose-intolerant, so why was mitochondria the powerhouse of the cell?

"Wait, *wait*!" Michelle said, pulling on Lexi's arm. "I need to sit next to Lex so I can talk shit the entire time."

"You were already next to me," Lexi replied.

"Yeah, but I need to be on this side so I can talk to Eilish too."

Lexi looked up at Jonathan, who was standing behind her. Over his shoulder was Gui. Gui gave her a shrug. He wouldn't have wanted to talk anyway.

Jonathan's elbows avoided the armrests, and his hands rested on his jittery legs. His fingers were twice the length of Lexi's. They stretched from one side of his thigh to the other. He looked tense, trying to take up as little space as possible.

"You can use the armrest," she offered.

"I'm fine."

"I can't tell if you're stubborn, or just trying to be nice."

He snorted. "I am not nice."

They had barely spoken two words to each other in months, and that was the first thing he wanted to say? It was both cryptic and ominous. There was a conversation brewing beneath the surface, clawing at the backs of their throats, yet neither of them knew what it was about, or how to initiate it. Lexi couldn't tell Jonathan what was really going on, and Jonathan was acting strange.

Hollywood trivia from decades earlier played across the screen. A question scrolled across the screen about a show that Lexi didn't recognize.

"Los Angeles," he said.

Voices across the half-empty theater shouted various answers, but then the answer appeared. Jonathan was correct. Michelle bent forward and gave him an approving nod.

"What is that show about?" Lexi asked.

"A funeral home," he said. "It's really good, but pretty dark. You wouldn't like it."

She didn't like being told what she would like, especially by someone who barely knew her. "Maybe I would."

"I'm not saying you shouldn't watch it, because you absolutely should. I'm just saying that it would depress you. Michelle told me about your movie tastes."

"Not that you asked," she said with an almost flirtatious spirit.

Jonathan flustered was not the same as other people being flustered. His voice didn't change. He didn't fidget. There was no indication that he was anything other than in complete control. It was impressive, but forced.

"So, you watch a lot of television and movies," Lexi said.

He shrugged.

"What do you like about them?" she asked.

He was reluctant to answer. "They kind of represent life, but kind of don't. Nobody talks like that. We say um, or we repeat ourselves. The real world is just sloppier. It doesn't matter how real we think a movie is, even if it's a biopic, it's never really accurate because the roughness is missing. Every movie does that. Real reality is not how people want to be entertained."

"How do they want to be entertained?"

He gave her a considering look. He wasn't accustomed to sharing his thoughts. He didn't seem to hate it as much as he thought he would. "With the idea of a story," he said. "What matters is how it feels. We're so affected by these fake things we know are fake and, I don't know, I find that kind of fascinating."

"Like a horror movie," Lexi said, trying to follow.

"Yeah, exactly. Why are you scared? You're not going through the haunted house, someone else is."

"I think that's called empathy."

He chuckled. "Yeah."

His voice was smooth, and his leg stopped bouncing. Maybe it was philosophy that made Jonathan come alive, or maybe it was the movies. Either way, Lexi could see what he and Michelle had been talking about all these months. Michelle loved movies. She wanted to be a director. If Lexi didn't copy her, Jonathan was never going to warm up.

Michelle was chatting with Eilish and digging into her bag for candy. The crinkling of the plastic was enough white noise to drown out anything within earshot. No one was paying attention to Lexi and Jonathan.

Jonathan noticed it too. "So, why don't you like the heavy stuff?" he asked, taking advantage of the opportunity.

Lexi shrugged. "I don't know."

"I doubt that." He placed his arm on the armrest, forgetting that he was supposed to be restraining himself. "You pay attention to everything. You just don't want to tell me."

"You're one to talk."

Jonathan opened his mouth, but then closed it. He grinned and said, "Touché."

The day at Cannon Mountain flashed through Lexi's mind. Jonathan had touched the back of her neck as if he knew something was supposed to be there. He was an Iron Dreamer, but that didn't mean he knew it. Jonathan wasn't supposed to have anything to hide.

What would be the harm in telling him the truth? His life was halfway to it already. His parents were gone. He wasn't particularly close to his friends. He could adapt to the isolation better than most. What if the future was where he belonged?

The three-month deadline was coming up. Lexi still didn't know which Iron Dreamers would pay the price for her oxygen, and she couldn't allow it to be Jonathan. Perhaps if he knew *just* enough, he could pull himself out of the simulation the way Lexi had.

She leaned over his arm and was about to whisper in his ear when the theater lights dimmed.

Jonathan inclined his head, careful not to move too close to Lexi and make the wrong assumptions. She blinked, caught like a deer in headlights. Jonathan was still as a statue, their noses mere inches apart. It would make more sense to kiss him than ask if he knew they were in a simulation.

"That d-day on Cannon," she stammered. "What were you—"

A sound check rang through the theater, shaking the seats—a friendly reminder that they had upgraded the speakers last year. The expression on Jonathan's face changed. He was anxious. She had touched a nerve, but lost the window.

"I'm going to get soda," she said. "Want anything?"

He inhaled and shook his head. He sunk into his seat, the cool, indifferent mask returning to his face. It wasn't quite rejection, but disappointment.

Lexi stepped over his legs and scurried down the aisle, realizing that she hadn't asked Michelle if she wanted anything. She rushed past the concession stand and threw the door open. She took a deep breath and welcomed the cold breeze that would soon be ushering in another storm. The attention to detail was truly otherworldly.

She was rocked back on her heels, enjoying the moment of peace, when she opened her eyes to find the attendant staring at her. He was leaning over the counter, resting on his arms, watching her with an amused expression. She waved awkwardly, unsure what else to do, and walked down the street in the opposite direction.

"Wait," he said. He moved away from the window and reappeared through a nearby door.

Lexi sighed, hoping that it wasn't an attempt to ask Eilish for lift tickets. The season hadn't even started yet.

The boy shoved his hands into his pockets and kept his head down. He looked to be no more than fourteen years old. He stopped in front of her and grinned. It was eerily familiar, yet a completely alien expression on a face so unassuming.

"You can't do that again," he said.

Her brow furrowed. "Excuse me?"

He looked over his shoulder, though no one was there. "This way."

Annoyed, she followed him up the sidewalk. She hadn't done anything wrong. He couldn't kick her out of the movies. They walked a few feet up the hill, out of earshot from the theater doors. The boy folded one hand into the other, and rubbed the back of his wrist.

"They don't like it when you interfere like that," he said. "You put everyone at risk telling Jonathan what's really going on."

Lexi froze. She didn't know what to say, or what not to say. It could be Mostafa toying with her, or Artemis testing her. Lexi had learned from the mishap with Mai to keep her mouth shut. An engineer would see this interaction soon enough and pull her out.

The boy smiled. "You're learning."

"Who are you?"

He looked to the stars, shifting his eyes as if moving from one constellation to the next. "Would you tell me what your plan was? After you told Jonathan that he was an Iron Dreamer, were you going to try to pull him? There's only two people in the world who can do that. You could have killed him."

The voice wasn't Artemis's. The mannerisms weren't Mostafa's. And the tone wasn't threatening enough to be Gal. Lexi didn't know who else was in Beta at that moment, and which of them was stationed in the North Country. If what he was saying was true, then he had stopped her from making a terrible mistake.

"Who are you?" she repeated.

"I think the real question is, who are you? I'm curious what you think. How do you decide what to do or what you want, when all the things that made you were made up? You used to call me *tio* when you were little, but I don't think you remember that."

Lexi jerked back.

It wasn't the phantom of her uncle. It wasn't even his voice. She was speaking to the real Tiago. The Dark Angel, who was inhabiting the body of an unsuspecting high school freshman. The occupation was invasive and wrong, and it made her afraid. What other lines was he willing to cross?

"I know that look," Tiago said, wagging a finger. "I wish I had time to explain, but I only have a few minutes."

This was Lexi's chance to show her value to the Senex. To prove that Tiago *did* need her in some way, and that she needed to continue her mission in Beta. She couldn't be pushed to the sidelines to let Jonathan's or the other Iron Dreamers' fates be determined by a detached third party. The Senex didn't care enough to be in charge.

"Where are you right now?" she asked. "Are you on Luna?"

"Maybe."

"Ugh." She threw up her hands, remembering the dead man's floating hands. "Why would you care if I'm putting anyone's life at risk?" she asked with an accusatory anger. "You don't care about anyone."

"I do care," Tiago said. He looked at his feet. "I thought I could do it remotely."

"Yeah, well. It didn't work."

"I know." His voice was small, nothing like what a terrorist should sound like. Then again, Lexi wasn't doing a particularly splendid job of predicting the domineering personalities of those around her.

"Is this the part where you justify all your actions with some self-righteous speech?" she asked.

"No." Her uncle crossed a foot in front of his ankle and balanced on the leg. "There are hard choices that need to be made, and really, I'm not sure if there's a way out of this without people dying. I've tried everything, and nothing seems to work. I have something now that might work. I can live with failure, but I can't say the same about the people around you."

"*Me*?" Lexi scoffed. "We're only doing this because of you. You're the one screwing everything up. I was happy with my life—"

"Then why did you pull yourself out?"

"I-I wasn't trying to."

Tiago rubbed his hands together, keeping them close to his ribs. It was an almost nervous gesture. "We have geniuses and generals in those pods, but a seventeen-year-old girl escapes. How?"

"That was just...no one knows how."

"You didn't wake yourself up. No Iron Dreamer can." He pointed to the back of his neck. "There's a suppressant in the main cord that prevents them from moving. It's like what your body does to keep you motionless in your sleep. If we didn't have that, Iron Dreamers would be jerking around and getting tangled up in the pods. We needed to paralyze them. It's impossible to override."

"Well, I did."

"Did they tell you about Cillian?" Tiago's line of questioning was as erratic as his responses.

"Uh, yeah. He's the first Iron Dreamer that escaped."

Tiago pointed a finger to his chest. "I found him. Beta has an imbedded failsafe that only I and one other can access. I programmed it years ago, but it was the first time I had seen it tested. I've been trying to recreate those conditions since, but without direct access to the Nest, I haven't been able to get it to work. I'm sorry about that, by the way. That must have been horrible."

"Wait," Lexi said, pinching her nose. "You didn't free Cillian?"

"No."

"So then who did?" Lexi could feel her chest tightening. "Who's the only other person who can do that?"

Her uncle smiled. The answer was obvious. "My wife."

Lexi tilted her head toward the night sky. Her eyes gazed upon the stars, but her vision was distant and unfocused. Somewhere in space there was a program running the rotation of the stars. Nothing was real.

"You weren't there when I was pulled," Lexi said, realizing.

"Artemis is the one who pulled you."

CHAPTER FIFTEEN

"Why would she do that?" Lexi asked. The betrayal of her circumstances and the lies surrounding it could sink in later; right now she needed answers before the engineers realized what was happening and pulled her out.

"Artemis needed the bait. It's just like her." Tiago chuckled to himself, reminiscing. "She wasn't a great engineer, but she is a strategist. She always finds a way to me."

"Well, I'm happy you're amused by this. She ruined my *life*."

He shrugged. "Maybe. She might have done you a favor, to be honest. The Iron Dreamers have no legal rights. If Beta is scratched, you'll be safe as a citizen of Sol. I assume they gave you my estate?"

Lexi shook her head, attempting to mitigate the multiple conversations. "Uh, no, not yet. Gal is fighting me for it, but Art—" She struggled to say the woman's name, refusing to praise her for anything. "I got most of the rights."

"That's good."

Lexi collapsed onto the sidewalk. From the moment she rose out of the pod, her life had been a lie. She hadn't even pulled the cord. Well, *that* part she had done, but only because Artemis had disabled the suppressant that kept her immobile. Artemis had been waiting for her in the Iron Sector, watching from the shadows like a bad omen. Lexi had been thrust from one lie to the next. Artemis's little puppet. At no point did Lexi have a say in what happened to her.

"I'm just cannon fodder," Lexi said, her voice just barely above a whisper.

Tiago took a step forward. "You're not cannon fodder, you're my family."

"You people only care about yourselves."

"Wait." Tiago's arms dropped by his waist, and his body went rigid. His eyes drifted across the street, seeing more than a quiet town in the middle of the night. The breeze was blowing, but it didn't flow with that metallic taste. Whatever Tiago was looking for, it was happening outside of Beta. "They're coming," he said.

Lexi's head spun. "Who?"

He placed his hands on her shoulders. It was an exceptionally troubling gesture from a fourteen-year-old. "Find it in your heart to forgive her," he said.

"Artemis?" Lexi asked, astounded. "No way. I don't want to be anywhere near her."

"Anger festers like an infection. I don't want to see that happen to you."

Lexi released a hollow laugh. She was mortified by the idea that real tears might be spilling from her face somewhere a thousand years away.

Her uncle was a terrorist. He could be spending what few minutes he had left to extract information from her as Mai had, but instead of an interrogation, he was worried about her. He had asked for nothing, only that she forgive his wife for using Lexi as a tool to hunt him down.

It's not that Lexi thought he would hit her or yell, but she did expect more indications of the harm he could inflict. She expected clearer signs on what to do. Good and evil were supposed to be obvious emblems of the wills of those whom they represented, not muddied intentions of nuance and perspective. Lexi didn't know how to navigate him.

"None of you are what I imagined," Lexi said, sniffling. "I can't seem to get any of you right."

"People are complex. You have to let them show you who they are." He pointed a finger at her. "And then you have to believe it."

For a moment she thought she saw a flash of his eyes through the boy. Her uncle had always been somewhat of an anomaly in their family, with hazel eyes that changed color from blue to green depending on the light. No one in the family knew where it came from. The Carvalhos had brown eyes.

"I guess now you want something from me in return? Information, or whatever," Lexi said.

Tiago shrugged sheepishly, which was a mannerism more fitting to his body. "They're here now."

A sharp pain shot through Lexi's skull. The sidewalk faded, and the brick wall of the theater turned to mist. She stumbled forward, and into the arms of the boy in front of her. His eyes went wide. Tiago was gone. The boy looked around, bewildered. He couldn't remember why he was standing outside, or who the girl in his arms was. Like a demonic possession, Tiago and Lexi were leaving their bodies as the phantoms took over.

Lexi lifted through the fog and into a familiar coldness. It wasn't the lack of warmth that ripped her from the nostalgia of her hometown, it was the recklessness of a future that had no idea what it was doing.

A dark hand hovers over her forehead. Azi stands above her, studying the dilation of her pupils. It's the same routine every time she's pulled. Except, this time, it comes with a grievance. Instead of the detached interest in her vitals, Azi's mouth is tight and his eyebrows are furrowed. She leans to the side and peers over his shoulder to a brooding figure.

Artemis.

"It was you?" Lexi demands to know. "Did you see that?"

Artemis clasps her hands in front of her. "The Dark Angel made sure that I did."

"You've been lying to me."

Artemis moves to the foot of Lexi's cot and out of strangling distance. She balances in a wide stance, buzzing with energy. Lexi's eyes narrow, and she's about to lash out when she realizes that Artemis is not on the defense. Her mind has moved past the conversation and onto something else.

"What's going on?" Lexi asks worriedly.

Azi pulls out his hollow and moves to the back, pretending to have something more important to do.

"The deadline has moved," Artemis tells Lexi. "The council will be here any minute."

"What, why? You don't mean...are they coming for an Iron Dreamer?"

Artemis sits onto the cot beside Lexi's feet, a bold move considering the fury still running through Lexi's veins. "Three of them."

The cord that was just connected to Lexi's skull drops to the floor. "The deadline isn't for another two weeks."

"I know."

"If you know, then *fix it*!" Lexi leaps off the cot, finding her balance so that she's standing over Artemis. The gravity in the Nest is not quite as strong as what's simulated in the North Country. The world is wrong. She stumbles forward and catches the edge of the cot. Maybe Artemis moves to help her, she doesn't know. Lexi stands before anyone can touch her.

The doors are too far for anyone to hear them, but like the metallic taste in Beta when an Iron Dreamer arrives, there is a feeling in the air when forces working against her are closing in. The tapping of Hatshepsut's cane grows louder. Lexi can't bring herself to turn. It could be a massive audience that's come to watch her be reprimanded, or they've brought three Iron Dreamers to slaughter in front of her.

"They're here now," Artemis says.

The déjà vu gives Lexi chills. Now that she's met the real Tiago, she can't help but see the similarities between husband and wife. They both put on a good show. Even their expressions of false compassion are the same. Artemis lifts herself off the cot and elbows Lexi in the side. Reluctantly, Lexi bows to the council.

"We had high expectations," Farhad says. "Too high, it seems." The bags under his eyes have deepened, sharpening the fierce features of his face. It's not from any guilt he feels for the ultimatum. "We made a deal, you and I," he says.

Lexi doesn't know the extent of the Dark Angel's capabilities. Her uncle has been evading the authorities for four years. He could have concealed them at the movie theater. There's a chance that Farhad has no idea that he approached her. She chooses her words carefully.

"I'm doing what you asked," she says. "I'm acting as bait."

He huffs. "A tree that has yet to bear fruit."

Gal takes her place beside him. Her hair flows freely over shoulders, sharpening her dark expression. Her eyes burn with quiet anger. Something about it rattles Lexi.

"Our deadline isn't for another two weeks," Lexi says.

"The shipment from Earth has been delayed," Farhad replies.

The words register logically. Lexi knows the consequences of a delayed supply shipment, but emotional register hasn't quite hit. She marches toward Artemis. "This is *your* fault," Lexi says, pointing a finger at her. "None of this would have happened if it wasn't for you."

Artemis shoots her a look so severe that it could cut ice. It's not a warning, it's a threat. The woman could probably space her without anyone noticing. Lexi doesn't care. She twists her body, either to turn toward the council or to wind up to hit Artemis, when Chen's arms seize her by the shoulders. He lifts her off the ground and pulls her away.

They're all in on it.

"Let me *go*!" Lexi screeches.

Farhad waves a bony hand, as if swatting a fly. "Someone silence her."

Chen enters a command into his balat, and slaps his hand to Lexi's chest. The nanotechnology of her balat crawls up her neck as if lowering her into a vault of lava. She lifts her head to escape, but she can't move. Not a finger. Not her legs. The balats aren't just for protection against space, or a tracking tool to navigate Sol.

They're prisons.

She thrashes at full volume, screaming at the top of her lungs. The council makes their best effort to ignore her until the balat covers her mouth. Chen pulls her past a row of engineers who pretend that nothing is happening. He holds her in his arms like a rag doll. She is helpless to do anything but watch.

Farhad turns to Hatshepsut and says, "High Councilor."

"Get on with it." The frail woman hunches over her cane, having responded so quickly that Lexi realizes nothing she said would have mattered. The decision to kill three innocent people was made before they even entered the sector.

Did Tiago know this was going to happen?

Azi's eyes dart from council member to council member, checking to be sure that he heard correctly. Lexi can't read Hatshepsut's expression. The frail woman appears to feel nothing. Azi holds the hollow in front of him, and Farhad nods impatiently. If Azi feels anything other than nervousness, he doesn't show it. He enters a command into his hollow the way he would enter any other command.

Hundreds of thousands of people died every day before the Senex appeared, yet the world spun madly on. But to the Senex, death is an event that happens to other people. It doesn't even graze their skin. There should be backlash for their actions, consequences for their callousness. And yet they'll be rewarded for their actions. One day they'll be truly immortal, and nothing will stop them.

Artemis stands behind a row of council members, blending into their shadow like mist. Gal's steely gaze is fixed on her. Artemis matches it, and they share a wordless exchange. Their beliefs are different, but both appear to have some semblance of appreciation for human life. Or maybe they just don't like that someone else won.

Lexi expects a ripple to move through the room, a sign that a light has been snuffed. *Some* sign that a life is lost. But air isn't sucked out of the room. The universe doesn't blink. For a moment, Lexi wonders if the world around her has collapsed at all.

"It's confirmed," Azi says.

If she weren't paralyzed, she would collapse to the floor.

Three people have died on her behalf—three people—because she was *breathing*. She doesn't know who they are, where they lived, or who their families are. Maybe the families aren't real. Lexi hopes they're not. The only solace in the senseless deaths is that the suffering left is just a line of code. There is no one real to mourn them. Just like the man in the tub.

Farhad walks toward Lexi. She tries to retreat, but the balat has a steel grip on her legs. He leans forward, breathing onto her face.

"Until you learn to close your mouth, it will be one Iron Dreamer every month," Farhad says, looking to the side as if eye contact is beneath him. "If you consume more resources than that, it will be two Iron Dreamers."

Farhad and the other council members shuffle out of the sector. Hatshepsut says something to her, and then reaches up to pat her on the shoulder, but Lexi isn't listening. The engineers don't acknowledge anyone as they pass, continuing with their work as if it's just another day in the office. The Iron Dreamers mean nothing. Whatever humanity the Senex once had died with Earth.

Chen waits until the council is gone to release Lexi's balat. She crumbles to the floor, vomiting onto the illuminated blue sea beneath her fingertips. She retches until the contents of her stomach are emptied, and then dry-heaves. Tears of pain burn her eyes.

Is this what it feels like to kill?

She shivers, and the balat soothes her with a wave of warmth. A moment ago, it was a straitjacket. Now it's trying to comfort her as if it's been a security blanket the whole time. Could a piece of clothing gaslight a person? She wants to rip it off. Leave it to Sol to create a device for both benevolence and suffering.

Artemis's feet step into view, but Lexi doesn't look up.

"Was it Jonathan?" Lexi croaks.

"No."

"I should know who they are," Lexi says, rubbing her wrist against her runny nose. "I should know them. I want to know their names."

"No, you don't."

"Where is Mostafa?"

Artemis makes a noise, as if Lexi is behaving like an immature teenage girl. "Interesting you'd ask for him."

"Does he know what you did?"

Artemis pauses before answering. "No."

"What about Zuchiris?"

"If you're going to determine who you trust based on how transparent they've been, I'm afraid you'll have no one to trust here."

Lexi mutters under her breath. "Bitch."

Artemis doesn't yell at Lexi, or deliver some witty condescending remark about who holds the power. What would be the point when Lexi possesses so little? Instead, the sentinel is calculating. Her mind is an assembly of gears and wheels, turning with incomprehensible direction. Her head shifts, as if debating, coming to a decision, and then changing her mind again.

"Luna wants to explore exoplanets," Artemis says.

Lexi frowns. "Okay?"

"Five years ago, they began putting resources toward traveling to a handful of systems nearby. If they manage to construct the engine, they could reach a new world within months."

"So?"

"You're too young to be interested in this, but the existential threat that humanity poses to the universe could be enough to alter it, especially if we manage to prolong our life expectancy, which I imagine we will. In a million years, we could become a virus spreading upon existence itself, inflicting our will as an expansive empire either built by our insatiable appetite, or conquered by it."

"That sounds...a million years away."

"The plan has already begun."

Lexi has no idea what that means, and doesn't care. She doesn't have the mental elasticity to focus on protecting the Iron Dreamers, and whatever existential crisis Artemis is alluding to. Lexi didn't go to college to manage a company. She didn't run for political office. These are problems for someone else.

"Sounds like a you problem," she says.

"I wish it was, then I could control it." Artemis rubs the side of her thigh as if wiping blood off her hands. "We need more time to evolve before we become everyone's problem. I would prefer that a species with the power to destroy worlds be a bit more benevolent than us, wouldn't you agree?"

Lexi could sweep it under the rug as a distraction to divert her anger toward an enemy that she and Artemis could share. The future had turned its back on Earth, accepting its death as a termination beyond their control, and moved on to the next planet to consume. The Senex were setting their sights on something else, somewhere else, and Artemis feared the consequences.

If Lexi had been contemplating the condition of the universe, or whatever it is that demigods think about, maybe she would be worried about humanity's role in it, but she doesn't care about a planet hundreds of light-years away.

"For once, can you just tell me what you want?" Lexi demands.

"Mm." Artemis studies the room, turning to Azi, who stands at attention, and the dozens of engineers and sentinels plugged into the simulation. There is something she wants to say, but she can't say it here. She says instead, "Believe it or not, I do care about what happens to you. I've watched over you since you were born."

Lexi scoffs. "It doesn't feel that way."

"It's not my strong suit," Artemis agrees, looking to her hands. "Feelings are more Tiago's area."

"I get why he cares. He thinks I'm a reincarnation of his niece. But why would you care about me?"

"Because you're a part of him," Artemis replies easily. "That makes you important to me."

"You are the weirdest couple." The simmering anger returns, boiling to the surface as Lexi remembers why she's there. "You could have left me out of it."

Artemis exhales slowly. Consoling is a difficult act for her. She'd rather save time and get to the point. "Pulling you out of your life may have been wrong," she says. "But that was never your life. It wasn't even Alexandria's. She was born on a sick planet and her friends died before she was your age. We had to bury her mother in contaminated dirt because there was nowhere else to go. You, on the other hand, will never know disease. You were born in the thirty-second century, with clean water and air."

Lexi dry-heaves again, having thought of Farhad systematically killing every Iron Dreamer until he reaches Jonathan. She can't think about anything else.

Artemis crouches to the floor, careful to keep her distance. Lexi can't stand to look at the woman who is to blame for all the misery in her life. Neither of them says a word, and the awkward silence is unbearable.

Lexi groans, lifting her head. "Just leave me alone."

"Hate me if you want," Artemis says, frustratingly at ease with Lexi's anger. "I meant what I said before. You are a survivor, and there are 700,000 people in those pods that I need your help to keep alive. Can you help me, or not?"

Agreeing with Artemis, even to save a single person's life, somehow feels like consent to the crimes committed against her. The fact that Artemis knows that about her is even more infuriating. How can Lexi have any choices when Artemis already knows what she'll decide?

Lexi nods begrudgingly.

Artemis leans back, inhaling with relief. "Tiago stays close to the North Country when you're there," she explains. "He wants to recruit you. For what, I don't know. Your mother mentioned a family trip for Christmas. That's our deadline." Artemis stands. Her feet shift slightly, indicating silent communication with Chen over Lexi's head.

"Why is Christmas the deadline?" Lexi asks.

"Because your mother never saw those flight prices, and an engineer didn't program them," Artemis says. "Tiago made her say that."

Lexi shivers at the idea of her mother being invaded. It's not editing a photograph of her; it's violating her in real time. It's changing her voice and her thoughts for another man's agenda.

Artemis pulls out her hollow and beckons Azi. "Assign her a study schedule," she orders him. "If the Dark Angel approaches, I don't want her mouth hanging open like an illiterate child. And pull Mostafa."

"Yes, sentinel," Azi replies.

Mostafa is lying supine in the sentinel chair, still connected to the simulation. The suit pulsates around him, flowing in waves as the nanotechnology mitigates the energy moving through his body. Beside Mostafa is another man and a woman that Lexi doesn't recognize. The three of them appear to be working together. Mostafa's body lurches, his chest rising half a foot off the chair like he's being pulled by strings. Azi removes his helmet. Mostafa leans over the armrest and rubs his eyes.

It comes as some relief that everyone's body, on some level, rejects the violent removal from Beta.

Mostafa looks up. He needs no explanation. Within seconds, he's read the tension in the room and understands the nuance.

"When?" he asks.

"Just now," Artemis says. "If Tiago is the one to tell Lexi the truth, she'll never trust us. She'll need a crash course in our history, and the future."

Being spoken about as if Lexi's not in the room is still annoying, but pointing out a simple manipulation technique doesn't make it any less effective. The order of operations of earning trust is generally, whoever discloses the truth first is the most reliable. It's not that Lexi trusts Tiago because he was the first to tell her what Artemis had done.

It's that Artemis has more to hide.

She looks Lexi over, but not in the clinical way Mostafa does it. Artemis is searching through scrolls buried deep within Lexi, like a sailor watching dark clouds on the horizon—she's seen the outcome, she's just waiting for it to catch up. "Stay with her," Artemis says.

Mostafa stands beside Lexi. She takes his arm, telling herself it's for the physical interaction, but there is no softness to his touch. The balat maintains its armor qualities. He guides Lexi through the Nest doors, moving gingerly to compensate for her wobbling legs, though he doesn't ask why until they're clear of the Iron Sector.

"The shipment was delayed," Mostafa says. It sounds like a question, but it's a statement. He already knows the answer.

"Yeah," Lexi croaks. Her throat is too dry to elaborate. She drops her gaze to the floor and watches the steps of a woman ahead of them transform the hallway into a trail of bioluminescent lily pads.

Mostafa isn't a friend exactly, but he's the closest she has to one. Michelle and Gui aren't real. Jonathan doesn't know anything. Zuchiris will back Artemis all the way, as will Chen, and anyone else who acknowledges the hierarchical role of the sentinels. Mostafa is the only one with rebellious eyes. If there is anyone on Sol who Lexi could talk to in a moment of loneliness, it's him.

"Three people are dead because of me," she says, her voice barely above a whisper. "It's my fault."

Mostafa can't deny it if he wants to be honest. Lexi's consumption of water and oxygen have thrown off the calculus of a city older than the Ottoman Empire. If she wants to live, the price is the life of another Iron Dreamer.

"I'm losing the game, aren't I?" she asks.

His face brightens as the memory flickers to life. A smirk tugs at his lips, caught off guard by the mention of a conversation that he had almost erased from his mind. "There are no winners," he tells her. "Although you have made it interesting."

"Glad I could be of amusement."

"What I mean is, I think it's important you're here. These events would have occurred whether or not you were pulled from Beta, but your reactions haven't gone unnoticed. You're a fresh set of eyes on a very old set of problems. You're...human. I think some of us have forgotten what that means."

"I'm a science project."

He shrugs. "So were we."

"Yeah, but at some point you were normal. I was cloned in a petri dish in a spaceship. Calling me human is a stretch. I'm *unnatural*."

"Nothing in this city is natural. Clothes, society, agriculture. They're all manmade. That doesn't make them bad. Meningitis is natural, but we made antibiotics. Sometimes the things we make are good." Mostafa looks to her mouth, his eyes distant, as if his mind is miles away. He hesitates, but his voice is gentle when he says, "Like you."

Lexi bites her lip, willing herself not to smile at the compliment. She's mortified by how desperately she wants to be accepted. She's never cared about those things before, yet she clings to him like a lifeline. She needs the comfort—something to hold onto as the storm rages around them.

Lexi has been cast in a role too big for her, and she's bombing on stage. There is no past experience that she can use as a guide. Every decision she makes is the wrong one, and now it's gotten someone killed.

Three someones.

She is not Alexandria. She doesn't have her personality or memories because she isn't her. Lexi doesn't even have her own memories. They aren't real. What's left when the moments that built her mind are unwoven from reality?

"It's been a long time since I truly cared about anything," Mostafa says. His voice is low, as if he doesn't want to be heard. He doesn't enjoy disclosing his personal thoughts. "It's interesting to watch you navigate this, and with heart. You care."

"Thanks," she mumbles, picking at her fingernails around his arm. "Feels like it's going to be used against me."

He doesn't argue against the possibility. Instead, he says, "I can find peace with however this turns out, so long as the course was shaped by empathy, and not ambition."

A small crease appears between her brows. She's caught between wonder at Mostafa's honesty, and embarrassment over the warmth spreading across her cheeks. She thought that he was observing her actions through a logical lens, but he was watching the other parts too. Like how much the Iron Dreamers' lives weighed on her. The uncertainty of their fate tortured her, and that's because she cares. She can't allow herself to discover how much.

His caramel eyes look to her with a vulnerability that makes her feel like she's trespassing on a private moment.

Mostafa is comfortable, even if it's while wearing one of his masks. It makes her feel accepted in his world. It may be one tiny sliver of a very large picture, but it's acceptance all the same. She stares at his mouth. There's not a thought in her mind. He catches her gaze and quickly looks away. The balat is hard as steel, but she can feel his muscles stiffen beneath her hands.

Mostafa should be in college studying political science, or going to parties and talking to pretty girls. He *looks* young, and there's a hint of youthfulness in his steps. But if time were allowed to run its course, his beautiful face and hair would have rotted in the dirt by now. It's like speaking to Alexander the Great.

They should have never crossed paths.

Lexi leans into his arm, and he softens his posture. They walk together in silence, enjoying the quiet hum of the station's mechanics. His strides are longer than hers. He shortens them to synchronize to her rhythm. She's still learning the differences between the halls, but she's caught sight of the same dark smudge on the bottom of one rounded corner. They've crossed the same place twice. They're going in circles.

"He approached you," Mostafa says in the dark.

Lexi sighs. She was actively avoiding the subject of Tiago and stopping herself from imaging the faces of the three Iron Dreamers in order to enjoy a moment of tenderness.

“He was pretending to be a theater attendant,” Lexi says, shivering at the encroachment. “He was just a kid. I thought he would at least look himself.”

“Tiago was always strange,” Mostafa says. A neutral mask settles onto his face. The blue lighting from the floor cuts so deep into his cheeks that they seem bare bone.

“You don’t like him,” she says, realizing. “Even before all this, you never liked my uncle.”

“I don’t trust him,” he corrects.

She snorts. “Who could trust anyone here?”

“It’s not that.” Mostafa shifts his shoulders, tugging at Lexi’s grip. She’s determined to hold onto him, and accidentally brushes the back of his hand. His legs continue moving in tandem with hers, but his chest goes rigid. It’s the first time that she’s touched his bare skin; the rest of him is covered in nanotechnology.

“What is it?” she asks.

Mostafa clears his throat. “He says a lot of words to mask his ambition.”

“Is that what he’s doing now,” she asks, “something ambitious?”

“I don’t know.”

“Does anyone actually know his plan?”

“Whatever it is, it will be dangerous. Tiago is reckless.”

Until she met her uncle—the real one—Lexi hadn’t given much thought to whether or not she supports the Iron Dreamer program. She wants it to be in operation for as long as she’ll be alive, but the moral implications of storing bodies as a problem-solving tool are ambiguous at best.

Lexi can understand the inability to maintain the resources to support them as wandering beings on Sol. If her presence outweighs the lives of three Iron Dreamers, then she can’t imagine the damage 700,000 people would cause. But Tiago wasn’t a hurricane. He didn’t roar or rage. He was thoughtful. An immortal trapped on a desert island wouldn't burn it to the ground. He knows the risks, and he's doing it anyway. It's like Artemis says; he has a plan.

"He didn't sound reckless to me," Lexi says.

Mostafa casts her a sidelong glance. "You've had one conversation with him, and now you're the expert."

"I'm just saying he didn't seem like that type of person," she replies defensively. "Maybe you've all been so stuck in your ways for so long that you can't see a different path."

"You're a child."

"And you're a bunch of geriatrics on a cruise ship."

Mostafa's cheeks rise, and he breaks out into a grin. He laughs. It's quick, like lightning, but it's a genuine wholesome sound. Lexi brightens, pleased to have extracted such a sweet sound from him.

"That's true," he says.

Tiago has included Lexi in every iteration of Beta since its beginning. Maybe she could use that as leverage to uncover his plan. At this rate, another Iron Dreamer will die before Artemis and Mostafa can track him. Lexi will have to reach her uncle before that, and make it look like a coincidence. Maybe, if the Senex know what he's planning, they can come to an agreement and avoid all the death and destruction.

Lexi lifts her head to Mostafa. He's running through his own list of scenarios. Her chest aches with the impending deceit. She can't tell Mostafa her plan. He'll be obligated to inform Hatshepsut. Lexi is not so naïve as to believe their blooming friendship will hold weight against whatever relationship has already been forged with the High Councilor. Lexi will need to keep her plans to herself, and cast her own sail into the wind.

She's going to contact the Dark Angel.

CHAPTER SIXTEEN

"My coes are told," Lexi says into her hollow.

Somehow, in the midst of all the confusion in Beta, she managed to remember the unintelligible contact information for Mai.

There's no guarantee that the call won't be traced. Lexi can only hope that everyone's reaction to Boole is testament to his skill, and that he'll conceal their conversation before security can be alerted.

There is no day and night on Sol. The rotation of the city, though hardly noticeable, is substantially faster than Earth. Sleep schedules are programmed off the old eight-hour routines, depending on the work shift. Not too unlike Earth in the twenty-first century, except that it is evenly spread out. Night crawlers and early risers don't exist. The city is as busy in the morning as it is at night. Lexi is on the administrator schedule to align with Artemis and the council in case they need her, for whatever reason. Like for an interrogation, or as a witness to murder. She will be alone for the next seven hours in the privacy of her own room. If there is a time to make contact, now is it.

She places the hollow on the ground, and a full-size hologram of a short woman with jet-black hair appears. The transparency is barely perceptible. If Lexi squints, she can swear that Mai is in the room with her, floating inches above the ground like a wraith.

"Ah, there you are," Mai says. While she sounds like a teenager, the tiny lines by her eyes indicate otherwise. Mai could be forty years old, or eighty. "You remembered the summons. I'm impressed."

"Yeah, what is that about?" Lexi asks.

"It's a spoonerism. My coes are told, my toes are cold. It's when someone moves letters around. A little misspeak is more subtle than a bona fide coded phrase and, no offense, lovey, but I didn't think you could handle that. Oh, this is just *delightful*. You've brightened my whole day! I have to admit, I didn't think you would call."

Lexi lifts herself off the cot. "I guess I'm desperate."

Mai crosses her arms and juts her hip out, leaning on one leg.

She's an American.

"I take it you need something?" Mai asks. "Seems only fair. Without you, I wouldn't have been able to secure an exclusive with Chancellor Nikau on Luna. I've been petitioning for that since their lights first turned on. *Ah*." Mai sings the note, pacing in circles, though from Lexi's perspective she remains in the same spot.

"I need a favor." Lexi takes a breath and says, "I need to speak with Tiago."

Mai raises an eyebrow. "That's not a favor, lovey. That's treason."

"So, you know who he is."

"Of *course* I know who he is." Mai flattens a palm to her chest as if offended. "There aren't many people who could play the role of the Dark Angel. That takes some serious skills, and Tiago's are legendary. Did you know that he hacked into a satellite when he was a student? A small-town boy in the middle of nowhere! Who *does* that? Anyhoo, what is it you want with him?"

Lexi doesn't need to know the order of operations. Whether Mai found Tiago and requested that he free Boole so that she could dig up a juicy story on the council, or Tiago needed Mai and Boole for his plans to dissemble Beta, is irrelevant. Mai is the only person Lexi knows with direct contact to the Dark Angel outside of Beta.

"I need to speak with him," Lexi says.

"Don't we all." Mai rolls her head. "I'm afraid I can't help you there. I haven't spoken to him since he went radio silent four years ago. For a man living in a confined space, he has a special talent for dodging people. One might think he doesn't like us very much." She chuckles to herself in a high-pitched song.

Mai is choosing her words carefully. It's not because of security. She just admitted to assisting in Boole's escape from Luna's prison. Her caution is for another reason. A sense of morality? Perhaps, after a millennium, maintaining a web of lies is simply exhausting.

"You two haven't spoken recently," Lexi deduces, "but has he contacted you in another way?"

"Not recently."

She stifles a groan. "Can you help me reach him or not?"

"Literally, or metaphysically?"

"I swear, you people." Lexi drops down onto the cot. She isn't accustomed to the duplicitous nature of the Senex. She has no idea how to recruit an ally, or negotiate with an enemy. "I guess you wouldn't care if it's a matter of life or death."

Warm breath brushes the side of her face, and a shiver runs down her spine. Mai can't possibly be in the room with her. The technology on Sol has been an unending rabbit hole, but the human body cannot be in two places at once.

Lexi jerks her head to find Mai in the middle of the room, still in the hologram.

Mai spreads her fingers, once and then twice. A crease forms between her eyes, zooming in on Lexi's face to assess her sincerity. "Hold on a minute. I didn't say *that*. I want to help you, but I'm going to need a bit more information."

"I'm breathing too much, and using resources," Lexi explains. "Every month I'm here, they kill an Iron Dreamer to make up for it. At least until a shipment from Earth arrives. I need to talk to Tiago to stop it." Lexi is careful to withhold the information about the deal with Farhad. If Mai learns that the plan is to take Tiago prisoner, and possibly space him, she may not be as inclined to help.

"Oh, the Iron Dreamers are clones, lovey," Mai says. "We can always make more. Carbon copies, in fact! Whatever is scratched can be replaced. I thought you meant a Senex. *Woo*, you scared me there."

"I shouldn't be surprised you don't care about clones."

Mai waves a dismissive hand, though her fingers are so slight, the motion has the dance-like quality of a ballerina. "You only feel that way because you are one. If you were one of us, you wouldn't be so concerned about it. Funny how that works, isn't it?"

"Tiago is concerned," Lexi counters. "That's why he's fighting back."

"Maybe. But it still took him three hundred years to grow a conscience about it. Or worse, it took him that long to grow the balls."

Lexi hadn't thought about that. "Will you help me, or not?"

"My goodness." Mai clicks her tongue. "You're a binary creature, aren't you? Must run in the family. I'll see what I can do, but I can't make any promises. Tiago isn't the sort of man you track down."

"I guess you'll have to do something spectacular to draw his attention."

Mai grins widely, clapping her hands. "Oh, I do love a show! I must warn you, though, it will come with a price."

Lexi tenses, having anticipated a bargain. "What do you want?"

"Don't look so alarmed. I don't need anything *now*, and when I do, it'll be small. I find the small things are the most worthwhile, don't you agree? I'll be in touch!"

Mai's voice rises on the last note. Lexi's room is soundproof—no doubt a security feature—but she casts a worried glance at the general area of the door. She's learned where the edges are, though they are melted away, and presses an ear against the cold surface. It's like trying to listen to crickets through a boulder.

Nothing.

She exhales a sigh of relief. No one's coming. She lies on the cot, determined to sleep and perform at her best tomorrow, but sleep eludes her. She tosses and turns throughout the night. After three hours, she debates whether to just turn the lights back on and pace her small room.

What will Mai do to draw his attention?

How long will it take?

Will he notice?

Lexi takes a breath and counts down from sixty.

Fifty-nine.

Fifty-eight.

Fifty-seven.

In the morning, after a few merciful hours of sleep, the edges of the door slip away and Chen stands in the doorway. He enters a command into his balat and turns on the light. Lexi holds her breath, anticipating a reprimand, but none comes. He is clueless about the conversation with Mai.

"Ready for your first full day?" he asks.

"Yep." Lexi jumps off the cot, perhaps too enthusiastically.

Chen gives her a suspicious look. "Let's go."

Artemis and Mostafa are already in the Nest by the time she arrives. Their bodies lie on the chairs, breathing steadily as if in a deep sleep. They appear the same from this angle. Lexi avoids looking at any of them in case she's able to identify Artemis. She's still not sure how to feel about the woman.

Azi and a few other engineers hover nearby, monitoring the displays without the usual tightness in their faces. It must be a slow day. Azi drags the cord for Lexi, avoiding her line of sight. She tries not to take his cold indifference personally.

"I've been told to warn you that this will be an intense day of activities," Azi says, gesturing toward the cot. He stands by the head of it, avoiding eye contact. "Act normal, is what you should do."

"Same old, same old," Lexi says in a joking manner.

Azi doesn't laugh. He continues to work on his hollow, holding the cord under his armpit until Lexi lies down. She's never been alone with him and doesn't know what to say. How do you ease the tension with someone when they hate you? Before she can ask where she'll be arriving, she feels the pinch, and the darkness swallows her.

Her vision was blurry. She pushed through the brain fog, reaching forward until her fingertips touched a cold, smooth surface. Her body rocked as if she were in motion. She felt a sharp jolt, her body jerked up until a restraint pulled her down.

A seat belt.

She was in a car.

"I'm not joking," Michelle said. "I *just* found out he had them. How crazy is that?"

Lexi's hearing was shifting in and out. There could be a faulty wire in the cord, or maybe something was wrong with her implant. She smacked the side of her head with her palm, as if knocking water out of her ear.

"What's wrong with you?" Michelle asked, turning onto a steep road. "You were, like, super psyched a second ago and now you're all quiet. Why do you two have to be so weird around each other?"

It was nighttime. Snow was on the fields. It twinkled in the moonlight like glitter. It typically snowed in the North Country in October, but it didn't last long, and it certainly wasn't over two feet deep. That kind of snow didn't begin until late November. She hadn't been gone long—a week, max. Was she losing track of time, or had the engineers shifted the time frame ahead? How could they do that with active Iron Dreamers in play?

"Uh, sorry," Lexi mumbled, squeezing her forehead. "I think I'm getting a headache. Must be...the weather."

It was a sloppy transition, but Michelle didn't notice.

"Isn't this awesome?" Michelle squeezed the steering wheel and bounced in her seat. "We haven't had a storm like this in years. I can't believe it's only October."

So, it was the end of October. Lexi had been at the movie theater last night, talking to the Dark Angel. The engineers hadn't moved anything, they'd just decided to drop a nor'easter on the entire Eastern Seaboard for no reason.

The car slid around the corner off the main road, and they hit the edge of the sidewalk. Michelle calmly maneuvered her tires as they struggled to pick a side. Sidewalks were impossible to differentiate from the road after storms.

"Are we late for something?" Lexi asked.

Michelle was well versed in the snow, but she veered toward the conservative side. If there was fresh snow on the ground, she normally stayed well below the speed limit.

"I told him eight," Michelle said. She tugged on a strand of her hair. Her anxiety skyrocketed when she needed to be somewhere. She could ask Lexi to send to a text to whoever she was talking about and let them know they would be six minutes late, but it would do nothing to soothe the angst of actually being late. It was the helplessness that Michelle hated most, or the fear of being a disappointment.

Why was she programmed that way?

They turned onto a side road and slowed to a crawl. The side streets hadn't been plowed yet. Michelle stayed inside the tracks of whoever had driven that path before her.

Lexi didn't live in the main part of town. She and Gui's family lived on the outskirts, where their families could live in silence. Most people lived in town. Though it was small, with no traffic lights or chain restaurants, Lexi didn't know who inhabited every single house. Especially now, she didn't care. What would be the point in learning about fictional characters?

"Whose house is this?" Lexi asked, eyeing each house as they passed.

"You brought snow pants, right?"

"Yeah."

She had no idea if she had or not.

Michelle turned onto a short driveway with a two-door garage large enough to fit a fire truck. The tires crunched as they rolled over the thick snow. The house was large, but without the typical North Country features, like a wooden frame or metal roof. A couple of lights were turned on, and the top floor was blocked by a tree. It was a nice house, and uncommonly suburban.

One of the garage doors rumbled to life and Michelle jumped out of the car. She barked a few words, and a deeper voice replied. She ducked under the rising garage door, disappearing into the darkness.

Lexi didn't have time for this. She had a terrorist to contact, and he wouldn't make himself known if there was a witness present. He could inhabit one body at a time. Lexi needed to find a way to be alone with someone, *anyone*, in hopes that Tiago would take the bait and try to speak with her. There was only one body Tiago couldn't use, aside from Lexi.

After half a minute of paralyzing indecisiveness, she took a breath and stood in the driveway.

Michelle ran toward her, sliding on the snow like her feet were skis. She wore sneakers even in the winter. "He has to warm them up," she said, gesturing over her shoulder. "He had to change the spark plugs, or whatever."

"Spark plugs?" Lexi shoved her hands into her pockets. The temperature was plummeting. "What is it, a rocket ship?"

"What? No, snow machines."

As if on cue, the engines revved from inside the garage.

Lexi had only been snowmobiling a couple of times. Her family lived on a snowmobile trail, but they didn't use it. Many of the people who did were tourists staying in their vacation homes. Lexi's family could hear them drive by in the middle of the night. Their headlights flickered through the trees like flashlights.

"I need to pee," Michelle announced. She ran into the house, leaving Lexi.

A dark figure stepped out of the garage. He held a helmet under his arm and another in his hand. He was wearing snow pants and a long-sleeve shirt. A cold wind blew through his hair. It would chill anyone else, but he didn't flinch.

"Hi," Jonathan said. His inflection dropped at the end of the word, as if he was sad that she was there.

Lexi pinched her lips and said, "Hey. So, we're snowmobiling?"

"Yep."

Lexi rocked on her heels in the awkward silence. In true small-town fashion, they didn't know how to talk to a stranger they had seen a hundred times. It created an awkward sort of familiarity. Like seeing a long-lost cousin at a funeral.

"Did you bring snow pants?" he asked.

"Uh, yeah."

Detecting something in her voice, Jonathan's head cocked to the side. "Yes, or no?"

"Let me check." Lexi ran to Michelle's car and dug through the back seat. Fortunately, they were there. She held them up over her head. Satisfied, Jonathan made his way into the garage.

The engines were painfully loud. The mechanical growls echoed off the walls. Lexi wanted to cover her ears, but didn't want to seem ungrateful. Despite the poor timing, she was excited. Snowmobiles were a rare commodity. Most of the locals couldn't afford them, and Jonathan had two.

An unmistakable difference between the machines caught Lexi's eye. She tugged on Michelle's coat and asked, "Is that a two-seater?"

"Yeah," Michelle said. "Why?"

"You and I are taking that one."

"Pff, no way. He gets to use these things all the time. I'm taking the single. You can ride with him."

"Michelle, I'm not riding with—"

"Could you guys move?" Jonathan asked.

Lexi mumbled an incoherent apology and stepped out of the way. Jonathan moved back and forth between the snowmobiles, prepping them for the ride. Michelle and Lexi stood uselessly by, awaiting orders that never came.

Jonathan guided one snowmobile to the driveway and then the other, as if unaware of Michelle and Lexi's presence. "Alright, let's go," he said, sounding tired.

"This is okay to do at night, right?" Lexi asked.

He inclined his head. "We can only go at night, actually. We need the headlights to see people coming so we don't hit each other."

The danger didn't exist, technically speaking. Lexi could hit a wall at ninety miles per hour and not die. Nothing around them was real.

Somewhere a thousand years away, Lexi was lying on a cot with a cord plugged into her head like she was a refrigerator, and Jonathan was in a drawer. The difference between them was that he was fully submerged in the simulation. If he died, the program scratched him. He would die for real. Lexi wasn't concerned for her safety. The element of immortality made her feel powerful.

Was that what it felt like to be one of the Senex?

Invulnerable?

Emboldened by her durability, Lexi agreed to sit on the back of the two-seater. If there was an accident, she could throw her body in front of Jonathan. The sentinels would just have to come up with some elaborate story as to why she showed up to school the next day without a scratch.

Michelle watched Lexi sit without a fight and beamed. She ran to the single, the rustling of her snow pants chafing against her legs only adding to her excitement. There was no mature way to move in winter gear.

"I doubt we'll see anyone," Jonathan said, handing Lexi a helmet. "But if we do, hold up a fist when they pass. It tells them that there's no one behind us. Michelle will be in front so she'll hold up one finger."

"The middle finger, most likely."

A gentle smile tugged at his lips. "Let's hope not."

The helmet was bulky and warm. She couldn't hear anything. The growls of the snowmobiles were muted by the thick padding. If she sat perfectly still, she could feel blood pumping through her forehead.

Jonathan swung a leg out in front of her and sat down. She nearly jumped back. There wasn't much room. Her knees touched the tops of his thighs. She tried to shimmy away. His back was inches from her chest. She couldn't scoot any farther back unless she wanted to fall off the seat. The snowmobile was suddenly too small.

Jonathan couldn't twist all the way around without bumping into her, so he turned sideways. All she could see were his eyes. She didn't know they were green.

"WHAT?" she screamed.

He flipped up his visor. "*I said, you're going to want to hold onto me!*"

Yeah, right, buddy.

He read her expression and shrugged. "*Your call!*"

Michelle zipped past them, and the cry of her snowmobile faded onto the street. It was not her first time. How much time had the two of them spent together?

Jonathan squeezed the throttle, and Lexi was thrown backward.

She threw her arms out in front of her and grabbed Jonathan's waist before the wind knocked her off. He was wider than she'd expected, and firmer. Lexi let go. It was awkward even through the winter gear. She jolted back again from another dip in the road. That would be the nature of the entire ride, she realized. She slid up to his back and held the spot just above his hips, resigned to her fate. Leave it to the North Country to make riding a tank so weirdly intimate.

Jonathan's chest shuddered.

He was laughing.

Lexi hadn't thought about how she felt about Jonathan. They were two teenagers on an adventure alone in the woods, and her arms were wrapped around him. It would raise a few eyebrows at school. She should have been asking questions. Instead, her heart pounded with stress. Her concern was keeping him alive. He was a pawn in a game taking place a thousand years from now, and Iron Dreamers like him were on the chopping block.

Michelle and Jonathan slowed their pace and turned right onto the sidewalk. They didn't worry about people because there was no one walking outside. There were no billboards or outlet stores. Nothing to remind them of the outside world, no extension of modernity's widening reach. Just a gas station and a couple of streetlights.

They crossed the main road and stopped at the entrance of the trailhead. The border of the forest was illuminated by a single streetlight like the entrance to Narnia.

Michelle stood above her seat and opened her visor. "*I'll follow you guys!*"

Jonathan gave her a thumbs-up, but Lexi tapped his shoulder. He took off his helmet and turned to face her. His black hair was disheveled and matted to one side. She had never seen anyone look so anxious and composed at the same time.

"What's wrong?" he asked.

"*Nothing!*" She took off her helmet. It was like screaming into a pillow. "Nothing," she repeated. "How fast do these things go?"

"Pretty fast," he said, trying to gauge her reaction. "Why?"

"Just wondering how we'll die."

He cracked a smile, and then his expression was unreadable. "The lake will be better, but it'll take a while to get there. We can get up to sixty on the trails, though."

Under normal circumstances, Lexi would have been thrilled to go snowmobiling. She would have fought to take the single, or at least negotiated for a turn on it. She would be keeping an eye on the stars to orientate to where she was. Her brain would be buzzing, her body would be alive. But all she felt was anxious, and she didn't know why.

She scratched the back of her neck. Attempting to behave normally, she said, "Alright, then. Do your worst."

"Well," Jonathan said with a smirk, "with the extra weight, it wouldn't be my *best*, per se, but I know what you mean."

Lexi chuckled. "Behold, a sense of humor."

"If that's what you want to call it." Jonathan said it with a preoccupied sincerity. He was behaving strangely, but being cryptic was typical for him. He was about to put on his helmet when he said, "Hold one finger up if we pass someone, since we're in front of Michelle now. And lean in the same direction as me. Otherwise, we're going to flip and probably die."

"That could be fun."

He laughed. It was more of a rumble than an outright laugh, but it was still nice to hear. She had never made Jonathan laugh before. The sound shook his body and moved through Lexi, shifting as noise was wont to do when traveling through different mediums.

Jonathan squeezed the throttle, and they flew into the forest's mouth. She wrapped her arms around his waist and ducked as a branch hurtled toward their heads. The narrow passage offered just enough space to stretch out their arms. There wasn't enough space for snowmobiles to pass each other. There was hardly enough space for two hikers.

The wind wormed its way through every fiber of Lexi's being. Snowmobiling at night was more of a physical sensation than a visible one. It felt like moving, but the eyes couldn't confirm. Snowflakes falling off the branches flew into the headlights like stars at warp speed.

Michelle was scrambling to keep up with Jonathan. She wasn't a bad driver.

He was just better.

When Michelle's lights finally disappeared, Jonathan started to show off. He made impossible turns, speeding toward a wall of trees seconds before cutting it too close. Each time, Lexi thought they were going to hit a tree, but Jonathan commanded the snowmobile with an effortless dexterity. He was in his element, swinging both legs to one side and pulling on the handlebar for a sharp turn. There were Formula One drivers only a few years older than him, so it wasn't entirely surprising that Jonathan would drive a snowmobile like a racecar driver. Lexi could see why he had waited for Michelle to fall behind. If she could see what he could do, she would try it too.

Lexi held onto Jonathan's waist for what felt like hours, likely leaving bruises on his hips whenever she braced herself for an impact that never came, but he didn't complain.

A part of her suspected that he was doing it on purpose.

After half an hour, the trees thinned and the scenery opened. Lexi marveled at the frozen lake. The snow twinkled beneath the mountains in a perfectly serene scene that Lexi wanted to run through. What was it about perfection that made humans want to disturb it?

The lake wouldn't be frozen enough to drive snowmobiles or trucks over yet, but if the cold kept up, the locals could go ice fishing soon. Jonathan slowed to a walking pace, hovering near the tree line and avoiding the lake. It was expert navigation of the shoreline. He seemed to know every rock and divot.

Michelle didn't own snowmobiles, and she lived on the opposite side of town. Lexi was concerned that she wouldn't be able to navigate the shoreline, and would crash through the ice. Lexi tapped Jonathan on the shoulder, and he held up his hand.

Wait.

The word entered her mind effortlessly, as if it was a message from the future. Had she heard it from the Nest? Or had it entered her mind some other way? Something was wrong. She took off her helmet and sniffed the air.

Metal.

A Senex was nearby.

Lexi's head was on a swivel. The snowmobiles weren't moving fast, but it was fast enough that the seemingly infinite row of trees blended together in an indecipherable blue-purple blur. She couldn't hear over the roar of the engine. Michelle was nowhere in sight. The only two Iron Dreamers for a hundred miles were in clear shot.

They were sitting ducks.

Jonathan pulled to the side and turned off the engine. Everything was muffled by the padding of snow. The contrast from the engines was jarring. Lexi's ears started to ring.

Jonathan swung a leg over the seat and stepped back. His mouth was tight. Lexi placed her helmet on the seat and took a tentative step toward him.

"What is it?" she asked.

"Don't be mad," he said carefully. "I don't know what to do."

A single set of footsteps crunched in the snow. They were growing closer. Through the trees, over Jonathan's shoulder, was a figure in the shadows. The outline of a man she hadn't seen for years began to take shape. It wasn't the phantom of a fourteen-year-old boy, or another borrowed body—it was Tiago himself.

The Dark Angel took a place beside Jonathan. He was wearing black snow pants and a thick sweatshirt, fitted to the scenery like a fish to water. He was born into an ancient forest beneath mountains older than the Himalayas, where the rivers cut deep into the rocks, and the roots were an interwoven song. It was Tiago who had been raised in the North Country, not Lexi. Standing in this province of the simulation was the same as walking through his memories.

Tiago folded his hands and rubbed his wrist. Though he had been in his thirties when he stopped aging, he looked younger. He had a baby face, masked only by the beard that covered his playful smile. His shoulders were hunched—an odd sight beside Jonathan's towering height. Tiago wasn't a man who liked to take up space, yet his presence sucked up all the air.

"Hello, Lexi," Tiago said. It was the voice from the recording with Alexandria. Soft and kind. It matched his face.

"It's really you," she said.

"You could say that."

She shouldn't be surprised that he had appeared. It was what Lexi wanted, after all; a meeting with the Dark Angel. She hadn't expected a face-to-face. It made him vulnerable. She tried to compose herself.

"Mai gave you my message." It wasn't a question so much as a statement. Lexi was surprised that the reporter had followed through on their agreement, and so quickly. Mai had made it sound like Tiago was impossible to reach.

Apparently, the devil honored his deals.

"I did want to speak with you," he said, tilting to his head as if listening to an unknown voice. "Unfortunately, I'm here for a different reason. What do you know about Azi?"

"Azi?" Her face twisted in puzzlement. She racked her brain for details on the assistant, but nothing substantial emerged. She knew his job, what he looked like, and that he didn't think clones were people. Other than that, she didn't know much about the man she interacted with daily.

"Not much, I take it," Tiago said, watching her closely. "I trained him. He's smart, but stubborn. A very black-and-white way of thinking."

"Funny, someone just accused me of that."

"He doesn't like it when the rules are broken," Tiago continued, ignoring Lexi like everyone else. "And you've broken a few rules."

"What rules have I broken?" Lexi asked. "Artemis is the reason I'm here. I was perfectly fine with my life before she pulled me into *your* mess. Maybe you should take it up with your wife."

"I do."

Lexi blinked. "What?"

"Where do you think she goes when she comes here? She talks to me."

Lexi stumbled back. Jonathan twitched as if to lunge forward and catch her, but he saw something in her eyes. She was mad at him too. He was no different than the Senex. He had been keeping secrets from her. Nobody trusted her with the truth. They used it as a weapon, revealing it only when the timing suited them.

"All this time, we've been trying to find you," Lexi said, "and Artemis already did. No wonder she didn't want Mostafa coming with her."

Tiago gave a small, almost indifferent lift of his shoulders. "She always finds me."

Lexi threw up her hands. It wasn't their love story that nauseated her. Tiago and Artemis deserved each other: they were both duplicitous schemers. What outraged her was the ease with which they controlled her life.

In Greek mythology, the gods played with humans the way children played with toys. They could move, control, and determine people's fates. The consequences meant nothing to immortals because they never paid a price for their actions. Tiago and Artemis couldn't be hurt. They couldn't die. As good as their intentions might have been, the stakes weren't high enough for them to practice caution. The Iron Dreamers were a means to an end. A tool for their self-righteous crusade.

"Has anything you ever said been true?" Lexi asked.

"Everything I say is true," Tiago replied.

"Then why is he here?" she asked, pointing to Jonathan. "I thought you said I was putting everyone at risk by telling him what was going on, and then you went and did it anyway."

Tiago looked to Jonathan with polite curiosity. Maybe he had forgotten that the Iron Dreamer was there. "Jonathan doesn't know the full story," Tiago said. "A few of the broad strokes, but nothing specific."

The first sign of genuine emotion bloomed on Jonathan's face. He hadn't dealt with the Senex as much as Lexi had, and wasn't familiar with their annoying tendencies. He didn't like to be spoken about as if he wasn't in the room, either.

"What are you not telling me?" Jonathan asked.

"You're distracting me," Tiago said, rubbing the back of his wrist. He turned to Lexi, his voice becoming urgent. "You need to pull yourself out like you did the first time. You need to do it now."

She tried not to sound scared. "What's going on?"

"Azi is trying to kill you."

Jonathan stepped between them as if Tiago was the one trying to harm her. "*What*?" he growled. "You never said anyone was trying to kill her."

"I didn't think he would do it today," Tiago said, as if that were an explanation. He walked up to Lexi and placed his hands on her shoulders. "You're suffocating. You need to pull, or you'll die. I can't stop it from here."

"Y-you're lying," she stammered.

"I have no reason to do that."

Lexi was perfectly safe in the Nest. Her guards were at the entrance, and Artemis and Mostafa were lying beside her. But why did she have guards? It hadn't been explained to her. If it was because of Tiago, why was he trying to save her now? Maybe something *was* wrong, and Azi had another agenda. If Lexi pulled herself out and everything was fine, no harm, no foul. If Azi was trying to kill her, then she needed to leave.

She weighed the bet, and it wasn't worth the gamble.

Lexi dropped to her knees, sinking deep into the snow. It was hard to believe that the last time she had attempted this maneuver was over six months ago. Tonight was eerily calm. The lake glittered as if all was right with the world. She reached for the back of her neck, groping for a cord that wasn't there. It was on a different plane of existence.

How was she supposed to reach it?

"This is stupid," she complained. "What am I supposed to be grabbing?"

"It's like waking from a dream," Tiago said, kneeling beside her. "You have to imagine yourself waking up, and then you have to reach for it. It's best to mirror the motions and move your arm here. Hurry. You only have a few seconds."

Lexi's teeth chattered, but not from the cold.

Tiago held out his arm, stopping Jonathan from approaching. Jonathan shot him an angry scowl. He was half a foot taller than Tiago, and could easily overpower him, but he obliged. The two of them looked down on her like looming watchtowers.

Lexi searched the back of her neck, imaging herself lying on an old cot in the future. She pictured a honeycomb ceiling and the rough texture of a thin mattress. She stretched. Like digging for a lost memory, she reached into the dark of her mind. A sharp pain shot through her skull. A familiar blue light bled through the trees like maple syrup—slow and sticky. It was working, but she needed to reach the light faster.

Something was wrong with her other arm. Her body was groggy, moving through a heavy fog. She took a breath and screamed, throwing her body forward to yank the cord with her one good arm. The tension released, and a hard blanket pressed upon her mouth.

No, not a blanket.

Her *balat*.

Azi is leaning over her. His onyx eyes are empty, as if he's only distantly aware of what he's doing. He restrains Lexi's right arm, blocking the controls of her balat. With her free arm she claws at her face, trying to pull the suit down, but her lips are met by the immovable wall of programmable metal.

Tears well in her eyes. The cot squeaks against the floor, but no one rushes to her aid. Her lungs are empty. In a few seconds, she'll die.

She shoots a furious glare at Azi, staring him down in her last moments. She may not be able to stop him, but she won't make it easy. Let him watch. Let him live with the guilt of murder for the rest of his unnaturally long life.

But then Azi's body is thrown through the air.

Lexi jerks forward, Azi's grip still around her wrist. He pulls her shoulder out of the socket as he flies over a nearby engineer. His body punches through a holographic screen and slams into the wall. The engineer jumps out of his chair, finally jolted by an event taking place in the Nest.

A set of hands grab her. She feels fingers press against her arm, and the nanites recede back to her chest. She gasps for air. It stings like fire. Chen lowers her carefully to the cot and runs toward Azi, holding a curved blade at his throat.

Azi is slumped on the floor, unconscious. The wall behind him shimmers and moves, the nanotechnology healing the damage before the structural integrity is compromised. They're nowhere near the vacuum of space, but Sol is a living organism, self-healing with an urgency that cannot afford risks.

Lexi coughs, trying to recalibrate the oxygen levels. She's about to thank Chen for saving her when she cracks open a watery eye and finds a woman at the foot of her cot instead. The woman's back is turned to her. Her shoulders rise and fall like crashing waves, having used all her energy to hurl a full-grown man into the air. Azi isn't moving. The woman may have broken his neck.

Lexi cradles her arm and croaks, "Thank you."

The woman turns. Her expression is guarded and hostile, but for once, it may not be aimed toward Lexi. Her cousin regards her and storms off, leaving Lexi speechless.

Gal?

CHAPTER SEVENTEEN

Lexi is sitting outside of Jonathan's pod when Mostafa finds her.

She's spent the last few weeks sitting on the hard floor of the Iron Dreamers. She doesn't know if this is where Jonathan is stored. The drawers all look the same and they aren't labeled. This is just where she was kept. One of the administrators told her that they tend to keep Iron Dreamers together if they are also in close proximity in Beta. Lexi and Jonathan were born in the same area, so this is the most likely location of his body.

Jonathan is the one piece of her hometown that lives. The one piece of her life that's actually real. She's spent most of her time lately in the Iron Sector, protecting his pod in fear that the council will choose him next.

The supply mission arrived a few days ago, but an Iron Dreamer had already been killed. Lexi wasn't in the room. She heard about it later—something about nobody wanting to deal with her emotional outburst. The guilt eats away at her. She's tried to decrease her breathing, but the numbers from her room haven't changed.

Mostafa takes a seat beside her on the floor. He follows her gaze in the dark, tilting his head to the drawer that Lexi has decided is Jonathan.

"It is weird," Mostafa says, musing.

"What's weird?" she asks.

"This." Mostafa waves a hand at the columns. "We could have built a bigger station to include the clones. Instead, we built a row of columns, and then another row, and then another. Before we knew it, we had 700,000 brains at our disposal. Why do we give them bodies?"

Maybe they shouldn't have made so many, then. How many Iron Dreamers does it take to design a force field, or nanotechnology? There couldn't be more than a few dozen people capable of such a feat.

Maybe the Senex just wanted a nation of people to rule over.

Lexi is too tired to engage in a philosophical debate. Her body is sore, and her shoulder is tender from having been dislocated by Azi. She's worn down by the justification for every choice made on Sol. She doesn't know what to do. Everyone makes sense when they explain their reasoning because the Senex have had years to assemble the morality of their positions, justifying them to each other and to themselves.

"The trial is starting," Mostafa says.

Lexi runs a shaky hand through her hair. It isn't long enough to pull into a ponytail, but it gives shape to her face and keeps her head warm. Years of lying submerged in amniotic fluid has turned her hair exceptionally soft.

"I'm not sure I want to go," Lexi says.

"You don't have to."

She shifts her hips nervously. "I, uh, thought you had come to chitchat."

"You want to talk?" he says, raising an eyebrow. "To me?"

"Sure."

Mostafa looks to the door. Life on Sol runs by a strict schedule. A shipment is late, and three people are killed. There is no flexibility, and the reminder causes his lips to press into a thin line. He leans over his legs and settles onto the floor, deciding that she's worth the trouble.

"We have time," he says.

Lexi smiles, too flustered to stop fidgeting. "Thanks."

"So, what do normal people talk about?"

She bursts with laughter. "How should I know? Even before this, country bumpkins like me weren't considered normal. There's a whole list of mainstream references I still don't know. It drives Michelle crazy."

"I'm a thousand years old, and I still don't know them."

"I guess you can check it out a few centuries from now. It'd be cool to watch a movie that was 15,000 years old," she says, imagining a pyramid being erected in a desert. "Imagine if the ancient Egyptians made movies. And the real Hatshepsut could explain what happened back then."

"They had movies."

Lexi jolts upright. "*What*? Are you telling me that technology existed in *ancient Egypt*?"

"No. I just wanted to see your face." He chuckles, pleased with himself. "I was going to tell you that aliens built the pyramids, but then I thought it might be too much."

"Yeah, I think so." Her giggles taper off as a sudden train of thought takes over. "You're the only one who's honest with me. I mean, you're dodgy about things, but you don't do it like everyone else." She picks at the edge of the balat around her wrist. "You might be my only real friend."

Mostafa pauses. "You have Jonathan."

"No, I don't. He's trapped somewhere in there, and he'll never come out."

"You'll be there soon," he says with a guarded tone. "If you still want that."

Lexi sighs, determined to lighten the mood. Things have been dreary enough lately. "Why would I want to leave when I have so much going on here?" she teases.

It could be the jitters of testifying at Azi's trial in an hour, or the longing that Lexi has felt from being away from the North Country for so long, but she could swear that Mostafa's open expression is a sign that he wants to talk.

Artemis had known where the Dark Angel was since the beginning, and she lied about it. She put Mostafa's reputation at risk, making him appear inept to the council. He never stood a chance. The net had already been cast before he entered the simulation. Lexi doesn't know what Mostafa and Artemis's relationship was like before the rise of the Dark Angel. If they had been close, then it would feel like a betrayal.

"It's not usually this interesting," Mostafa says, leaning back onto his hands. "Most days are boring. BetaVu is about as interesting as it gets around here."

"Is that why you all want to leave the solar system, because you're bored?"

"When humanity is anxious, we move. That's how we discovered continents."

"No, you. Do *you* want to leave?"

"Ah, I see." He smiles sweetly. In a voice that sounds suspiciously like flirting, he says, "You're digging to me."

"I'd like to know what you think," she says, trying to keep her cheeks from flushing. She hasn't seen that maneuver on his face before, like he has a secret that he wants to share with only her. She pulls at the balat around her ankle, though of course it doesn't move.

"I agree with Artemis," he says.

Lexi tries not to groan.

Mostafa releases a forced laugh. "It pains me too, believe me. I'm still upset with her. But Tiago's plans have been unreliable in the past. He jumps before looking. I don't like either option, but if there's anything I've learned, it's that the conditions change, but we're vulnerable to the same fallacies. Maybe it's best that we stay."

"People don't change," Lexi says.

"Well, that depends."

"On what?"

Mostafa turns to her with a curious expression. "On what you want."

"Good thing you have 18,000 years to figure that out."

"If time were our problem, then we would have figured it out by now. Stretching the day doesn't always make it more productive. We've fallen into routine and predictability, and it makes us feel safe. Many of the Senex are fine with the way things are." His eyes weave through the space between them, searching for answers. "What do you want?"

Lexi wants her life to go back to normal. Sol isn't her responsibility. She didn't burn the world, or assemble the makeshift replacement of it. If everything goes according to plan, then she won't have to help find a solution. She'll be long gone, lost to the storyline of the past, and back to a place where she knows what to do.

The immediate challenge is protecting the Iron Dreamers. She can no longer bear to think of them. There are so many. Capturing her uncle ensures their safety, and wipes her hands clean of the charge. No one person should be held responsible for so many unsuspecting victims just trying to go about their day.

Lexi draws her shoulders together and shrinks into herself. "I want to go home," she says.

Mostafa's gaze drifts past the columns. "I understand."

"Would you come visit?" she asks, sounding too eager. She lowers her voice to keep from sounding like a little girl. "I mean, when I'm back in the North Country."

"It could compromise your assimilation into the simulation. I would be a reminder of Sol, and the outside conditions. Don't you want to forget?"

"I don't want to forget everything," she assures him, though she doesn't know what she means. "Would you visit?"

He regards her with a hint of fascination. It could be a medical fascination. He did study psychology, after all. "If you want that," he says.

"I do."

"Then I'll come."

Lexi bumps her shoulder into him. It's like pressing against a steel tower. He doesn't look at her, but leans into it, swaying gently alongside the low hum of the Iron Dreamers' columns. It's the largest collection of water on Sol. The Iron Dreamer pods are a self-contained network independent of the rest of the station, recycling every molecule within their own ecosystem. So long as the power stays on, the Iron Dreamers will never starve.

Lexi expects silence, hours of it, and is secretly hoping that she and Mostafa can sit in harmony forever when Mostafa's hollow dings. He huffs irritably at the interruption.

"The Luna delegates have arrived," he says, reading the screen. "We need to meet them in the transport bay."

"Not me too?" she asks.

"The only interaction they'll have with you is at the trial, where you'll answer a few questions and that will be it. If you want to garner sympathy from the Lunans, they should have more interaction with you."

She rolls her head at the additional layer of political intrigue. "Why am I not surprised this is another manipulation tactic?"

"Everything is," he says with a half-hearted shrug. "It's not always nefarious. Saying hi to a stranger on a hiking trail doesn't mean you're trying to manipulate them. You just want them to feel friendly toward you. It's the same with these small interactions. If you don't take control of the narrative, it leaves room for other people to do it."

Lexi frowns. "That's a sad way to view the world."

"The world is dead." Mostafa snaps the hollow to his side and stands, holding out a hand to Lexi.

She looks to his palm. His hands aren't like Artemis's. Mostafa's are smooth and soft, lacking the minefield of callouses. He wasn't trapped on Earth for as long, nor was he responsible for mechanical work on Sol.

Lexi reaches up and is surprised by the warmth of his touch. His fingers wrap around her wrist, and he pulls her swiftly to her feet. She's seen him compete against Zuchiris in wallball, but hadn't realized how strong he is until she's pulled off the ground like a featherweight. She tries not to picture what muscles lie beneath his balat.

"Why is there a Luna delegation here?" Lexi asks.

"Zuchiris was supposed to explain this to you."

"He might have, but I don't always understand what he's saying. I think he gave me a book on the history of the Mining Boom treaty."

Mostafa snorts quietly. "If you ask him to say it differently, he'll try a few methods until one of them works. Just tell him that a book doesn't help."

"Ah, he's direct."

"Very." Mostafa presses a hand to the wall and the door melts away. They make their way down the hall, arm in arm, heading in the direction of the cargo bay.

"Why do I need Luna's sympathy for the trial?" Lexi asks. "Who cares what they think?"

"We're not permitted to prosecute Azi without their vote. He's one of theirs." His voice drops as if talking about a piece of property, or an animal.

Her brows furrow in confusion. "What does that mean?"

"Azi—the original one—died shortly after the construction of the Solarium in a depressurization incident. We weren't able to retrieve the body, but we had genetic samples and requested that Luna clone him."

"He's a *clone*?" Lexi asks, recoiling as if physically struck by the revelation. "Then why has he been giving me such a hard time?"

"I don't know. The cloning program is controversial," Mostafa says introspectively. "He may be a clone, but he still possesses the genetic material to be a Senex. The Azi you know is over five hundred years old. Clearly he was battling something within himself. We should have caught it sooner."

Lexi scoffs. "What a hypocrite. We were the same the whole time, and he was looking down on me. Why would someone behave like that?"

"People will find any difference between themselves and others. It's your skin, then your country, then your town, narrowing the population until they've moved so far down the line that all that's left is themselves."

"You're saying Azi felt alone?"

"Possibly."

Lexi pictures the original Azi floating through the darkness, spinning head over feet past Jupiter and Saturn, frozen for all eternity. One day he might be sucked into a planet's orbit and burn up in the atmosphere, or fall into the gravitational well of a star. But space is mostly empty. Sol could be long gone, and Azi's body would still be floating through the universe, preserved in its ghostly state.

Mostafa guides Lexi around a corner. The pull of gravity is stronger here; they're moving toward the outer edge of the station. Mostafa opens a room that is not designed like any other chamber on Sol. Instead of conserving light and energy, the expansive room is brightly lit with gentle yellow lights. The walkway at their feet stretches to the back to meet a wall of stars.

Two groups stand on either side of the walkway huddled together. On the right are the Senex that Lexi is familiar with: dark balats and stern expressions. On the left are long flowing garments and boisterous voices. The men and women wear elaborate, colorful designs, which leave their skin visible in certain places. They don't wear balats. They appear unconcerned by their proximity to the nothingness.

The invisible barrier that separates a breathable atmosphere from the hostility of the void reaches high above them. There is room enough for a ship to land, but it's docked outside. A circular protrusion to the left appears to be the tail end of a ship. The ceiling features a large circular pattern of blue, pink, and yellow flowers that glow in multiple layers of rings. If this room were the entrance to a hotel in space, it would be a five-star resort in Hawai'i.

It's a waste of energy. The lives of two Iron Dreamers are apparently not worth more than keeping the lights on for the Lunans.

"This is something," Lexi says.

"They have a greater appreciation for art and music," Mostafa agrees. "They've taken liberties with their wing."

Jovial laughter erupts from the Lunans.

Artemis stands in the middle of them, conversing with the delegates like old friends. Her balat is set brighter than usual. The muted black she prefers is drowned by the bright waves of blue and green swirling across her chest. They soften the blue in her eyes, muting the otherwise sharp silver. Lexi has never seen her come to life—not from interacting with people. She's only seen Artemis operate under stress.

Artemis smiles upon seeing them, her face glowing with geniality. "Ah, here she is. Lexi Carvalho."

Lexi wants to correct her. Carvalho is not her last name, it's her mother's maiden name, but she's been advised to emphasize her connection to Tiago to help ensure her claim to his estate.

He has made Carvalho a powerful name.

"Lexi, I'm pleased to introduce you to the delegates of Luna. This is Freya, who assists the ambassador with the mining treaty." Artemis extends a hand toward a tall woman with fair skin and red hair, who nods politely. "And this is Priya Patel, who manages Luna's satellite stations around Earth." An older, dark woman with black hair woven into an intricate pattern above her head steps forward. Her cheekbones are sharp and her eyes hawk-like. Her fierce beauty is almost oppressive until she smiles and shakes Lexi's hand.

"Pleased to finally meet you, Lexi," Priya says sweetly. Her hands are warm.

Lexi notes that their last names are not always mentioned. It's reasonable, considering that many of the Senex either changed their names to those of famous figures when they boarded the orbiters, or were the only survivors of their entire family and don't want to be reminded of the people they lost.

"And this is Kai Ihaka," Artemis continues, sidestepping a tall figure. "Chancellor Nikau's first advisor."

A bald man with facial tattoos turns from another man with whom he was conversing. Kai's head is cleanly shaven, though the temperature on Sol is kept well below comfortable. The tattoos swirl around his face and eyes in a faded blue-black. He neither smiles nor frowns, simply regards Lexi with passive apathy.

"They've brought their support staff with them as well," Artemis continues, "who you will have more time to commune with after the trial has concluded." Artemis guides Priya away from the group, chatting loudly and happily, but Lexi knows her ways. She's pulling Priya to the side to speak with her discreetly, meaning that Priya is either the most likely to ally herself with Artemis, or the least.

The Lunans smell of flowers and spices. They press their fingers together in silent snaps. Lexi catches one of them and realizes that an image of her is being sent to his hollow. The snapping triggers a photograph. The support staff closes in and bombards her with questions.

"How are you enjoying life on Sol?"

"Have you been adjusting?"

"Is this what you imagined?"

Lexi presses her lips into a thin smile, uncomfortable with the attention. She lets their questions continue unanswered until Mostafa appears by her side. She takes his arm reflexively.

"We should make our way to the Council Chamber," he announces, gesturing toward the door and ushering them down the walkway.

A Luna woman in bright yellow garb places a hand on Mostafa's forearm, bumping Lexi's hand out of the way with a casual obliviousness that feels intentional.

The Lunan's face is round with large features. Isolated, none of them would work. Together, they weave an effortlessly harmonious face, one that is foreign yet familiar. The striking beauty is unlike anything Lexi has seen before. It is the first time that anyone has actually looked like one of the demigods of fate. She appears to be in her late twenties, but the youthfulness is masked by a maturity forged by the endless march of time.

Mostafa holds her gaze, the tension thick between them. "Hello, Isadora."

"Will you be joining us at Dorian's later?" she asks without greeting, as if they had been together only moments ago. "It would do well to have some fun after all this nasty business. I hear they've brewed their autumn special. That's your favorite, isn't it?"

"I'm afraid I have other arrangements," Mostafa says, in a clipped tone.

"Of course." Isadora lists her head lazily toward Lexi. Her smile is kind, but her expression is not. "To babysit Artemis's new...protégé?" The "p" is carried out with false hesitation. Isadora wants to say "pet."

"Woof," Lexi deadpans.

Mostafa straightens his neck, stifling a laugh, and says to Isadora, "I'll see you at the trial."

Isadora pouts, but releases his arm and returns to the rest of the delegates. She glides toward them like a ballerina, chatting excitedly despite the impending murder trial. Artemis gives Mostafa a quick, taunting rise of her eyebrows as she passes with Priya.

Mostafa waits for everyone to reach the end of the walkway before dropping his arms. He locks his hands behind his back and keeps a wide distance, reverting to his typically aloof behavior. The mask has returned.

"Ex-girlfriend?" she asks.

"That's not the word I would employ for it," he replies, distracted. "I thought they would use someone else."

Mostafa marches past her before she can ask for clarification.

They follow the delegation at a slower pace. The bubbling excitement of the Lunans can be heard from the hall. Lexi watches them with horrified fascination. "They know they're going to a trial, right?" she asks. "Why are they acting like we're going to a football game?"

"The Lunans are liberal with their cloning program," Mostafa answers. "If Azi is sentenced to death, they'll just make another one."

"That's how *everyone* is born?"

"The Senex are sterile," he says matter-of-factly. If Mostafa feels anything about losing his family and being unable to make a new one, the emotion is guarded. More likely, he's long since come to terms with being the last in his line. "The Iron Dreamers are technically capable, but childbirth is dangerous as it is; in a pod, it's nearly impossible. Cloning is the safest method to reproduce, and the final product is guaranteed."

"The final product," Lexi mimics.

Mostafa looks down to her, his face empty of warmth. "Anger is not the emotion you want to project. The fear from before would be ideal. The more pathetic you look, the more likely the Lunans are to side with you."

"Excuse me? I wasn't afraid, I just..."

Don't like Isadora.

"Azi can't be released," Mostafa says, sparing Lexi the admission. "The Dark Angel is following these events somehow, and he could use him. If the Lunans don't agree to take Azi, or space him, it could jeopardize our entire mission. You still care about what happens to the Iron Dreamers, yes?"

"Yes, of course."

"Then look pathetic."

Lexi attempts to hold on to her anger as a shield against the impending sense of dread, but genuine fear begins to chill her bones. She hasn't given much thought to Azi. The hypocrisy of his behavior when he himself is a clone is off-putting, but also not enough to strike terror. Her real concern is anyone who isn't on trial.

Who else hates her enough to try to kill her?

The Council Chamber is lit in the same color palette as the transport bay. Three circular rows of elevated seating surround a platform with a metallic image of Earth carved into the floor. The chamber is large and imposing, with high ceilings and no windows to provide any indication of where they are.

The delegation fills the empty seats in the front row. They continue chatting, as if they're in a movie theater and the trailers haven't started. Artemis takes a seat in the middle row alongside Priya. Their faces are polite, but Lexi knows Artemis well enough to identify a somber conversation from the crease forming between her brow.

"You're here," Mostafa says, leading her to a seat in the third row, next to the aisle.

The chair molds to her body like the sentinel chairs, but far more comfortable. It pulls closer to the workstation, aware of her height. A flat screen on the tables illuminates, pushing up a holographic image of Azi and the details of his arrest. She grips her armchair.

"It will be a long trial," Mostafa warns, sliding his hand in a graceful motion over the screen. "If you need anything, wave your hand like this, and food or water will be transported to you from underneath."

She arched an eyebrow. "I didn't know this place had take-out."

"Try not to abuse it," he says, and leaves to take a seat next to Artemis on the other side. It might have been a joke, but she can't tell.

Sol's council members arrive from the back, taking their places opposite the Luna delegation. Gal and Farhad are among them, sitting a few chairs from Hatshepsut, who waddles slowly to her seat, which rises from the ground in preparation. Lexi catches sight of Isadora. She sits beside Kai. She must be high-ranking if she's sitting next to a chancellor's advisor.

Within minutes, the chamber is packed. It buzzes with energy until two men approach the center platform with a stretcher between them. The stretcher hovers, seemingly suspended by an invisible cord. On it, a man lies on his back, motionless and unbound.

Azi.

The balat restrains him in the same way he tried to use Lexi's balat against her. There's a sick satisfaction from seeing his helplessness. One of the guards enters a command into his balat and Azi slides off the stretcher, dropping into a rigid stance. Even his fingers are locked in a wide spread. It must be terribly uncomfortable. The balat extends past his neck and his mouth. Only his eyes are visible.

The chamber hushes to deafening silence.

Isadora rises from her chair and walks toward the center. She takes a place beside Azi. Her brown, curly hair flows freely around her, appearing almost red in the lighting. She places a gentle hand on Azi's shoulder and gives him a reassuring smile. He seems to brighten from it, his eyes hopeful at the sight of her.

Isadora is Azi's lawyer.

She interlaces her hands and paces slowly, using the anticipation of her words to draw out the dramatic silence.

"My fellow Senex," she begins, "the circumstances that have brought us here are tragic, but not a crime. Azi Abba was acting in self-defense. Our laws allow a person to protect themselves when they feel that they are in danger, and Azi had no choice but to act in order to protect us from the forces that work to destroy everything we have built. As an engineer standing on the front line of the threats that move against us, he knew the danger and took action. The prosecution will attempt to convince you that this was an attempted murder, but that is far from what happened. I ask that you listen closely, examine the circumstances that have brought us here, and realize that Azi Abba was acting in self-defense."

Lexi jerks back in her chair as if slapped.

Self-defense is Isadora's strategy? She's alluding to the Dark Angel, using him as the real enemy. Lexi can understand her taking that angle, except that Isadora is attempting to connect Lexi to it, as if she's working with her uncle, and implying that Azi was justified in protecting not only himself from her, but the other Senex as well.

Isadora returns to her seat and a handful of the Luna delegation clap. Notably, Priya does not join them. It's Artemis's touch. She's weaving the web and planting seeds. Lexi hates it that she feels safe watching Artemis work. She can't help but feel that a greater force is protecting her—even if that greater force's intentions are ambiguous at best.

The trial crawls at a snail's pace. Lexi fades in and out of focus at the legal jargon. A man she doesn't know and wasn't listening to when he said his name acts as the prosecution. Instead of brief introductions and the interrogation Lexi had been expecting, Isadora and the prosecution go back and forth, presenting the evidence and their claims. It's not like the court proceedings Lexi used to watch on *CSI*. The lawyers don't call a witness for hours.

It's civil, boring, and pompous.

Azi remains motionless behind them. His body is frozen like stone on display. It seems cruel and torturous to keep him trapped in the same position for hours.

A flash of his face as he was watching her die sends shivers down her spine, and clarity strikes her like lightning.

Justice.

Isadora finally calls for a witness, and requests Gal. Lexi's cousin rises from her chair and approaches the center platform, ignoring Azi with every fiber of her being.

A representative from Sol and one from Luna hold Gal's right arm. Their heads dip and they focus on the screen on her balat. They're observing her vitals. It must be a lie detector feature. Gal doesn't seem to mind the security.

"Gal Carvalho," Isadora says, "you were the one who attacked Azi Abba, correct?"

"I object to the use of the word 'attack,' " Gal says.

"Noted, Miss Carvalho. Please tell us in your own words what happened."

Gal stares Isadora down and clicks her tongue, her defiance bouncing off the walls. "I had just completed my twenty-eighth mission in Beta cycle 2.3a when I heard a choking noise a few chairs down from me. When I removed my helmet, I saw Azi holding onto Lexi's arm. Her balat was initiating level three preservation mode."

"How did you know that it was a level three?" Isadora asks, walking toward the Luna delegation. "He could have been administering a stress medication, or addressing some other medical event within Beta. How do you know that Tiago wasn't attacking her, and using her body as a means to access Sol's control system?"

Gal's head twitches slightly. "Her body convulsed."

"Convulsed," Isadora echoes. "Why did you not simply ask Azi to stop? Why did you have to throw yourself at him and fracture his C2? Under normal circumstances, an attack of that magnitude would warrant imprisonment in your new installation. The Forest, correct? I believe that's what you call it."

Lexi's head snaps to Azi. She assumed his balat was in that position to restrain him, not to support his body. Azi has been *paralyzed*. Gal doesn't hold back. She is physically incapable of moderation. Lexi looks to Mostafa, who had already anticipated her reaction. He holds out a hand as if to say, "Relax, he's fine."

"I didn't have the time," Gal says. "If I had taken a second too long, then Lexi would have died. Any injuries Azi sustained could be fixed later. Lexi's death couldn't be fixed."

Isadora frowns dramatically, as if her confused performance is airing on national television. "But isn't Lexi a clone?"

"Yes."

"Then her death could be fixed."

Gal looks to Isadora with a stony expression. "By that definition, so could Azi's."

An amused murmur settles through the chamber. Hatshepsut slams her cane onto the floor and the excitement recedes. She gestures to Isadora to continue.

Isadora paces in the short distance between Azi and Gal. Seeing her cousin standing near Azi, she isn't sure how Gal was able to launch him so far.

"You're currently in a legal dispute with Lexi Carvalho over your family's estate, is that correct?" Isadora asks.

"Yes."

"You would be entitled to the largest estate on Sol if you won the claim, correct?"

"That's correct."

"Why would you attack Azi Abba so aggressively that you could paralyze a fellow Senex over the life of a clone?"

The shift in questioning is jarring. Lexi leans forward in her seat.

"I abhor violence," Gal says, her voice unsteady, but managing its stubborn resilience. "I thought we had agreed to end senseless murder. It's what separates us from the past."

"You abhor violence?" Isadora asks. "Interesting coming from someone who paralyzed a man."

"She *is* my cousin. I'm not going to let her die."

Lexi falls back into her seat.

Gal has been fighting her for months, yet the moment she thought Lexi was in trouble, she risked everything to save her. She doesn't even regret it. Her jaw is stubbornly set, flicking away Isadora's attempts to discredit her with an unwavering commitment to her personal code of ethics—however those are arranged.

Gal withdraws from the stage. She's not pleased with the turn of events. Lexi knows the expression. It's a common one in the northeast.

Loyalty is currency, asshole.

When Lexi is called by the prosecution, she walks to the center platform. She feels every set of eyes on her. If anyone was falling asleep before, they're awake now. She keeps her distance from Azi. She doesn't want to risk standing too close, or seeing his face. The last time they locked eyes, his were empty. She never wants to see them again.

Since Lexi was in Beta during the "incident" and only semi-conscious, the questions are limited. She provides the play-by-play, describing a night of snowmobiling while carefully excluding the unexpected appearance of the Dark Angel. When Sol's prosecutor is finished, Isadora approaches. The bright yellow of her dress is a shocking contrast to the dark balats of Sol's residents. Lexi entertains the possibility that she'll be a sympathetic ear.

"Lexi Carvalho," Isadora says, playing with each syllable on her lips. "That's not your name, though, is it?"

Lexi tenses. "Uh, no."

"Carvalho is your mother's maiden name. Your father is from Québec. His last name is Bouchard. So, you're actually Lexi Bouchard, or is it Alexandria Bouchard? It gets so confusing."

"Lexi Carvalho is fine."

"Yes, I'm sure it is." Isadora turns toward the assembly, extending her hands as if welcoming a hug. "The Carvalho estate is quite an accomplishment. Tiago Carvalho, may he rest in peace, played a pivotal role in our success, and pushed the boundaries of what was possible. We couldn't be more grateful for his contributions."

Luna wants to believe that Tiago is dead, and that the Dark Angel is some unknown vigilante with comparable skills. Lexi is struggling to reconcile the actions of a legend with the terrorist who's trying to keep her safe. To everyone else, he might be the Dark Angel, but to Lexi, he is a guardian angel.

Without his warning, she could be dead.

Isadora turns to Lexi. "If Gal were to be convicted of attempted murder, your claim to the Carvalho estate would be uncontested, would it not?"

Lexi sucks in air between her teeth, realizing the image that Isadora is trying to paint of her: that she has ulterior motives and cannot be trusted. She looks to Artemis, unable to resist the urge to be saved. Artemis raises her eyebrows and shifts, signaling that Lexi should shrug off the accusation.

"I'm not really sure how it works," Lexi says truthfully.

"That's how it works," Isadora replies. "Have you heard of the trolley problem?"

"No."

"It's a thought experiment. A trolley is heading toward five people who are tied to the track. If you pull a lever, then the trolley is diverted to a different track that will kill just one person. Do you pull the lever and kill someone, or do nothing, and let five people die?"

Lexi is sure there is a right answer, she just doesn't know what it is. "I don't know," she says.

"Are you aware that your presence consumes excess resources? And that for every month you're here, an Iron Dreamer is scratched until additional supplies arrive?"

Lexi waits for an objection from Sol, but the prosecutor does nothing. The treatment was the same for Gal. Either criminal trials are so rare in the future that every ounce of theatrics is squeezed for entertainment value, or none of the Senex were lawyers before they came to Sol.

"Yes, I'm aware," Lexi says.

"The longer you're here, the more people die—people of impact who invent and create art for all of humanity. If Azi Abba pulls the lever to protect the lives of five people, is he committing a crime? Or are we the criminals for sitting back and letting them die for one person?" Isadora turns to the congregation and bows, and walks off the platform.

Lexi is left speechless.

Isadora didn't ask her a question. She just wanted to highlight the price of allowing Lexi to live, and bring to light the value of the other Iron Dreamers in comparison. They are inventors and artists, and she's the niece of a celebrated engineer.

Nepotism.

Lexi doesn't want to give Isadora the satisfaction of seeing her rush off the platform to her chair. Fortunately, nobody notices as they whisper amongst themselves. A man with skin dark as night rises from his seat with the Sol delegation and moves to the platform.

"My fellow Senex," the man begins. "Thank you for your attention. The ruling is as follows: Azi Abba has been found guilty of attempted first-degree murder, and is sentenced to death by spacing at 0200 hours. Thank you."

Azi may have screamed.

With half his head covered, it's hard to tell if he's furious or terrified. Without mayhem or protest from the congregation, the two guards drag him away like a lifeless marionette. The assembly rises from their seats.

Lexi's hands grip the side of her chair, suspended in emotions with which she has never grappled. She's beginning to understand Alexandria and the wild unrest capable of raging within her chest. Whether by her doing or not, another person will die.

She checks the time on her screen and gasps.

It's 01:54.

"You don't have to go," Mostafa says, standing over her.

"Yes, I do."

Lexi pushes her chair back and walks past him. Her mind is in a daze as she follows the crowd of people down a set of halls. It's like walking through a dream. The room they stop at is dark, small, and bare, with a set of large doors leading to the void. The doors fly open as Azi enters. The chamber is pressurized. It must be where technicians can exit the station for repairs.

Azi's sentence is repeated by a different man. Words are spoken. Priya embraces him. The hug is weirdly intimate, given what Lexi had assumed was a professional relationship, but maybe they had been friends before. Priya gives him a sad smile and rejoins the assembly.

Azi is given no last words.

They exit the room and go into the hallway. The guards follow last, and seal the door. Azi remains in his rigid stance, his eyes darting between council members and the Luna delegation. Even at his execution, they refuse to lower his balat and release his head.

Azi flies out through the back doors.

The trial is concluded.

Azi is dead.

CHAPTER EIGHTEEN

Rose screamed.

Lexi's sister jumped onto the bed, squealing with delight at the queen-size mattress. Most apartments their parents rented in Portugal had twin-size beds. Lexi and Rose typically shared a windowless room or couch, while their parents pushed two twin-size beds together in the bedroom. This place was much larger, and equipped with all of the American amenities.

Rose ran to the refrigerator and held a glass beneath the ice dispenser. "There's no reason to go back!" she chirped.

Lexi's mother didn't explain how they found such a luxurious apartment in the middle of town. Tourism in Porto had boomed since Lexi was a kid. Real estate companies were buying up properties and renting them to tourists, leaving the locals with inflated housing prices that they couldn't afford.

A lot had changed.

"Alright, everyone unpack and we'll go get some food," her mother said.

Rose was an organized individual. That was just her programming. She laid out the clothes on her side of the closet, and folded the rest in drawers. If there wasn't order, there could be no peace. Lexi threw her bag in the closet.

"You're not unpacking?" Rose asked, frowning. "We're going to be here for like, two weeks."

Lexi shrugged.

The truth was, Beta was feeling less and less real. Lexi was gradually losing her ability to focus. She was watching a movie that she already knew the ending to, and faded in and out of interest depending on the scene. Every delayed flight, water bottle, and cloud in the sky was a design by the engineers. It was a pre-planned world without risk. Beta was a fantasy.

The real threat was outside.

Azi may have been killed, but there were players in Sol who wanted to see the Dark Angel succeed. What if they captured them? What if they captured her uncle?

The trial had woken an unsettling angst within her. The Dark Angel had caused far more problems for the Senex than a loyal servant like Azi, yet they had discarded him so easily. The punishment for Tiago would be more severe. She didn't have the imagination to conceive whatever torture the Senex could conjure. The punishment for Lexi, if she failed, would be no different.

It was either her or him.

Artemis was nearby, as were Mostafa and dozens of others. The sentinels had taken their places throughout Porto as bartenders, tour guides, students, and city workers. Everyone was aware that it was a trap. It couldn't be this easy. But they had to take the bait anyway. If the Dark Angel was signaling a move in Porto, then that was where they needed to be.

Her family walked the cobblestone streets to one of their favorite restaurants on the eastern side of town. Where New England excelled at brick and durability, Porto took every opportunity to be the quaint artistic city of the north. The sidewalks were laid with elaborate patterns of swirls and designs that stretched throughout the city, giving Lexi an excuse to keep her head down. She watched her feet stroll over the designs.

The city was built on a hill overlooking the Douro River. Every road in Porto was sloped. Her parents liked to stay near the top of the hill to avoid the tourists. It may not have been what Porto truly looked like a thousand years ago. It might have been a small beach town with a thousand people. The fact that the engineers cared enough to provide such unnecessary intricacy for the Iron Dreamers' spoke of their commitment to authenticity.

Her family sat around the table, reading the dinner menu. Her mother's Portuguese was much better than Lexi and Rose's, and her father didn't speak a word of it. Lexi remembered more when she was a kid, but as schedules became busier, her family had spent less and less time in Portugal.

Lexi rubbed the side of her head, struggling to remember the translations. She had asked an engineer if the language could be downloaded into her brain—or any other skill, for that matter—and the engineer had laughed. That wasn't how it worked.

Her parents chatted excitedly, deciding what tapas to order for the table. Rose argued with them a few times. She was a half-hearted vegetarian, and didn't want to order beef. Lexi had been too busy with the events on Sol to take a moment to process the loss of her family. She missed them. She missed her mother's hugs and her father's laugh. She even missed Rose's terrible cooking. Could Lexi miss something that had never been real?

Tears welled in her eyes.

"Oh, honey, what's wrong?" her mother asked.

Lexi covered her face, overwhelmed by the warmth of her mother's words. That was what she missed most: *love*.

No one on Sol cared about her. No one loved her. Look at how they treated Azi—a man who had lived among them for centuries. They held a sham trial and tossed him out the door. Lexi wouldn't live half that long, and she would receive a fraction of the compassion. She was alone in a world she didn't recognize.

Lexi's body shook as she attempted to contain the waves of grief crashing upon her. The love had never been real. It was a memory of the Senex that they themselves had long forgotten. She was mourning the loss of her family as they sat across the table from her. She was mourning what never was, and what would never be.

"It's nothing," Lexi said, wiping her eyes. "A migraine, I think."

"I have some ibuprofen," her mother said, digging through her bag.

Lexi took the pills, though they would do nothing. Unless an engineer dosed her with a sedative, it would be a figment of her imagination.

The server approached their table and their mother ordered. Rose's ear for other languages wasn't great, but she cared about food.

"I thought we were getting fish?" Rose asked.

"Codfish is for Christmas Day," her mother said.

Lexi excused herself and headed to the bathroom.

She walked past the other tables, wondering who among them were Iron Dreamers. Statistically speaking, none. But if there was even one, would they want to know the truth? That they were in a pod a thousand years in the future, orbiting the sun in a technological wonder constructed from the ashes of humanity's crimes?

Or did they want to enjoy their meal?

Lexi ran down the stairs and slid the wooden doors closed behind her. The bathroom was a dark sanctuary, with a black sink and a wicker basket for towels. She placed her hand on the counter and closed her eyes. The door behind her slid open.

Mostafa.

Lexi jumped. She reached behind him and closed the door. It didn't lock, it was merely the entrance to the bathroom. On either side of the sink was a private toilet with additional doors. Technically speaking, anyone could walk in on them.

"What are you doing here?" she hissed. "And why do you look like you?"

"I prefer my own skin." He moved to the sink and leaned against the wall. He crossed his arms and looked her up and down.

He wore a dark brown leather jacket and jeans. She could see why he preferred his own skin. She preferred it too. It was startling to see him in regular clothes. She had only seen him in the balat. Once upon a time, he had lived on Earth. He had worn jeans and sneakers, and talked to girls in bars. Lexi was the outsider. She was the one walking through their memories.

"I was told to tell you to 'get it together,' " he said, mimicking the impatience of a familiar voice.

"Artemis," Lexi snorted, wrapping her arms around herself. "Is she the server?"

"No. I think she's learned to keep her distance." Mostafa bounced against the wall, deciding whether or not to step forward and comfort Lexi, or give her space. "Happy birthday."

She gave him an amused look. "You know my birthday?"

"Artemis had something planned," he said quickly, shrugging it off. "Of course, our current predicament cancelled that."

"She doesn't like it when I'm mad at her."

"She doesn't," he agreed. "In your country, you're allowed to drink now, yes?"

"Not in the United States. My parents let me drink here, though, since the legal age is eighteen in Portugal. Not that it matters."

Lexi buried her face in her hands. She knew that her parents weren't real, and never had been. She knew that her sister was a phantom, and Gui and Michelle were probably programmed to be her friends. She knew that nothing she had done had mattered until now. This was the first time she had done anything real, and it was just to be bait as the real powers battled it out.

"Are you going to be okay?" Mostafa asked. The kindness was unfamiliar to him. The words spilled from his mouth as if it pained him to say each word.

"I just keep thinking about Tiago," she confessed. "Are they going to kill him? I mean, he did try to save me. Feels kind of weird to aid in his capture, or whatever it is I'm supposed to be doing."

"Gal saved you."

It pained her to admit that he was right. "Yeah, but Tiago warned me."

"You would never have been in that position if he hadn't started this. You would be an Iron Dreamer in a pod, enjoying a holiday vacation with her family and living a normal life."

The assumption for months had been that Tiago's desire was to free the Iron Dreamers. He had argued for years to end the Beta program, but his pleadings fell on deaf ears, and then he disappeared. He killed the first man in a pod only by accident. The intention was to pull the Iron Dreamer out of Beta. He wanted to free them.

"What if he's right?" she asked, holding out her arms. "This is kind of messed up."

Mostafa stiffened. "Okay, I'm all ears."

"What do you mean?"

"You don't like the plan we have, so what's the new one? Do we stop Tiago? Do we do nothing? Where would you like to place 700,000 people? Tiago's plan. Artemis's plan. Either way, it's a course of action with consequences. What's your decision?"

Lexi blinked. She hadn't expected to be put on the spot. She didn't have a plan. She didn't know what to do. That was the whole point. That was the *problem.*

"I-I don't know," she stammered.

Mostafa pushed off the wall. He paced in the tight space, keeping a distrustful eye on the door. The bathroom was downstairs, and they could see through the thin space between the doors. No one was spying, yet he was wary.

"It doesn't add up," Mostafa said, pressing a finger to the mirror to check the thickness. "Tiago knows the variables better than most. He knows the population, and our limitations. He can't release the Iron Dreamers. It would kill us."

"Maybe he's lost his mind."

Mostafa smiled, amused by an inside joke that predated her birth. "He can be crazy, but not stupid."

"What is he to you?"

A crease formed between Mostafa's eyebrows. "He's not everyone's uncle. If I had been his family, or had any technical skills, I would have had a much easier time. Sol wasn't always what it is now. In the early days, the only people who mattered were scientists and mechanics, or anyone with skills that could be directly applied to building a space station. It didn't matter if you were a Senex, if you couldn't contribute to the construction, you were useless. I thought they were going to space me to save air. I survived by putting my faith in someone I knew would be important one day."

Someone pulled on the door and Lexi slammed it shut. "One minute!"

A voice on the other side barked in German.

"How did you survive?" she asked.

"Hatshepsut," he replied, lifting his shoulders quickly. "I did whatever she asked. When a bureaucratic system was eventually structured and she became the leader, she ordered that a room be built for me. I had made a wise investment."

The pieces fell into place. The colors that painted the image of Mostafa and his relationship to the High Councilor were beginning to make sense. Not everyone could have a technical mind. What happened to those who couldn't rebuild civilization with their bare hands?

"You didn't say what Tiago is to you," Lexi pointed out. "All of you have a way of answering questions without actually answering them."

"Maybe it's because we're afraid of what you'll think of us." Mostafa lifted his head suddenly, turning an ear to the ceiling.

Lexi couldn't hear anything, but she felt that an important moment had interrupted. "What is it?"

"Artemis." Mostafa gave Lexi a stern but empathetic look. He took her hand. "We need to go."

"What about my family? I can't just leave them here."

"You have to."

Lexi had to leave her family to find Tiago, but she had to leave them in more ways than one. She had to let go. She had to face the truth.

Mostafa had watched every single person he loved die. It might have been the slow ticking of time that took them, or a blast from two nuclear wars. One way or another, everyone he had ever cared about was taken from him. Loss was a heartbreak with which he was familiar.

"Okay, one min—" His head shifted, hearing another message from the ceiling. His face darkened, adjusting to the orders. "We need to leave."

The man waiting on the other side of the bathroom scowled at them as if they were newlyweds taking advantage of a dark room. Mostafa pushed Lexi through the downstairs level and found the back door leading to the street.

In this world, Lexi was strong enough to keep up with him. She followed him down the road, turning right into the shopping district. The sun had set and the humidity was moving in. The old lampposts shone dimly in the fog. It was a Monday night and most of the stores were closed.

The streets were empty. Lexi didn't know what they were following, or where it was leading.

They ran until Mostafa flung an arm into her chest.

Three bodies lay on the sidewalk behind a row of cars. Lexi couldn't see their faces, or tell if they were breathing. Mostafa scanned the road and cautiously approached them. He held a finger in front of the two older men's noses. The third person's head was slumped. Lexi couldn't see his face, but the shine in his messy black hair suggested a teenager.

"These two were sentinels. They were pulled." Mostafa swore under his breath and said, "Run."

"I'd rather you stay," Tiago said.

A figure stepped out of the shadows. His unique body language was unmistakable. He stepped out of the fog smiling bashfully, as if he wasn't the force wielding the danger.

"What have you done?" Lexi asked. Somehow, she knew that Tiago was to blame for the bodies. It could have been the way he folded his hands, or the shy expression on his face, but he radiated guilt.

The three bodies were hunched, heads leaning over each other's shoulders. They looked to be asleep. She could swear their chests were moving. How was it that sentinels were booted from their phantom bodies? Lexi didn't doubt Tiago's skill, but the multitasking of all these achievements was stacking up. Someone was helping him.

Boole.

Tiago took a step forward, and Mostafa held a protective arm in front of Lexi. Tiago held up his hands to signal that he was going to stop moving, and only wanted to reveal what was in his pocket. He pulled out a small flash drive. Compared to the technology on Sol, a flash drive was incongruous. It was old and ugly, and didn't belong in the thirty-second century.

"This will put an end to the lies," Tiago said, holding the drive up. "Once I install this into an Iron Dreamer, their life support systems will shut down, and Beta's programming will be scratched. We can start over, and move away from slavery. We can't keep doing that. If we end it today, we can use the time to build up the resources for clones to live with us, and let them reproduce naturally. This is our chance for the human race to start over. We can go back to what we were."

"You're going to *kill* them?" Lexi asked in abject horror. "I thought you said you were trying to free the Iron Dreamers."

"I never said that," Tiago said, his voice thick with emotion. "I don't want to do this, Lexi."

Mostafa's mouth parted for words that escaped him. His arm remained locked in front of a stunned Lexi.

Tiago studied them. Judging by his calm, collected manner, their unsettled expressions were about what he'd expected. He had prepared a speech. Perhaps he thought he could convince them to side with him. A smile was tugging at the corner of his lips, foreshadowing what he anticipated to be an inevitable victory, when he caught sight of motion over Lexi's shoulder.

Tiago's face dropped. A mixture of pain and longing etched into the creases of his face. A silent testament to years of pain that never left his body. His eyes followed the figure until she passed by Lexi and Mostafa. Artemis took her place between the two opposing forces—where she had always belonged.

Against her better judgment, Lexi released a sigh of relief.

Artemis wore a red leather jacket and black boots. Her hair was tied into a high ponytail, the blonde tips bouncing in the low light. She looked ten years younger. Was this what Artemis and Tiago had looked like in the old world? Just a couple of kids from the woods.

Artemis pressed her lips together, but her cheeks betrayed her. "Hey, Ti."

"Hello, Artemis," Tiago replied, also unable to suppress his smile.

It pained Lexi to see. For all his faults, he loved Artemis. He feared her. He respected her. Lexi felt like she was intruding on a private moment.

Artemis held out her palm. "Give me the catalyst."

"Oh." Tiago's gaze fell to his feet. "I was hoping you'd want to talk."

"About what?"

"Your day. Life on Sol. Whatever you want."

Her arm dropped. She sighed, or snorted—Lexi couldn't tell. The complexity of their relationship was too lived-in to be untangled by outsiders. Mostafa and Lexi were frozen in place, caught between the ancient forces of a hurricane and a tsunami.

"I woke up an hour before my alarm," Artemis said, swinging her arms in an amusingly innocent way. "I spoke with the shield mechanic about the nitrogen layer. And the maples are being tapped. We should have that in the next few months. Remember real maple syrup? Not that grainy shit from New York. The real stuff. They've mapped the shift vectors for the warp drive."

The last words punched through the air like thunder. Tiago's eyes grew wide. Whatever Artemis was talking about, she had saved the best for last.

"But the Einstein field equations—" Tiago said.

"They're past that now. Construction was set to begin, but it's been delayed because of..." Artemis twisted dramatically, holding her arms out.

Tiago put the flash drive back into his pocket. His focus grew distant. He took a step to the side, shifting his weight as he labored on a thought. Mostafa watched his hands, preparing to jump at a moment's notice and steal whatever the catalyst was, but Artemis flashed him a warning glare.

The exchange with Tiago balanced on a tightwire. Any movement could snap the tension.

"What's going on?" Lexi whispered.

"She thinks she might be able to change his mind," Mostafa said, his voice so quiet that it was barely audible. "We're about to find out what's really going on."

Tiago paced back and forth, jittery with excitement. He was a scientist to his core, intrinsically curious and thoughtful. In light of the emerging information, he was consumed by a whirlwind of fresh ideas that he couldn't help but tinker with. His hands were meant to fiddle with inventions.

Maybe Artemis could reach him. Maybe she *could* put an end to it.

"Trappist One?" he asked. "Incredible."

"We can't have that power," Artemis said. "We'll do there what we did on Europa. We'll take the local ingredients and plant life from it, and then we'll move on to the next system and do it again. We'll do it *everywhere.* In a billion years, there could be a hundred civilizations sprouting across the galaxy, and we'll be the empire that rules them all."

Tiago crossed one leg in front of the other. "A billion years is a long time from now, Arty. We could evolve past suffering. Look how far we've come in just a thousand years."

Artemis choked a hard laugh. "I know you saw what they did to Azi. We're not past anything."

Lexi looked to Mostafa. The trial wasn't aired, it was a private session. Even the residents of Sol didn't know much about what had happened. Mostafa shrugged, unsurprised that Tiago had found a way to observe the events that had transpired.

"We're united now," Artemis continued. "That's the only reason we're not at each other's throats. But as soon as we're going to other systems and planting our flags in the dirt, the old wars will come right back. We haven't evolved. There are no biological markers to indicate that any substantial psychological advances have been made. Until it's in the DNA, the pull toward violence will always be in our brains. Look at you." Artemis gestured to his pockets. "Is that not an act of violence?"

Tiago dropped his head, placing a hand on the outside of his jeans. His hands moved gracefully, but they were as calloused as Artemis's.

"This is different," he said sadly. "This will put an end to centuries of enslavement. I can't live with the guilt anymore. The Senex need to find another way. You say we haven't evolved, but we can learn to do that. We can alter the brain chemistry of the next Iron Dreamers. We can remove their reptilian instincts, and erase the violence, and set them free."

"Set them free *where*?" Artemis demanded.

"Well, not these Iron Dreamers," he admitted. "People later on. We'll build a bigger station, or find an exoplanet for them. We have plenty of time to figure it out. We just need a shock to the system right now. Something to force us to try something better. I have no choice."

"That's what we all say right before we do something terrible."

The Senex didn't answer questions directly. They relied on subtext and distraction to avoid lying. They danced around interrogations like bridge trolls, shamelessly dodgy and dismissive. To watch them do it against each other was mesmerizing. Artemis and Tiago were carrying on two separate conversations, yet understanding each other all the same.

Tiago shook a finger at Artemis. "I see now," he said with satisfaction. "You freed Cillian. I just got there before you could."

Mostafa stepped back, the realization smacking into him like cold water.

The sound drew Tiago's attention. He had forgotten that Lexi and Mostafa were there. He chuckled and pointed to his wife, and told Mostafa, "Maybe you should arrest her."

Artemis's jaw set. "We cannot be allowed to leave."

"I'm impressed," Tiago said, allowing himself to be pulled back into her orbit. "The Beta program provides everyone with the things they desire. Threatening to destroy it would align Sol and Luna for a while. Cillian was a good choice. The distraction would be enough to give you time to delay the warp drive. I'm not sure what your plan was going to be after that, though, the diversion is just a quick fix."

Lexi snorted under her breath.

Artemis had a plan. Her view was so macro-scale that she would balance the world against the weight of a single individual. Nobody knew her plan, but Artemis wouldn't have distracted the two orbiters simply to delay the inevitable. She needed those years to finalize her main strategy.

"You're so disciplined," Tiago said, voice warm with respect. He turned to Lexi and Mostafa and said, "She never loses focus, have you noticed that? She just makes you think she has. Even when we were kids, I couldn't read her mind. I actually tried a few times when she first went into Beta, but her brainwaves didn't register." He chuckled to himself and looked to his wife. "I don't suppose you'll tell me what you're planning?"

"No."

Tiago held a finger to his chin, focusing on Artemis's tactic rather than her strategy. "Cillian is where you messed up. You wanted him to be the enemy, but you didn't account for my location in the Iron Sector, and the effect he would have on me. It hurt me, finding him like that. I hadn't appreciated what we were doing until I met him. You wanted Cillian to become the Dark Angel. But instead, it was me."

"It had to be someone," Artemis replied. She shrugged with a forced stiffness, as if she didn't even believe the callousness.

Tiago nodded thoughtfully.

He knew his wife. After a thousand years, how could he not? He knew her ruthlessness, her calculating nature and relentless certainty. Despite it, he accepted her. That was what it must be like to be seen, Lexi thought.

She was witnessing the idyllic representation of love. Possibly the only real example of it outside of Beta.

Minus the murder part.

"Why didn't you come to me?" Tiago asked. "I could have helped you."

Artemis shook her head once, holding back what should have been tears, but was probably nullified by her body's programming. "I'm sorry."

"You didn't trust me."

"I did, I just...I couldn't risk it."

"What were the odds that I would get in the way?"

"6.10 percent."

"Oh, yeah." A faint chuckle slipped past his lips. "Too high for you."

At some point, Artemis had learned the Senex were developing a technology they didn't deserve. Like Oppenheimer with the atomic bomb in World War II, she feared the power that humanity could wield. Their extended lifespan was roughly 18,000 years. That was plenty of time to find a key to immortality. Artemis knew that, ultimately, they were going to be a group of people that lived forever.

What if the golden age of life in the universe began because of humanity's tendency to tamper with nature? True immortality meant that an uncivilized species, unchecked by disease or the natural hostility of asteroids and other celestial bodies, would have the time to establish dominion over all of them. A galactic empire beyond their wildest dreams.

Artemis needed a battle, and an enemy.

If someone threatened the two orbiters' primary think tank, it would allow her a window of opportunity to come up with a plan to delay construction. She was thinking millions of years ahead when no one else would. And so the battle over Beta began, and the rise of the Dark Angel. Artemis had orchestrated it all.

Lexi was just a side character in the crosshairs of greater powers.

"Do you agree?" Artemis asked. Her voice was tight, but a hint of hopefulness leaked through.

Artemis walked slowly toward Tiago, stepping out of the lamplight and into the shadow. It plunged her silhouette into darkness. Each foot was carefully placed on the ground, one after another, like a hunter in the woods. For the first time, the self-appointed namesake made sense. Artemis was a creature of the night. The goddess of the hunt.

"That will kill people," Artemis said, pointing to Tiago's pocket. "Do you really want their deaths on your conscience?"

Tiago's shoulders rose. "Everybody's already weighing on my conscience."

"Come home," she said softly, testing the waters.

"I don't want to do this. You know I don't. No matter what I do, there's no winning. I could continue to watch the slavery happen, or stop it. It doesn't matter. I carry so much guilt. How do we do this to people?"

"We'll find a different way. Just you and me."

Like prey sensing a predator moving in, he shifted absentmindedly to the side. His subconscious was doing the heavy lifting, but he grinned arrogantly and said, "You can't build a simulation without me."

"And you can't design a world without me."

Artemis and Tiago were moments away from possibly killing over their convictions, yet there they were, cracking jokes.

"If you could get me out of this, what would you do?" It didn't sound like he was really willing to withdraw his plans, just like he wanted to entertain the possibility of coming home.

"I would send you to Earth," she replied too quickly. "It would explain your disappearance and the communication failures. Azi could be the Dark Angel."

"Only after I did something for you, though. Why Earth? What is it you need there?"

She shrugged in an innocent, mockingly casual way.

Mostafa positioned himself at an angle behind Artemis, moving forward to match her pace in Tiago's blind spot. Lexi was left alone to stand dumbly with her hands by her side. She felt useless. If Artemis jumped Tiago, Mostafa would be close enough to attack. Tiago was too distracted by Artemis's pleading to notice another player.

The third body stirred from the corner of Lexi's eye. She squinted in the low light, trying to make out his body through the fog. She recognized the dark unkempt hair. Tiago had dragged him all the way from the North Country to inject him with a virus and destroy the simulation. It would kill him.

It would kill the Iron Dreamers.

Jonathan shook his head, and held a bleeding palm to his brow. He blinked rapidly, trying to see where he was. He noticed the bodies of the sentinels on either side of him, but he wasn't alarmed. When his gaze fell on Lexi, his eyebrows shot up. He wasn't surprised to see her either. How much has Jonathan known, and for how long?

Tiago sensed the rustling. His window was closing. He gave his wife a grief-stricken, apologetic look, and sprinted to Jonathan.

"*No!*" Lexi screamed.

They all ran to protect Jonathan, but only one of them ran to Tiago.

Lexi threw herself upon the Dark Angel, smacking into his chest with the full weight of her body as Gal had done. Tiago fell like a rock, rolling over Lexi as the two of them tumbled down the road. Lexi spread her arms, so familiar with the sensation of falling that she could have maneuvered herself over the slope at highway speeds.

She caught sight of Tiago lying on the ground and lunged for him. He wrapped an arm around her waist and easily tossed her to the side. His strength was mutant-level. He had programmed his own power, and it was amplified beyond what Lexi could match. She slammed into the side of a car and crumpled to the road. She was dizzy and breathing heavily from multiple rib fractures.

Shocked, she pressed a hand to her side. She wasn't supposed to feel pain. Her balat may have recreated the fractures for real.

And then there was Artemis.

The hunter came up behind Tiago and wrapped her body around him like a snake, jerking them to the ground. She locked her legs over his hips and one arm around his neck. Tiago's arms reached back and tried to grab her throat. All compassion and love were lost from their eyes. Centuries ago, they were probably warriors on the battlefield fighting side by side. Now there was a cold indifference between them. Lexi didn't know what war did to a person, but it had done it to them.

Tiago was bigger and stronger, Artemis was the more skilled fighter. She arched her back against the street, pulling Tiago's hips and pushing his chest upward to cut off his windpipe. He gasped for air, frantically reaching for Artemis.

She was pulling him apart.

Lexi saw her chance and sprang into action. She scrambled across the road and dug through Tiago's pockets. He pushed her away with weak swings. Lexi grabbed his wrist and held it overhead, giving her the opening to reach for the flash drive. Tiago croaked, and a blast of his air caressed Lexi's cheek. She froze, gaping at him.

"Lexi," Artemis groaned.

"Sorry." Lexi grabbed the flash drive and, without thinking, smashed it on the ground.

Tiago might have howled if he weren't suffocating. He swung his arms one last time before collapsing into Artemis's arms. He closed his eyes, his body limp. She held him like that for what felt like an eternity, either untrusting of his demise or mourning it. After a beat or two, she released his body like a rag doll. Her face was too calm for a woman who had just killed her own husband.

"Is he..." Lexi asked, leading.

"He's not an Iron Dreamer, Lexi. He can't die here." Artemis's voice had returned to its superiority complex.

They had foiled Tiago's plans. Jonathan was alive. The Iron Dreamers were safe.

Months of anxiety was finally coming to an end. Lexi could feel the weight of the world drain from her bones. Tiago's weapon was destroyed. Whatever havoc he was going to wreak next would take years of planning. Life could go back to normal in the meantime. Now that they knew what he was capable of, the engineers could reinforce the security measures.

They would be ready for him next time.

"What did he want Jonathan to do with that, eat it?" Lexi asked, studying the splintered pieces of plastic. "Did the drive only *represent* a virus, and it's actually a line of code that can be in a bunch of places at once, or was that it? Did we get it?"

Artemis's lips curled into an approving smile. "Those are the questions to be asking." She rose from the ground and circled Tiago's body. "I don't know."

Mostafa was crossing the street, holding Jonathan up by the arm. Jonathan was taller than him, but skinnier. Mostafa could have probably thrown him over his shoulder and carried him to the city center. He lowered Jonathan to the ground and Lexi threw her arms around him, her relief tangible.

Jonathan was out of place, and not just because he didn't live in Europe. He was wearing snowboard pants and a thick coat—gear far too extreme for Portugal's mild winters.

Mostafa looked to Tiago's body and said, "I can't track him if he's not here."

"I know, shit," Artemis said, rubbing the back of her neck. "I couldn't risk that virus getting into an Iron Dreamer."

"A what?" Jonathan said, speaking up.

The three of them regarded him with cautious suspicion. It reminded Lexi of when she first appeared on Sol. Everyone had looked at her like that, and now she was doing the same thing to Jonathan. She was beginning to understand how it felt to hold all the cards.

Artemis shot an irritated glare at Mostafa. "You were supposed to get him out of here."

"You should listen to this," Mostafa replied. He tugged on his leather coat and leaned against the hood of a car.

Artemis's eyes narrowed, noting Jonathan's winter gear. Her mind was still reeling from the confrontation with Tiago. It had physically shaken her.

"How did you get here?" she asked Jonathan.

He was assessing the integrity of his circumstances. He didn't appear to be entirely clueless on what had transpired. His eyes lingered on Lexi. Deciding he had nothing to lose, he gestured toward Tiago and said, "He told me teleportation. Not sure how much I believe that, though."

Artemis gave a hand signal to Mostafa, and they held a quick exchange, switching between speaking and Sessiz—a precaution Lexi assumed was due to Jonathan's presence, not hers. "There were others in this designation. Why bring Jonathan?"

Mostafa shrugged. "Not everything has a deeper meaning."

"Mm."

While they conversed, Lexi asked Jonathan, "Teleport? Like, you just appeared?"

"Pretty much," he said, wiping the blood from his hands on his snow pants. His knuckles were raw. "I basically blinked and I was in Portugal.

Your uncle said it was some future tech. I didn't believe him at first, but he showed me these things and...I'm pretty sure they're impossible."

"What did he smell like?"

"What?" It was not the direction Jonathan wanted to go.

Lexi was pulled into a trance, entangled by the memory of an oak tree and the smell of bark. "We need to leave," she said, jumping to her feet. "I mean, *leave* leave."

"Why?" Artemis asked.

"I know where Tiago is."

Artemis didn't doubt her, but she needed to hear it anyway. "Are you sure?"

"I'm sure," Lexi said, her hands trembling. "He's in my room. He's been there the whole time."

CHAPTER NINETEEN

Lexi collides with the floor.

She has a death grip on the cord. Now that she can identify the location of her body, she can pull herself from the simulation at will—a party trick that will come in handy in the future.

She runs for the row of sentinel chairs, her feet wobbling as she adjusts to the gravitational laws of a new world. Artemis bolts upright, ripping the helmet off her head and running toward the door. A set of hands in armor catches Lexi before she trips on the helmet. She's in her real, crappy body again. Mostafa places her on her feet and runs after Artemis.

Lexi looks over her shoulder to grab the fourth person, only to remember that Jonathan isn't there. They left him behind. They abandoned a teenage boy in Portugal with no money, or means to get home.

One crisis at a time.

Lexi runs for the door and finds Chen waiting for her. His orders to guard her are not void simply because they're faced with a new obstacle. The two of them sprint through the dark, running so quickly that the lighting lags behind them. Lexi holds her hands up to stop herself from slamming into a wall.

"What's happening?" Chen asks.

"Tiago's in my room," she says.

Dim blue light glows from around the corner. Someone is at her door. Lexi slides to a halt, taking position behind the wall and signaling to Chen. Lexi peeks around the corner. Mostafa and Artemis are standing in front of Lexi's room, their expressions vacant and defeated. A handful of guards

Lexi doesn't recognize stand behind them. They're motionless, the light bouncing off the edges of their jawlines making them look like statues in a dark museum.

The air rushes out of Lexi. "Where is he?"

"Gone," Artemis says.

Mostafa waves his arm, and a screen appears by the door. "According to the readings, oxygen is only used when Lexi is in the room," he says. "Except for today."

"He was in the room whenever she was," Artemis says. "Masking tech."

A shudder runs through Lexi.

She has never been alone on Sol. All those times she heard footsteps and thought it was the natural sounds of a space station, it wasn't. There had been another person in the room with her. All the time they spent looking for Tiago, he had been sitting mere feet away, following Lexi into her room under the shield of invisibility.

That's why he appeared in the forest. He knew she wanted to speak with him. It wasn't because of Mai. She probably didn't even know how to contact him.

How often had he stood over her bed and contemplated what to do with her?

"I should have known," Artemis says with disgust. She squeezed her eyes shut, struggling to contain her anger. "Bastard stole my tech right from under me. All this time we thought you were—"

"A mouth breather?" Lexi finishes. "You were killing Iron Dreamers because you didn't want to face the possibility that Tiago was still on the station. You just wanted to blame me."

"I couldn't convince the council with these numbers," Artemis says, pointing to the screen. "I knew he was alive."

A cold fury moves through Lexi. She crosses her arms and says, "I guess you're juggling too much."

Artemis's jaw locks.

Zuchiris rounds the corner and marches to Artemis. His face is red and sweaty. "He ran through Sanitation and I lost him," he says between breaths. "He didn't look good, Arty."

Blue lights slowly begin to brighten upon the wall across from the door.

"The council is coming," Mostafa says.

Artemis casts a worried glance at Lexi. Her eyebrows arch, analyzing a series of possible outcomes. The timeframe that she's normally allowed to work with has been torn to shreds. These are not the conditions under which she likes to operate. She has seconds to make a decision. She turns to Zuchiris and says in a nasally voice, "Clean that up."

Zuchiris chuckles.

Another inside joke.

He casts Lexi an assuring glance before running out of the room. Apart from the Nest, Zuchiris doesn't leave Artemis's side. Why would he be sent away at a time like this?

Mostafa waves a signal to the guards, and they move to the end of the hallway, unseen and out of earshot. He lowers his head, his voice severe. "We need an extradition."

Artemis's eyes glint with amusement. "Is that a moral compass I see, Moose?"

"It's logical," he assures her, straightening under the accusation. "We need someone who can move in and out. She's our best chance."

"I'm aware."

"Then extradite, or do you not care what happens?"

Artemis closes her hollow. She plants her feet, her glare so threatening that she could justify any savagery she commits. There's a line somewhere, and Mostafa crossed it.

"I have been watching over every iteration of my niece for three hundred years," Artemis says carefully, enunciating each word as if issuing orders. "Every birth, every first step, graduation, broken heart, and death. I have been with her since the dawn of her *existence*. You gave up on people, Moose, but I'm still here. I'm still trying to figure this out." Artemis takes a breath, trying to collect herself to her normal demeanor. "I'm glad you finally found it in your dusty-ass soul to find an interest in something, but if you challenge me on this again, I will space you into the fucking sun."

Lexi had assumed that Artemis became a sentinel because of her technical abilities, or maybe some world-building skillset. But Artemis had endured two nuclear wars and navigated through a scorched wasteland. She might be a sentinel not because of a tangible skillset, but because she can get whatever she wants. Maybe she's simply ruthless.

Unequivocally and violently ruthless.

The guards split like the Red Sea, making way for a fragile being half the size of Lexi to wobble through the entryway. Hatshepsut taps her bony fingers on the wall. If Tiago left evidence, it's long since lost its value. The High Councilor surveys Lexi's room and slams her cane. The floor absorbs the cracking like snow after a storm.

"A rat in a sewer," Hatshepsut says. She twists her asymmetrical body toward the council, speaking to Farhad. "Now we have an explanation for the oxygen consumption. Have Cillian released at once. It's Tiago."

Farhad's head is visible over the front row of the council. For a man craving the spotlight, he's picked an ironic time to sink to the back. His mouth twists in reluctant submission as the council members voice their confusion. It's easier to blame Lexi and Cillian. They're Iron Dreamers. Clones. The council struggles to grapple with a terrorist being one of their own.

Hatshepsut bores her dark eyes into Artemis. "Where will he go?"

"Mars," Artemis replies. "Maybe Psyche 16, if Luna has Rohan stationed there."

Hatshepsut shuffles across the floor. "Mostafa."

Mostafa steps forward, shrinking back to servant mode. "Yes, High Councilor."

"Lock down every transport. Nothing gets in or out. If we're lucky, the Dark Angel is having a stupid day."

"He'll mask the ship," Artemis interjects.

"One can hope for absentmindedness."

Farhad steps forward. "What of the aiding and abetting? We will need to include it in the security hearing."

Hatshepsut waves a dismissive hand. "Yes, yes. Let's get on with it."

The council follows Hatshepsut into the hall. Mostafa settles into his place behind her. Now that Lexi knows the reason for his loyalty, she can't fault him for responding to her every beck and call. Without the High Councilor, he might not have an estate, and without an estate, he might not have rights at all.

Lexi moves to follow, but Artemis grabs her by the arm. The two of them wait until the lights from the council fade.

"What's the security hearing about?" Lexi asks.

Artemis looks both ways and pushes her into her room. It's only when the cracks are sealed, leaving behind a smooth flat wall, that she speaks. "They're going to charge you for aiding and abetting a terrorist, and then send you to a station around Earth for twenty years as punishment."

Lexi loses her balance, but Artemis's grip keeps her upright.

"They won't believe you didn't know Tiago was in your room," Artemis continues, "and even if they do, they don't know what happened in Portugal. The entire event was concealed by, I suspect, Boole, as payment for Tiago freeing him. Tiago likes to...collect favors. All the engineers saw before it went dark was you and Mostafa running into a blind spot where Tiago had just entered. Mostafa will be questioned, but ultimately shielded by Hatshepsut. They'll find it easier to blame you."

The blind spot means there is no evidence. Nobody heard the conversation. Nobody witnessed Tiago's admission or his plans to kill the Iron Dreamers. It's Lexi's word against an empty chamber. The pieces are stacking up, and not in her favor.

"But you were there," she says.

Artemis's breath hitches, replaying the events from the day. "Tiago had me shielded from the moment I landed. The Nest thought I was in Croatia."

"You two, I swear," Lexi snaps bitterly. "So, you'll protect each other, but forget the rest of us?" She rips herself from Artemis's hold and pinches the space between her eyes. "Just tell them what happened."

Artemis pauses for a beat too long. "I could."

"Then *do that*."

"If I do that, then yes, you won't be blamed. The council will honor your deal and send you back to Beta. You can go back to your life, and maybe over time, you'll forget this ever happened."

A month ago, Lexi would have begged for that without a second thought. Returning to Beta doesn't change the politics of Sol, or the decisions happening outside of the North Country. She has no power. The best she can do is be the bait. She doesn't have the resources or the knowledge to go toe-to-toe with the Senex. She just wants to keep her people alive.

"I know you want to save the Iron Dreamers," Artemis says. Her mouth tightens, preparing to tell Lexi what she wouldn't tell Tiago. "I think we can save Earth."

"Wh-what does that mean?" Lexi stammers, hesitant to feel an ounce of optimism.

"A group of Iron Dreamers are testing Venus's atmosphere to terraform. They don't know that it won't work because we didn't give them Venus's metrics, we gave them Earth's. The Iron Dreamers are *this* close to figuring out how to reverse the damage. We just need to give them more time. The council will halt the expansion plans if they think Earth can be rehabilitated."

"Are you telling me there's a chance we could go home?"

A shadow of sorrow crosses her features. "It would be tens of thousands of years before those changes took effect. You would never live to see it, Lexi."

Lexi had only ever looked at the Earth once. There are satellites still in orbit, and the images are accessible on their hollows. Research teams monitor the storms and wind speeds, but the clouds are impenetrable. The sickly gray-yellow skies never open. Instruments are occasionally sent down to the surface to collect samples. It's hot, windy, and heavy. The air is too toxic to breathe. The winds could rip paint off the wall. And the atmospheric pressure is steadily increasing. Zuchiris said that even before they left, it had been like swimming thirty feet underwater.

Basically, it was hell.

"What was the North Country like?" Lexi asks.

Artemis stiffens, caught off guard by the question. "What do you mean?"

"Was it really the way you had it in the simulation? Were those the mountains? Was that the wind?"

Artemis probably hasn't thought about the North Country in years. Maybe she doesn't remember. Maybe she doesn't want to. If Lexi had been left behind by the last collection of humanity, that's where she would run too. Artemis had probably returned to the North Country in search of safety, only to find a carpet of ash and corpses strewn across the scorched wasteland.

"Yes," Artemis whispers. The pain is genuine. Having been confronted with too many emotional exchanges for the day, Artemis looks away to readjust. She tilts her head as if stretching a muscle and says, "Yes, it was accurate."

A wave of sympathy washes over Lexi.

Loss isn't a competition. Saying goodbye to an artificial world is no different than to a biological one. She's beginning to realize that they're both real in their own way. Worlds are created for humans to live in, and no one is the wiser. People are made with whatever components they deem fit, selecting their experiences at will. Reality is such a fluid concept that the Senex monitor constants like pi just to figure out if they're in a simulation or not. Nobody really knows anything.

Lexi erupts with laughter.

She can't stop. She doesn't know what's come over her. Her body shakes, pushing a ring of laughter through inconsistent bursts that bounce off the walls. Every emotion from an overwhelming day floods her at once. Pain. Loss. Anger. She doubles over, wiping the tears from her eyes. Artemis regards her with polite confusion.

"You mean to tell me that you had all this technological power," Lexi says, wheezing between breaths, "and you couldn't stop the school septic system from blowing? There was shit everywhere for, like, three days."

A smile cracks across Artemis's lips. "That actually happened."

"And what about the road to Cannon? I mean, make it one degree less steep and we could have gotten there so much faster."

"That was the gradient."

"What are these details you remember? I couldn't even *draw* a bike if my life depended on it."

"The trick is to draw two triangles. Everyone just draws one."

Lexi's mouth hangs open in comical shock. Artemis shifts from the awkwardness, and then releases a chuckle in response. She covers her mouth as if not to be rude, and then its contagiousness spreads to her.

"It was a strange place, even back then," Artemis says, giggling. "You know they made us wear gloves during class in case the ceiling caved. What did they want us to do, shovel ourselves out?"

"So my life was always going to be super weird."

"Pretty much."

Suddenly, Artemis and Lexi are laughing uncontrollably, acknowledging the absurdity of the situation and the circumstances that have brought them here. It's a conversation that says everything by saying nothing, and it feels good. It's nice to hear the light-hearted notes coming from Artemis, and it's nice to share the absurdity of humor with her. It might be the first moment of genuine warmth that settles deep enough into Lexi's heart to linger.

Lexi wipes the moisture from her eyes. "What ridiculous thing do you want me to do?"

The ghost of a smile remains on Artemis's lips. She runs a hand through her hair, checking the braids. If she had been a few inches taller, she would have made quite the Viking. "I need you on that station. To terraform Earth, we'll need Luna's resources, and they won't be easy to convince." She checks the time on her arm. "Will you do it?"

Lexi wants to save the Iron Dreamers.

There are 700,000 people whose lives rest on the whims of alien forces. The Iron Dreamers don't know that the rulers of their world aren't gods, or even a single divine being keeping watch over his creation. It's just people. Nameless faces they will never meet, trying to squeeze out a new tool from them. Even under the best intentions, that's a dystopian power imbalance that Lexi can't stomach. It's simply unfair.

Artemis wants to save the galaxy. The sentinel's fear lies in an existential future so far away that it's too ludicrous to consider. Too far to be tangible. Artemis is planning a fate billions of years out, grappling with the variables on a scope wider than anything Lexi can imagine, and that's been the problem since the beginning. What's the expression? "A society grows great when old men plant trees in whose shade they shall never sit."

Nuclear war tore through the skies because no one thought ahead. The power of the sun in the palm of their hands, and all they did was poison their own land. If it weren't for the insatiable greed of short-sightedness, maybe Lexi would have been born in the real North Country, under a blue sky, with fresh lakes, instead of an artificial pod of cold metal.

It would be easier for Lexi to push the problem off to someone else. It could be a future Lexi's problem. All she has to do is ask Artemis to tell the truth, and the council will send her back to live out her days in the simulation. But the next Lexi will think the same thing and push it off. At some point, the chickens come home to roost.

It needs to be *someone's* problem.

Lexi will never be able to live with herself, knowing that there was something she could have done to save future generations of Iron Dreamers and she buried her head in the sand. There is a real North Country out there. The trees and animals may have been destroyed, but the mountains are still there. With the single-minded determination of the last of humanity, people could live in the forests again. The rivers could return.

It will take thousands of years. The Beta program will continue on until then, and millions of Iron Dreamers will live and die within a simulation they'll never know exists. Those people can never be freed. There is nowhere for them to go. But someday, generations from now, Lexi will be one small piece in a bigger plan that gives humanity a planet to call home. She could help save the future for more than just her own people.

She could save everyone.

"What about Jonathan?" Lexi asks, tying up the loose ends. "We left him in Portugal."

“I’ll get him out.” Artemis’s clipped word choice concerns Lexi, but knowing the sentinel, she won’t waste her breath explaining the entirety of her plan to Lexi anyway.

“I’ll go,” Lexi decides.

Artemis visibly relaxes. “Thank you.”

They sprint to the Council Chamber. Hatshepsut bangs her cane to the floor when they arrive, and the last of the members take their seats. The chamber is lit differently this time. Instead of red, it’s the familiar blue. Without the Luna delegation to fill the seats, the chamber is mostly empty. The center platform is raised higher than it had been for Azi’s trial, with three people seated behind a dark table. Hatshepsut is in the center, Farhad to the left, and a woman Lexi doesn’t recognize to the right.

Artemis gives Lexi a reassuring squeeze of the arm and takes a seat on the other side of the chamber, leaving Lexi with a row of empty chairs.

There’s a relief that comes from knowing a verdict ahead of time, even if it’s a bad one. There’s no dread or anticipation, just the feeling of wanting to get on with it. She already knows what’s going to happen, and what she needs to do.

“My fellow Senex,” Farhad begins, standing from behind the table. “We are here this morning to address the troubling events transpiring in Beta that pose a direct threat to our national security. As you are aware, the Dark Angel has been plaguing us for years. We were close to capturing him today, but our plans were thwarted by Lexi Carvalho, who has been facilitating his objectives since her arrival.”

Lexi sucks in the air between her teeth.

She knew it was coming, yet it’s still a shock to hear.

“This clone has allowed four Iron Dreamers to be killed to compensate for the Dark Angel’s oxygen—who she has been concealing in her living quarters,” Farhad continues. “She threatened the security of the mission by speaking with Mai Bunma. She conspired to save him from capture just hours ago, utilizing a dark spot and masking technology, both of which are illegal practices. Everywhere she goes, the Dark Angel escapes. I move to sentence her to spacing, effectively immediately."

Before Azi, spacing was a punishment that hadn't been enacted in centuries. Now they were handing them out like candy. Even as a thought experiment, the prospect of being tossed into space again paralyzes her with fear.

"Do you have evidence to support this claim?" the woman to Hatshepsut's right asks.

Farhad taps his fingers, having expect the question. "No, Councilor Sophie. We don't have physical evidence to present to the committee, but may I ask that you consider what other possibility could exist? At every turn since Lexi Carvalho's appearance, the Dark Angel has evaded capture. We must consider that he's the one who freed her. Who better to aid his mission than a witless clone?"

Councilor Sophie appears older than her voice. Lexi remembers her from the Forest when she first arrived from Beta. Sophie had been the one to suggest that she be freed. At the time, Lexi thought she was an intern, or a trainee of some kind. White lines are woven into Sophie's black hair in thick chunks, as if dyed to follow the pattern of a zebra, and short wrinkles fold at the corners of her eyes.

She is no apprentice.

"Not just a clone," Sophie says, "a naturalized citizen. We voted on Lexi Carvalho receiving 51 percent of the Carvalho estate this morning. If official criminal charges are to be pressed against a citizen, then it must move to trial. May I suggest a different solution?" Sophie turns to Hatshepsut, who nods. Sophie continues, "I agree with your observations, Council Farhad. Lexi's appearance is suspiciously timed. I move to hold her in the Forest until the Dark Angel is apprehended."

The Forest is a prison. It is not a station around Earth. It's not where Lexi is supposed to be.

A quarter of the council members mumble their discontent, but the majority vote in approval. None of them hesitate to send an eighteen-year-old girl to a prison designed to drive people mad.

"Lexi Carvalho will be moved to the Forest effective immediately," Hatshepsut says, and she slams her cane into the floor. If the High Councilor has qualms about the sentencing, she doesn't show it.

Artemis, too, is indecipherable. Her body is rigid, but her face reveals nothing. It takes all of Lexi's self-control not to rush her.

Farhad leans forward, pressing his palms deeper into the table. He does not take a seat. Hatshepsut sighs heavily. "Something else you'd like to say, Councilor?"

"I would like to address the matter of Number 521a," he says.

A chorus of grumbles echoes throughout the chamber. Some of the members had already begun to leave.

"That's a matter for the Beta Committee. This is a security hearing," a taller man with dark skin says. He sits next to Artemis, towering over her and the rest of the sentinels like a sequoia.

"Number 521a has become a matter of security," Farhad says sternly. "I have requested temporary security clearance for head engineer Ronaldi to provide the necessary information to the council."

An engineer Lexi recognizes from the Nest appears from the side door, passing by two guards. She carries a hollow in her arms, cradling it like a book she can't tear her eyes away from. She doesn't appreciate being the center of attention.

"Tell us the status of the Iberian Region," Farhad instructs her.

The woman scrolls through her hollow. "Number 521a is causing a disturbance in a city. Um, yes. Number 1280i has noted his behavior. We estimate that she will approach by the end of the day."

Jonathan.

Lexi hadn't given much thought to the codes used to classify the Iron Dreamers. Number 521a must be Jonathan. They left him behind after the confrontation with Tiago, and now he's roaming the streets asking for help, trying to figure out what's happening. If his actions are the beginning of a chain reaction, it could lead to the Iron Dreamers being scratched, and the simulation rebooted.

It would kill them.

Artemis and Hatshepsut share a quick exchange—nothing so bold as a hand signal in a room full of sign language experts—but poignant.

"There is no evidence that this will lead to a chain reaction," Sophie replies. "He's a boy in a strange city. Artemis will—"

"Artemis," Farhad sneers dismissively. "If she hadn't been hundreds of miles away, perhaps we would know what transpired today."

At the mention of her name, it could be Artemis's chance to tell the truth. Her plan has failed. Lexi is being sentenced to the Forest—not a station near Earth. Artemis needs to tell the council why there was a black zone when they faced Tiago, and why her true whereabouts were shieled from the Nest.

But she doesn't move. Her elbows sit comfortably on the armrests, and her fingers are laced with all the ease of a patron at the theater. Her head tilts to the side, as if too curious to intervene. Lexi can't tell if it's because of anger, or apathy.

"Why don't they do a Mandela maneuver?" an agitated voice asks.

"We're past that," Farhad insists.

"What is the current off-course rate?"

"Off-course rate is at 0.0015 percent," the engineer replies. "If Number 1280i approaches 521a, we estimate that it will push the iteration up to 1.2 percent, and increase exponentially."

A frenzy moves through the chamber. The walls respond to the turmoil and change from blue to yellow.

If Jonathan speaks to another Iron Dreamer and plants a seed in their head, the chain reaction could spread through the system until it reaches every Iron Dreamer. Like realizing they're in a dream, they might have an *itch* that urges them to wake up. It could wreak havoc. Any progress made would need to start over as they wait for a new set of clones to reach maturity.

Tiago didn't need to plant a virus.

Jonathan would become one all on his own.

The artificial intelligence that regulates Beta follows the decisions made by the Iron Dreamers. Their actions have a direct impact on the events that transpire within the simulation. The system is too complex for the Senex to handle from the outside. There are real people in there.

The Iron Dreamers can't believe the sky is blue their whole lives, and then one day it changes on them, and everyone acts as if it had always been pink.

A Mandela maneuver is a last-ditch effort by the sentinels to alter events without causing a chain reaction. Lexi read about it during her studies with Zuchiris. Nelson Mandela had lived on Earth and became South Africa's president, but many people believed that he had died decades earlier in prison. Millions were convinced of it. From the names of peanut butter brands to cartoon characters, there had been multiple incidents of the masses collectively believing that something was true when it never had been, and the phenomenon had occurred on Earth.

Knowing that humans in the real world could fall for the same false memories, the sentinels are occasionally able to insert changes into the simulation to cover up mistakes, but not often. They can't overdo it. The simulation is a living, breathing world of its own.

If Lexi could just talk to Jonathan...

Hatshepsut slams her cane. She shifts her head until her neck cracks, growing impatient.

"This iteration has forty-seven years remaining," Farhad says, rushing to his proposal. "To avoid a system-wide failure and a fundamental altering of the program, I move to compress the schedule to five months."

Lexi covers her mouth before she can scream.

"Five months," Hatshepsut says, frowning with skepticism. She turns to the engineer and asks, "Could it be done that soon?"

"Um, possibly." The engineer avoids eye contact with Farhad and scrolls through her hollow. He would have chosen her for this meeting because she is the most pliable. The engineer scrambles to provide a more desirable deadline. "A year would be sufficient."

A year to kill 700,000 people.

"High Councilor, I must object," the man next to Artemis says. "This iteration has been fruitful. We have progress being made on multiple fronts, including intelligence trades for the warp mechanics. May I remind you that without those, we cannot travel to the Trappist exoplanets. To scratch the iteration now would be to delay our own progress. We should let it continue until the scheduled deadline in forty-seven years."

"We are 0.0015 percent off target," Farhad reminds him, approaching the front row. "The Dark Angel has completed his mission and infected the Beta program. If the public were to learn of this, our fellow Senex, they would question this council's competence. We must terminate this iteration before the poison spreads. Waiting a year to see what happens does nothing but prolong the inevitable."

"High Councilor," the man says, looking over Farhad's shoulder to address Hatshepsut. The *audacity*. He must be a sentinel. "This is an inappropriate discussion for the Security Council. The Beta Committee hasn't processed this deviation, as it is still en route. Had

Councilor Farhad alerted us to his intentions, we would have brought the relevant documentation."

"The off-course rate concerns me," Hatshepsut says, neither agreeing nor disagreeing. "It's bigger than we've dealt with in some time."

"They may be Iron Dreamers, but they are people," the sentinel says firmly. "They're members of society whether they know it or not. We can't kill them."

Until today, managing the simulation has been a matter of oxygen shipments, resources, and logistics. Scratching the program is an entirely different matter. It's genocide. The Senex aren't turning off their computers and rebooting a video game; they're killing people, for what, convenience? How are the Senex any different from the world leaders they criticized a thousand years ago for pressing a button to launch nuclear warheads?

Hypocrites.

The Iron Dreamers have been tools for so long that the Senex don't see them as people. They're numbers on a screen. Processors to provide solutions for the water system beneath the Solarium, and Lagrangian mechanics in the cargo bay. The Senex have grown too complacent in their comforts. Artemis was right. They're not evolved enough to rule the galaxy.

They're not evolved enough to rule a school board.

"They're clones," a woman says. "We'll make more."

The sentinel turns to her and coolly asks, "Are you volunteering to be the one to kill them?"

"S-sir, no," the woman says, faltering. "I'm supporting the decision to do in a year what we were planning on doing in forty-seven years."

"Most of the Iron Dreamers would have lived out their natural lives by that point. Under the conditions you're suggesting," the sentinel says, emphasizing the last word, "we'll be killing 846 children."

The sentinel is putting his foot down. He's protecting the Iron Dreamers, as he should, by laying out the details. It's not enough to say "murder." A single word sanitizes the violence. The council needs to know precisely what they're requesting, and that some of the deaths will be children. It's the details that strike the heart.

Sensing a set of eyes on her, Artemis turns to Lexi and gives a quick nod as if to say, 'Yes, he's good.'

"I'd like to know what Artemis thinks," Sophie says.

Artemis doesn't like to announce her opinions. She weaves her plans in the shadows. She rubs a thumb across the top of her hand as she chooses her words—a motion eerily similar to the Dark Angel's.

"The off-course rate is 0.0015 percent," she says, dropping her voice to a monotonous pitch. "We've managed rates 3 percent higher than that, though it has a 45 percent probability of failure. However, if we scratch the program in a year, we lose progress on multiple fronts. We cannot make guarantees on the Trappist expeditions without the M-series Iron Dreamers. You would delay the mission by another twenty years."

Artemis is using what they want against them. The council wants to explore exoplanets in search of another world to live on—or worlds to conquer—and she's telling them they'll have to wait if they pull the plug on Beta.

Nice.

Some of the members fidget uncomfortably in their seats. This is not a discussion in which they often engage. They don't want to navigate the ethical nuances of birthing millions of people in pods under false pretenses; they just want to enjoy what's working.

Humanity can justify anything in the face of obliteration. On the brink of destruction, the Senex devised a plan that would allow the Iron

Dreamers to live blissfully ignorant lives in a simulation, while supplying the future with technology they needed.

But that was centuries ago. Why haven't they reassessed the program?

Lexi is beginning to understand Tiago. She doesn't agree with his tactics, but the Dark Angel isn't without his moral reasoning. No wonder he turned to extremes.

They don't want to discuss it.

Hear no evil. See no evil.

"Excuse me, ma'am. I have an update," the engineer says. Farhad stands over her shoulder, a foul grin stretching across his face. "Number 1280i has approached 521a," she tells the chamber. "The off-course rate has recalibrated. It's at 0.30 percent and rising."

"Jonathan, goddammit," Lexi hisses under her breath.

Hatshepsut nods once. "The Beta Committee will gather their documents and present to the Security Council their findings with a recommended course of action in three weeks' time. The sentinels will attempt to mitigate the disturbance in Porto in the meantime. I would like to prevent scratching this iteration." Hatshepsut looks to Farhad with a stern, unapproving glare. Then she turns to the engineer. "In the meantime, you may begin preparations in case this iteration needs to be scratched. Start with the nonessentials. Dismissed."

Artemis slams her hands on the table, wordless, and full of fury.

The three council members exit the center platform. A handful of members who Lexi assumes are part of the Beta Committee talk frantically amongst themselves. Artemis turns to Lexi, regret and anger painting her face as an outcome she hadn't conceived of overrides her trajectory.

Lexi's not angry.

She's not anything.

She sees it like a tsunami offshore, feeding on the restless water and growing taller and taller until the world beneath is masked in darkness. Her feet refuse to move. They are rooted in the sand, condemning her to drown.

Lexi is going to prison.

And the Iron Dreamers will die.

CHAPTER TWENTY

Lexi is carried through the halls.

Her feet drag along the floor, hardly triggering the lighting that's meant to recognize her. She has no belongings, so there's no reason to bring her back to her room to pack. Even the suit of armor she wears doesn't belong to her. Chen huffs from the dead weight and swings Lexi into his arms, cradling her like a child. She asks for Artemis.

They're going to kill the Iron Dreamers.

The Beta Committee could present enough evidence to postpone its elimination, but it was scheduled to end in forty-seven years anyway. Lexi was only ever going to live to be sixty-five.

That's it.

She would have preferred to never know when she was going to die. There's something about seeing the end date that makes the Beta program feel even more like a chilling exercise in control, rather than a simple problem-solving tool. The Senex pay no price for the deaths of hundreds of thousands. It's an entire world run by people above consequence.

Humans haven't changed at all.

Lexi is thrown to the ground.

She slides across the floor and slams into a wall. Chen scrambles to his feet, throwing out an arm into the shadow. His fists swing in the dark, but they are hitting no one. There is no second set of lights. There is no one else there.

He's gone mad.

Two guards rush past Lexi and are systematically tossed aside. There is an extra person among them. An invisible man.

Realizing the hall is too narrow for both guards to attack, they rise from the ground and move one at a time, but it doesn't matter. The first guard has his head bashed into the wall, the second snaps backward as blood rushes down his face. Chen claws at his throat, his back arching. Terrified, Lexi crawls away.

Chen takes one more breathless gasp of air before slumping into a hidden set of arms. The figure places him gently on the floor.

Lexi can't hear footsteps or breathing, or see the outline of a man, but she hears a man's voice.

"Sorry about that."

"*Zuchiris*?" she breathes, squinting into the dark. She feels a hand grab her wrist and drag her to her feet. She takes a step back, unsure where to put her eyes. Zuchiris doesn't drop the masking technology. "What did you do to them?"

"I didn't kill them."

"Oh, great."

"Did you want me to?"

"No, it was sarcasm." She looks to their bodies. "What's going on?"

"I'm getting you out of here." Zuchiris slides an arm around her waist and throws her into his arms. As soon as he does, the technology extends to her. She looks to her hands, twisting them and marveling at the seamless transition from body to air. She's completely invisible. If she weren't being carried, she would trip. She bends her legs into her chest, worried that her feet will smack into a corner.

"I thought you were Tiago," Lexi says, realizing. "And they will too."

There's a smile in his voice when he says, "You're finding your weapons."

"They'll think he's aiding my escape because he's the only one they know of who has this tech. Hatshepsut knows you have it, though. You must be banking on her not saying anything. She's still on our side?"

"There aren't sides in this mess."

A fog of blue stretches down the hall. It shouldn't be smudged like that; the light on Sol is sharp. They must be in the residential arm, where the humidity is increased to mirror an atmosphere. A woman is walking toward them. Zuchiris slows to a halt, holding his breath. Lexi covers her mouth. The woman passes by, unaware of the two sets of eyes watching her.

How many times has Lexi been spied on like that by Tiago?

Zuchiris presses his hand beside an unexceptional door. Though they remain masked, the door registers them. It glows softly, illuminating like sunlight in the early morning. Zuchiris is careful not to touch the sides as they pass through the doorway, pulling Lexi in tight so that no contact is made. When the door closes behind them, the entire room brightens to a breathtaking forest.

Rows of trees extend toward a familiar mountain range. The high ceiling is of a cloudy day, with rain looming in the distance like a typical thunderstorm in the North Country. The walls stretch up, showcasing their towering pines and mossy rocks. A couple of leather couches and wooden tables are positioned in front of bookcases. If woodland elves from fantasy novels were real, this would be their abode.

Zuchiris lowers Lexi to her feet.

"It's beautiful," she says.

"It's Tiago's room," Zuchiris says, dropping the invisibility. "Well, now it's yours. Mostly. Artemis's estate is on the other side. So, if this whole thing doesn't go tits up, you can hang out here someday."

Lexi can see why Gal had fought so hard to claim the Carvalho estate. It's not the Solarium, but it's the most luxurious and comfortable living quarters that Lexi has seen. It's massive, and feels like home. It's better than most homes on Earth.

"Am I staying here?" Lexi asks.

"No, we're just waiting."

"I can't believe you choked Chen."

"He wasn't going to be okay with this," Zuchiris says, rubbing his chest. "He wasn't going to be okay with throwing you in the Forest, but he follows orders. I'm not super persuasive. Why risk it when I can knock him out?"

Lexi chuckles.

The door slides open, and Zuchiris moves in front of Lexi. His massive shoulders crouch into a charge, ready to pummel the intruder, then he relaxes. Lexi peeks over his shoulder and gasps at the incongruous sight.

Mostafa and Gal carry a man between them. The balats are stiffened near the joints to take some of the weight, but they look like they've hauled him over a mountain.

The man's head is slumped forward. He's too skinny, and his head is white as a sheet of paper. Mostafa drops him onto the couch with an air of indifference. Gal lifts his face to check on a pair of green eyes. Lexi's heart pounds in her chest and she runs toward him, a surge of protectiveness throwing her onto the last living piece of home.

Lexi shoves her cousin out of the way and presses her hands to the sides of Jonathan's face. She holds him the way he had held her at Cannon Mountain. His skin is slick and soft. His hair and eyebrows are gone. He looks like a ghost. She runs her hand down his arm, testing the balat. Its settings are still the defaults. He doesn't even know what it is yet.

"Hey, can you hear me?" she asks.

Jonathan's head rolls. He's dazed, but conscious. He blinks a few times before his eyes land on Lexi. "What's going on?"

"Excellent question." Lexi stands, furious.

Mostafa is exhausted. The bags under his eyes are muted by the lighting of the forest, but his face is drained. He lifts an arm to enter a command into his balat without explanation, focused on the next step.

Gal, on the other hand, looks ready for a fight. She rests her fists on her hips, prepared for a confrontation—maybe hoping for one.

Lexi points to Jonathan. "What is he doing here?"

"You should be thanking us," Gal snaps. "We're saving his life."

"You ruined his life."

Gal tosses her hair. "If the Beta Committee fails to convince the council to change their mind, he'll die in a year anyway. What were you doing at the hearing, sleeping?"

Lexi bites back a retort. Gal is right. The situation in Beta has become much more tumultuous. The council could kill the Iron Dreamers if the sentinels don't figure out a way to save the program from a chain reaction that Jonathan unwittingly started.

"Is Jonathan coming with me?" Lexi asks Mostafa.

Mostafa doesn't lift his head when he answers, "Yes."

"We *all* are," Gal says. "Except for Zuchiris."

Zuchiris nods. The shrug in his body says the same word it always says when the curtain is pulled back to reveal the stage. *Artemis.*

A dull thud vibrates through the chamber. The back of the room drops the forest and a transparent glass unveils the stars. If Lexi ran forward, she would fall into space. Tiago's rooms have direct access to the outside. No other living quarters on Sol have that. The maintenance alone requires an exceptionally adept mind. Tiago must have built this place himself. He was always planning on an escape.

A wall of slow-moving metal crosses in front of the opening.

"We're getting on a ship," Lexi says flatly. "You're joking."

"We don't have teleportation," Mostafa says. His voice carries a peculiar blend of humor and indignation, making it hard to tell if he's joking.

Mostafa's position on Sol is a comfortable one. His responsibilities aren't so significant as to hold the lives of others in his hands, but he works for the council and therefore is a beneficiary of the comforts that come with high orbit. His disappearance won't be a mystery. Even Hatshepsut will have to acknowledge the insubordination. A single miscalculation, and Mostafa could be charged with conspiracy. Everything he's accomplished could unravel from a single decision to do the right thing.

Lexi places her hand on his forearm. He looks to her hand. His jaw tightens, but his eyes soften despite himself.

"You're coming with me?" she asks.

"Yes."

"Why?"

He clears his throat, caught off guard. He seems adrift in the warmth of kindness. To compensate, he hardens his voice. "Because Gal has no diplomatic skills, and you don't know anything. They'll space you both." He grins, more at ease with empty flirtation. "You need me."

She shoves his shoulder gently. "That's just what you say to all the girls."

He releases a genuine laugh that brightens his face. His eyes sparkle with a playfulness that sends a jolt through her. "You don't want to know what I tell them," he says.

Lexi pulls her hand away, her face flushing. She thought she could keep up with his wit, but he's a few centuries ahead.

"Why would Gal help us?" she asks.

Gal's performance at Azi's trial was impressive, but not enough to convince Lexi of her intentions. As Farhad's whisperer, Gal would be able to accomplish more with the tools left behind by Tiago. The estate is probably a goldmine of experimental technology. All of that, and yet she's coming with them. It would be in Gal's best interest to let Lexi sabotage herself. It doesn't make sense.

Mostafa shrugs. "You'll have to ask her."

The ship docks with Tiago's chamber. Lexi holds her breath, uneasy with the mechanics. Nanotechnology is embedded into the ship's exterior to allow for maneuverability and to air-seal based on the parameters of the framework. The tiny pieces flutter to the side as they reach for the edges of the room. Though the layer is only a few millimeters thick, it is airtight and completely opaque.

Jonathan's head droops, probably tired from holding itself up for the first time in his life. He watches the ship from the corner of his eye, trying to decipher the havoc into which he's been thrown.

A ramp extends to the floor, punching through the forest like an alien invasion, and a man and woman appear. Their balats stretch over their heads to fit as a spacesuit. The woman strolls to Lexi, and the helmet recedes. Artemis's expression is wild, every ounce of mental fortitude focused on the mission. The man remains atop the ramp, taking a wide stance and crossing his arms like a guard.

Artemis pulls Lexi toward the couch, wasting no time on introductions.

"The trip to Earth is two weeks," she says, her voice uneven. "It is long and miserable, and the conditions won't improve when you arrive. Station 23 is a prison masquerading as a gas station. You will find no friends there. It has a ship that's equipped to handle Earth's atmosphere, which is why Gal is going with you. You'll need to convince Luna to let you board, which is why Mostafa is going with you."

Lexi's heart races. "What about Jonathan?"

"He'll cause too much trouble." There is an assuredness in Artemis's voice that is normally reserved for Tiago.

"What is that supposed to mean?" Lexi asks.

Artemis pulls Jonathan off the couch and slings his arm over her shoulder. She's too short to reach his armpit, but he wobbles under the new gravity. His gangly body falls forward. He'll take longer to learn how to walk than Lexi. Mostafa grabs his other arm and huffs with irritation. He's taken issue with Artemis's schemes before, but something about this grates on him differently.

They half-carry, half-drag Jonathan to the ship. The whole time, Jonathan doesn't say a word. No questions, no demands, no protest. He simply accepts the impossible. Lexi isn't sure what to tell him when he snaps out of it.

The calm before the storm.

"What is Jonathan?" Lexi asks, following them aboard. It would have been easier to leave him in the North Country. Pulling him out of Beta is a big move. He's only the third Iron Dreamer to experience it.

Or at least, the third to survive.

The man on the ramp steps forward and takes Jonathan from them, grabbing his torso with a single arm. He moves at twice the normal speed and half the normal caution. The teenager is a paperweight to him. Lexi makes a sound of protest, but it is quickly extinguished by a crack at the chamber door.

The guards have found them.

They sound pissed.

Artemis leans forward onto the ground and crawls, rubbing her hands across the floor as she recedes. A dark purple light shines beneath her palms and pieces of nanotechnology shoot out like vines. She's erasing evidence. She follows Jonathan's trail to the couch, eliminating any sign that he was there.

"Jonathan is an activator," Artemis says. "We don't use them often, but when we do, we put them at the end of an iteration. They have a tendency to disrupt things. That's why the off-course rate is impossible to reset at this point. If he were anything other than an A-series Iron Dreamer, we might have been able to pull a Mandela maneuver. But Jonathan won't let it go. He never does."

Lexi frowns. "Who is he?"

"A general." Artemis takes a breath. "He led our forces in the First Nuclear War. He almost put an end to it too, but he was assassinated."

Lexi's eyes bulge.

That explains why Artemis didn't want to explain why Jonathan wasn't in the recording with Alexandria. He was a few years older and already at university. He probably didn't know Alexandria; they just happened to be from the same area.

Lexi stares at the ship and imagines the bodies inside, wondering how a small-town boy from the forest became a general.

"I need him off Sol," Artemis says, following her gaze. "He's more use outside of Beta."

"You mean he's more use to you."

"Call it what you want."

Everything in space is too far away. What if she can't return to Sol within the year? What if all the Iron Dreamers are killed while she's busy running Artemis's errands? Lexi needs to know that she did everything in her power to stop their deaths, even if she has no power to speak of.

"What about the Iron Dreamers?" Lexi demands. "I'm supposed to just get on this ship and forget about all those people?"

As if needing the reminder, Artemis says, "There's nothing you can do."

The guards override the door, peeling it back by a few centimeters. Any wider, and they'll be able to see who's inside.

"We need to go," the man from the ship says. The balat recedes down his face, revealing light brown skin and a black beard. Tattoos reach up his neck to where a pair of dark wings peak above his balat. Lexi has seen that tattoo in her hometown enough times to recognize the patron saint. He's ex-military.

Did he know Jonathan?

"We can't save Earth if the Iron Dreamers are killed," Lexi argues. "They're the ones figuring it out. Without them, you have nothing."

"Wars are fought on multiple fronts. You take this off my shoulders, so I can handle the Iron Dreamers."

"And I'm supposed to just trust you now?"

Artemis sighs. "If I can trust you with Earth, can you trust me with the Iron Dreamers?"

In truth, the plan hasn't changed. Lexi has already agreed to go to the station and perform in whatever Artemis's plan is to rehabilitate the planet. The timetable has advanced, creating an additional layer of complications, but Lexi's priorities haven't changed. If Earth can be saved, then she needs to save it.

Artemis takes Lexi's silence as permission to push her up the ramp.

Mostafa and Gal stand on either side of the doorway, while Jonathan sits behind them in the belly of the ship, his balat molded to the chair as if it's eating his chest. He's coming out of his daze. There are a million questions swimming in his eyes. How could Lexi answer them? How could she tell him that every single person he's ever known is a phantom?

The guards wedge a piece of equipment into the door. They're trying to force their way inside. Artemis looks over and huffs. When technology doesn't bend to the will of man, sheer willpower ought to do it.

"Zuchiris," Artemis says.

"On it." Zuchiris disappears, and a breeze blows by them.

Artemis folds her hands. "You could stay here and help save the Iron Dreamers, maybe, or you could leave, and bring Earth back to life. You're not running away. You're on a different mission. A very important mission."

"Don't talk to me like I'm a child."

"Jesus, Lexi, pick a battle."

The ship terrifies Lexi. Leaving the Iron Dreamers terrifies her. Jonathan is safe, but there's still one more person in the simulation. Mostafa said that there are three Iron Dreamers in the North Country. That means there's another one in a pod that she might know. Is she just going to leave them behind?

And yet Earth is home, the birthplace of humanity. If there's even a chance that the rivers can return, then it would put an end to the Beta program. Cloning practices would cease, and people could return to their lives on solid ground. There is nothing Lexi can do except focus on the bigger picture, and prevent other generations of Iron Dreamers from suffering the same fate.

Lexi throws her arms around Artemis.

Shocked, the woman freezes.

Lexi is surprised by her own emotional outburst. She doesn't agree with many of Artemis's decisions, but she is trying to save millions of people. Artemis softens as much as she can. She raises one hand and pats Lexi on the shoulder. It's awkward. Lexi chuckles. She doesn't know when she'll see her again.

"Touching, really," Gal groans. "But if we don't get a move on, we're all going to the Forest."

Chen howls in pain, clutching his hand as an invisible force breaks his fingers. Zuchiris only has a few centimeters to work with, and he makes each one count.

Lexi pulls away from Artemis and says, "Tell Zuchiris I said goodbye."

"Go," is all Artemis says before she runs to a bookshelf and disappears behind it. The chambers of husband and wife have hidden compartments between them. No wonder Tiago was able to steal the masking technology from her.

Lexi runs into the ship, feeling the force field between the doorways move through her like a blast of air. She shivers, thankful for having moved quickly before remembering it was there. The ship is gutted, empty aside from four tall chairs welded to the floor. Lexi takes a seat beside Jonathan, and the five of them are sealed into the dark.

The tattooed man runs past them and up the center platform. He plants both feet, waving his hands over a wide set of screens. Lexi doesn't have a moment to marvel at the cockpit before the walls fade to transparency, giving way to the stars. Jonathan's eyes go wide. They could be floating through the abyss. If he didn't understand that he was in space before, he's painfully aware of it now.

"What is this?" he asks.

Lexi rests her hands on her lap as the nanotechnology connects her to the chair, pinning her in place. She reflects on the last few months, and begins with, "It's the year 3124. The Earth has been dead for a thousand years."

ABOUT THE AUTHOR

Ashley Christine is a STEM communicator, consultant, and commentator for science fiction literature, movies, and television. She is from a small town in northern New Hampshire where she learned outdoor skills, survival, and how to keep up with Olympic athletes. After attending the University of New Hampshire and Southern New Hampshire University with a BA in Applied Mathematics, she briefly worked in politics before deciding to travel the world to study French, Russian, and Arabic. Deciding to pursue her passion for science, she moved to California to work as a STEM communicator on social media, and has been given the opportunity to work on movie sets, consult writers, and inspire a generation to have a love and curiosity for science. She currently lives in Los Angeles, California.

Mango Publishing, established in 2014, publishes an eclectic list of books by diverse authors—both new and established voices—on topics ranging from business, personal growth, women's empowerment, LGBTQ studies, health, and spirituality to history, popular culture, time management, decluttering, lifestyle, mental wellness, aging, and sustainable living. We were named 2019 *and* 2020's #1 fastest growing independent publisher by *Publishers Weekly*. Our success is driven by our main goal, which is to publish high-quality books that will entertain readers as well as make a positive difference in their lives.

Our readers are our most important resource; we value your input, suggestions, and ideas. We'd love to hear from you—after all, we are publishing books for you!

Please stay in touch with us and follow us at:

Facebook: Mango Publishing

Twitter: @MangoPublishing

Instagram: @MangoPublishing

LinkedIn: Mango Publishing

Pinterest: Mango Publishing

Newsletter: mangopublishinggroup.com/newsletter

Join us on Mango's journey to reinvent publishing, one book at a time.

www.ingramcontent.com/pod-product-compliance
Lightning Source LLC
Jackson TN
JSHW032300230525
84103JS00001BA/1
* 9 7 8 1 6 8 4 8 1 7 3 8 2 *